Marianne de Pierres w̶ now lives in Queensl̶ d
and two cockatoos. s
Television and a Postgraduate Certificate of Arts in
Writing, Editing and Publishing. Her passions are
books, basketball and avocados. She has been actively
involved in promoting Speculative Fiction in Australia
and is the co-founder of the Vision Writers Group, and
ROR – wRiters On the Rise, a critiquing group for
professional writers. She was also involved in the early
planning stage of Clarion South. Marianne has
published a variety of short fiction and is collaborating
on a film project for Sydney-based Enchanter
Productions. You can find out more about her at
www.mariannedepierres.com

Find out more about Marianne de Pierres and other
Orbit authors by registering for the free monthly
newsletter at www.orbitbooks.net

BY MARIANNE DE PIERRES

DARK SPACE

BOOK 1 of *THE SENTIENTS OF ORION*

marianne de pierres

www.orbitbooks.net

ORBIT

First published in Great Britain in 2007 by Orbit
Reprinted 2009 (twice)

Copyright © Marianne de Pierres 2007

The moral right of the author has been asserted.

A CIP catalogue record for this book
is available from the British Library.

ISBN 978-1-84149-428-9

Typeset in Caslon 540 by Palimpsest Book Production Limited,
Grangemouth, Stirlingshire
Printed and bound in Great Britain by
CPI Mackays, Chatham, ME5 8TD

Papers used by Orbit are natural, renewable and recyclable
products sourced from well-managed forests and certified
in accordance with the rules of the Forest Stewardship Council.

Mixed Sources
Product group from well-managed
forests and other controlled sources
www.fsc.org Cert no. SGS-COC-004081
© 1996 Forest Stewardship Council

FSC

Orbit
An imprint of
Little, Brown Book Group
100 Victoria Embankment
London EC4Y 0DY

An Hachette UK Company
www.hachette.co.uk

www.orbitbooks.net

Rosemary Mina de Pierres (née Vincent)
1926–2006
'A wild and precious life'

ACKNOWLEDGEMENTS

I would like to thank a few people.

Launz Burch, ever my biology consultant. The ROR-ettes for putting up with me submitting this for critique in six different incarnations.

The loyal 'Patchers' who have waited for me to produce another book.

Tara Wynne for those encouraging e-mails.

Lastly, Darren Nash, whose patience, gentle persistence and guidance helped me through.

AUTHOR NOTE

I have taken extreme liberties with the Italian language. Please do not look for grammatical accuracy – you will not find it. This is the far, far future!

The awful shadow of some unseen Power
Floats though unseen among us – visiting
This various world with as inconstant wing
As summer winds that creep from flower to flower–
Like moonbeams that behind some piny mountain
                                                                shower,
    It visits with inconstant glance
    Each human heart and countenance;
    Like hues and harmonies of evening–
        Like clouds in starlight widely spread–
        Like memory of music fled–
        Like aught that for its grace may be
        Dear, and yet clearer for its mystery.

Hymn to Intellectual Beauty
Percy Bysshe Shelley, 1816

ENTITY

Dark space is not really dark.

Neither is it empty.

Nor lonely.

Beings roam the corridors between galaxies and the gargantuan tracts of dark energy. These creatures, though self-nourished, will on occasion merge and barter their knowledge of the universe with each other – the true nature of neutrinos for anti-quark jokes, the complete catalogue of variations in time/space rifts for amusing anecdotes about the behavioural idiosyncrasies and anomalies of their most exotic particles, the reason for the left-handedness of the universe, for . . . love.

They adore collecting data and keeping secrets. But more than anything they enjoy arguing over the truth about death.

Gluttoned with knowingness, they pride themselves in their comprehension of the incomprehensible. No concept is beyond their understanding. No action is beyond their ability. They attain knowledge from the exponential synergy of interaction.

Yet they are denied the knowledge of one thing . . .

Applied history download, alternative version (including aural anecdotal evidence).

Accessed by Artificial Intelligence 339997^ Wanton.

Extropist stream to Vreal Studium via Scolar hub.

Jo-Jo Rasterovich's verbal recount of first contact:

'I got lost way out past the edge of Orion's Belt on account of crap uuli navigation software. (Don't buy it, people!) Last inhabited place I'd seen was some naff planet called Foregone that wouldn't even give me shortcast rights.

'I tried to mag-beam right back to Mintaka's civilised worlds to get some new nav but my beam credit expired (lousy floating banks). I sent a SOS to the nav centre on Foregone but the naff buggers probably thought it was a local radio station.

'I had no choice but to use res-shift. I ran a debug on the nav and it seemed to work so I charted a shift back to Hum-Uuli figuring if they paid me to keep quiet about the nav I'd have enough lucre to top up my mag credits (course, I never would have kept quiet afterwards). It was a dumb risk, I know, but without shifting I was likely to be stuck gassing around beyond Foregone so far past my next rejuve that the salvage crew'd be lucky to find my bones.

'Turned out the nav was still bugged. I *calmed* way too close to unmapped space about thirty LYs from Hum-Uuli. The particle analyser went jammy on me.

Told me the atom count had fallen to .04 and that I was on the edge of a gas tube that tracked way up out of the galactic plane. Last thing I remember was the infrared array playing shadow puppets. These . . . *things* . . . like freaking huge leeches were hanging, sucking at an area in the tube. One of them, a great bloated bastard, dropped right off and shot out at me. I only had one thought in my head as I watched it come.

'*I am so fucked.*

'It swallowed me whole. I felt like I'd been dropped down the bitch of all volcanoes. Life support died and so did I. Amazing thing was, I woke up again.'

End verbal recount.

Studium Narrative Summary:

After Jo-Jo Rasterovich returned to inhabited space, news spread through the Nations of Orion Sentients that he had encountered a new being. Governments sent envoys escorted by nuclear-armed warships to meet and greet. It was concluded that the mysterious entity – quickly given the name Sole – that had reanimated Mr Rasterovich was not only benign but of an order of intelligence greater than anything previously known or imagined.

Sole, it appeared, was God.

Better still, Sole seemed willing enough to share information with the Sentients of Orion. But only on a strict system of barter: one clearly delineated feat of cleverness on the part of the Sentients in exchange for new knowledge or a key to knowledge.

This turned out to be a cryptic and often unsatisfactory arrangement but crumbs from Sole's table were valuable even so. And anyway, Sentient history has been built on never understanding anything fully.

NOS exported a select few of their best minds to Sole's local area (a couple of rather inferior ones managed to squeeze past as well) but Sole, though patient in the manner of any quasi-eternal being, didn't seem able to interact successfully with the chosen minds.

For a time a stalemate occurred, without an exchange of ... anything. Sole and the chosen academics eyed each other from a ship-to-God distance.

The ship's little colony of eager minds with not enough to do turned quickly to a nasty claustrophobic cauldron. The first murder occurred within three Foregone-weeks – a Geneer vac'ed 'accidentally' after winning the daily Minds Tournament twelve consecutive times.

Whether motivated by a desire to stop the obvious disintegration of the colony or not, Sole instigated some bridging steps to enhance the communication process between quasi-eternal and Sentient.

How Sole communicated effectively its plan to the proletarian wastrel Jo-Jo Rasterovich is a complete mystery to Sole-aphiles and it has been deemed that in their initial contact Jo-Jo had been somehow altered to *make it so*.

Jo-Jo Rasterovich conveyed Sole's desire for a selection process preceded by a *procedure*.

Sole-chosen Sentients submitted to an event they

dubbed *shafting* where their brains were altered so that their minds operated in distinct layers. In humanesques like the Lostols and Ceruleans (rumoured to have originated from a singularly blue planet on the far edge of Orion) the procedure occasionally resulted in psychoses. Non-humanesques like the uuli displayed no observable change.

The selected Sentients called their tutelage an apprenticeship and a graduate therefrom a *tyro* and once the ground rules for selection had been set, the race began in earnest.

Scientists came first, all types and species. When it became obvious that most would be rejected they were forced to look outside their fraternity. Reluctantly, they invited in professionals from other disciplines – all fine thinkers as well but, because of their place in the course of things, intransigents.

Radical thinkers from the philosophers' city of Scolar also bid for entry but were resoundly denied a chance to meet with Sole by the multi-species organisation that had set up the whole event.

This body of bigots called themselves the Group of Higher Intelligence Affairs and rejected the applications of Scolar-based academics on the basis that their unquantifiable methods were likely to endanger the Sentient-Sole relationship.

Even the outlawed, secretive trans-humanists (indeed, that's what they call us!) attempted to place a member using subterfuge. The member was discovered and expelled.

Jo-Jo Rasterovich the 33rd, contract minerals scout of rather dubious integrity and the original 'discoverer' of Sole, remains the only un-learned person to have open access to New Bubble space. He was, after all, the *first contact* and no one could take that away from him.

The Studium concludes that this humanesque should be the focus of further attempts (by us) to contact the Sole Entity.

NB: It should be added that, these days, Rasterovich is more entrepreneur than scout, having sold his personal recount the length and breadth of Orion's Arm for an untidily large sum.

MIRA

I've heard you are beautiful.

Insignia was whispering to her again. This time the words were lucid. It was not always that way: mostly the voice in her mind was a mere hum, punctuated by peaks and troughs of half-formed words, as though the effort required to shape them into something she could understand was too great.

Could Insignia hear her replies? She did not know really, but still she spoke to it – it had been her only companion here when there had been no other.

Tonight is graduation, she explained.

Insignia sighed and Mira Fedor felt it as a pressure in her chest, a slight involuntary lift of her shoulders.

I have been alone for a long time . . .

Since my father died, said Mira.

She hoped her words might prompt it to say more but the biozoon's presence subsided back into an irregular drone. As always, Mira felt its withdrawal keenly, and yet today would be the last time.

She inspected herself in the gilded mirror. Today, for graduation, she wore her familia's traditional five-thousand-gold-thread fellala with its blood-jewelled silk velum. The velum's rubies burned under the chandeliers. Faja had sent it to Mira from their villa in Loisa as a sign of her sisterly pride – for only one ceremonial robe remained in their familia now. It was heavy and stiff, and restricted her movement, but it gave her belief.

Smoothing loose tendrils of her dark hair under the headdress, Mira allowed excitement to twist her lips into a smile. It was said that for Fedors, first *union* with a biozoon was like a wedding night. The moment of her life's purpose had finally come, and it was not too soon, for dark, impulsive thoughts lurked near.

Her need for *union* with the Cipriano Clan's organic pilot ship had become a craving, a hunger in her mouth that she could not satisfy, an ungovernable heat in her lower belly. Such feelings were improper for a Baronessa – but then, a Baronessa had never harboured the Inborn pilot gene before: indeed, a *woman* had not.

The Studium bells tolled, jolting Mira from her reverie: the formal ceremony was beginning. She gave her room the barest of glances despite knowing that she would not return. Her years here had been at best disagreeable. She had detested the sly behaviour of the other aristos and the way they hung off the young Principe, Trin Pellegrini, as if he granted meaning to their lives.

'You *are* different,' Cochetta Silvio had drawled loudly enough for all at one dreary patrizio soirée to hear. 'So sombre, Baronessa. So *thin*.'

And, of course, there was the unspoken thing, the thing Cochetta was too refined to mention but which stood between her and the other aristos in the way that an infectious sickness created its own distance – her hereditary talent.

'Different? Si, thank Crux,' Mira had replied. But the sting of the snub stayed with her.

She dragged the heavy doors of her room closed with two hands and stepped out into the vast portico. The nano-filtered baroque arches lent Mount Pell a soft, almost benign appearance – so deceptive when the real Araldis sweltered under intolerably dry heat.

Mira let the view down to the Studium menagerie calm her: *All their taunts will mean nothing after today*. Straightening her shoulders, she sealed her velum and set the filter to hide everything but her eyes. Then she descended the central helicoidal staircase to the grand ante-room.

The entire Studium attended graduation, even the untitled Nobile. Now, as she entered, they jostled for position alongside the patricians like a gaggle of ornately feathered birds. Threading her way between them, Mira took her place on the dais to the side and a step behind the young Principe, Trinder Pellegrini, and his cousin Duca Raldo Silvio.

'Bonjourno, Baronessa,' said Raldo. He stroked his stiff moustache with practised affectation and gave her a smirking sideways glance.

'Duca,' she acknowledged with suspicion and the barest curtsy. Since when did Raldo Silvio use his guile on her?

On her other side Trinder Pellegrini dipped his head – enough to satisfy courtesy – but did not speak. In fact, he had not spoken to her for months now, not since . . .

'*Patrizios*, please be seated.' The Principe's maestro appeared at the edge of the dais. The ante-room's smart acoustics dispersed his command as if it were a whisper spoken directly into each person's ear. When satisfied that the audience was settled, he announced simply, 'The Principe.'

Utter silence fell as Franco Pellegrini, dressed in sweeping olive-velvet Studium regalia, strode to the centre of the dais. The silk inserts of his sleeves ruffled down past his waist in a dramatic display of his status. Unable to walk on the ludicrously high platform of her dress shoes, his wife Jilda was chair-lifted to the side of the stage. Only the toes of her footwear showed past her hemline.

Though he was in later middle age, Franco retained all the physical qualities of a younger Latino male. His thickset body and heavy patrician features hinted at an irrepressible virility. Mira thought he looked more determined and assured than his son. He had certainly been a forceful leader – as had his ancestors – though she had never seen him in true performance mode before. She had not been invited to Franco and Jilda's court for reasons of politics. When the Pellegrini familia left Latino Crux they had invited only those of their clan who supported the Machiavelli politic. Yet the Insignia Pilot familia that they so desperately needed to fly their ship were of the Castiglioni ideal. The Pellegrinis had ever since played a double-edged game of inclusion and exclusion with the Fedors. Fedors were necessary to them but they would never be given a chance to influence the court.

Mira's sorella, Faja, had warned her of this when she had been preparing to attend the Studium. 'And it is just as well, Mira,' she said. 'Court is a place for rapists and societal cannibals.'

At the time Mira had shrugged off Faja's words as theatrical but her later acquaintance with the Silvios had added an uncomfortable flavour of meaning to them.

As Franco began to announce the list of successful baccalaureates, Mira's stomach fluttered. Her feminine degree in Latino Studies, Orion Literature and Genera would be among them. What no one knew about, though, was the knowledge that she had carefully – secretly – acquired about the designs and functional procedures of air and space vehicles. The long nights of complete absorption learning about flight: a labour of love in voluntary preparation for the thing that she so desired.

'Pilot First' was a discrete decoration that would be bestowed at the end of the ceremony. *Then* she would be properly honoured. Pilot First would confer on her a vaunted, influential position and Cochetta Silvio and her brittle friends would dare not speak aloud their demeaning thoughts of her again.

Mira left her place and curtsied before the Principe to receive her Literature laurel, her expectation of what would come next leaving her deaf to the perfunctory applause of the audience.

Soon. Soon.

The Principe cleared his throat when he had finished. 'Our history on Araldis is still only fleeting, a little over two hundred years, and in that time there have been only three pilots of Inborn Talent able to fly Insignia,' he said.

Mira's heartbeat quickened.

'Each of those pilots was a descendant of the Fedor

Barony as has been tradition from the very early days on the planets of Latino Crux. The Fedors were chosen for union by the biozoons after the First Exchange, an honour to be preserved for as long as their line existed. Accordingly they were bestowed with the Inborn gene.

'Today is an auspicious moment in our history. Today the honour of Insignia Pilot will be transferred to a new line, as the Fedor birthright has come to an end with the Inborn gene falling to a woman. Throughout history, Orion's finest geneticists have not been able to unlock the biozoons' secret – but now there is a way: a way that will allow us to bring new blood to this remarkable skill. In preparation for this, Trinder Pellegrini will be our Insignia Pilot designate. Trinder, *mio figlio*, step forward to receive your honour.'

No! Was it her or Insignia who cried out in her mind? In the moment of uncertain silence before the applause, Mira Fedor lost her self-possession. She stumbled down from the dais and through the ante-room in front of the many eyes that narrowed in amusement and curiosity.

Her instinct to flee the Studium steered her through the Grandioso Foyer and out onto the mosaiced promenade. As she reached the edges of the Studium menagerie she tore the tear-wet velum from her face. A flock of purrcocks ca-cawed and scattered as she sank to the mirrored path.

Sinners! Insignia is mine by birthright! Trinder Pellegrini cannot fly her. How can they think of attempting transference of my Inborn gene? What will happen to me if they do?

She knew – and shirked from the thought. *Insanity.*

Clipped footsteps on the tiles. Mira stiffened. Only the Cavaliere walked in such a fashion.

'Baronessa? May I be of assistance?' The tight-lipped Cavaliere bowed politely in front of her.

'I feel a little unwell. The importance of the day, you understand.'

He nodded, his face masked in formality. 'The Principe has asked that you attend him in the guest chamber of the Palazzo Pellegrini.'

Mira trembled. 'Of course, but I must change. The weight of these robes has left me a little faint.'

'In that case we shall accompany you.' He clicked his heels together.

Mira stood, resealing her velum, darkening the filter, cutting off any sense of familiarity between them. 'I do not need an escort. I am familiar with the whereabouts of the Principe's guest chambers.'

The Cavaliere's lips tightened. 'Then we will order an AiV for you and escort you there. It will await you outside the Grandioso Foyer.'

'As you wish.' She tilted her head and walked stiffly back to the Studium.

Once inside, Mira lifted the burdensome folds of her ceremonial robe and staggered up the staircase to her room. Fear and compulsion lent strength to her shaking legs.

She flung the doors open and found an older Galiotto servant folding her clothes into neat piles. Mira had seen her before, in the refectory and turning out the rooms, commanding the younger ones with a single gesture or curt word.

'What . . . are . . . you . . . doing?' she panted.

The servant curtsied. It was the heavy, slow movement of an older woman with weary joints. 'I have been instructed to pack your clothes, Baronessa,' she said, returning to her task.

'To go where?' demanded Mira in a shrill voice.

'I do not know, Baronessa. The concierge will make those arrangements.'

Mira stared at the Nobile servant, collecting herself. 'Of course, forgive me. It is just that you startled me. Now I must change. Give me a travelling robe and I will dress.'

The Galiotto complied, selecting an ochre fellala and exterior-rated velum from the pile.

Mira took them and stepped behind her screen. She slipped off her beaded ceremonial robe and slippers and exchanged them for the plain fellala, coolant stockings and terrain boots.

'Are you planning to go outside, Baronessa Fedor?'

Mira stepped around the edge of the screen, trying to assemble her frayed thoughts. Should she be evasive, or should she simply ignore the question? Would the Galiotto alert the Cavaliere?

But the servant merely held out her over-cloak. 'You would not do well without this.'

'Thank you,' said Mira.

The Galiotto still did not look at her. 'What the Principe has done this day is not right, Baronessa. Fedors are blessed with the Talent. That is the way it has always been,' she whispered. 'Some things should not change.'

Mira grasped the woman's wrist. 'You have heard?'

The servant swayed a little. 'My daughter Tina is

bonded to the Principessa. I knew . . . many of us knew before this.' She waved her hands at the floor to signify the graduation ceremony below.

Mira's thoughts flew to the young Principe. How long had Trinder Pellegrini known she would not get her entitlement? Had he known of this when he had taken her to the Tourmaline Islands? Had he deliberately courted her without a chaperone and then abandoned her?

'Baronessa?' The old Galiotto drew her attention to the shortcast. The screen was signalling a waiting audio call.

Mira was caught in a wave of desperation. She shook the woman's arm. 'What is your name?'

'Alba.'

'Alba. How do the lesser Nobile travel up and down the mountain?'

The woman took a slow breath as if she needed time to answer. She lifted her face to Mira. Cataracts had dulled the vibrancy of her dark eyes. That she had not seen fit to have them treated was, perhaps, her badge of honour. Mira knew that many of the older familia were inclined to such habits, resisting the newer technologies.

Not so the Principe.

Fresh fear spurted through Mira's veins. If the Cavaliere found her, she would be trapped, and though a small part of her mind struggled to be rational – *the Principe may simply want to offer me handsome recompense* – her stronger instincts could accept only one assumption: *gene transference.*

'Please,' she implored. 'The 'cast . . . it is the Cavaliere. They have an escort for me.'

Alba unwound the high neck of her fellala. Her skin was soft and puckered like worn suede. Mira forced herself not to avert her gaze; she had never seen old skin before. Nor had she seen anything like the myriad of finely etched lines on the woman's breasts. They might have been fine age wrinkles save for their violet hue and intricate patterning.

Alba Galiotto traced some of them with a blunt finger.

'Women are forbidden to mark their bodies,' said Mira automatically.

'Baronessa, when you see these marks again you will understand why I choose to help you.' Resting in the crease of her breast was a biometric stripe – her badge of trusted seniority. She peeled it from her skin without flinching at the pain and handed it to Mira. 'This will enable any general transport. Take any one from the loading bay behind the cucina.' She placed a small towel over her bleeding skin and deftly rewound her robe to keep it tightly in place.

Mira slipped the stripe onto her arm under her sleeve. It burrowed into the crook of her elbow with a slight sting. 'They'll know you helped me.'

Alba shook her head. 'Even the Principe would not dare disrobe me in a search. There are some compensations for age, Baronessa.' She gave a hollow laugh and returned to her folding.

Mira stood for a moment, uncertain.

'You should go now. The Cavaliere are not patient,' said Alba gently, as if prompting a ragazza.

'Blessings, Alba.'

'Blessings, *speranza*.'

*   *   *

In her travelling fellala and light boots, Mira was able to lift her knees to run. She flew along the floor of the lengthy portico, past the aristos' chambers and the helicoidal staircase, to the far end of the building. The servant's stairs were narrow. Food spills crusted the rough hessian stair-matting and the stairwell smelt of rancid cooking oils. The Cipriano crest, inlaid to the wall, had been spattered with red wine. No one had been reverent enough to wipe it clean.

At another time this lack of respect might have surprised Mira but the lesser Nobile seemed well contented enough. So might she have wondered at Alba Gallioto's actions and the strange vivid markings on the woman's breast but instead her mind was locked into two tunnels of need – escape and Insignia.

By the time she had reached the ground floor and located the door to the cucina . . . the two desires had coalesced into one.

Sole

manifestspace

yearn|seek seek amid|among light b'long farway
look'm secrets <luscious luscious>
cross'm void|
find|amid amid liquid swirl halo dust
little creatures|many many
how'm function??

TEKTON

Belle-Monde was named in the inimitable vein of sarcasm that marked the humanesque species apart from others. Far from being a *beautiful world*, it resembled a corroded iron ball.

Tekton was not accustomed to such a solemn vista. Seen from space, his home planet Lostol was a twirling topaz with pristine polar ice at either end like virgins' caps. A jewel suspended in space, elegantly looping a Type B star.

Belle-Monde's closest star was Mintaka, the last notch in Orion's Belt. Tekton's trip there had been by resonance shift to the Bellatrix system, then on to Alnitak and Mintaka, followed by dreary sub-shift propulsion to Belle-Monde.

It had given him plenty of time to absorb all available information on the discovery of Sole Entity and the subsequent placement of the pseudo-world Belle-Monde in its vicinity. The screeds of speculation and the smaller amount of fact led him one conclusion.

The Entity had wanted to be discovered.

Why, after all this time?

It was a question he pondered over as a distraction from the discomforts of space travel. Already his delicate skin was suffering from dehydration and he longed to return to Lostol for complete skin rehabilitation.

Instead he'd had to put up with an inferior exported light therapy that left him feeling itchy and overly taut.

It was not a way to be feeling as he stood for candidature. As a wealthy archi-Tect in his own right, he could afford more luxurious travel but the controlling body of this project, The Orion League of Sentient Species – OLOSS – insisted that all candidates travelled on *their* ships.

So typical of bureaucrats.

Yet Tekton knew he shouldn't really complain. OLOSS were picking up the tab for his travel, using taxes collected for and siphoned into the 'betterment of sentient species' fund.

'Candidate Second Godhead Tekton, your Belle-Monde moud is trying to contact you.'

Tekton dragged his gaze from the viewing port. A little thrill ran through him at hearing his potential new title. Godhead to a God.

The *Newland*'s Lostolian purser stood diffidently at his shoulder, eyes watering. He had been Tekton's only comfort on this last leg of his trip, understanding mannered deference *and* Tekton's dietary preferences.

'Thank you. I will tell my fact-aide to enable my in-com.'

The purser hovered. 'May I say on behalf of all Lostolians, candidate, that we support your favour with the Entity. We wish one of our own to be the first to evolve. We wish you to represent our race and design beautiful things in our name.'

Tekton nodded and graciously opened his robe so that the purser could gaze upon his naked body – a show of gratitude and good faith.

The purser devoured the sight. 'Should you ever need me, I am at your service. I shall log my name and credentials with your moud.'

'No need – the memory of your assistance will stay with me long,' said Tekton, closing his robe with practised ceremony. But, of course, by the time he turned back to the port he'd forgotten the purser entirely.

'Welcome to Belle-Monde, candidate Godhead. Your mind reconfiguration is scheduled for tomorrow. Is there anything you require?' The new moud entered his mind in a dignified if stilted tone.

'I'm not sure,' Tekton replied. According to the OLOSS fact sheet, the compulsory mind alteration provided the only way for Sole Entity to communicate directly with humans. The specifics of the process varied from sentient to sentient and were a matters of much debate. 'First, I shall need an escort to my quarters. Then I wish to review the current lists of other tyros and their projects. I'd also like you to replicate my dietary needs.' Tekton directed his fact-aide to download the ingredients and method of his preferred Lostolian dishes. 'I should like *properly* prepared Carminga livers for my evening meal.'

'Yes, candidate Godhead. A servant will pick you up. I have your disembarkation allotment.'

Tekton gave a delicate, amused snort at such a crude method of organisation. He would have things to get used to. The pseudo-world had been hastily refurbished from OLOSS monies and, like their chosen methods of transport, was said to be quite primitive in its amenities.

He deduced from his pre-orientation that there was no first-class or privileged anything. Everyone received equal material status on the basis that everyone was there for the same reason – that they might gain enlightenment. Glory of candidature was supposed to be reward enough. Knowledge represented a triumph over materialism.

Quaint.

On Tekton's world prestige was valued. Lostolians believed that it brought out the best in the Lostolian mind. Power and status allowed Tekton the freedom to imagine anything. He was not used to being limited by mean practicalities. Indeed, he had been involved in the design of some of his world's most significant constructions: the splendid bridges of the Latour moons, the Great Diorama Well of Mapoor, the Floating Palaces of the Armina-Pulchra Raj.

Yet this new discovery, Sole Entity, this being of limitless intellect – if intellect was a term you could even attribute to it – had drawn Tekton as surely as the Magnets of Need drew asteroids away from the planet Misako.

The attraction grew stronger when he heard that his cousin Ra had already been selected for this great honour.

Although Ra was behind Tekton in seniority at the Tadao Ando Studium, the younger man's aesthetic brilliance had made him Lostol's first candidate.

Tekton hid his outrage at being overlooked and set about seeking justice by wooing the Chancellor of Tadao Ando's unappealing daughter.

Carnal pleasures still amused Tekton where most of his colleagues appeared to have long forsaken physical intimacy for other things. Tekton believed that physicality gave a temporal aspect to his designs that the pure aesthetes like Ra had discarded. In fact, Tekton's students copied his style and had dubbed it 'Mortalis'. They carried on an unhealthy rivalry with Ra's aesthetes.

After some excruciatingly unpleasant lovemaking sessions with Doris Mulek, the Chancellor's puffy offspring, Tekton garnered her support for his petition. He was duly summoned before an OLOSS committee for an interview and examined to see if his body was healthy enough to withstand the mind-reconfiguration process.

Within a week of the interviews he was on his way to Belle-Monde.

And now he was there.

Carrying only a small holdall of skin lotions, Tekton transferred into one of the fat little transport ticks sucking the side of the sub-light vessel. The sturdy craft were the favoured method to courier passengers and cargo from ship to world.

In a matter of tumbling minutes after boarding the tick he was disembarking through a tube into the dismal welcome station.

Couldn't Sole have chosen a more hospitable sector of the galaxy in which to reside? he wondered.

The livery, a basic modifiable, approached with Tekton's face on its display. When Tekton touched it for confirmation, it bowed deeply.

'Welcome back to Belle-a, Belle-a—'

Tekton had a surprising urge to slap its malfunctioning resonator. Instead he followed it to the taxi. Physical force was not something that Tekton had ever considered using before.

At least – not his *own*.

After instructing Tekton to take a seat and wait, the livery attached itself to the outside of the taxi. Tekton sat primly in the swaying dark and opened himself to the fleeting impressions as artificial lights and sentient heat flashed by.

An appreciable time later the taxi stopped. The livery disengaged itself and held the doors aside. 'Please follow me, candidate Godhead.'

Tekton's bags were already waiting in his new rooms.

Though well enough ventilated they smelled of cleaning fluids and the soft-edged furniture suggested that an uuli had once occupied them. One wall in the living room showcased a rather kitsch 3D of a gigantic Selenat waterfall, while another displayed an illuminated map of Belle-Monde that doubled as the taxi phone.

'Is Godhead Ra in similar quarters?' he asked.

'I believe so, Godhead Tekton.'

'Good.' Tekton walked slowly through to the Studium node and sleeping room and back again. He examined every surface for emission: uuli excreta would not be acceptable.

Not at all.

TRIN

'Trin darling, could you not spend tonight at home?' the Principessa pleaded.

She leaned against the mock-ornate dressing-room door, drunk and weepy, her formal fellala crumpled and stained. Her thinning dark hair was captured into lank strands and had been wound through a royally jewelled hairpiece.

Franco hadn't slept at home for a week. He had a new young mistress, or so the servants said.

'And do what, mother? Pour your drinks? You have an entire family of Galiotto slaves for that,' Trinder said coldly.

'Servants are not company.' The Principessa smoothed the fellala with a vein-knotted hand, choosing her next words with care. 'I hoped we could celebrate your graduation. I w-would enjoy your company. You go out so often.'

The Principessa Jilda Pellegrini had a talent for eliciting guilt, just as she was gifted with many faces. For Trinder's father, Franco, she maintained a calm, accepting mask that never questioned her husband's string of affairs with young, eager women. Privately, though, like now, she shed that face for another – one ruined with sorrow and swollen with drugs.

When he'd been younger Trin had thought the finest

off-world whisky was her perfume. She would lie on the edge of his bed at night and weep. Perhaps she thought that, in the dark, he wouldn't know. He hated the wetness of her cheeks, the heaviness of her body draped across his legs in bed.

He'd sought his father's company to escape the suffocation of the Principessa's need but Principe Franco Pellegrini always dismissed him with the same excuse – a world to rule.

Trin sensed other reasons for his father's lack of interest, only he dared not seek them out for fear of what they might tell him about himself. Instead he nursed his hurt and turned it on Jilda.

Tonight he chose his words with precision and delivered them like thrusts. 'You should bathe more often, mother. It might make you more attractive to others. And besides, I am spending the evening with company of my own age.'

The Principessa pressed her tumbler to her mouth to stifle a sob. She turned and left without another word.

Trin dispatched his guilt to the same corner of his mind where he kept his anger, and finished dressing. Dismissing his valet, he flew his AiV down Mount Pell to Riso's Bar. His friends were already there, crowding up the tables around the ginko-containment films: Thomasi and Kotta Pellegrini, the Silvios and the Elena cousins – his gang.

Riso's was as daring a place as they would risk, even for graduation celebrations. In most of the Dockside bars familia were not welcome and not safe.

When he became Principe, Trin planned to drive

all the familia-hating ginkos out of Pell. Only the ones that served or provided entertainment would be permitted to stay. Franco and Grandfather Aldo had been stupid to allow them entry to their new world.

Trin knew the arguments for it – he'd just spent three years in political science at the Araldis Studium. The immersion-texts were full of explanations of how the Cipriano Clan had purchased and settled Araldis and had then realised that they had neither the population nor the breadth of skills to sustain a mining economy.

But how short-sighted to accept just anyone. Hadn't they learned anything from the cultural catastrophe of Latino Crux? The one time he had challenged his father about it he'd received a cold, unforgiving stare.

Trin strode towards his friends, putting Franco from his mind..

'Trin!' called out Thomasi.

'Cousin! Pilot First, by Crux,' said Kotta.

'Don Trinder, you un-bastard, where have you been? We have had to drink without you. Congratulations.'

Trin soaked in the salve of their clamour for a moment before taking a seat between Chocetta and Lancia Silvio. They fell apart like halves of sliced moist-fruit, making room for him against their ample thighs. Lancia threw lima pellets at the containment film around the uuli, and clapped as the creature changed colour.

'You know that it is the pain that makes them change,' Trin commented idly.

Lancia laughed and threw another handful.

The uuli squealed, its membrane flaring luminously. Most eyes were drawn to it.

Trin looked away, annoyed. Its helplessness bothered him. How could the stupid creature allow itself to be treated so?

Chocetta slid her hand along his leg. 'My turn tonight, Trinder?'

Picking up the jug of wine, he drank deeply from it. 'If you say so. I have lost track.'

She lifted her aquiline nose in the air, mock-aggrieved. He'd been sleeping with the Silvio Marchesas on alternate nights, and sometimes with both of them together, during their last term at the Studium. He knew it should have been exhilarating, two women, but their constant need for reassurance and attention spoiled things. He could smell his mother on them and the same weak familia-women's way. No doubt both wanted to bear a Pellegrini child. But it would not be them that he chose. *Never them.*

As if sensing his distraction, Chocetta leaned closer, pinching the flesh of his forearm under his fellalo. 'Did you see Mira Fedor go *loco* at the announcement? How unsurprising.' She raised her skilfully drawn eyebrows.

Mira Fedor. Trin hid a flare of embarrassment with a shrug as the memories ambushed him . . .

Crimson-grained Tourmaline Island sand.

'Why did you invite me here, Trin Pellegrini?' Mira Fedor asked.

She sat away from him on the shifting line between wet and dry as he wallowed in the surf. 'Is the eccentric Fedor female not beneath a Principe's son? Or do I make you curious? Or maybe it is simply that my familia is too distant to have me properly chaperoned?'

'Which do you think?' Trin parried, shocked at her direct-ness, her perceptiveness. He could see the outline of her body through her bathing skins. Strange to be close to such a thin, fine-boned female.

'I cannot decide.'

He let the waves roll him closer to her.

Mira did not retreat so he kissed her on impulse, to see what she would do.

Surprisingly, she kissed him back. Her hands slipped down the outside of his bathing skin. She touched his stomach with tentative fingers that created only fear in him.

His ardour softened.

What if she told people that the Principe's son was soffice?

Suddenly, he pushed her away.

Mira rolled up onto her knees as if slapped but he could not tell her that she scared him – that women scared him.

Without another word Trin ran to his AiV, leaving her behind . . . stranded . . .

The consequences of that night had lived on, for the next day Trin had purchased bravura from a dealer at Dockside. A safeguard, he told himself. So it would never happen again.

It never had – the bravura kept it that way.

While Trin and Mira kept their distance from each other, she excelled in her studies and he began to fail. Bravura addiction ruined his concentration and stole his focus. He hated her for it, but he hated his father more for what he had done this evening. Trin did not want Mira Fedor's heritage. He had no wish to fly

Insignia – in truth the thought frightened him. But mostly he did not want the guilt of her insanity upon his shoulders.

This evening, when Mira had fled the grand ante-room before the entire Studium, whispers began immediately – would she go the way of her most famous ancestor, mad Lancio Fedor?

Now, as Trin drank Riso's wine, the Cavaliere would be taking her to the palazzo to see his father.

'What is wrong, Trinder?' wheedled Chocetta.

'He is moody over Mira Fedor,' said Lancia.

'That's because he dated her.'

'I did not date her,' Trin said harshly. He pulled Chocetta onto his lap and called for another jug.

Chocetta began to kiss his face while Lancia stroked his neck and hair, but their thick oil-perfumes made it hard for him to breathe. Their giggles and dirty whispered promises suffocated him. He stood abruptly, pushing them off, making an excuse that the wine was poor and that he would demand another. Then he stumbled to the bar and ordered a fresh drink, slipping two tiny bravura slices under his tongue. When the wine and bravura collided, his confidence returned. Trin took some steadying breaths and returned to the table. But the Silvios had moved on to his cousin Thomasi, and ignored him. Annoyed at their capriciousness he looked around for an alternative to satisfy the stirrings that the bravura had awoken.

Riso's – apart from their tables – was filled with non-familia. He contemplated leaving but the court bars and ristorantes on Mount Pell bored him. Dockside was safe enough while he was with friends – but not when he was alone. Perhaps he should AiV out to the border towns for some variety?

As Trin stood, undecided, a group of familia women entered, dressed in seductive brocade evening fellalas. They headed straight for the bar, trailed by two Palazzo Cavaliere.

The most beautiful, and oldest, of the women bestowed an inviting smile on him as she passed. Her breasts showed through the lace of her fellala and her hips swayed in a way that sent tremors through him.

Trin picked up his drink and followed her.

She told him that her name was Luna and teased him with her eyes over the rim of the drink he bought her.

The Silvios stopped necking with Thomasi, and watched.

Aware of their jealous scrutiny, he leaned closer. 'Luna?' he laughed. 'Are you madness?'

She caught her bottom lip with her teeth. 'I have been called that.'

Trin felt the bravura heating him. There was something dangerous about her. Her slenderness suggested she might be an eccentric, like Mira Fedor – only far, far more beautiful. Intoxicating. With eccentrics you never quite knew . . . A few such familia, picked for their special talents or attributes, had been permitted to come when the Cipriano Clan abandoned Latino Crux. Fedors had been selected for their piloting skills. Trin wondered what Luna's familia had brought to the new world – aside from sheer magnificent beauty.

'Are you going to dance with me or simply admire?'

He glanced at her minders. Something in their aspect

nagged at him. 'Who are you to have Palazzo minders, beautiful Luna?'

She flushed a little. Her eyes flashed. This close he could see the tiny age lines round her lips. 'Don't you know?' she whispered.

Trin ran his fingers along Luna's brocaded arm and brushed the palm of her hand. 'Tell me.'

She slipped off the high-backed chair and melted into his arms. 'Later, perhaps. But first I would like to dance with a handsome *young* man.'

Her slight emphasis on his youth prickled a warning against his skin but the bravura's urge was stronger. Insistent.

Luna chose the dance – formal courting steps usually reserved for couples on their wedding night before they left the celebrations and went to the marital bed. Using it in this context – a ginko bar with a stranger – was so shocking that it heightened Trin's exhilaration.

He mirrored her ritual movements. His arousal had him sweating and breathing heavily.

She finished coyly with her back to him.

Indifferent to who was watching now and what they were thinking, Trin thrust his hips against the crease of her flanks and slipped his hands around her to cup the stiff brocade that hid her breasts.

Luna jerked her head back with a little *faux* cry.

By some unspoken agreement, her minders, hovering close, pulled her away from Trin.

Before he could react they had cloaked her and hustled her out. He staggered as if he had been robbed and left punch-drunk.

The Silvios pounced on him in a moment, pulling them back to their table.

'Did she dump you, Trinder?'

'Trinny, Trinny.'

'Did she leave you rovente, poor darling?'

'Ohh. Aah,' they mocked. 'Take it out on us.'

Furious, Trin brushed them aside and grabbed a jug from the table, swilling down the entire contents in several gulps. The bar began to swirl around him. Cold shivers crawled across his overheated body. He looked around wildly for a focus, something to quell the nausea.

Uuli.

It slithered dejectedly in its transparent containment film. Streaks of mucus coloured the sides, creating a kaleidoscope. Its pathetic manner infuriated him. *For Crux sake . . .*

Trin climbed onto the table and smashed the empty jug into the containment film. It gave a pressure-change thud as it cracked open.

'Get out. Get out,' he shrieked at the uuli.

It blazed scarlet and shrank from him.

He reached in and grasped it with both hands, intending to release it. But it shredded, lumps of mucus sloughing onto his fingers.

'Trinder!'

'Trinny – no!'

They were shouting at him now. All of them. Not just the Silvios.

'Come here,' Trin shouted at it. 'I'm trying to help you.'

The uuli screamed and churned through a rainbow of colours.

Rough hands dragged him down and took him to Riso's den.

Riso stood by his desk, rigid with rage, staring through the wall film into the bar. He turned slowly. 'If the uuli dies, even Franco won't be able to afford the bill. Here's my favour to you,' said Riso, his voice thick with fury. 'I will not call the Carabinere. Go home and sober up. Never come here again. Your behaviour blasphemes against the name Pellegrini.'

Trin laughed at him.

'Spurious *idios*,' spat Riso. 'Throw him out.'

Trin's father woke him the next day.

Half drunk still, Trin dragged the covers up over his chest like a ragazzo shrinking from a bedtime monster.

'I risked a great deal last night for your future,' said Franco, coldly. 'Making you Pilot First will cause discontent.'

'I did not ask for that honour, father. I do not wish to be Pilot First. I wish to be Principe.'

Franco's thick lips contracted into a cruel line. 'Then you must learn the value of things.'

'What do you mean?' asked Trin.

'I have decided that tomorrow you will accept a position in the Carabinere, working for Jus Malocchi. The cost of replacing Riso's uuli will be deducted from your gratis.'

Trin grappled for the pieces of the previous night. 'It died?'

'Yes. Aside from its visceral injuries, that particular subspecies of uuli does not tolerate the Araldis atmosphere. That was why it was sealed. You should have known that. You have bought an OLOSS humanitarian inquiry to my door when I have other matters, more important matters of concern.'

Trin hid his shock behind a sullen look. 'I thought the containment was just an affectation, one of Riso's circus tricks.'

'The only circus tricks at Riso's were yours.' Franco stared at his son.

Trin sensed another unspoken grievance threatening to upset his father's composure.

'Why did you attack it?' Franco said eventually.

Trin opened his mouth to explain but the words wouldn't form. Franco would not believe him. He sat up straighter instead, forcing himself to drop the covers. 'You care nothing for ginkos, Papa.' He used the diminutive deliberately.

But Franco was unmoved by it. 'No, I do not,' he admitted.

'Then why are you doing this? I do not wish to work for the Malocchis. The entire family is loco. Like the Fedors.'

Franco's stern expression softened the tiniest bit. 'In that case, my suggestion is that you are on time for your interview.'

MIRA

Liveried vehicles crowded the tarmac behind the Studium cucina, their chauffeurs trading insults and boldly nudging each other as they waited for the graduation festivities to end.

Mira pressed the biometric stripe on her inner arm to the lock of a battered TerV that crouched between a large passenger AiV and a victuals haulier. When the door sprang open she slipped inside and dimmed the windows. If any of the chauffeurs had noticed her, they would be too distracted by the mayhem – she hoped – to realise that she was the Baronessa Fedor.

She fumbled with the navigation screen until it displayed a map for the Fleet hangars in Dockside. *There!* She set the tack, and as she watched for a gap among the jostling liveries, her mind ricocheted between past and present. Insignia's entreaties had become such a constant in her mind that she hardly knew it from her own inner voice. Had it been so for her father – this endless monologue? Perhaps the stories of her ancestor Lancio Fedor were true? Perhaps insanity had truly claimed him? Indeed, it felt as if it would take *her* at any moment – due to fear and anger and disappointment at the very least.

Auto-drive sent the TerV climbing out of the Studium surroundings to follow a well-dusted path downward. Within a short time Mira had a panoramic view up at the Pell range. The Menagerie was a patchwork of brilliant hues linking the Studium to the Museo under one transparent dome. In the afternoon light the dome glistened like an enormous soap bubble.

East along the range, familia crests glowed in their dome fields above the lavish gilt villas. Mira saw the Silvios' Purrcock and Crossbow and the Elenas' Black Rainbow where their domes intersected midway down Mount Pell with the base of the Pellegrinis' Berga-Lion Carrying Serpent.

Far away in the small town of Loisa, the Fedor Bear, Feast and Pearl was reflected only in the small stained-glass entrance of the Villa Fedor – there were no protective domes on the plainlands.

When Mira's great-grandfather had been Pilot First – the one who'd led the fleet from Latino Crux to the new world – the Fedors had lived on Mount Pell. That had changed when Mira's parents had died. The Principe had seen to it.

Mira thought wistfully of her grandfather. The archivolos showed him dressed in a matt black fellala that made him seem extraordinarily tall and thin. His skin had been deathly pale from the time he had spent in vein-sink.

All the early Cipriano settlers had acquired milky space-farers' skin by the time they had reached their destination, yet as they began melanin treatments their colouring turned to the lustrous crimson of the modern, acclimatised Araldisian.

Not everyone had fared well with the augmentations. Melanin allergy was not uncommon and sometimes developed after the boosters had accumulated in a person's system. It had claimed Mira's own father and when her mother died from birth complications Mira's older sister Faja was left to bring up her younger sibling.

The Principe had kept them on a modest gratuity, enough to maintain a villa on Mount Pell. Later, after their parents' deaths, he had the girls shifted to one of the plainland towns and had decreed that only one of them would be educated at the Studium. Faja had given up her own chance at that for Mira.

Faja, what will you think of Franco's diktat? Mira wondered.

Near the foot of the mountain the TerV changed direction to circumvent the large, flat, functional cato-plasma edifice of Carabinere Centrale, and descended further.

Dockside had its own dome, a modest crimson-tinged field that married into the floor beneath the purple and red rock mountains. The Fleet hangars adjoined the docking stations, sharing the same launch infrastructure but with separate entrance and exit portals for the main-tenance staff and pilots. The Assailants were taken up into space on rotation twice a year to blow out the dust.

Mira raked through her memories of the hangar layout. During the first year of her Studium course she had concocted a research rationale to visit the Fleet – the history of Latino warship poetry or something simi-larly esoteric. To her disappointment the biozoon had been hidden from view by a large X-ray-resistant canopy. Her guide had explained that biozoons were always a target for bandits and that although Insignia had not been flown in twenty-odd years – since Mira's father had died – the Principe kept his premier ship closely guarded.

Insignia had felt her presence, though. *I sense one of you.* It spoke in her mind.

Mira had clapped her hands to her head in shock.

'Baronessa?' Her guide had looked at her with concern.

'A sudden headache, signor, nothing m-more,' she had replied.

The murmurs had started soon after, like a small babbling stream of half-formed words. If she concentrated she could make sense of some but for the most part it was like a language she had learned once and then forgotten.

Mira believed it was Insignia. Yet other possibilities haunted her and there was no one to speak to about it, no one to reassure her.

Occasionally clear meaning would break through the babble, as it had this evening. Now all she longed for was to see Insignia without covers, to know that it was real, to understand the forgotten language, to know she was sane.

Mira's ears popped and the TerV wallowed a little as she entered the Dockside preserv-field. Within a few seconds a Carabinere automon made contact.

She muted the shortcast transmission, ignoring it, and peered through the windows. There was no sign of the curious Carabinere, only the pandemonium of Dockside.

The launch and arrival docks were unsightly masterpieces of adaptation, reassembled from the gigantic vieships that had transported the larger part of the

Cipriano clan from Latino Crux to the new world of Araldis. Scattered randomly around them were the *grown* catoplasma buildings that were so common on Araldis. Only the Palazzo and the Studium were built with traditional stone materials, mined at great cost from the bluestone deposits on the far side of the range.

An AiV swooped low over Mira without apparent care for its safety and her TerV adopted a stop-start pattern to avoid colliding with the traffic that crowded the piazzas.

Mira stared out with interest. She did not share the Latino aristo abhorrence of other races and species. She had taken foreign genera subjects at the Studium, as was traditional for Fedor pilots, and in recent times her sister Faja had forsaken convention to give shelter to abandoned mixed-species bambini at the Villa Fedor.

Not that Mira or Faja's egalitarian viewpoint altered outsiders' perspectives: Araldisian aristos were arrogant and ignorant, or such was the common opinion.

Everyone, even the aristos themselves, knew that wealth drew others to Araldis – the lucre to be made on the small mineral-rich world on the far edge of the Orion system.

As Mira drew closer to the launch pads, the Fleet hangar became distinguishable from the rest by the clan crest on its vast roof near where it adjoined the main landing terminal. Inside the entrance was a manned checkpoint. Mira set the TerV to park itself in the nearest common bay and climbed out.

The acrid smell of solid-fuel waste that never quite escaped through the exhalation nanos of the preserv-field, choked her. It was hotter down here too, the climate control almost negligible compared to the manufactured fresh breezes of the Studium menagerie. Her lungs cried out for gentler, cooler air and she engaged the breather in her velum. Beneath the faint hiss of filtered air she listened for Insignia, but the ship had become strangely silent.

Another AiV swooped in low, this one bearing Carabinere symbols.

Mira hurried to the entrance. The door opened automatically into a long corridor. According to the signage, one way led to the public docks, the other to the Fleet facility. She turned in the direction of the Fleet and a soldier in Fleet colours stepped out from the security cubicle. His fellala was crumpled and loose as if he had been sleeping in it, and he wore no hood. 'What is your business, signorina?'

'Marchesa Chocetta Silvio. I-I have a pre-arranged research visit to the Fleet.'

'Pardon, Marchesa. I will confirm this.' He returned to the cubicle and scanned his deskfilm. When he could not find mention of any research visit he reached for the shortcast.

Mira quickly stepped around to the entrance of the cubicle and laid her gloved fingers on his wrist. 'My Studium assignment is late and graduation is soon.' He would not know it had been today, surely?

The soldier smiled at her. Mira read much into that smile – a tincture of boredom and the desire to brag to his amicos that he had escorted one of the famous Silvio Marchesas around the hangar.

'I suppose we could call it an oversight, Marchesa, perhaps?'

She nodded slowly, making her eyes smile in return. 'I will need to see the Insignia.'

He halted in the process of entering the release codes. 'Aaah, then you are out of luck, Marchesa. Insignia was relocated but an hour ag—'

A siren blare drowned out the rest of the soldier's words. With quick fingers he reversed the unlocking process and ran outside.

She followed him as far as a pair of dust-coated doors. Beyond them a large AiV was disgorging a troop of Carabinere. The Fleet soldier stood to attention. Several Carabinere approached him and after a quick exchange he gesticulated back inside.

Me. They want me. Panicking, Mira hurried down the corridor towards the public docks but the corridor ended in opaque double doors that refused her entry. She pushed up her sleeve and tried her biometric stripe.

To her relief the doors slid open, letting her into another corridor which branched into a myriad smaller passageways. Each tributary harboured a dozen tube entrances. Lights flashed above each, announcing the tube's number and status: *arrived, holding, departing*.

At the distant end, past several checkpoints, the central passageway opened into the general embarkation station.

Mira hesitated for a moment: the embarkation station would be crowded and better for concealment, but the Carabinere would expect her to go there. She imagined them clamouring down the corridor behind her at any moment, could almost hear their boots and the clatter of their rifles.

Mounting fear drove her into a branch picked at random, following the dilapidated, ribbed conduit to the closed hatch of a ship. There a wave of confusion broke over her. Insignia had been relocated. Where was she running to? Her mind pressed outward like a prisoner seeking escape.

Are you in distress?

'Insignia?'

I do not know that one.

'Who are you?'

I am Sal. The strength of your brain patterns roused me. I have not communed in a long while.

Mira's breath caught in her throat. 'A-a biozoon. Are you a hybrid?'

My current sentient companion is not an Intuit so enmeshment is not viable. I travel adequately as an AI, although he has shut down my feeders. My previous companion was not an Intuit either but he still allowed me to feed. I miss him.

'But your feeders keep you . . .'

Sane? Is that what you think? 'No excellent soul is exempt from a mixture of madness . . . What is madness? To have erroneous perceptions and reason correctly from them . . . Those who danced were thought to be quite insane by those who could not hear the music . . . Sanity calms but—'

'Sal?'

Who are you? I ordered no live feed for dinner.

'But I thought you . . .'

I wonder if I've been changed in the night? Let me think. Was I the same when I got up this morning? I almost think I can remember feeling a little different. But if I'm not the same, the next question is 'Who in the world am I?' Ah, that's the great puzzle!

Mira clasped her head to stop the nonsensical prattle. 'I am in difficulty. May I come in?'

Her mind suddenly fell silent as if the voice had never existed. Only the pop of the pressure seal on the shiplock persuaded her that it had been real.

Lifting the hem of her fellala she stepped inside. A motion-sensor alarm immediately began to pulse. She hesitated – perhaps she should leave? But the hatch swung closed, sucking in stale station air with it.

Haaahaa . . . I have you now . . .

'Sal?' Did the ship mean her harm? Mira tried to remember what the tube's status light had shown – *holding*, she thought.

She felt her way deeper inside, following the gradient downwards to what she supposed was the cargo hold. Her eyes adjusted slowly in the dim interior light and dizziness forced her to cling to the cooling metal railing. Blasts of air poured from the enormous air-conditioning vents above her.

She descended a narrow set of stairs. When she reached the bottom she stood among shadowy crates, wondering what to do next.

Sal?

The biozoon remained silent but she could feel its presence as if it were . . . sulking.

A whine of hydraulics started up and a lift cage clunked free from the ceiling. Mira ducked between the crates. Should she just declare her presence? Or would the ship's captain hand her straight over to the Carabinere?

The lift cage dropped into its floor gig and a Balol with an erect skin frill slid open the cage door and stepped out. She arced torchlight around the hold.

'Anything?' The voice came from above, from the railings.

Mira glanced up and saw the outline of a humanesque male: Latino height, but slim.

The Balol made an irritated hissing sound. 'Maybe . . . if you would turn on the floodlights, Jancz.'

Mira crept backwards on her hands and knees until she found the wall. Feeling her way along she eventually encountered a handle. She eased it up and pushed. The door sucked a little air as it opened.

The Balol swivelled the torch in her direction. 'Did you hear something?'

Mira didn't wait for the man's reply. She slipped through the door and pressed it gently shut. She stood with her eyes closed for a moment and waited.

When she opened them she saw that this section was lit by the same lo-fluorescent nightlights as the rest of the hold. But rather than containing crates it was stacked high with odd round objects, each one at least half her size and crusted with a sticky yellow substance. The smell coming from them was a sweet, pungent odour of decay that made her eyes water. The objects seemed to be exuding heat, and through her tear-stung eyes she thought she could see that they moved a little. There was something about them . . . a vague recognition that stirred in her memory – something she had learned about at the Studium, perhaps?

The door behind her swung inward, knocking her to the floor, and a light shone into her face, leaving her blind to whoever wielded it.

'Araldisian,' said the Balol in a thick voice.

Another beam of light converged with the first,

causing Mira to shield her eyes against the amplified glare.

'Not just an Araldisian, Ilke. Brush off your manners – we have royalty aboard.'

Sole

manifestspace

little creature/wrestle wrestle
thought thought/wrestle/want want
m'need'm change
make'm better?
fake'm worse?
find'm secrets <luscious luscious>

TEKTON

That evening Tekton tucked into fresh pond liver and sipped a flat Lostolian wine provided by the pseudo-world's auto-servery, while his fact-aide reviewed the list of Sole's apprentices and their projects.

The implanted memory organiser had developed an annoying rasp on the trip to Belle-Monde, suggesting that it needed a service. He logged it in for maintenance through his new moud and requested a replacement. The AI told him they were in a gro-medical replacement phase and it would take several weeks.

Tekton sighed and set his teeth to tolerate the grating voice.

'Prior to your arrival Sole Entity had eight apprentices. Of that number only five are humanesque.'

'Who are the humanesques?'

'Second Godhead Ra of Architects, First Godhead Lawmon Jise, First Godhead Dicter Miranda Seeward, First Godhead Dicter Javid Jivviddat and First Godhead Geneer Labile Conit.'

Ra? How has my arrogant-cock cousin already made second? What deviousness has he wrought to do so? 'And where can Ra archi-Tect and the other apprentices be found now?'

'I believe the humanesques are all in the ménage lounge situated on Circle Five,' said the moud.

Tekton told the wallmap to summon a taxi and sought Ra out.

The ménage lounge was somewhat of a surprise: a circular golden cage with plush perch seats on different levels and exotic plants that snapped and undulated at each other behind glass. Not at all the normal OLOSS conservatism. A large filmdis on the ceiling ran OLOSS news updates and an uuli slithered to and fro over a hum, creating discordant harmonics.

Ra sat at a table alone, wearing an opaque mask across his eyes and circling his drink around an image cube.

Tekton approached him directly, allowing his robe to fall open in greeting. 'Cousin, how well do you fare?'

Tekton's cousin was slim, hairless and blessed with the fine, tight skin of the purest Lostol blood. Time at Belle-Monde, though, had already caused damage, and Ra's face and neck had developed tiny fissures like those in drought-cracked earth.

'Better than you, Tekton – having already begun my apprenticeship.' Ra didn't bother to remove the mask to make eye contact, nor did he open his robe to return Tekton's customary respect.

Tekton recorded his rude behaviour with his fact-aide. The Lostol Studium Convocation took a dim view of lack of respect and Ra's minor breach of protocol might prove to be a useful wedge at some point.

To push his point Tekton removed his own robe

altogether and sat naked before his cousin, ignoring the glances from the humanesques at the other tables.

'Soon to be remedied, cousin Ra. I would not wish to diminish your success by beginning *with* you. My status will be equal to yours soon enough.'

'Your delusions are surpassed only by the narrow-mindedness of your designs, Tekton. You will stew in your own goslee livers. Already, as a reward for being apprenticed, I have been given the key to variable sight,' said Ra. 'The benefits to my design facility are immeasurable.'

'Variable sight?'

Ra ceased toying with his drink and removed his mask. 'I can see the full electromagnetic spectrum.'

Tekton's long intestines tightened, not only at the strange appearance of his cousin's new eyes but also at the likely ramifications of such a gift on his design imagination. 'Congratulations, Ra. What . . . cleverness has brought you such a reward?'

Ra touched the spinning image cube in front of him and activated it.

Tekton watched the model flower into a replica of a section of space. Fiery anti-gravity reactions formed in the shape of a rectangle.

'A Neo-Brutalist Aedicule.' Ra smiled with satisfaction.

'You mean a doorway,' snorted Tekton.

'But in space, Tekton. And what is behind a doorway? Have you thought of that?' For the first time Ra looked at Tekton's face. His eyes were segmented. The pink had disappeared. 'No, you wouldn't have. Fine as your designs are, you have such a *grounded* imagination,' he added. 'Earthly.' Ra snapped the cube shut and stood, his robe still firmly closed. 'Goodbye, cousin. I imagine you will be having transformation tomorrow. Perhaps it might affect your imagination for the better.'

A Geneer and a Dicter seated at the bar watched with bright intentness as Ra left. Even the uuli on the hum everted its flange in interest.

Tekton put his robe back on and, without speaking to any of them, returned to his quarters and lay on his bed in a fury. He let rage swamp him, indulging in its comforting aftermath of righteousness. Ra had always been impossible but now his cousin's competitive instincts bordered on psychopathy. *Does Sole Entity monitor such deviations from the psychological norm?* he wondered.

With no audience for further discussion other than himself, his anger drained into fatigue.

Tekton sank into a bath of emulsifier, instructing the moud to play the welcome message. The President of OLOSS, dressed in egalitarian fatigues and with an elaborate dress ring threaded through his ear web, appeared in place of the Selenat waterfall.

'Archi-Tect Tekton, please be welcomed to Belle-Monde. You have been selected to trial your suitability to study under the wondrous Entity known to the sentient species as Sole. Should you be successful you will remain under the Entity's tutelage until either it or you seeks to relinquish your contract. All we ask is that you submit to regular evaluations and monitoring by our trained staff . . .'

Tekton drifted off as the President's welcome was replaced with a monotonous disclaimer. Eventually he grunted at the moud to silence the film.

His final thought before sleep claimed him concerned the uselessness of a mind that had to shut down regularly to recharge and rearrange. He resolved in his last wakeful seconds that this would be his first request to Sole: sleeplessness.

How else would he stand a chance of inhibiting Ra's ascendancy?

Tekton's *shafting* occurred precisely at 0817 hours in a room referred to by the livery as the Arena. The Arena was the only building on the surface of the pseudo-world, aside from the landing dock. The thick, transparent amphitheatre walls gave a clear and altogether uncomfortable view into the dark space where the Entity resided.

The humanesque technician, a Balol matron with thick skin ruffles around her neck and wrists, instructed Tekton to record another disclaimer specifically for the reconfiguration. She then directed him to climb inside a slim, tall container.

Tekton found Balols on the whole irritating and often odorous, but comforting in their attention to detail. This one's thick ruffles suggested her seniority so he complied with her request.

As she secured the container's cover, a waft from her inactive skin folds became trapped inside with him. He sat straight-backed and concentrated on controlling his gag reflex. It would never do to regurgitate. Imagine the repercussions.

At first nothing happened. He stared through transparent barriers into space beyond and waited.

Then he lost any semblance of cognition.

Afterwards Tekton likened the physical experience to having his brain violently sucked out through a tiny hole in the top of his skull and syphoned back through a straw.

As the pressure of the reconfiguration process built, the greater became his fear that the arrangement and order of his mind would be irrevocably lost. He experienced long, intense moments of sheer animal panic in which his subconscious survival instincts urged him to flee.

As he regained consciousness he discovered blood in his mouth and on his body where his taut skin had torn. Deep bruises already showed on his shoulders where he had flung himself against the sides of the container.

Tekton also discovered that his panic had been in part validated. His mind *was* irrevocably changed. Two distinct voices filled his head where a conglomerate consciousness had existed before.

The livery helped him out of the container and handed him liquid refreshment. He sipped the juice, listening closely to the two streams of thought. One, he realised after a time, spoke a torrent of unassailable reason while the other was a bubbling cauldron of creative emotion.

Tekton became exultant.

Where humanesque neurophysiology had previously doomed him to for ever be the victim of both, acting in concert as they had, now he was able to separate the two entirely. One was no longer inextricably linked with the other. He could *choose* which voice to follow. He felt social customs and personal desires tease apart from pure knowledge and roll into individual slots. He felt clarity and a sense of infinite possibility blossom.

The Balol interrupted his revelling introspection.

'You have been accepted to commune by the Sole Entity. It will now communicate directly with you. Because the Entity is invisible, the amphitheatre will decode and provide some imagined definition for you.' She added under her ruffle, almost to herself, 'We find this helps.'

Space fell at Tekton. Where in one breath he had been staring out into distance, in the next he was out in that cold distance. His free mind primal-screamed about vacuum and weightlessness, while his new logic-mind calmly deduced that either his senses had been tampered with or the Entity was somehow protecting him – he was alive and breathing, after all. In his first act of duality he shut his free mind off, and floated.

Sole appeared around him as rippling dark distortion, a glutinous shimmer beyond Tekton's understanding. He hung in Sole's space (or thoughtspace?) like an insect stuck in glue and pondered what wonders Ra would see with full-spectrum sight.

A trickle of acuity began to flow into his pristine logic-mind. It became a gurgle and then a gush – a torrent of connections forged, soaking into his brain as if it were a blotter. But the sensation ceased abruptly as the blotter soon grew saturated. Sensations gave way to an implicit message not spoken but absorbed.

Show/beauty.

* * *

Tekton reflected on his brief communion with the Entity for the next few days. Beauty was what the Entity sought. How did one show a god beauty?

His tyro stipulated no time constraints or deadlines, only that he comply with the observers and (this being the important subtext) bring acclaim to Lostol.

Tekton therefore divided his time between voicing design ideas for something beautiful into his moud-caddy, and inspecting the scope of the pseudo-world.

The tyros' sector was a small sliver given over to Sole's students – Circle Five, to be exact – and the rest belonged to a semi-ordered combination of OLOSS scientists and their support staff, a joint humanesque and organic-AI team.

In the larger part of the pseudo-world the physicists and astronemeins worked on a feverish, non-stop obser-vation of Sole.

While the moud answered Tekton's most pragmatic questions, he was compelled to take his deeper ques-tions back to the ménage lounge and meet the other humanesques. He also needed company. Tando Studium, his alma mater, was a busy, social place to work and Belle-Monde felt oddly lonely.

As Tekton taxied over to the lounge for the first time since meeting Ra, he asked the moud to tell him about his colleagues. Dicter Miranda Seeward, it said, was the director of the Advanced Surgical Facility on the planet Ikar.

Labile Conit – who would not disclose his place of origin – had studied at the famous Yeungnam Studium school of Geneering.

Javid Jivviddat was celebrated for having found a

cure for the uuli repeater virus. (Personally, Tekton thought it not such a great accomplishment – what would OLOSS miss about uulis? The colour of their slime?)

Lawmon Jise, on the other hand, was someone to be impressed by. He had shaped the new OLOSS charter – a most skilful, subtle piece of legislation that kept the arbiters of power among the sentients in perfect balance. Though Lawmon-ing for the most part bored Tekton, he couldn't help but appreciate such political genius. Negotiation and manipulation were useful skills for anyone. He must get to know Jise.

Tekton entered the lounge, keeping his robes firmly shut. The tyro humanesques ignored him. Perhaps Ra's superior manner had made them cautious. So he set about disarming it.

'I should have introduced myself earlier. I am Tekton archi-Tect from Lostol. You have already met my cousin Ra. Permit me to say that blood ties do not indicate common personality traits on my world.'

Dicter Miranda chuckled while Labile Conit scowled into his drink. Tekton disliked him instantly – but that was not an uncommon phenomenon between Geneers and archi-Tects.

'Your work on Ikar is highly regarded, Dicter Seeward. I'm surprised you could be spared to come here,' Tekton said agreeably.

'Spared, archi-Tect? Surely you mean that this would be an obvious progression and reward for me.'

'That as well.' Tekton forced a polite smile to his lips.

'The case for all of us,' added Labile Conit.

'Indeed, Labile Conit. You, Dicter Miranda, Dicter Jivviddat and Lawmon Jise are all celebrated individuals – at the top of your professions. I am honoured to be in your company.' However much the flattery irked him, Tekton knew it would salve the damage done by Ra's arrogance. Academics differed little in that regard. 'Tell me, have I received the wrong impression, or are the OLOSS scientists here disinterested in our . . .' he searched for a word '. . . programme?'

'Their interest in us is purely experiential,' said Miranda. 'As long as we present for regular scans and keep out of their research area they are happy. Astronemeins care only for matter and gravity. The fact that an invisible consciousness exists has thrown their paradigms into disarray.'

I can imagine, thought Tekton. 'And tell me, how fare your projects?'

Suspicion fell over their faces like a shadow cast by an eclipse.

An uncomfortable silence settled until Lawmon Jise cleared his throat. 'We have found it better not to discuss such things in leisure hours,' he volunteered.

'But Tekton is new to Belle-Monde and is excited about his project,' Labile Conit interrupted. 'It would be rude of us not to let him share it.'

Tekton looked from one attentive face to the next. As quickly as it had appeared, the shadow had gone. Now they leaned toward him intently. He felt flattered at their interest and it swelled his akura. 'Of course I have yet to define my project exactly but Sole has asked me to—'

'Stop.' Lawmon Jise had risen to his feet, extending

a commanding hand. 'Shame on you, Labile Conit. Shame, shame, shame.' His voice was musical and mesmerically imperious. Tekton imagined him wielding it like a cut-throat among OLOSS politicians.

'If the truth be known, and it should, we have found it better not to discuss our projects at all. There is then no room for dispute.'

Tekton felt profoundly grateful to the Lawmon – an 'esque he could trust. Towards Conit, on the other hand, he felt an almighty rush of childish fury. His logic-mind rushed in to prevent any nonsense. *Academia is academia, Tekton. You are the fool for thinking anything else*, it chided him.

'Of course. I see,' said Tekton. 'Now, let me buy you all a drink.'

Tekton continued his regular visits to the ménage lounge. He took great pains to hide the fact that he had no inspiration and was despairing that he might have contracted geniusblock.

He thought of confiding in Lawmon Jise but pride forestalled him.

Then, during Happy Hormone shooters hour some weeks after his *shafting*, Tekton witnessed an appalling event.

Every spare second thenafter his free-mind replayed the sight and sound of Jise and Miranda's untuned flesh slapping and whumping as the two academics met and tussled astride the bar – unable to settle their differences in anything but a wrestle. Something about the ripple of Dicter Miranda's thighs gave Tekton shivers of creative wonder.

In fact, he found it impossible to subdue his erection for most of the following Mintaka-day. *What structures can I build that would emulate such sensual flow?*

So taken was his free-mind with the images that afterwards even his logic-mind could barely recall the bone of contention between the two, a point of argument over the medical and legal efficacy of fungi in the treatment of cross-species disease. (Were not, indeed, most fungi bordering on legally sentient anyway? Lawmon Jise argued.)

The point of discussion mattered not to Tekton but the event sparked an idea and he immediately set about sourcing the raw materials to realise his revelation.

TRIN

Jilda Pellegrini's chauffeured luxury AiV delivered Trin
to a smooth low-slung building midway down Franco's
Mountain.

Seated in his vast office, Carabinere Director
Malocchi didn't bother to move his feet from his desk
when Trin entered. Instead, he continued to inhale on
his Cusano and gaze at the picturesque windo-view of
the auburn landscape.

'Good morning, Signor Malocchi.' Trin chose deference in favour of arrogance. Let the loco director think
he was compliant.

The Malocchis had been handling the Cipriano Clan's
security since before settlement. They served the
Pellegrinis dogmatically but without, Trin believed, the
correct heartfelt respect. Trin had always thought that
their belief was in what they did, not in who they did it for.
If he were in Franco's position, he would denude the
Malocchis of their rank and bring in new blood. But
Franco was too dependent – or, perhaps, too indebted.

'Your title here will be Lesser Adviser.'

'A Lesser Adviser to what?'

'What you have been brought up to do, of course –
nothing. You will be given an office and in it you will stay.'

Trin became hot with embarrassment and anger.
'Why would I do that?'

This time Malocchi turned his head. 'Because I have told you to.'

'You cannot *tell* me to do anything. The Principe may be punishing me for a foolish error but I am still his son. Treat me poorly and, in the end, it will be *you* who will be castigated!'

Malocchi gave him a keen stare. 'You do not know, do you?'

Trin's skin prickled. 'Know what?'

'Why you have been sent here.'

'I killed an uuli: accidental and unfortunate. The Principe thinks to teach me about responsibility.'

'The uuli. Aaaah . . . yes. But it is not the uuli for whom you have been cast down.'

Cast down. Trin's mouth felt dry, as if he'd taken too much bravura. The hot prickling of his skin turned to shivers of alarm. 'You speak nonsense, signor.'

'In Riso's Bar you did the courting dance with a woman – is that not so?'

Trin shrugged, unsurprised that Malocchi had such information but unable to see its importance. 'So . . .'

'Did you not think it odd that the woman whom you so inappropriately and publicly pledged to bed was minded by Palazzo Cavaliere?'

'There are many Cavaliere in the Palazzo. I hardly notice them.'

Malocchi leaned back in his chair. 'Perhaps, then, you should sharpen your observation skills.'

'What point are you dancing around, Signor Malocchi?'

Malocchi let silence fill the space between them, savouring whatever revelation he was about to spring, taking flagrant pleasure in the matter. 'You performed a mating dance with your father's newest concubine.' He laughed then. Belly-deep and cruel.

Luna. Trin trembled through every part of his body.

Malocchi wiped the laughter from his eyes. 'Now you see . . . I think it best that you keep out of the way.'

Trin clung to his bravado. 'I-I will not do as you bid.'

Malocchi inhaled and blew out a long stream of acrid yellow smoke. 'Franco has made it clear that he wants to hear nothing about you. If there should be the slightest whisper that you are *not* doing as you are instructed then I believe you may find your gratuity affected. And worse. But of course,' he smiled openly now, enjoying himself, 'that is none of my business.'

Trin left Malocchi and returned to the Palazzo but his father would not see him. The door Cavaliere presented arms before blocking his path when he tried to pass.

Frustrated, he hastened to the sitting room and checked his gratis rating on the familia e-boards. A bulletin had been posted stating that his status had been suspended temporarily. He could he not procure anything that required gratis without the Principe's approval. With no other 'external' income, Trin had no tender. His thoughts flew first to his depleted bravura supply.

Panicking, he searched out Jilda. She was seated at her faux-Regence window, sober. He stood between her and the view, motioning the shutters to close. She would not ignore him as Franco had done.

In response to the sudden darkening of the room, the lights brightened into a splendorous, twinkling affair.

'Restore my gratis, mama,' he demanded.

She looked away from him. 'I cannot, my son.'

Furious, Trin punched the shutters. But Jilda kept her composure.

He stared at her with suspicion. She wore a new morning costume, uncreased for once, and her eyes seemed clear, almost bright. Beyond her, through the patinated screens of her sleeping area, he could see her bed ruffled and turned down on both sides. 'What promises has he made you?'

'Do not speak of your papa in that tone, Trinder. He is doing what is right, what is needed. I have spoiled you. An uuli, Trin. How could you do such a thing after Franco has risked all to make you Pilot First?'

'It was an accident. And what do you care for an uuli?' Trin was beset by an urge to hit Jilda. The smallest of attentions from Franco and she became compliant to a man who had no interest in her. How could he, Trin, have been bred from such a pathetic woman?

Instead, he inhaled deeply, composing himself. There were other ways to hurt her. 'He is not punishing me because of the uuli, mama. Ask him about his new mistress. Ask him about her taste for younger men. And then remember that I am your son. My failings are yours. And in the end Franco will make *you* pay for them.' He motioned the shutters open and the lights dimmed. 'He won't stay in your bed for long, you know. The new woman he has is far more beautiful.'

As Trin let himself out of his mother's apartment he saw, to his satisfaction, that she was crying.

Unsure of what to do next, he called the chauffeur to take him back to Centrale. Deep in gloomy thought, he saw nothing of the staggering view as they descended Mount Pell. The rugged vista of purple iron rock and red dust plains were as opaque to him as the workings of his father's mind.

The Galiotto chauffeur roused him from his brooding. 'Should I wait, Don?'

Trin shook his head. 'I will summon you later. I have . . . business here.'

The Galiotto nodded but proffered no further comment.

How long, Trin wondered, before all the Nobile knew of his fall from favour?

He located the main administration section and asked to be shown to an office.

'There are no available offices in Centrale,' the young woman to whom he had spoken told him. Around her, others hid their faces behind their deskfilms, smirking.

'But there must be. Where will I go?' Childish anguish overwhelmed him and tears threatened.

A dark-haired Cabone working quietly in the corner spoke up. 'I have not been here long but I think there may be a vacant office in the malformed section.' She touched her deskfilm and searched through the building plan.

The others glanced at each other with barely suppressed astonishment – the young Principe in an office in the malformed section.

The Cabone scowled at them and stood up. 'I will show you if you would like,' she said.

Trin nodded gratefully and followed her out into the

corridor. She led him down to the refectory level, deliberately keeping a distance between them.

'What's your name?' he asked after a few moments of walking.

'Rantha.'

'Why are you the only one who would help me, Rantha?'

She shrugged. 'Perhaps they enjoyed your humiliation. It is not often the Nobile see the Crown discomforted.'

'And you?'

'Your tia Marchella has helped me. I am returning the favour because you are one of her familia.'

Tia Marchella Pellegrini? Trin's interest sharpened. What had his loco tia done for this young woman? And why did she think she could speak so baldly to him of it?

He mustered some hauteur. 'I am still the Principe's son and I find your forthright speech insulting.'

'Insulting? What would you do about it? What sway do you hold with the Principe on this day, Trin Pellegrini, that I should be frightened of it?'

He absorbed her blunt point as though swallowing a lump of Araldis ore.

Rantha stopped abruptly and turned to him. 'You need not feel humiliated. You have been sent out to work – what is so bad in that? I would take your problems this instant to be rid of mine.'

Trin's laugh was tinged with bitterness. 'Your problems, little Cabone. How great could they be?'

In a deliberate gesture she flattened her fellala across her belly. The mound of a growing bambino was unmistakable. 'My . . . man pledged to me that if we were intimate he would remain infertile. He lied and left me like this. Now I am unwed. When the Malocchis find out I will be without means.'

'You will still have your gratis.'

'There is no gratis for one such as I. The only person on Araldis who would look to my future is Marchella Pellegrini,' she replied.

The bitterness and regret on Rantha Cabone's face made Trin feel guilty. He pushed the feeling away. After all, it was not he who had fathered her child. 'Perhaps you should not have gambled so?' he said.

'Yes, you are right. I should not have trusted a familia man.'

Thankfully the conversation faltered as they were forced to stoop under a bulge in the ceiling. In a bent-over fashion they continued on down an ill-formed narrow corridor.

At the end they found a small windowless room where the polymer-grown building had rooted itself to the side of Mount Pell.

Trin stared in disbelief. 'I cannot be here.'

Rantha sniffed the air and looked around. 'Industrial Services will activate your film. This one looks old. And your environmentals will need servicing. I can smell mould.'

A buckled deskfilm hung over a large lump of ore on a desk littered with shrivelled data-sponges. A single chair and some uneven wall shelving comprised the only other furniture.

Rantha gave him a single direct look. 'I apologise for my . . . manner. I am easily angered these days.' She turned and left.

Trin slumped into the chair. What to do now? His welling self-pity was tempered by annoyance. *Jus Malocchi will pay for this. And so will Franco.*

He reached for the deskfilm. He laid it flat and stabbed his finger at the thin, scratched screen. It switched itself on and tried to straighten, flickering for a while before the picture resolved. He used the administration menu to find the climate controls, which he boosted.

Dust stirred all around him and the enviromentals rattled into life trying to filter it. Aggravated by the clutter on the desk, Trin collected the sponges and shoved them onto the sagging shelves. The force of his action knocked other precarious piles to the floor.

In the space behind them Trin glimpsed a bubble – a result of the catoplasma malformations. As a ragazzo he had burst similar bubbles in the AiV hangars at the Palazzo. He lifted the shelving aside to have a better look and on impulse he jabbed a finger into it. The polymer coating punctured as he expected, but then the wall around it crumbled. Immediately he felt a draught of hot outside air.

Trin scrambled back to the deskfilm to boost the climate controls to cover the temperature change and quickly locked the door. Then he returned to the hole and carefully felt around the inside. The crumbling of the wall appeared to have left a gap between rock and building.

How far along does it go?

He slipped his head through the hole. In one direction was solid seam. The other way was a crevice with hot daylight flooding down it. He guessed it might come out near the upper AiV pads.

Widening the hole enough for his body, Trin squeezed

through and flattened himself against the rock. It was hot to touch and the space was only barely wide enough. He edged along the distance towards the light and peered out. Sure enough, across a small expanse of rock he located the AiV pads. The discovery both pleased and displeased him. The structural fault might prove useful – perhaps he could come and go from the building without being observed – yet it also seemed to emphasise the disrespect with which he was being treated.

Trin returned to the office and began looking for things to block the gap up. Pushing the shelving back into place, he replaced the stacks of sponges and sat down at his desk. He flicked idly through the film menu, wondering what to do. Malocchi had given him no tasks.

He reached for a random data-sponge and laid it against the deskfilm. It displayed details of familia births, deaths and marriages.

Trin's irritation evaporated into curiosity. First, he searched the statistics for his immediate family, his cousins Josef, Pesca, Antonia, Juni, Deboraah, Aldo. Then he moved on to Franco's generation: tia Marchella, tio Kotta, tia Mari. Slutty tia Ghia, he realised, had been lying about her age. And tio Kotta's first wife had been a ginko. The records showed that the marriage had been annulled. *And hushed up!* His curiosity flared into a tiny surge of excitement. He glanced at the shelves. Perhaps the sponges held information that would keep him amused for a time . . .

Attaching a number of them to the film, Trin settled deeper into his chair and read until hunger drove him out.

*　　*　　*

Like Malocchi's office, one wall of the Centrale refectory was a window given over to the panorama of the mining plains. Today, though, Pellegrini A and B mines were invisible because of a gargantuan wall of dust. Only the silver-snake conveyors winding their way into the storm, like tributaries to a larger stream, gave any indication of the mines' positions.

Trin stood and watched, relieved to be safely on Mount Pell. Only once had he been caught in a dust storm, when he had flown out to meet with a bravura dealer. Even now he could feel the panic of choking.

'Don Pellegrini?' The ragazza serving behind the food-warmer interrupted his thoughts. 'Pardon, but you must wait in line to be served.'

Embarrassed and angry, Trin stepped back to the end of the queue. When his turn arrived he held out his plate the way the others had.

She piled it inelegantly with food. 'Signor Malocchi has asked me to inform you that your food costs will be deducted from your first pay.'

Trin kept his expression carefully neutral. The ragazza was Scali or Cabone. Of all the Nobile they were the familia that he valued most – the ones he had played with from childhood. They weren't obsequious like the Galiottos or arrogant and obsessive like the Malocchis and the Montfortes. This situation was as uncomfortable for her as it was for him.

Ignoring the curious looks of the other diners, he took his food to a corner seat and ate without speaking to a soul. As he sipped his mocha, waiting for its essences to fortify his poise, he became aware of another presence.

Rantha.

She stood uncertainly before him. He glanced across to the next table and noticed that the women from her office had spread their frittata plates out so that there was no place for her.

Trin had no wish to ally himself with this angry, pregnant Nobile but she seemed as friendless as he – and, he reminded himself, she had helped him. He needed allies here, not enemies. Rantha worked in a section that saw and heard most things.

He nodded to the empty chair opposite and forced some unfelt charm into his smile.

'Grazi,' she whispered as she sank into the chair.

Over the next day Trin familiarised himself with the extent of the recorded data. He discovered that the cross-reference organics were inadequate and unable to generate a report or factfilm.

He called Rantha.

'Scalis handle that. I'll route you through to one of them,' she said.

'Fine.' Then, after a moment, he added: 'Are you well?' On his damaged deskfilm her crimson skin looked oily and peculiarly sallow.

'Sick,' she whispered. 'Ask for Joe Scali. He is helpful and . . . nice.'

Trin checked the Industrial Services directory. A surprised voice in IS told him that Joe Scali would be there within a short time, and, scuzzi, but could he give them directions?

Joe Scali arrived juggling diagnostic sticks and a frothy mocha in a tall mug. He had thick dark hair and a well-muscled physique that looked more suited to troubleshooting conveyor-belt automats on the plains than the delicacies of programming organic trees.

Scali wrinkled his nose with distaste as he looked around. 'I did not know there was an . . . office here.'

Trin grimaced. 'You Scalis do not get out enough.'

'Si. And I detest that.' The young man gave a heart-felt sigh.

It made Trin curious. 'Why not reassign, then?'

'I was with Carabinere out in Ipo. Got in a disagreement with the Cavaliere – a Montforte.' He rolled his eyes. 'Next thing I was back here.'

Trin nodded. 'Malocchis and Montfortes . . .' He held up crossed fingers.

'Thicker than my mama's cannelloni.' The Scali eyed him keenly. 'I am guessing that you might have suffered from a similar problem. Why else would the Principe's son be confined in a . . . cave?'

'Because I killed an uuli.' The words were out before he realised. *And flirted with my papa's woman.*

Scali whistled and rolled his eyes again. 'Any reason?'

'An accident that I have no wish to speak of . . . Now, I need a tree that will cross-check all these . . .'

'I am Josef.'

'Well, Josef, can you do this?' Trin pointed to lists on the menu.

Scali's eyes opened wide in astonishment when he saw the lines that Trin was tracing. 'What do you want all that for?'

Trin waved his hands at the piles of data on the shelves. 'These records are useless for anything. I wish to change that. Can you do it, Nobile?' he cajoled.

Scali sipped his mocha. 'Si. Perhaps.'

'Rantha Cabone tells me that you are the best in your section.'

'Rantha, eh?' He raised an eyebrow. 'Man-hater, that one.'

'No.' Trin surprised himself with his mild defence of her. 'She thinks you are . . . how did she put it . . . *nice*.'

Scali cleared his throat with embarrassment and picked up his empty mug. 'I will give this my priority, Don Pellegrini, but I cannot be sure of the outcome.'

Trin nodded his understanding. The Ciprianos had brought only rudimentary processing organisms with them to Araldis. They should have been superseded, so the Studium interactives informed him, but the great cost of starting a new society on a brand new world had demanded that the funds be syphoned elsewhere.

Far-cast communications were worst affected by preserving the primitive system. Far-news was always delayed and scant. Most of Araldis hadn't even heard about the Stain Wars until the forces concerned had been skirmishing for half an Araldis year.

The Scali familia showed the most aptitude for managing the crude biosystem but even they were often lost when it came to growing new applications.

Trin slid his hand from his pocket and opened it. Multicoloured bravura grains rolled around his palm. 'Could you could keep it quiet from Signor Malocchi?'

Scali glanced nervously around the office as if Jus Malocchi might jump out from behind something. 'Is it as good as they say?' he whispered.

'Better.'

A light sweat broke out on the technician's upper lip. 'As you wish, Don. But should anyone ask me, I will tell them that you said Malocchi ordered the new programme, eh?'

'Call me Trinder.' Trin pinched a couple of precious grains into Scali's mocha.

After two sips the swelling between Scali's legs was tenting his fellalo.

Trin and Scali burst out laughing.

TEKTON

Tekton's design for Sole flowered in his free-mind. The trouble was, his logic-mind regularly reminded him, that he had the idea but not the material with which to construct it.

So Tekton buried himself in study. Somewhere there had to be a metal that rippled like liquid in its solid state. Yet it seemed that everywhere he searched Ra had been before him – consuming information at a shocking rate. There were traces of him on the Vreal Studium's geological data files: his signature in the mineral catalogues sign-on, his credit on the OLOSS assay register.

Ra had become a foregoing malignant ghost.

Was his cousin trying to second-guess him? Or were their ideas uncannily taking them to the same places?

Tekton's free-mind liked to think it was the former, indicating that, perhaps, Ra might feel somewhat threatened by Tekton, despite his apparent arrogance.

Tekton's logic-mind, however, told him that this notion was based purely on ego and that evidence suggested that Ra merely had an inquiring mind and a strong work ethic. And if knowledge was power – Ra was growing more powerful. So be warned!

To distract himself from what, his logic-mind also hastened to tell him, was creeping paranoia, he took up perving.

It was easy enough to justify his actions as empirical observation. However, justification had become a sort of moot point now that his mind had been re-formed. His internal life had become all about choice, in which he could as easily turn off recrimination and doubt as peel a Balol ugli-peach.

And Tekton loved it.

He set about wooing Dicter Miranda with the sole (he excused himself the pun) ambition of gaining a closer inspection of her thighs.

On their first date he took her for a shuttle ride around Belle-Monde. As the creaking tug wallowed its way around the pseudo-world close to Sole-space, Tekton wondered what Sole was thinking, or if, indeed, Sole thought at all. When you knew almost everything, what would there be left to wonder about?

To his disappointment, Miranda was wrapped in a voluminous silvery garment that covered most of her flesh. Tekton mind-instructed his moud to alter the enviro setting to 'uncomfortably warm'. He then apologised for it, grumbling excuses about the pseudo-world's poor maintenance.

By the time the heat began to make him feel a little light-headed, however, there was little show of Dicter Miranda's flesh.

'How marvellous this feels, Tekton – I've been cold ever since I got to this damn place. Might even sweat off a few joules. Or is that jowls?' She laughed heartily. The act of mirth filled her false cheeks with air and wobbled them.

The frisson of delight Tekton experienced nearly equalled that of the night when he had witnessed her 'thighs' in action (though he had taken to keeping his robe tightened in company, so as not to alert his colleagues to his feelings). He felt so gratified by her display that he picked the scorched lobster for lunch and ordered up a bottle of Lostol vintage spritzer.

Miranda's eyes sparkled at the extravagant fare. 'You do know how to treat a girl. Now Tekton, tell me *all* about you – and about that rather deliciously brooding cousin of yours. We're dying to know.'

She flirted and bantered as she polished off the best part of his month's complimentary food allowance.

'And what of your affairs, Miranda? Have you sorted out your differences with Lawmon Jise?'

She sniffed, giving her best impression of grievance. 'The man is impossible – such a pedant. Not a person to trust either, Tekton. Why, I heard he was offering information on your project – for a price. Of course I declined the knowledge. This is not a competition between us, is it, Tekton? We are more a family. A brilliant, clever family, of course.'

At that point Miranda lifted the tail of her shift and crossed her legs, showing a large measure of undulating thigh flesh.

Something in the artful timing of it triggered a thought. *Moud? Has Dicter Miranda been on any other dates recently?*

Date is a difficult term to define, Godhead. However, she has been in the company of others.

Who?

Most regularly, Lawmon Jise.

What do you mean by 'in company'? Evenings? Have they been sleeping together?

Yes, Godhead.

Thank you. Dear, devious Dicter Seeward – but not devious enough.

Tekton told the moud to instruct the tug to cut short the slow approach and finished up the date early, before cognac, leaving Miranda with a courtly bow on the docking bay. No matter how much she inflated her cheeks, he vowed silently, she would not entice him to disclose an iota about his project premise – nor would he buy her spritzer ever again!

Tekton went back to his rooms in a huff.

'Moud. Tell me where Lawmon Jise is located. And how I might spy on him.'

The moud floundered for a moment. *Could you give me more information, Godhead?*

'What privacy rules have been set in place?'

Each occupant may secure their rooms if they so wish.

'How many do so?'

All – with the exception of you, Godhead.

'Even Ra?'

Most certainly Godhead Ra, Godhead.

'Has my room been entered by anyone?'

Yes. You did not set the privacy conditions.

'Who?' Tekton could not keep the shrill note from his mind-voice.

Sentient?

'YES, sentients!'

Lawmon Jise, Dicter Seeward and . . . The moud took what Tekton imagined to be a deep breath. *Ra.*

'Good Sole!' mind-shouted Tekton. 'What were you thinking, letting them in here?'

You did not stipulate your wishes. The default is programmed to an open room.

'Why? What was this place before? A bordello?' Tekton snapped.

The moud took another 'breath'. *Yes, Godhead. It was.*

MIRA

'Remove the mask,' said the man in clumsy Latino.

No hand extended to help her; no apology came for knocking her down. Breaking the seal on her velum, Mira folded it back and climbed shakily to her feet. Her shoulder blade felt bruised and her neck was already stiffening.

'What are you doing here?' The man spoke again. He stood on her left, the Balol on her right. The female's musky odour was so strong that it overpowered the astringent scent of the objects behind her.

'Please. I-I cannot see,' Mira protested shielding her eyes from their flashlights with her hands. 'I am here by mistake . . . an accident.'

The man uttered a few discordant sounds and switched his light off. The Balol lowered the beam of hers to the floor.

Mira blinked several times to refocus her eyes. The pair stood close together. The man looked unkempt but not dim-witted. His blanched hair and elongated physique suggested that he had spent time in space, and she sensed that he was older than he seemed. His features were misaligned, crooked – not an easy face to forget.

The Balol wore no clothing over her amour-thick skin and bore many ridges of decoration scars on her chest and arms. Mira could not recall the significance of them: Balols were not a species she had chosen to learn about; their coarse habits had always made them an unattractive study subject. She had preferred the musically gifted uuli and the simple bellodina.

'Then tell me, signorina, why is the entire Araldis Carabinere roaming the docking tubes in search of you?'

She tried to identify the man's origins and could not. The humanesque diversity in the Orion system exceeded anything on Araldis.

He stepped forward unexpectedly and began patting her body for weapons.

Mira trembled under his rough, invasive handling. 'This is not necessary – I am unarmed and I am unused to—'

His fingers halted on her bruised shoulder and gripped her until she cried out. 'Not used to what? Trespassing? I could push you straight out of the lock for that, or inform the Carabinere that I have you. You think you can stand here and make demands?' he snarled.

The pain robbed her of speech and she could not stop her body swaying under his grip.

Sensing that she was close to fainting the man let go of her and stepped back

Mira bent forward and swallowed gulps of air while the Balol sent the beam of her light darting from ceiling to wall, searching for something.

'What is your name?' the man demanded.

'Marchesa Silvio,' Mira answered.

'Try again, signorina. I know what Cips look like. You

are too lean and angled. You could not be a Crown aristo.'

Mira felt anger rise up and subdue the fear in her belly. She straightened. She would not discuss her pedigree with a common humanesque. 'You have expertise in Latino lineage?' she asked coldly.

He hesitated as if her mild question had thrown him. Then the shortcast device on his wrist chimed and drew his attention. 'I'm afraid your holiday is over,' he told her softly.

Mira's heart quickened. If the Carabinere had found her then she must strike a bargain with this man. She would not let Franco and Trinder Pellegrini take her Inborn Talent. 'If you hand me over to the Carabinere, I shall explain to them that you are harbouring an illegal life form in your cargo hold.'

The man forced a laugh. 'What would a Latino crossbreed know of illegal life forms?'

Mira summoned the haughtiness she had practised well as defence against the Silvios and the Elenas. 'More than you know about nobility, signor. I am an educated woman – do not underestimate that. I also have a sound deductive ability. The smell and composition of these objects is as undeniably alien as your companion. And if your cargo were legal you would not be coupled to this isolated berth, you would be attached to quarantine. I assume you must be paying someone well to go unnoticed.'

The man crossed the space between them with frightening speed. 'How does your education and breeding help you when this happens?' He jerked a knife from a shoulder harness beneath his jacket and pressed it to Mira's throat.

She retreated from the sharp pressure on her windpipe, stumbling backwards, falling.

He leaped forward, pinning her down, and she felt his male urge swelling against her abdomen. For a long, terrifying moment she thought that he would abuse her. His ragged breath and grasping fingers told her that he was thinking about doing so.

'Signor,' she pleaded.

'How did you get onto my ship?' he whispered into her ear. 'How did you override the locks?'

Mira strained her neck to turn her head aside and put some distance between their breaths. 'I-I am an Intuit. Your biozoon let me in.'

The man rolled off her and sat back on his heels in surprise. 'Not possible. Intuits are as rare as quixite and female Intuits . . . I have never heard of one. Anyway, the organic component of the ship is inactive.'

Mira lay still, fearful that any movement might bring him back closer. 'You can never entirely repress its cognitive processes unless you kill it, in which case your ship would not be able to fly.'

'What has the ship said to you, then?'

'It told me that it is starving, that you are keeping it in silence. I asked it for help and it let me in. That is all.' She did not tell him that she thought the biozoon was unstable.

The man stared hard at her. He was not a person, she thought, who believed in trust.

'Who would miss you if I used this?' He brought the knife up before her face.

Mira closed her eyes to his cruel expression. 'I would rather be dead than in the hands of the Carabinere. Yet truthfully I would prefer neither. I can . . . *will* use my talent to harm your ship if you alert them.'

'You cannot do that.'

He was right. She could not – at least, not without serious injury to herself. 'If I can stay here until they have finished their search then I will go without interfering.'

The man pressed the knife to Mira's throat again. This time, though, she could feel the length of the blade's sharp edge across her neck, in the killing position.

'Jancz?' growled the Balol in a warning tone. 'Listen.'

Mira opened her eyes.

The man, Jancz, had become still and alert.

A moment later the dim floor lights went out and the air became thick and silent.

The Balol flashed the beam of her light to the ceiling vents.

Sal? Is that you? Have you stopped the air?

You said you would wound me? The biozoon sounded hurt.

No. Understand that I am bargaining for my life. It is a game.

What game?

I am hiding from humanesques who would close down my . . . my feed. Your captain would hand me to them.

'What have you done, Intuit?' Jancz hauled Mira to a seated position. He sheathed the knife and pinched the front of her throat with his bare fingers, constricting her breathing.

'The – ship – is proving my point—' she gasped.

'Unprove it!'

'What – of – me?'

Jancz's grip became intolerable. It was as if he would

squeeze words from her mouth, or crush her breath. Little explosions of light pinpricked her eyelids and her senses diminished. She could hear nothing; feel only the pressure.

Sal – please accept – as truth! Mira begged. *Give back – life support – or he will – kill me.*

A torrent of chatter entered her mind. *Pain analysis: cutaneous nociceptors – unmylinatedC fibres – transmitting at .04999 mps along the laminae II and III of the dorsal horns. Glutamate released on the spinway to the thalamus and on up to Brodman areas 3,2 and 1 . . . stress authenticated.*

< Sigh> Very well.

Slowly, the darkness began to abate and once again Mira could see the outline of Jancz's nose and the smooth, low line of his brow. A downward blast of air chilled the perspiration on her face. The numbness receded as the fingers at her neck loosened enough for her to cough violently.

'I want you off my ship, Intuit.' Jancz's voice carried a hint of breathlessness.

With shaking hands Mira massaged her hot, swollen throat to enable herself to speak. She tried to crawl away from Jancz and failed, her limbs too weak. 'Transport me – to the plainlands – to Loisa – and I will – forget what I – have seen.'

Jancz sprang upright. 'Where did you say?'

'Loisa?' Mira repeated.

He turned to the Balol and they exchanged smiles. 'Come.'

He dragged Mira to her feet and through the door back into the main hold. The lift cage took them to a mid-deck. From there they walked a loop of corridors, past a well-appointed galley and infirmary to a set of cabins.

Jancz appeared to select one at random and pushed Mira inside. 'I will consider your offer.' He stepped out and the door snapped shut between them.

Mira sank to the floor and sobbed.

When her tears and shaking finally subsided she looked around the cabin. To her surprise it was plainly but quite luxuriously furnished, with a large bed and screened-off personal-hygiene fixtures. Though she longed to clean herself properly she settled for a wash and a tentative examination of her shoulder. The bruising was severe but the skin was unbroken. She felt past the mirror mirage, searching for a lotion to reduce the inflammation. The mirror image burst and she encountered someone's – a male's – personal effects: body scents, lubricating gels and other appurtenances that warmed her skin with embarrassment.

Mira withdrew her hand and the image reinstated itself. Returning to the bedroom, she tried to open one of the many cupboards. *Locked. All locked.* She tapped the sensors on the bedhead array. All the cupboards in the cabin opened at once to reveal an extensive library of recreational simulations. She pulled one out at random and put it back quickly, shocked by the vulgar contents.

A fearful thought took her. *Sal? To whom does this room belong?*

You will make me sad again, asking questions.

Is it the captain's room?

Yes. No. Your questions are too difficult.

Please concentrate, Sal. Will Captain Jancz sleep in this room?

Him? No. No . . . no . . . no . . . not allowed. Never. The biozoon drifted off then, refusing to return despite her pleading.

Jancz did not return until the next evening. Mira knew it was evening from the cabin display and the fierce hunger in her belly: more than a day without food and the worry that he might come for her if she dared to try to sleep.

'I've decided to accept your proposal.'

To her relief he beckoned her out into the corridor and along a distance until he stopped at an open hatch lit by a down light.

'Now down!' he ordered.

The entry to the ship's lug was a single flexible ladder encapsulated in similar material to the conduit that attached the ship to the station. With deliberate – and, she hoped, infuriating – dignity, Mira collected the loose outer folds of her fellala in one hand and stepped onto the ladder. The climb tested her balance but she managed to negotiate it without falling.

Below the bottom rung was enough room for a person to crouch, swivel and slide through another small hatch into the cockpit of the lug.

The small craft was already vibrating with life and an interior light switched on as Mira entered, feet first. Three harnesses hung like soft skeletons against the side behind the pilot's seat. Behind the co-pilot's position lay rows of tightly stacked crates.

Mira stumbled straight into the co-pilot's seat, her

fingers skittering along the controls searching for the hatch command. If she could shut him out . . . but Jancz was there, leaning over her before she could finish her thought.

In the lug's bright interior light Mira saw him closely for the first time. The irregularity of his features was not unpleasant so much as unusual, but his eyes were devoid of any expression that Mira understood.

'Hands off, Baronessa. Or I will remove them for you, right there.' Jancz drew an imaginary line across her wrists with a chopping movement.

Mira snatched back her hands and folded them in her lap.

Jancz turned and began checking the latches on the crates. One latch rattled and as he tightened it she caught an impression of neatly stacked sheets of a material that was unfamiliar to her. It resembled catoplasma – but hard and brittle-looking.

Jancz snapped the lid shut and climbed into the pilot's seat. He set the navigation coordinates and the lug wallowed against the side of the ship. 'Ilke,' he said. 'Release.'

Mira heard the coupling grate apart and felt the lug set free from the ship. She sank back into the harness and closed her eyes, thankful to be nearly away from the disturbed biozoon, thankful to have evaded the Cavaliere and the Carabinere.

When she opened them again the remnants of an Araldis sunset were streaming through the window. She watched with relief as Dockside's graceless collection of buildings fell away behind them.

Within a short time they had crossed the fringes of

the sprawling open-cut mines and pock-marked under-grounds. Evening had encroached, bathing everything in a pleasant vermilion haze; phosphorescent lights flared alive around the mines, charging the air with an eerie beauty.

Mira's gaze was drawn to the distant but brightest display of all, Pellegrini A; the expansive ever-widening mineral-laden gouge that ensured the Pellegrini familia their wealth and power. Scattered between those open-cut scars were the rainbow glows of the underground mines, coded for night identification – the only evidence of some system, in fact the only system, among the mining mêlée.

Araldis's abundant mineral and the Cips' inferior geological expertise had been a lethal combination. Collapsed mines were common in the warren of diggings. Only recently, under pressure from OLOSS, had Franco begun to employ seismic measures to avoid loss of life. *Too late for those at the Juanita mine*, Mira thought. The most recent accident had killed over a hundred. Faja had sent a shortcast of the news to her at the Studium.

Now, gazing out at the mines, Mira imagined what their thoughts had been as they ran out of air, trapped below the fall of baked rock. *Did they feel as I do?* she wondered. Right then she missed the comfort of Insignia's presence. She strained to detect its hum but found only silence, as though the distance between them was insurmountable.

Where are you?

The engine thrum wooed exhaustion into her body and she dozed, not waking again until the lug abruptly changed altitude.

Jancz had not spoken to her during the trip – another thing to be grateful for. Mira blinked sleep-blur from her eyes and strained forward to see the city lights. 'On the western edge there is a large AiV park.'

'I know it,' he said curtly.

His familiarity with the city bothered Mira somehow, but she didn't dwell on it, wanting only to leave his company as soon as possible.

As soon as the lug landed she left the co-pilot's seat and waited near the hatch. When Jancz released the lock, she spared no word of parting for him.

His words, though, followed her down the narrow hydraulic steps. 'Forget me, signorina,' he said. 'And the Carabinere will not find you.'

Mira gave a tight nod, unsure that she could trust him with any such pact. Outside in the heat she sealed her velum and slipped into anonymity between the rows of AiVs. Strangely, though, the lug did not shift from its landing spot.

What is he doing, she wondered, glancing back, *waiting like that?*

Mira avoided the TerV-stop crowded with miners waiting to be transported to their shift, and walked the short distance to Villa Fedor by way of several small, unlit viuzzas. With each exhausted step she expected to hear Carabinere sirens. They would look here for her soon. She would seek Faja's counsel and then leave.

Villa Fedor was a modest villa – by Mount Pell standards – situated in the familia district of Loisa. There was little to distinguish it from the surrounding buildings, aside from a small outhouse in the desert garden of imported red lostol grasses and teranu prickly tongues, and the Bear and Pearl crest, shimmering across the gate facade.

Mira avoided the main entrance and placed her thumb into the side gate's authenticator. It shaped around her digit and released the lock. She risked spiking her ankles with prickly tongue to reach the side entrance unnoticed and repeated the action on the door there. When it accepted her tissue sample she stepped into the small, plain parlour.

Discordant noise spilled out of the room on her right. Through the door she glimpsed several bambini arguing, two humanesques against two aliens.

'This is our world. We get it when we want it.' One of the humanesques rested her hand possessively on the ballada table.

The alien korm – the largest of the four – whistled and chirped in excitement. The fur on its blue-grey skin had begun to bead in distress and its soft beak was open, baring a row of savage teeth. It fell back on its huge hind legs.

'We are here first,' said the other alien – a crossbreed – in stilted Latino.

'So what?' said one of the humanesques.

The korm's crest spiked alarmingly and Mira stepped in to intervene. When the bambini noticed her presence in the doorway they all bowed hastily.

Mira gave them a slight nod. 'I am Baronessa Mira from Mount Pell. The Baronessa Faja says the table must close down for the night.' She leaned over and pulled out the magnet key.

The humanesques gave her sulky looks but dared say nothing. They knew that Baronessa Mira Fedor attended the Studium with the Pellegrinis and the Silvios.

'You may go now,' Mira said.

As they left the room she swayed and reached for the wall.

The cross-breed's neck gills fluttered with concern. 'Baronessa Mira, are you well?' it asked.

The korm whistled and clicked, dropping down onto all fours.

'Mia sorella,' Mira panted. 'Quickly!'

TRIN

Within a few days Joe Scali grew the extraction sets that Trin wanted and distilled them into Trin's organism access.

Trin then set up cross-reference checks for all the data. By the end of the first day he realised that his i-texts from Araldis Studium were inaccurate and misleading. The discovery sent a shiver of pleasure through him. A whole alternative history of Araldis dwelled among these neglected records.

He returned to the Palazzo that evening in a lighter mood – able to shift the guilty weight of his flirtation with Luna and the uuli's death to a more distant place.

Tina Galiotto brought him dinner to his room, fussing over him as she always had, pleased that he was home for dinner. In the end he sent her away and ate his food by the window, watching the dust storm still blowing itself out over the plains. The tumultuous display of wine-red dust painted a more exhilarating picture to him than the store of flesh holos in his cupboard. In truth he had barely viewed them. Araldis was his pleasure – the world he owned.

Jilda appeared at the door as Trin poured the last of his wine from the decanter. He hadn't drunk since the night in Riso's Bar and he'd missed the warm courage of alcohol in his belly.

'What do you want, mama?' He did not bother to turn and look at her.

'Marchella Pellegrini is coming to visit in a few days.'

'Tia Marchella? Here in Pell? What has happened? Has there been a revolution?' he joked.

Jilda drew a sharp breath. 'She and your father have things to discuss.'

What can Franco have to discuss with his much-loathed sorella? Trin swung around in his chair to look at Jilda. She seemed angry, and again appeared to be sober.

'What are you trying to tell me?'

'You are to be the next Principe, Trinder.'

'Of course.' He scowled. 'What does that have to do with tia loco?'

'Be watchful of her. She wants change and I fear she may seek to depose you.'

'How? And with who? Herself?' Trin laughed – but a fleeting memory of Rantha's unabashed praise for Marchella sent his body tight with fear. He yawned rudely to hide it. 'An amusing joke, but I think you drink too much wine.'

'Do not pretend with me, Trinder. I know how much you want to be Principe. Remember who bore you into this life.'

'And bore me you do, mama.'

Jilda clicked her tongue with impatience and swept out of Trin's room.

His mood turned dark again. He stripped off his clothes and sprawled sideways on his bed, not bothering to remove the covers. The headboard's carved beasts jeered 'Bravura addict' at him and he rolled away from their scorn. Eventually he fell into a fitful sleep, only to wake hot and thirsty.

Naked, Trin roamed the frieze-covered halls of the Palazzo until he found his way to Franco's private bar. In the darkness he poured himself a measure of his father's prized cognac and tossed back the contents. *There, papa!*

'Lostol cognac is the finest – the most expensive. It is meant to be sipped, Trinder.'

He froze. The intruder's voice flowed around him like an embrace rather than a reprimand. In the flare of a spark he saw Luna light a cigarillo. The pungent smell of chang-lo leaves caught in his throat.

'What are you doing here?' he demanded accusingly.

Luna unfolded her exquisite limbs from the shadows of a smoking chair and glided towards him. The muted light enhanced her beauty, as if he were dreaming perfection.

She placed a cool hand on Trin's bare chest. 'We didn't finish our dance.'

Desire flooded him. It intermingled with anger and made his skin feel hot. 'Do you know what your flirtation cost me?'

She smiled at him – a glimpse of pale teeth. 'I have expensive tastes and Franco will not be here for ever. Perhaps when you are Principe you will remember how it is between us.' Her hand slid down the length of his naked torso.

On reflex his hand reached for her breasts. They were heavy and soft beneath her sheer costume – a woman's breasts. Trin wanted to have her; have Franco's property. But as Luna stroked his back and murmured suggestions in his ear the fear rose. He had no bravura with him.

Sensing a cooling in his response she knelt, cupping him, her head bowed with intent. 'Let me pleasure you, young Principe. A taste of things to come.' She breathed warmth onto his groin and licked the fine hair matt of hair that covered it with her sharp tongue.

Trin's fear climbed higher and higher in his chest until he found himself gasping. 'Get up!' He tried to pull Luna to her feet but she resisted, fixing her lips to the tender most part of him.

Trin felt his shrivelling response. 'No!' he whispered.

Luna's lovely neck arched back; her eyes widened with coy surprise. 'What is it, bambino Principe? Are you afraid of women?'

He pushed her to the floor and left.

Are you afraid of women? Luna's taunt hovered in Trin's conscious thoughts the next morning as he pored over her records.

Like that of the Fedors Luna's pedigree was eccentric. Unlike the Fedors she had no claim to special pilot talents: only womanly ones. Unsurprisingly, she came from a line of gifted coquettes; her mama had been Aldo Pellegrini's first mistress, the famous Shelba Lanzano. Luna had not only chosen to discard her mother's name but, according to Customs records, she had spent years travelling off-world. Little wonder that Trin had not known about her.

When the organic had sifted all Luna's data, Trin was shocked to learn the enormity of her gratis. What drove Franco to keep his mistress better than his wife, he wondered? Pellegrini men had a reputation for licentiousness – not stupidity. Scanning further, the records revealed only one other notable item: Luna's ownership of a small underground mine called Juanita, located between the vast Pablo tunnels and Pellegrini B.

Next, Trin delved into the export register and found that the Juanita mine produced very little – yet it was ranked in the top tier. He could find no documentation of its mineral content.

When he had exhausted his information search on Luna, he turned his attention to Marchella Pellegrini. Yesterday's idle game of spying had acquired new purpose. If his position as the next Principe were to be challenged by his tia and if Luna il Longa chose to entangle him in her own games, then he would not be played for an idiot.

But Marchella's records were scant and uninteresting apart from one detail – her outright ownership of the lucrative Pablo underground mines. Strange that Franco had allowed such a thing. Perhaps he had paid his eccentric sorella to leave Pell?

The mine was certainly the best provided for on Araldis. Marchella's gratis log showed that an extraordinary amount of her earnings was spent on stocking Pablo with provisions for the small workforce she employed there. Trin found this puzzling. Perhaps she merely had a misplaced sense of philanthropy – and no head for economics.

Aside from this inexplicable dispersion of her earnings, his maiden tia had no ready secrets to un-closet. No illicit bambino to protect. The record of her current residence was imprecise. She moved too often for anyone to keep track. Her gratis was drawn on from Dockside to Chalaine-Gema. The only fact that Trin could substantiate was that she rarely came to Mount Pell. *Why now, then?*

Unable to arrive at an answer, Trin moved on to Franco. *What do I wish to learn? Everything* . . . a man who would dissect a woman for her genetic code so that his son might have her talent . . . *and nothing* . . . and yet cast that son from his home without the means to survive.

Trin instructed the organic to chart the Principe's personal expenditure but it refused to display that information. Frustrated, he tried a lateral approach.

'Compile the safety violations incurred by Pellegrinis and the higher-caste familia – and their outcomes,' he told it.

Trin discovered a surfeit of offences: safety issues, claim jumping, unfair trade, tax disparities, exortortionate machinery hire and conveyor tolls – yet almost all the cases had been dismissed by OLOSS's visiting judiciary. He could see only one explanation for such repeated leniency: his father was bribing the judge.

He searched more stored data, meticulously copying every useful scrap of information to his own sponge.

Rantha called him up at midday. 'You wish to eat?'

'No. I'm busy,' he said, annoyed at being interrupted. She frowned and signed off.

Trin didn't think of her again until a few hours later when she stood before him with a plate of overly soft linguine. The sauce had stained her fellala. 'I thought you might be embarrassed to eat with me, so I brought food here.' Her face was puffy from crying.

'No. I was busy,' he said, truthfully.

'Busy? Here?'

He rotated the deskfilm so that she could see Scali's data tree. 'These records of all these things are logged but rarely used for anything.'

Rantha shrugged. 'So?'

Trin spoke her name to the deskfilm. Tabbed reports overlaid each other. 'See? You are pure-bred Cipriano. You have three fratellas and your gratis rating is seven. It would be higher if you did not spend it all on outsys texts.' He wagged his finger mockingly. 'You are not contributing anything much to our cultural development, Rantha Cabone.'

'Cultural development? On Araldis? This place is for men and ginkos.' She lowered her voice. 'I do not think Signor Malocchi will like what you are doing, Don Pellegrini.'

Trin's smile faded to a scowl. 'He put me in this worthless position. What are the point of records you cannot use?'

'It depends, I suppose . . . on how you use them.'

Trin stared at her. Rantha was clever enough to know that he was planning something. Perhaps he had showed her too much. 'Grazi, for the meal. We could meet tomorrow in the refectory?' he suggested.

It was her turn to stare. He was offering her a trade-off – to keep silent about his delving in return for his company.

'Si,' Rantha said slowly. 'You mean sit together?'

He nodded.

She smiled and Trin glimpsed the gentle young woman beneath her touchy manner. But he had no wish to get to know that person – who, he knew, would need honesty and devotion.

Trin returned to the Palazzo late and had dinner in his room again. Despite Rantha's caution about Malocchi, he was determined to continue delving. Not only from determination, he realised: he was also enjoying himself. Secrets attracted him far more than ideals.

The next morning he reviewed his data sponge, seeking out patterns and connections. The low productivity and high returns of Luna's mine bothered him. He sensed it was in some way connected with the large gratis that Franco awarded her.

Trin attached a number of archival sponges to the organic and requested the trade reports for previous years. One caught his attention – a visiting dignitary who had requested a lotion bath at a meeting. Intrigued, Trin sent a shortcast to the trade department residente, Lotte Perrone.

'Your access has been downgraded along with your gratis, Don Pellegrini.' Perrone barely concealed his smug satisfaction.

Furious, Trin flew his AiV down the mountain to the trade building in Dockside and strode to the front desk.

'Don Pellegrini.' The pretty ragazza at the desk stopped him cold with her simpering delight.

He recognised her – a cousin of the Silvio twins – and in a breath he switched from angry to charming. 'Bella . . .' He grappled for her name until he saw her ID. '. . . Christa.'

She dipped her head coyly. 'I heard whispers that

you were working with Signor Malocchi. Something discreet and important, si?'

Trin thought of his malformed office. 'Si. Confidential. In fact, that is why I have come to see you . . .' He told her what he wanted.

The girl's smile wavered after she had searched for the file. 'Pardone, Don, but that is privileged. Sealed by your own tia Marchella. Lotte Perrone would chew me up with his morning pastrami if I let you see that.'

Trin nodded sympathetically at her while he tried to think of another approach. *Marchella Pellegrini again. Why did Franco or old Principe Aldo put Marchella in charge of a trade negotiation? Why are the transcripts privileged?*

Unwittingly Christa Silvio gave him a lever. She cleared her throat and smoothed the outer folds of her fellala. 'Do you know Joe Scali?'

'Si. Mio amico intimo,' Trin lied. 'You should accompany us to Riso's or Panchetta's some time. He is loco company.'

Her face lit up. She was more beautiful than Chocetta and Lancia Silvio and Trin's groin tightened involuntarily.

'When?' she asked.

Trin leaned across her desk so that his breath fanned her neck. 'Just as soon as you've copied that transcript for me.' He drew away slowly, giving her a moment to digest what he'd said.

Christa's eyes widened as she weighed the risk against the reward. How much did she desire Joe Scali? As she began to unlock the file, Trin detected the faintest sheen of perspiration on her forehead. 'Can you take it with you?'

He pressed his data sponge into her hand.

She attached it to her organic and copied the transcript, glancing nervously towards the other offices.

When it was finished, Trin retrieved the sponge, slipping it beneath the folds of his robe. 'I will shortcast you tomorrow when I have spoken with Joe.'

She nodded, her eyes watery with fear. 'Don?'

He nodded in a reassuring manner. 'I will not forget.'

Heart pounding, he returned to Centrale and hurried to the refectory to keep his promise to Rantha. She was not there but the bain-marie ragazza waved him over. 'Don Pellegrini, your amica Luna il Longa was looking for you,' she said as he drew close.

Trin's heart contracted but he forced his tongue to work. 'I have no amica. Unless you would you like to be?'

The ragazza giggled.

'I want minestrone,' he said casually. 'Could you bring it to my office?'

The ragazza's hand shook as she poured the hot, meat-laden liquid into a beaker and snapped the lid shut. Trin thought the tremor was a result of his teasing until a voice spoke quietly in his ear.

'There are no Palazzo privileges here, Maestro Pellegrini.'

Trin stiffened. Jus Malocchi stood at his shoulder. 'Are you too busy to attend proper meals? I wonder what keeps you so occupied?'

Carefully Trin waved away the soup. The ragazza met his gaze briefly. He saw sympathy in her eyes, and a warning. Malocchi did not usually come to this side of the refectory; he ate in his own private dining room.

Trin gave a polite bow and mumbled an apology. Once out in the corridor, he ran to his office. With trembling fingers he began killing off his newly grown programme. While it destroyed itself he left a short-cast message for Joe Scali. 'The cave is closed due to a rockfall.' He then encapsulated his data sponge and slipped it into the courier's chute.

By the time Malocchi and his elite guard arrived Trin was playing lupa on his deskfilm. They ransacked the office and found nothing, but Malocchi didn't look convinced. He swept the deskfilm onto the floor where it flickered and died. 'It seems I made a mistake about you. You should have something challenging to do.' His words were mild, innocuous, but his voice held an edge of threat.

Trin lounged back in his chair, feigning surprise. 'I hesitate to accept, signor. I am so unpractised at working.'

'Accept?' Malocchi frowned. 'That is an intriguing word.'

Trin cocked his head. 'How so, signor?'

'Are you mocking me, Pellegrini?'

'Most definitely not, signor.' *You bastard cazzone!*

Malocchi walked the three steps to the door. 'You will be sent to Capitano Christian Montforte at the Loisa Carabinere branch. Take nothing from here. You will be body-searched before you go.'

'Your father wishes you to attend dinner this evening,' said Tina Galiotto as she packed Trin's clothes. The tears running down her plump cheeks fell unchecked onto his bed.

Trin had no words of comfort for her as he dressed in the formal attire that she had laid out for him. Her show of emotion embarrassed him.

As soon as he could, he escaped his room and walked down the helicoidal staircase to Franco's private bar. The smoking chairs loomed large under the flickering light of Lig candles. The wax-scent of the three-legged Ligs pervaded most of the residences on Mount Pell, their odour a welcome deodoriser against the rising fumes of Dockside.

Franco waited for him, cupping an empty balloon glass. He wore a gold-thread semi-formal fellalo and casual silk slippers.

'I had no knowledge that she was your consort, father.' The words burst from Trin without forethought.

Franco froze in the act of pouring. His face tightened into something unreadable. 'I do not wish to speak of this.'

'And I do not wish to go to Loisa. The border towns are primitive.' *Please don't send me there.*

'Capitano Montforte will teach you about respect.'

Trin quivered. 'So I *am* being punished.'

Franco almost drained his drink in one swallow and turned to his son. 'Malocchi tells me you were abusing your position by seeking out sensitive information. What were you looking for, Trinder?'

'He gave me no office and no reason to be there. I had to find ways to amuse myself. Besides, what could be too sensitive for a future Principe to know, papa?' Trin countered.

'Despite what you think, Trinder, Principes earn their position. I have no intention of denying you your

birthright, if you see reason. You have too many of your
mama's weaknesses in you. You must outgrow them.'

Mama. Always that. 'So am I not worthy because you
wed a weak female, or because I danced a fucking song
with your woman?' Dangerous to goad Franco but he
couldn't stop himself now. The righteousness, the anger,
welled in an uncontrollable spurt. 'What of the special
talent you would rip from Mira Fedor's flesh? Am I still
worthy to receive that?'

Franco's hand trembled, spilling the last few drops
of the cognac. He stared at his son. 'Mira Fedor has
eluded the Carabinere.'

'Eluded?' Trin gasped and then laughed. 'A familia
woman has *eluded* you?'

'When she is located you will be recalled and we
shall proceed with the gene transference.'

'What if I have no wish to be Pilot First? What if I
do not want to have her genes mingled with mine?'

Franco didn't speak, nor did he break eye contact,
his gaze as remorseless as the Araldis plains.

Trin wavered first. He reached for a glass and poured
the rest of the decanter into it. Quick, fierce sips
relieved the pain of his insecurity.

Thankfully, Jilda's thin voice wavered into the angry
space between them. 'Trinder, are you in there?'

'Si, mama,' he managed. He stepped out of the bar
into the familia dining room. Jilda saw his shaken
expression and went to him, wrapping him in her arms
and her wine-perfume. Trin stood stiff in the embrace.

Behind his mother a woman in a worn ochre fellala
gave him an amused smile.

Jilda relinquished her hold. 'Trinder, you remember

your tia Marchella? She does not visit Pell very often nowadays.'

Trin took in Marchella's intelligent face and ragged, unbound hair. She was not that much older than him but her manner was weary and aged. She drew on her rolled tobacco and held his gaze. Familia women were not permitted to smoke but his tia, as he'd heard many times over, lived outside such customs.

'Bonjourno, Trinder,' she said. 'They tell me you are gifted in the art of dalliance – just like your father.'

Jilda clicked her tongue in a disapproving manner and beckoned them to their places at the table. 'Marchella, you trouble-make still. How is it that you never learned manners? Franco is a Pellegrini and Principe. Of course women will want him. And his son.'

Trin couldn't drag his stare from Marchella as she moved to her allotted place at the table. *Does she know about Luna?*

'I have manners, Jilda. What I did *not* learn is the art of submission,' she said.

Before Jilda could reply, Franco joined them. He sat at the head of the table, offering no customary familia embrace for his sibling.

Tina Galiotto moved silently around them, removing Franco's and Trin's slippers and unfolding napkins onto their laps.

Marchella refused her help and performed the rituals herself. 'Yes. Infidelity is one of those traditions that our men adopted when they stole our choice to have children.' Marchella stared directly at Jilda. 'Tell me, Jilda, do you have amicos?'

Jilda's hands fluttered in protest.

Franco jolted from his seat and leaned across the table as if he might slap Marchella's face. 'I will not have such filthy conversation in my house: conduct yourself properly or leave. What did you come here for anyway, mia sorella?'

'I want to know, Franco: why do you continue to hoard the best of everything for your Enclave?' she asked. 'On the plains, the miners live and work in dangerous conditions. It is not necessary.'

Trin sat straight in his chair, distracted from his own troubles by Marchella's temerity. The woman was like an island stoat with a fleshy fish in its teeth.

'This is not a suitable discussion for dinner.' Franco bestowed another warning glare on her. 'A young world like Araldis cannot afford the widespread luxuries of the established OLOSS planets.'

'It is not about luxury, Franco. It is about *your* greed.'

It was true, Trin knew, that the mines ran on archaic technology – rubber conveyors and primitive mechanical crushers. Even the screens were metal. But he did not think Marchella was speaking of those things.

'Your feudalism stops our world from progressing. You keep Araldis in check as if it were one of your women.'

'What would you know about acting like a woman, mia sorella? You choose manliness over your true sex. That is the truth.'

'At least that way I have a choice. That way no man can force me to bear his bambini.'

Franco hit her then, in front of Jilda, Trin and the Galiotto servants.

Marchella fell from her chair, stifling a cry.

Trin found himself half out of his seat. He looked to his mother but she did nothing except call for a dressing for Marchella's bleeding mouth. The Principessa had seen this before and she seemed almost pleased that Franco had asserted his right.

Yet Trin had never heard Cipriano traditions so vehemently and shockingly challenged before. He believed it was his choice as to when and with whom he would father children, and that no familia woman had a right to refuse him. At the Studium he had heard whispers of a secret women's group that opposed Franco and the old traditions but they appeared to be nothing other than ginko-incited grumblings.

Marchella climbed slowly to her feet. Her gaze met Trin's as she retook her seat, dabbed her mouth with the cloth and delicately drank down her small glass of wine. She seemed neither repentant nor cowered. She seemed . . . satisfied.

This was for me!

The calculation of her act shocked Trin almost as much as Franco's violence.

A Galiotto entered the silence carrying a large silver platter. Jilda clapped her hands with appreciation. 'Aaah, polenta dumplings!'

JO-JO RASTEROVICH

Jo-Jo Rasterovich was a Cerulean, a blue-planet kid. At least, that was how he thought of himself. The truth was (and Jo-Jo had some difficulty with that concept) that his family hadn't lived on that world, in that constellation, for a thousand years. Yet something deep in his often-rejuvenated psyche stayed immovably Cerulean. He even still thought of the blue planet as 'Earth' although most of the Orion Sentients had never heard the name.

Sole Entity had entered Jo-Jo's life just in time to save him from a rather unpleasant permanent biological death (or perhaps Sole had caused the death, in which case the point was moot). Adrift on the edge of an uninhabited system due to some dodgy navigational software that he had purchased cheaply from the Spiral Arms swap-meet in Vega and which had bugged his propulsion start-up, Jo-Jo had strayed into an uncharted gas tube.

Instead of low-density X-rays, the space anomaly was crammed with high-density microwaves. The last thing Jo-Jo remembered, as life support faded, was the propulsion bay glowing blue as he tried uselessly to cold-start his ship.

When he regained consciousness the propulsion system was back on line and breathable air flowed sweetly. One part of him felt unhappily as if it had just been tipped out of a freeze-dried sachet and mixed with ice cubes into a lumpy consistency. Another part of him suggested running diagnostics to see what had caused the problem.

Jo-Jo staggered to his bridge-cum-bedroom and lit up a fat smoke of chang-lo hemp. Something BIG had happened. Something WEIRD. Jo-Jo hadn't run a full diagnostic check since he'd earned his licence. Even then he'd failed to do it properly and had had to bribe the astrogator to pass him.

His mind felt like it had been crapped on, rolled in and dissected.

He toked deeply, hoping that the killer cannabis might reglue things but all it did was activate the smoke alarms. In among the warm fog of the hemp and the unnatural patterns of his altered thinking, he felt a presence enter his mind.

<you'm in distress. prevent'm decay you. chose'm inhabit mind you. problem without'm alter you.>

Jo-Jo inhaled so deeply that the butt burned his lips. *There's nothing out there,* he told himself sternly, *but a big fat bundle of microwave radiation. Oh, and those leech-shaped things. But I imagined them.* He fumbled in his utilities bag for a second scoob and sucked noisily until he passed out.

Later, when the narcotic hangover cleared, his mind had two new and persistent voices in it. Jo-Jo was left to confront the fact that he'd discovered another type of life (or it had discovered him, because for all intents and purposes it had killed him and then resurrected him: no sentient species he knew of had the ability to do that) which had altered his mind, and that perhaps he should make the most of it.

So Jo-Jo set about making a living off the story that he'd discovered Sole Entity, a benevolent type of god-thing that had strayed in from the fathomless stretched space between galaxies.

He paid no attention to the nagging feeling that he had forgotten something really important, or the sneaking notion that Sole Entity was not in fact benign but rather more like a cosmic-sized feline toying with a blind, legless lizard.

The story, as it stood, earned him enough lucre to purchase a biozoon from a black-market slaver and have it luxuriously appointed in a manner suitable for a wealthy space-nomad bachelor. He dubbed the bio-craft *Salacious II* and planned to live out the rest of his life travelling through lesser-known sections of the galaxy.

In general Jo-Jo liked other sentients well enough, particularly humanesques, as long as he didn't have to spend too much time with them. He had a particular dislike for some of the slug species on Lucas's World and found he had a severe allergy to korm odours.

But mostly he preferred his own company.

He washed infrequently, swore aloud when he liked, and kept a substantial array of bizarre recreational flesh-simulations for which no one could reprimand him. His relationship with the hottest sexpot sims of Galaxy Productions was as close to perfect as Jo-Jo could imagine.

In short: he didn't want a wife.

His closest, most terrifying scrape with a real woman

(which had rather set the seal on his bachelorhood) had been on the planet of Ikar. He'd been delivering a Sole recount to a theatrette bulging with Studium smarts. Afterwards, a woman with several degrees, more than her fair share of chins and equally shivery thighs (which he could see through the strips of material that wound around her legs like snakes) asked him to stay behind for a drink. The faint repulsion he felt at her physical appearance was well offset by the swollen credit voucher she waved under his nose.

They drank and caroused vociferously, until Jo-Jo found himself behind rows *hess* and *thess* of the theatrette with his face trapped between the woman's thighs.

'Can't breathe,' he snuffled.

'I'm assuming that you are having trouble breathing,' she warbled. 'I am told that it is the most erotic move-ment in my repertoire. I can clench for indefinite periods of time given the right mood. And you, *God-discoverer*, have put me in the mood.'

'Let go,' gasped Jo-Jo.

But the smart didn't seem to hear him.

'I don't mean to be forward,' she continued, 'but you could be the recipient of other such delights for a small favour. I could be persuaded to perform in a number of ways, including my formidable chin massage – *my* chins massage *you*, ha! ha! – in return for an introduc-tion to God.'

Chagrin was too insipid a word to describe how that made Jo-Jo feel. The woman was bribing him with sexual suffocation. Furious and desperate, he resorted to a move told to him by a court-martialled special-forces hermaphrodite on Bosun.

He bit her pubis with all musterable ferocity.

As the smart collapsed in pain, her legs fell apart.

Jo-Jo struggled to his knees and wiped his damp face on the plush theatrette seats. Then he climbed to his feet and ran like fuck.

For months afterwards he had nightmares, which only abated if he drank vodka chasers and played Malconfunk arias after his evening bong.

Despite the *chin and thigh* affair, Jo-Jo's Sole-wealth bought him another hundred years of rejuve, which fitted in nicely with his desire to continue exploring. As long as he returned periodically to a civilised world with the necessary technology to do a disease appraisal, everything in Jo-Jo's life was, to use a Cerulean term, hunky-dory.

Then Sole mind-spooked him again:

<observe'm>

Jo-Jo took some time to decide that the mind-voice and its pretentiously commanding greeting was real – so to speak. In fact he ignored it until his head reverberated like a tuning fork.

<**OBSERVE**>

<Sole?>

With a flash of quick thinking Jo-Jo ordered his shipcom to 'record and convert patterns to something audible'. The 'record' bit was actually redundant. As a precaution against getting so stoned that he couldn't perform basic ship functions, he'd instructed *Salacious II* to monitor constantly his neural activity. When his brain turned to mush it administered him a fluid flush and a vitamin boost.

The 'audible', though, was a better signpost to Jo-Jo's personality than a Rorschach test. See, Jo-Jo was a person who liked to verbally restate things. If a problem was outside his ability to solve (as things often were), he would find inumerable different ways to say, *Crap, that's hard*, or *Fungul, who but a teranu brain-master would know that?*

Restating gave him comfort.

He also liked to hear things out loud. Somehow it made the whole process of mind-talk with an unfathomable energy entity less wholly bizarre.

The audible came through precisely 1.263 seconds after he heard it in his head, causing a slight echo effect. Jo-Jo eyeballed the ship's filmdisplay as if he could look at the Entity.

'You just don't get the "person" thing, do you? I have a name. J-O J-O RAS-TER-O-VI-CH.'

<return'm> – Sole's voice, generated through *Salacious II*'s decoder and replayed, lacked inflexions. Corresponding fractals of the thought energy, mutated across the bridge's main filmdis like algae. <return'm Belle-Monde/present'm ménage lounge>

Jo-Jo spent a moment recalling the ménage lounge. His flawless mind-catalogue of bars and clubs was a source of some pride to him. *Uncomfortable chairs, gaudy urinal. Distinguishing features: uuli hum and exclusive academic clientele.*

'But I have business on one of the teranu worlds,' he protested.

Actually he planned to attend a symposium on how to enlarge the pleasure centre in the humanesque male cerebrum – but he didn't think he needed to be precise.

Although he wasn't entirely sure that Sole couldn't read his mind as well as talk in it.

<change'm plans>

'Er . . . no,' he said out loud and with feeling. 'Fuck off.'

The long silence that followed suggested that Sole had taken his advice and Jo-Jo climbed into his bridge hammock with a self-satisfied grin. 'That showed it,' said the master of restatement.

Not long after, however, a peculiar sensation began to seep through him. It started in his toes and fingers and crept upwards along his body until it converged in his head. His mind fell into thin slivers as though someone had carved through his skull with a large egg slicer.

Only, in Jo-Jo's case, the egg was soft and made a *God*-awful mess.

Sole

manifestspace

little creatures| cross'm void void
cleave'm|thoughts thoughts
commune'm|change change
Expand'm|way way
Find'm secrets<luscious luscious>

TRIN

Trin flew straight to Loisa after dinner. He didn't speak again to Franco or Jilda and took only a small reticule of clothes, the remains of a canister of bravura, his bora – a pouch containing his hereditary seals – and the lucre he'd found in Jilda's bureau when he'd been looking for calmatives.

He flew at a reckless speed, wishing only to put distance between himself, his familia and the Palazzo Cavaliere who shadowed him. *You are having me watched now, papa? What is next? Imprisonment?*

Luck favoured Trin's carelessness and the air traffic was scant as he left the Dockside environs and swept onward into the mining belt. Below him the rainbow of mine lights streamed and flickered in erratic patterns across the ground. He fixed the nav-set, then switched to Autopilot and slumped against the window.

Marchella's words disturbed him still. If her visit had been designed to draw attention to the plight of the mining towns then she had uncanny timing. Trin had cared little for the poor conditions in the belt previously, yet now he had been banished to one without the immunity or privilege of name. The irony irritated him.

He drifted into gloomy thoughts and, eventually, sleep.

Some time later Autopilot woke him from his wine-drowse, bleating for landing instructions. Ignoring all normal air protocols Trin sent the AiV into a spiralling descent into the darkened, narrow viuzza in front of the local Carabinere building. His escort landed in a more orderly fashion in the well-lit AiV bay at the side.

The dust-dimmed solar ground lights revealed a building similar to the flat-roofed elliptical familia offices in Dockside. It was surrounded by equally plain villettes of the Nobile, and beyond them Trin caught a glimpse of the simple mud-and-cellulose casas of the non-familia and ginko workers.

In the short walk up the path to the Carabinere building, the searing wind caught in his throat like hot smoke and dried the perspiration from his face before he felt it grow damp. He sealed the hood of his fellalo against it. Loisa had no protective bubble like Dockside or Pell. He had heard that the building environmentals battled to keep structures cool enough for comfort. Death from dehydration was common enough among the miners.

Urgency sent Trin banging on the door. How foolish to come in unexpectedly at night: even with his fellalo sealed he could perish out here in this hotwind. *Will the Palazzo Cavaliere help me?* What had Franco instructed them to do? Surely he did not wish his son dead?

A shadowy movement inside caught his eye. Was someone in there? He banged again, calling out, but the movement was not repeated. It was as if he had imagined it.

In the clutch of panic, Trin retraced his steps to the

AiV and set the cabin temperature to its coolest. He would be comfortable, and he would not give the Palazzo Cavaliere the satisfaction of asking for their help.

He lit the last of his hemp and inhaled with deliberate determination. When the smoke had calmed his fears he laid back the seat and slept.

'Pellegrini?' A bull-necked Carabinere in an immaculate white-dress fellalo roused Trin from a cramped slumber. Light had barely reached far enough to lend colour to the day but already Trin could feel the rise in the air temperature. He shifted and unwound his legs, realising that the grinding sound in his dreams was the straining AiV engine. The air blowing on his face now was barely cool.

'Pellegrini?' The Carabinere's voice again – muffled through the cabinplex.

Trin slipped back his hood and swept the pile of hemp ash from his clothes, embarrassed at the state of his dress. He squeezed the 'kill' command on the exhausted engine and opened the cabin.

'*Don* Pellegrini,' Trin replied.

'I am Capitano Christian Montforte.' The man's voice was clipped with disapproval and he didn't extend his hand. He waved his pouchfilm before Trin's face. 'Jus Malocchi says you are to be kept occupied but are unused to work. How in Crux will that be of use to me here?'

Trin glanced towards the building. 'Do you not keep your station manned, Capitano? I could not raise a soul last evening.'

'It *is* manned, *Don* Pellegrini. But only for those with real emergencies.'

Trin swallowed down a quick rise of anger. 'My reticule is in the back,' he said.

'Then I suggest you bring it with you.' Montforte turned on his heel and walked away.

Trin wavered between belligerence and the knowledge that it would gain him nothing. The heat was already suffocating and he badly needed to bathe, so he dragged his reticule from behind the pilot seat and followed Montforte inside to a catoplasma-grey room that was – by the look of the dusty floor and the red trails of excreta – only rarely cleaned.

They both unsealed their hoods.

The Capitano wore his hair short and his face clean. His cheeks were full-fleshed like those of a man who enjoyed his food. 'We have no Galiottos here. Our cleaning nanos are replaced once a year and when they fail we must wait for the next batch,' he said.

Trin lifted his gaze to the walls and ceiling and the cracks in the internal joins. The quality catoplasma, he supposed, had probably gone to the local Duca and his chambers.

'This is your office. I am in there.' Montforte pointed to a door on the other side of the room. Then he slid aside a partition next to the shortcast unit. Behind it was a tiny space with a bed and pinched-out shelves set into a rounded alcove. A small cooking unit stood tucked into another corner, and the smell of engine oils drifted through the air vents from the services yard behind. 'You will live here.'

Trin hid his shock. How could he live in such a place? 'What is my occupation?'

Christian smiled in a way that made his face puff

out. 'You are my aide. This can be interpreted in any way I choose.'

Trin's stomach began to ache, whether from hunger or displeasure he could not tell. 'When will they bring my food? I have had no breakfast.'

Christian folded his arms over his taut rounded stomach. 'No one will *bring* you food here, Pellegrini. You must become accustomed to different ways. The food you will procure for yourself from the market.'

'Procure? With the 'esques and the ginkos?'

'Si. I will advance you some lucre to purchase what you need. It would not do for Franco's only son to starve.'

'But it is reasonable for him to perish in the hot nightwinds?' Trin retorted.

Montforte affected a carefully puzzled look, the thick flesh of his forehead folding into deep creases. 'You speak in riddles, young Don. Now, you should bathe and change. Then you will proceed to Villa Fedor and interview the Baronessa Faja. Her sorella, Baronessa Mira, is to be detained by us at the earliest possible moment.'

Trin stared aghast at the Capitano. Surely Montforte knew of the circumstances – the reason – behind Mira's disappearance.

'Would another be more suited for such a task? I am – as Signor Malocchi has stated – uninitiated in the manner of Carabinere work,' said Trin.

'Two of my most experienced men will accompany you. They will assist with any difficulty you may have.'

You mean spy on me, you cazzone bastard.

'When you have bathed and changed, present yourself

to the depot next door.' Montforte nodded and disappeared into his office, closing the door.

Trin washed in a small cubicle and pulled a clean fellalo from his reticule. He fumbled his way into it, the folds tangling without Tina Galiotto's patient hands to assist him. *What sort of a poor fool cannot dress himself?* he thought bitterly. *What sort of fool allows his papa to decide his life?* He could hear, almost, his tia Marchella's laughter.

He called Joe Scali from his pouchfilm.

'Don Pellegrini, is that you?' Scali sounded nervous.

Trin smoothed his tunic down. 'Nobile. Did you receive the gift I sent you?'

'Si. I believe so. M-many thanks.'

'Perhaps you will you bring me a return gift at your earliest convenience?'

Joe nodded, understanding his meaning. 'Er . . . of course . . . and are you well entertained? I hear you have left the Enclave.'

Trin's chest tightened. 'Yes. I am with the Carabinere in Loisa. I am tolerably entertained. And you?'

'Actually, Don, I have a new amica.'

'An amica?' said Trin, surprised.

'Si. Rantha and I . . .' Joe tapered off sheepishly.

For some unfathomable reason the news displeased Trin, as though Rantha had in some way betrayed him. 'I must be going. Come and visit me sometime. The view is splendid.' He held the tiny screen to his window so Joe Scali could see the cluttered service yard behind.

Scali's eyes widened in shock. 'Are you content?'

'Of course, Nobile,' Trin replied with little conviction.

*   *   *

'Vespa and Seb Malocchi?'

A group of men in dusty fellalos looked up from where they sat on crates. Their faces were as deep crimson as those of the miners who came to Dockside, and as parched of moisture. Each one sat before an equipment bag, checking the contents. Trin wondered if their deliberate care was a method of time-wasting. Though they were shaded by the workshop's high roof and fanned by the huge engineering coolers, his robe thermostat told him that the temperature was unforgiving. Yet none of the men had sealed their hoods for assisted cooling. He resisted sealing his own although the perspiration was already streaming down his body.

'I'm Vespa,' said one in surly tones. 'What of it?'

Trin set his jaw. 'I am . . . Pellegrini, Christian's new aide. He has told me you will accompany me to Villa Fedor to interview the Baronessa.'

'*Don* Pellegrini? An aide?' said Vespa. He glanced to the others who barely bothered to hide their smirks.

A man at bottom of the circle with a more agreeable expression stood up and extended his hand. 'I am Seb Malocchi. Take no notice of my rude fratello, Don Pellegrini. The heat makes him soffice here.' Seb tapped his head. 'Better than here, I think, eh?' This time he cupped his groin. 'I for one will be glad to escape this stinking heat and visit the cool of Villa Fedor.'

In spite of the vulgarity, Trin felt a moment of gratitude to the man. 'Buono.' He gave a stiff smile.

Seb waved his hand towards the hangar bay. 'Choose your chariot – any except this one.' He pointed to Trin's sleek, liveried AiV, which had been towed in and placed in a diagnostic gripper. An analytic hand probed inside it, blasting an air-water mix into the engine cavity. 'Some loco soffice ran the cooler all night with it stationary: seized the motor. Apparently he was afraid of the hotwinds.'

The circle of men roared with laughter.

Trin felt the rush of bloodheat to his face. How foolish of him – Seb Malocchi had meant him no kindness at all.

He walked away from them, straight-backed, fuming. He would leave here at once. That notion propelled him into the first Carabinere vehicle he came to, but he faltered when he saw the controls. Unfamiliar icons danced on the display – a more complex selection than his personal AiV. He slipped his hand tentatively inside the pilot glove, feeling again the frustration of his own limitations.

'It is not permitted for you to be unaccompanied, Don Pellegrini.'

Trin located the voice at the cabin door. A Cavaliere stood, leaning inwards with his hand cupped around his rifle. His tone was unapologetic.

'Am I your captive?'

'Only if you try to leave here alone, Don Pellegrini. The Principe has ordered it so.'

Trin's fingers curled to a fist. 'Remember who the next Principe is, Cavaliere,' he said clearly. 'For he shall remember you.'

The Palazzo guard released the grip he had taken instinctively on the door frame and straightened to make way for Seb and Vespa Malocchi.

Seb climbed straight to the front of the vehicle. He

slapped Trinder playfully across the back of the head and slumped into the second pilot seat. 'Now, now, Pellegrini,' he said with impertinence. 'Don't be like that.'

'Baronessa Fedor? It is Don Trinder Pellegrini. I have come to pay my respects.'

'Carabinere, Baronessa,' said Seb, speaking over Trin's shoulder. 'We have questions to ask you.'

The masked woman moved closer to her viewer. 'What nonsense is this? Since when do the Carabinere call on me? And since when has the young Principe been one of the white ones?'

'Let us in, Baronessa,' said Vespa.

Faja Fedor released the gate and met them halfway down the path to the villa. She was dressed in a full velum. 'What is it you want?' Her voice sounded thin through the velum's amplifier.

'To be invited inside, Baronessa, would be a beginning,' said Trin.

Reluctantly she beckoned them through the coldlock into her parlour, a largish room – though not by Palazzo standards – decorated with soft sapphire drapes, winding ornamental candelabra and hand-woven rugs that bore the Fedor crest. Each must have come with the familia from Latino Crux – such things could not be procured on Araldis. Nor could the inlaid-pearl occasional tables and the slightly shabby ceremonial chairs.

Trin recognised them as copies – valuable in their own right but not comparable to the authentic Pellegrini originals. For a time in Latino Crux it had been a fashion to duplicate the valuables of the patricians.

A thin, unsightly humanesque woman brought them cups of cold Latino-bean coffee and Pan di Stelle biscuits on a tarnished silver tray. The stars were misshapen and the chocolate pale for lack of cocoa.

Trin noticed the little signs of impoverishment. He waited until the woman, after serving the refreshments, had left before he addressed the Baronessa. 'Where are your familia servants?'

Faja Fedor unfolded her mask so that he could see her face. He was struck by how little she resembled Mira and by how much more typically Latino in bone structure and colouring she was.

'My circumstances are my business, Trinder Pellegrini,' she replied.

'Not when we have an order to detain your sorella,' said Seb Malocchi. 'Your business has become ours.'

Faja raised her eyebrows in shock. Trin noticed they weren't thinned in the artful manner of the court women – their masculine breadth lent her face strength.

'What can you mean by "detain"? Mira is not a common criminal, she is a patrician, blessed with the Inborn Talent.' She turned to Trin. 'Is this a graduation hoax, Don Pellegrini?'

'It is most serious, Baronessa,' said Seb swinging his legs up to rest on a pearl table.

'On what charge do you propose to detain her? What has she done?' Faja stood, hands clasped as if one restrained the other.

Trin shifted in his chair, wishing he was somewhere else. Was it possible that Faja Fedor knew nothing of Franco's declaration? Had word not filtered through to her of his intention?

'It is what she has *not* done. She has been ordered to surrender her Inborn Talent to the Principe. Instead she has chosen to evade his direct request. Your sorella is a runaway, Faja Fedor,' said Seb.

Faja unclasped her hands and curled them into two fists. Her voice trembled. 'You would steal her genetic right? How is that possible?'

'The Principe has technology that can make it so.' Malocchi was enjoying himself.

'Then *that* would be the crime, signor. Should I see my sister, I would praise her for fleeing from such a transgression of justice.'

Seb Malocchi leaped to his feet in a lightning movement. 'What would a woman know to speak of justice, Baronessa? Should I inform the Principe that you contest his judgement?'

Trinder saw Faja teeter on the brink of a dangerous retort – one that might see her arrested. The Carabinere provoked her with a practised tongue.

Instinctively he intervened on the woman's behalf. 'Have you seen or heard from Mira Fedor, Baronessa? That is all we would know from you.'

Faja sagged back down onto her chair, visibly fatigued. 'My pardon, Don Pellegrini. I am shocked, as you can see. The answer to your question is no, I have not seen or heard from mia sorella.'

Trin stared at Seb Malocchi. 'I am satisfied with this.' He glanced to the corridor. 'Where is Vespa?'

Seb sat down again and reached for the plate of biscuits. 'Searching the villa, Pellegrini. Join him if you like. I am sure Baronessa Fedor will entertain me.'

*   *   *

Trin escaped from the parlour into a cool, dark corridor that ran the length of the villa. But it did not deliver him from his discomfort. Fedor ancestors gazed down upon him with as much accusation in their faces as Faja. In the wavering pixel of each Pilot First's depiction he recognised the same thin, strained appearance that Mira had inherited.

Of the women, though, he saw only the traditional robust Latino figures and fleshy faces. Mira Fedor truly was a genetic peccadillo. *More reason not to have her DNA mingled with mine. What miserable providence has brought me to her home – as if I was complicit in Franco's plan?*

Noise spilled from a partially open door further along the corridor. In what should have been the villa's formal dining area, two pale-skinned young humanesques played with shuttles, while others sprawled casually on the old-wood table. In one corner a large scaled creature with a birdlike head squatted, chewing rhythmically. They glanced at Trin briefly, but with little interest. Vespa Malocchi had spoken of Faja Fedor's penchant for taking in aliens and bambini. 'Ginko lover,' Vespa had called her. Then he had spat on the floor.

Trin followed the corridor through the villa to the rear coldlock. He let himself out to the portico. He had not the taste for Seb and Vespa Malocchi's bullying game – the stifling heat was preferable company. He would wait there until the Carabinere had finished their dealings.

But the view onto Villa Fedor's dry-garden disturbed him more: thorn bushes, a flaking-dry algae pit and irregular tufts of dried red Lostol grasses leading to a squat, dust-stained outhouse. Trin craved for the sight of the Menagerie's controlled environment, its lush vine-growths, mauve faux-trees, and the idiotic purr-cocks that he hunted for sport when he was bored.

Discontentment took hold of him and dark thoughts shadowed the ungovernable brilliance of the day. He left the shade of the portico without sealing his hood. If he perished in the sun, perhaps that would be deliverance of a sort. His mother would weep for him – but she would be alone.

Then he heard a strangled cry.

Trin stepped in among the thorn bushes, searching for the source of the sound. In the thickest clump he found a naked sulphur-skinned ragazza with pale blood leaking from a wound on her head. *An aqua species*, he thought. He had seen them before in Riso's Bar. This one had pebble-like breasts and layers of external skin-folds covering her pubis. He stared at her madly fluttering neck gills. 'What has happened?'

Peculiar sounds poured from her mouth. She reached out a finely webbed hand.

Trin had never touched ginko skin before. Instinctively he retreated but the ragazza's desperate, imploring look filled him with guilt. Still he hesitated, wondering if she were contagious with something – or loco, perhaps.

Before he could decide, the intensity drained from her eyes and she fell back, unconscious.

Dead? He could not tell. She didn't appear to be breathing. He considered leaving and pretending he had not seen her, but her vulnerability prickled his conscience.

Trin lifted her awkwardly, holding her against him.

To his shame, the pressure of her naked body stirred excitement in his groin. He leaned his torso away from the contact and stepped out of the thorn bushes, shouting for help.

The humanesque servant peered from the coldlock along the portico. When she saw Trin's burden she cried out and beckoned. 'Come. Carry her to the infirmary.'

He followed the woman inside and up the villa's central stairs. By the time he laid the ragazza on a bed his arms were shaking with the effort.

'Her name is Djeserit. Her familia left her behind on Araldis. She had become too difficult to manage is my guess. Miolaquas mature early,' said the woman. 'Please, signor – while I examine her wound you must restrain her. If she awakens she will become violent. May I suggest you remove your gloves or they might become stained with blood.'

Trin stared at her. *But what of my hands? What of her alien blood on my skin?* Yet he could not say the words. The woman's solicitous care shamed him. 'Is she alive? I see no breath,' he said.

'Si, alive, but not breathing.' She pointed to the ragazza's neck gills, which lay firmly shut. 'She is in shock and her body is using stored oxygen. I must persuade her to land-breathe again.'

'You know healing . . . er . . .'

'Istelle. And si, I know a little healing.' She gave him a gentle smile, which transformed her severe features into something more comely.

The ragazza stirred, her legs suddenly flailing.

Trin stripped off his gloves and held her. Djeserit felt lean and papery under his hands – there was nothing soft about her, unlike the familia women. His body betrayed him again, responding to the touch of her. He pressed himself flat against the bedside to disguise his growing erection but Istelle was in any case distracted by her ministrations – murmuring quiet reassurances while she treated the wound.

Djeserit began to breathe with her lungs again in noisy, carking gulps.

Trin released her in surprise, stepping back.

'She is crying. Beautiful, isn't it?' said Istelle. She stroked the ragazza's thin hair tenderly. 'Djeserit, it's Istelle. Don Pellegrini found you and carried you inside,' she whispered into the ragazza's smooth earbud. 'Tell me what happened.'

Djeserit opened her flat-lidded eyes and blinked several times, swivelling her head like a confused checclia. Suddenly she seized Trin's hand and kissed it.

The sensation of her lips on his palm set his blood throbbing.

'Djeserit, what happened? Why were you outside?' Istelle urged.

But Trin didn't wait to hear the answer. He fled the room and the sensation of Djeserit's mouth, like a fresh burn, on his hand.

A squealing sound woke Trin before dawn. At first he thought it was the uuli as he tried to free it from the containment field in Riso's. Then, heart pounding, he realised it was the emergency shortcast.

'Fire . . . grain stores . . . shootin' up like a twister.' A man's voice: guttural – 'esqe but not Latino.

The station relay told Trin that the message was

originating from the northern edge of Loisa. He located the grain silos on the town map and verified the correlation. Following the procedure that Christian Montforte had left for him, he coded the alert through to the duty crew in the compound. Then he called the Capitano.

Christian appeared on his viewer, scowling. 'Si?'

'An emergency call has come in. The caller says the grain silos are on fire. It has come in from the right vicinity.'

'Can you smell anything?'

'Pardon?'

'Get outside and sniff the air. Can you smell anything?'

Trin left Christian's impatient glare and walked the few steps to the rear coldlock. He cracked it open and waited for his senses to stretch past the nullifying blast of the heat. *Yes*. It was there. The acrid taste of smoke settling on the back of his tongue like burned food.

He returned to the shortcast. 'Si. I can taste something.'

Christian swore in another language. He lifted his arms above his head and stretched himself awake. The movement of his body revealed a figure in bed behind him. Her armour-like skin and neck frills were unmistakably Balol. Trin had seen such females at Dockside, in the transit lounges, and once, as he procured bravura in the oily shadows of a freight bay, he had observed one overseeing the docking of a luxury ship.

The men had called Faja Fedor a 'ginko lover' – what, then, did they make of their Capitano?

'. . . I'll meet the duty crew there. Come with them,' Christian was saying.

Trin forced himself to listen to the Capitano's instructions. 'But—'

'That is not an invitation, Pellegrini!'

Christian ended the shortcast, leaving Trin to stare at the blank film.

Trin's insides trembled with a mixture of fear and excitement: he had not been close to a fire before. Because of the high oxygen quotient in Araldis's air, and as a future Principe, it had always been forbidden for him to take such a risk. A sudden frisson of liberation took him; perhaps there was some small compensation to be found in the indignity of his denouncement.

Following the Emergency Directive, he switched the shortcast to the Emergency Vehicle Frequency and let himself out through the coldlock into the compound.

The duty crew were already dressed and loading their vehicles.

'Capitano says I should come,' he said to a man he thought to be Seb Malocchi.

Malocchi inclined his flash hood towards the workshop office. 'Find a firesuit in there. We'll be gone in a few minutes. We won't wait,' he shouted.

Trin struggled into the suit with no assistance – and no hindrance. Where were the Cavaliere? Why were they not here?

'Last chance to catch a ride, Pellegrini,' a voice crackled through the flash hood's transceiver.

Trin squashed all the seals tight and went back out into the workshop.

'The Cavaliere have been recalled to Pell,' added Seb Malocchi, as if reading his mind. 'They have a *situation* up there as well.' He was piling kitbags on top of each other.

Trin climbed into the back of the remaining TerV as Malocchi secured them under webbing. 'What situation?' he asked.

Malocchi didn't answer. The vehicle swung out onto the bare redcrete viuzza and took several fast sharp turns to orient itself north. Trin banged his head against the window slits as he tried to peer out.

The TerV sped past the dust-white villettes of the Nobiles and into the non-familia section of Loisa where row upon row of cramped mud-and-cellulose cabins huddled together creating shade for each other.

'You know how to use these?' Malocchi again.

Trin turned awkwardly, half swinging from the holding straps.

Malocchi slid a crate across the floor, then himself after it, wedging in alongside Trin. He popped the crate's lid and pulled out several items. 'First Responder Kit – you take one of these when we stop and help anyone you come across that's hurt. See: burn-gel, cold compress, trauma pads, valve shield, infection swipes, skin-restore, blood-stopper roll.' He tucked each item back inside as he listed it.

Trin heard the words without comprehension. He did not deal with people like this: not with their blood and their wounds and their panic.

'You got it, Pellegrini?'

Trin nodded automatically.

'The grain silos are flaming,' another voice joined Seb Malocchi's in his hood. 'The truck is already there. So are we – almost. Can barely see the sky for merda . . .'

The TerV jerked to a stop. Trin waited inside, handing the kits out to the line of fire-suited men emerging from the other vehicles. When he had passed out the last one he hesitated, suddenly not wanting to leave the safety of the truck.

Outside, the sky had blackened as if overtaken by an eclipse, and despite the flash-hood's extractor poisonous fumes crawled into Trin's airways. A babble of voices competed over the transceiver but Christian cut across them all. 'Anyone not on a pump, there's someone injured over by the processor. Take your FR kit and get to it.'

'No one is free, Capitano,' replied another.

'Pellegrini!' Seb Malocchi motioned to him.

The rush of excitement Trin had felt back at the compound evaporated as he forced himself out of the TerV.

Fierce gouts of waxen smoke unfurled into the air from three silos. Groups of Carabinere battled with their tiny, ineffectual cold-foam tanks and nozzles to keep three more from doing the same. Flakes of hot polymer rained on the mask of Trin's flash hood, melting dints in the heat-resistant goggles. The ambient heat sent his suit temperature soaring dangerously.

'Follow me,' shouted Malocchi.

Trin sucked on the fluid tube and peered through the hot plastic rain for the processor. *There*. A tall frame at the end of the row of silos housing smaller bins and an elaborate loop system for grain separation.

Trin shouldered his kit, following Malocchi slowly. The might of the flames mesmerised him, as did the AiV that flew tight circles around them, spurting cold-foam from its belly tank.

What foolishness . . .

Without warning the flames plumed outwards, engulfing the AiV. It disintegrated, sparking a series of miniature explosions. Trin ran for the cover of the processor and flung himself full length under a bin housing.

Malocchi was already underneath the same bin, bent over a collapsed figure. He beckoned Trin over, pointing at his kit.

Trin rolled to his knees, suppressing his urge to flee back to the TerV. There was no safe place in the vicinity of the silos, he told himself. Safety was in the Palazzo back on Mount Pell. He thrust the kit at Seb Malocchi.

The man threw open the lid, rifling through the contents until he found the burn-gel. Trin stared down at the injured 'esque. Pieces of blackened clothing had been seared into his body tissue where skin should have been. Trin turned away from the charred head.

Dios! No hair, no lips.

Sickness rose in his throat and disgorged itself. His flash hood suctioned away the worst of the vomit so he could still breathe, but it could not neutralise the stink of his own weakness and fear.

The 'esque spasmed once, twice, and them became still.

Mercy.

Malocchi took a valve mask from the kit and laid it across the 'esque's blood-black face. He fitted the valve onto his own air supply and began a pointless attempt at resuscitation.

Then a fourth silo exploded as if birthing a universe.

Panicked, Trin scrambled from underneath the bin housing. He would not die here.

Malocchi saw his intention and abandoned his task. He ran after Trin but became tangled in the resuscitation hose still attached to his air supply. It tripped him and he fell heavily, twisting his leg underneath his body.

Every instinct shrieked at Trin not to wait, not to turn back for him: from the corner of his eye he could see the flames leaping to the fifth silo. If it reached the final one it would engulf them both.

'Wind shift . . . fall back.' Christian's order was a distant crackle. 'Evacuate . . .'

Trin could see the TerVs already pulling out. 'Montforte!' he screamed into his pickup.

'Pellegrini . . . where . . . you?'

Another thunderous crack and the bottom fell out of the flaming silo, sending an avalanche of smoke rolling down the tarmac. It swallowed Trin and obscured his line of sight to the remaining vehicles. 'Near the processor,' he gasped.

'For Cruxsakes . . . back here. I . . . lose . . . Principe's son . . . useless cazzone.'

Useless cazzone. Christian's words stopped Trin like a blow to the head, right there, in the billowing thick whirl of the smoke stream.

How many times had he thought the exact same of others? Countless.

If he died here, he would be as inconsequential as them: as pathetic and ignoble. The idea was more overpowering than the fire roaring behind him. He wanted to spill his rage into the fire. *I am important! I am . . .*

For no reason of valour – only the knowledge that

the balance should be tipped – Trin returned to the fallen Carabinere and took the shears from the FR kit strapped to the man's back. With precise strokes he cut through the hoses, releasing Melocchi's twisted foot.

Malocchi gripped Trin's shoulders and leaned gratefully against him.

Trin helped him to his feet. 'Montforte!' he shouted again. 'Montforte!'

But there was no reply. And he could see nothing through his melted goggles now, or feel much, save a sense of rectitude.

Their intertwined walk turned quickly to a stagger – Trin had never borne the true weight of another man before – and his muscles betrayed him. Collapse would take them soon, anyway, when their breathers faltered. He began to cough uncontrollably – they both did, bent over with the heaving and gasping of it. So much so that neither of them saw the TerV looming ahead through the smoke.

Trin rode in the Capitano's vehicle past the line of evacuated mud casas and white villettes, back to the compound. With trembling gloved fingers he detached his hood and gulped in the cooler cabin air.

'The wind will push the fire north onto the sand. It will burn itself out. We have evacuated the edge of town to be sure. But I think we are fortunate it will not spread there,' said Christian.

Trin stared at him aghast. 'I risked . . . you risked your men for mere grain?'

'For our main food source. Si,' he said flatly.

'But there are stockpiles at Dockside.'

'Our grain is allocated on a priority system that must be approved by the Principe – it is the same for all our imported commodities. It is unlikely that he would risk depletion of the familia central stores.'

'Are you saying that my father would let you starve?'

Christian gave a grim but unreadable smile. 'You stink, Pellegrini.'

Trin became aware of the foul stickiness of vomit on his face and neck. Somehow it did not seem as important as it should.

Christian called Trin to his office when the new duty crew signed on. The Capitano reeked of scorched polymer and the blisters on his face seeped little rivulets of fluid onto his silk innersuit. His expression was morose and dull with fatigue as he slumped in his chair.

Trin knew his own skin had not fared much better and the throbbing of his burns gave him an odd sense of fellowship with the Carabinere.

'Nathaniel Montforte will relieve you on shortcast for this shift. You saved one of us today. Sleep and recover,' said Christian. 'And salve those burns.'

The Capitano's consideration took him by surprise. 'Grazi.'

Yet when Christian left Trin found it impossible to relax. Energy coursed through him still like an unsteady pulse. He washed in the cramped basin and donned fresh clothes.

Young Nathaniel Montforte hung behind him as he applied burn-gel from the office medikit. It was awkward – doing these things for himself.

'What was the fire like, Don Trinder? Did it scare

the seed from your balls? I heard you saved Seb Malocchi,' prattled Nathaniel.

But Trin had no interest in feeding the younger man's imagination. 'I will take transport to the market for food,' he said.

Out in the compound Trin discovered that his AiV had been repaired and shifted to a corner. He made his way over to it, half expecting to be stopped, but unlike the Cavaliere the duty crew paid him no attention – save for the hissing-motor and muffled-laughter noises that they made.

Trin settled his AiV in the vehicle bay adjacent to the Bear and Pearl gate façade of Villa Fedor.

Istelle answered the gate-call and let him in. She waited in the coldlock for him. 'Do you have news of Mira?' she asked.

He stiffened. 'That is Carabinere business.'

Despite his rebuff Istelle's smile stayed warm. 'I am very fond of the younger Baronessa. I don't want to see her hurt.'

Trin was taken aback. The 'esque woman seemed to have no grasp of a servant's manners.

When he did not reply her smile faded a little, and she escorted him down the ancestor-crowded corridor to the cucina.

Faja Fedor was bent over a vat of stew. She glanced up, surprised. 'An early visit from the Carabinere, Don Trinder? Hoping to find my sorella hiding in the pantry? Behind a jar of pimento, perhaps.'

'I come from the fire,' Trin said simply.

She frowned, mollified. 'What news of it?'

'Loisa has lost its grain stores but only a few lives.'

Faja sighed as if the news made her tired. 'That is good news and bad. There will be food shortages now.'

'How is the ginko?' he asked.

She stabbed the stew with her ladle. 'We do not use that word here.'

'What is she, then?'

'Her mama is a miolaqua and her father a Lostol. So in fact she is part 'esque. Only she has many of her mama's features.' Faja eyed Trin closely. 'Tell me why you would care, Don Trinder, when it was your men who did this to her?'

He shrugged to hide his embarrassment. Vespa Malocchi had bragged of menacing the ragazza. He had handled her a little, he said, because of his curiosity about her strange skin. But she had run from him. 'What would you have me do? Shoot a Carabinere? Today they risked their lives to save your grain supplies.'

'Their courage in the face of a fire does not give them rights over a 'bino.'

'Hardly a 'bino, Baronessa,' Trin argued. *She could not be and stir such things in me.* 'Your words stray towards sedition. Little wonder that your sorella has acted improperly. What values have you taught her?'

Faja took a step closer to him, her head tilted to one side, her dark eyes fierce with intent. 'Would you really take Mira's Inborn Talent for your own? Would you steal from the genes of our ancestors?'

Trin retreated. The woman had a presence; ways of making him feel uncertain. The same as Mira had that night on the beach, and his tia Marchella at dinner.

'A woman cannot be Pilot First. You know that as well as I.'

Faja swayed as if she had been slapped. 'I do not think that you and I know the same things at all.'

Trin gave her a sharp, dismissive look. Faja's aggression alarmed him – even the voracious Silvio sorellas knew how to curb their stronger opinions.

'I have other matters to attend,' he said curtly. Conscious of the Baronessa's glare at his back, he walked to the end of the corridor where Istelle waited.

'Djeserit has recovered now,' Istelle whispered as she opened the coldlock. 'Thank you.'

Though Trin did not reply, her words took some of the sting out of Faja Fedor's boorish manner. He stepped outside the lock, wondering why he had come. What had he expected? Comfort? Respect? He stared at the waves of heat billowing from the redcrete. The viuzzas of Loisa were so barren and hostile compared to Dockside and Pell.

'Don Pellegrini?' The low, urgent voice came from the shadows of the portico.

He turned. 'Si?'

A naked hand extended towards him. Trin recognised the mottled skin and took an involuntary step forward. What was the ragazza doing here? Waiting for him?

Djeserit's fingers closed on his glove and she drew him along the side of the villa and down the edge of the dry-garden. Not a word passed between them until she opened the door of the oval outhouse that contained two beds, a table stand, a tiny cucina and a washroom.

'What is this?' Trin asked, stepping inside.

She shrugged – a curious full-body movement that brought her to the tips of her toes – and closed the door. 'The Baronessas lived here when the villa was being built.'

Impulsively, Trin reached out and touched the healing gash on her forehead. 'Are you improved?'

Djeserit smiled, her facial skin tightening until her eyes almost disappeared. Without warning she pushed the door shut and locked her arms around his waist.

The pressure of her body sparked an instant wash of desire in Trin. He tried to push her away but she clung to him with surprising strength, hugging herself close to the swell in his groin.

He stripped off his gloves and ran a hand across her dry, papery cheek.

She turned her lips to it and tongued the skin between his fingers. Even her tongue felt parched and abrasive.

'What are you doing?' The words strangled in his throat.

'I am ready for quenching but here . . .' she rolled her eyes up under her lids and gestured in the direction of the villa '. . . they do not understand such things. The Baronessa only knows of quenching in the ways of the Latino. When the man says. When the man wants. I am not Latino and I want . . . now.'

Trin felt another rush of desire. Djeserit's strangeness fuelled his passion, as if repulsion was his true attractor. She was bold and vulnerable at once. But more than that . . . she was alien and unrestrained.

He lifted her into his arms and carried her to the bed. She wore a simple working fellala without thermal layers. Underneath it he could feel the protected parts of her lotioned skin – so soft and malleable compared to her face. He lifted her robe and peeled back the lower layers of his fellalo so that he could lie on her. Explosiveness built inside him as he pressed himself into her. Their union was quick and difficult, her anatomy not a complete fit for his.

Afterwards she clung to him, making disjointed carking noises. They did not startle him this time. He brimmed with elation – he had performed without bravura.

'More.' Her breath was light and quick against his neck.

Methodically Trin refolded his robe and sealed it. 'Tonight, late,' he said. 'Can you come here?'

Djeserit nodded. 'Under the cucina there is a wine cellar. I use it to get away from the 'esques. They don't like to come outside.'

'They taunt you?'

'Si. But I am not afraid of them. Not like your Carabinere.' Her face tightened with fear and her eyes disappeared under their lids as if she had gone to sleep.

Trin felt the pangs of a mistake he could not undo. He had soiled himself with a ginko. He was a ginko-lover.

Djeserit hugged him again but this time he stood impassive in her embrace. When she had gone, he left along the side of the villa, thankful that he would not have to look Faja Fedor in the face.

MIRA

Mira woke on the floor of the little hall with her sorella's face blurred by nearness. She tried to sort the sounds coming from Faja's lips but they emerged as drops of noise without form. The room was a blur of shapes. Her feet felt bloodless and distant. Faja lifted her to them, propelling her along the corridor to the cucina. She helped Mira to a low seat, returned to the door and locked it.

Mira inhaled the food scents. Her stomach contracted with hunger. 'I have not eaten,' she whispered.

Faja hastened to her with a plate of minestrone from the huge pan on the cooker. As Mira sipped the soup her vision cleared. Faja's house fellala was stained with food and sweat-crumpled, even in the cool of the house. Her rich crimson skin glowed with the cooking heat and beads of moisture dotted the line of her dark hair.

Mira's sorella felt the scrutiny and set the ladle down, wiping her hands on her apron. She poured Mira a drink from a tall jug and brought it to her. 'Can you speak now?'

Mira took a deep and shuddering breath, unsure where to begin.

'I know some of what has happened. They told me the Principe would take your Talent. The Carabinere were here just a few hours ago,' said Faja.

Mira jerked upright, ready to run from the cucina, but Faja pressed her back down. 'You are safe for tonight, cara. There has been a fire and the Carabinere have other things to divert them.'

Mira trembled with relief and then began to sob. Seeing Faja had made it more real.

'Madre de Dios,' said Faja with uncharacteristic softness. She clasped Mira tightly. 'Tell me what happened.'

'The Carabinere came for me after graduation. I ran . . . to find Insignia. But she is gone. The Principe has moved her and I can no longer hear her in my mind. I hid on a ship at the landing station. The captain, he wished to kill me, but the ship was another biozoon. I-It helped me. What will happen to me, Fa? Without Insignia . . .'

Faja kissed the top of Mira's hair. 'Without Insignia you will be strong.'

Mira inhaled her sorella's thick scent, calmed by its familiarity. It had been this way when they were younger: Faja giving comfort to her just so.

'It is not just for you that there are troubles, 'bino. The city's kranse stores are gone, burned down – *whoof!* – like that. These last weeks the Carabinere sirens bleat day and night. The miners are angry with the familia, but Franco Pellegrini does nothing to improve things for them. *Nothing.* And now . . . he would take our birthright away.' Her voice shook on the last word. She drew a quiet breath. 'I must speak quickly to you of an important matter.'

Mira stared up at her. 'What matter?'

Faja disappeared into the large pantry. Mira heard her heavy-footed tread down the stairs to the cellar.

She returned with a bottle of aged wine. Mira knew its quality from the clear tawny colour.

'Where are your servants?' asked Mira.

Faja handed her the cup. 'The Galiottos have been recalled by the Principe. He has heard that I am giving refuge to alien ragazze,' she said.

Mira sat a little straighter. How long had she been away at the Studium? Several years. She had not come back in that time. It had not seemed right to flaunt her learning in Faja's face.

'Do you know how I can afford to care for these un-familia?' asked Faja.

'Our gratis?'

'Pfft. That does not scrape the skin of my expenses. I cannot beg the Principe to buy korm shell or uuli nutrients. No, I have only been able to do this through the grace of a patron.'

'A patron?' Mira was alert now and distracted from her own concerns. 'Who?'

Faja took a generous swallow of her wine. 'Marchella Pellegrini.'

Marchella Pellegrini? Franco's estranged sorella! Mira knew the name – most familia did – though she had never met her.

Faja saw her puzzlement. 'Some believe that Marchella should be head of the familia instead of Franco. If intelligence and courage stood for anything it would be so. But Ciprianos are the most intransigent of our clans. They think only of the men . . . the men . . . The men say they left Crux for the sake of our future. That is a lie, Mira! They left for the sake of *their* future: to keep their women restrained. Things had begun to change on Crux. The many wars had opened our eyes to other ways.'

Mira stared at her, open-mouthed. 'No. That is not so. We left to arrest the dilution of our race. When our women were raped during the wars, it led to much interbreeding with our enemies. That is why they altered the terms of our fertility. To protect us.'

'You sound like a Studium lecture, Mira. Have you not thought to look past the official canon?'

In truth she had not. In her time at the Studium her mind had been immersed in Latino poetry and ship schematics, and ways to avoid Lancia Silvio. 'W-what other truths do you know?'

'I – *we* believe that our clan leaders wish only to strengthen their patriarchy – that our race was never in danger of dilution.'

'The Fedors would not have fallen for such a thing! Why did they volunteer to pilot the migration?'

'Maybe they thought it would preserve the Inborn Talent, for we do not truly know why or how we are blessed.'

Worry, not hunger, churned Mira's stomach now. 'The Principe believes he can cut the gene from me and transfer it to his son.'

'Franco wishes much for his son. It is Franco who should experience a transference – transference of command.'

Mira took a sharp breath. Faja spoke treason. 'You must not say that,' she begged her sorella. 'You are the prudent one. The steadfast elder Baronessa Fedor. I am the loco; the eccentric.'

Faja swallowed the last drops from her glass of wine

and poured another; her cheeks glowed brighter with her rising passion. 'You are not the only one with dreams, Mira. Why do you think I have taken in these bambini?'

Without warning she parted the folds of her tunic and revealed intricate lines and patterns etched into her flesh.

Mira gasped. 'I have seen that before – on a Galiotto woman at the Studium. She gave me her biometric stripe. That was how I escaped.'

'It is the sign of the Pensare.'

'I thought they were only an invention of the Nobile.'

'No invention, cara.'

Mira cupped her fingers around the rim of her cup, absorbing what she had just learned. 'Why did you keep this from me?'

'So that you could find your own path, mia Mira. I did not wish my bitterness to be yours.'

'You are not bitter.'

Faja's serious expression softened. 'When you look at me you see only a mama, because our own did not survive. But I am not just that – I am many things and not all of them admirable or biddable. It is time that you knew this and made your own choices. The Pensare can help you.'

Mira's skin prickled with alarm and a measure of anger. 'How can they help me? Can they deny the Carabinere? Can they stand before the Principe and command him not to take my Talent? And if they could help me – why would they? Who am I to such insurgents?'

'Their opposition is subtle but that does not make it less. And they would help you, Mira – they have already have – because you are a woman.'

'What if I am a dishonest woman who deserves no help? Do they not discriminate?'

'You have not learned enough yet to understand that we are only pushed to corruption by circumstance. It is not our natural inclination. If the Pensare can improve the circumstances of our women then one soul will be no different from another. All will be matched. And remember, we are of the Castiglioni! The Pensare have learned to revere our beliefs. Who better than us to steer the transformation?'

Her sorella's rapt expression stirred Mira. Yet she found it impossible to relinquish the stone of mistrust lodged deep inside. 'The familia women I know would not care for your help. They hated me for my thin body and truthfulness.'

'Your slenderness is a different beauty, Mira. Have I not told you that many times?'

'My difference is not here.' Mira slapped her sides. 'It is in *here*.' She touched her forehead. 'Even from you, Fa. I have no care for home and place. I long to be free of it all.'

Faja nodded. 'It is the Inborn Talent. Pilot are wanderers.'

'Then perhaps I should give myself to the Principe. Perhaps without my Talent I would fit better.'

Faja stood, frowning, and began throwing bluish-purple legumes into a bowl. 'If you are inclined to indulge in such self-pity then perhaps you should.'

Mira bowed her head.

Her sorella went to the cooker and lifted an enormous tray of fritters from the oven. 'We will talk more later. Take your meal in here and sleep in the lodge. Only a few of the bambini know of your presence. I shall instruct them not to speak of it to anyone.'

She dropped several fat fritters on a plate in front of Mira and carried the rest from the room.

Mira sipped more wine and greedily fingered the fritters into her mouth, uncaring that her chin became slick with fat.

'Have you unlearned all your manners on Mount Pell, Baronessa?'

Mira dabbed her mouth guiltily.

Istelle stood at the door, smiling. The Pagoin humanesque's spider-thin limbs seemed frail compared with the solid Latino shape, but the warmth of her smile made her face into something beautiful.

Mira ran to embrace her.

'Poor darling,' Istelle murmured, stroking her hair the way Faja had. 'Faja has told me of your ordeal. Why did you not come sooner?'

Mira thought of Jancz. She could not speak of him, even to Istelle. 'I have been m-moving to avoid the Carabinere.'

'How have you survived?'

'Friends have helped me.'

'Well, you are safe for the moment. Come with me to see the new bambini.'

Mira followed Istelle along the familiar corridor to a room decorated with rich brocade wall-trim and furnished with several lace-covered cradles and an armchair. Istelle lifted a bambino from one of the cradles and settled it in her arms. It suckled on a latte bladder, its fist curled around Istelle's thin finger. The others began to cry, hearing movement.

'You have your hands full there, 'Stelle.'

'Their mother was a Pagoin. She was killed in the Juanita mine collapse. Their father is still alive but he is filled with grief and refuses to see them.'

'What happened at Juanita? I heard many different things.'

Istelle shrugged. 'Some say it was deliberate, others say an accident. Faja believes the Principe does not insist on enough safety.'

Mira watched her rock the bambino. 'It suits you,' she said softly.

Istelle smiled. 'I've been blessed, Mira. You know I was born wombless. That's why my husband abandoned me. Yet I find myself with more love and more children to care for than I could have dreamed about.'

'I think *they* are the ones who have been blessed, Istelle.'

Mira stayed with Istelle until a little before midnight when Faja came to find her.

'Come while I finish,' Faja said.

Mira followed in Faja's shadow. 'So many bambini now,' she whispered.

Faja nodded. 'It seems that more and more are being abandoned. It has become known that we will not turn them away. I suppose that is how the Principe heard.' She pointed into Mira's old room. 'Djeserit – the miolaqua – asked for you.'

No sense of familiarity claimed her when she entered the room. Her Fenice four-poster bed and armoire had been removed to make room for the korm nest. The korm was roosting on it now, making soft crooning noises. Only the amber-tinted walls were the same.

'Why do the Carabinere want you?' Djeserit lay in a sack on a simple bed opposite the korm. The scent of lotion rose from the cloth – her skin was being mois- turised as she rested.

Mira sighed. 'They would take something of mine.'

'But you cannot deny the Carabinere, Baronessa.'

Mira paused. She could not explain the nuances of her world to this ragazza. 'Why do you ask?'

Djeserit turned her head away. 'Baronessa Faja says you are very clever. How do you know if a man is . . . noble?'

The question took Mira by surprise, sparking memo- ries she had tried to disregard – Trin Pellegrini kissing her on the beach, wanting her, then pushing her away.

She took some moments to let them pass before she answered. 'How do you judge any person? Perhaps by knowing yourself.'

Djeserit tossed and turned in her lotion sack, discontented.

Mira wondered if she should pursue it further but Faja called her out into the dimness of the corridor. 'The lodge is clean enough for you to sleep in – like old times, cara. Lock the door to it, though. I do not believe that our city is as safe as it was. I will contact the Pensare and in the morning we will take you to a safe place. The Carabinere will never know you have been here.'

On impulse Mira embraced her sorella, brushing the lines on Faja's forehead with her lips. 'Grazi.'

Faja drew back. 'For what? Honouring my sorella?

You have always come first in my life, Mira, when you were a bambina, after our mama and papa were gone.' She cupped her thick, blunt-fingered hand gently against Mira's face and then disappeared down the dark corridor.

Mira sighed. Faja had been mama to her, but who had been mama to Faja?

She made her way through the rear coldlock and followed the line of dismal teranu grass through the dry gardens to the lodge.

The small outhouse felt more familiar to her than her own bedroom. Nothing had changed inside: the same beds and a small organic cucina and bathroom that she and Faja had lived in when they had first been relocated to Loisa.

As the pressures altered to adjust to the influx of heat Mira chose the bed closest to the door – her bed – and fell quickly asleep.

The exact same noise of pressure change woke her a few hours later. She lay there, breathing quietly. *The door*. She had not locked it.

A soft curse and the door closed.

Warmer air surged around her. Someone was in there. Not Faja. Or Istelle. An intruder?

Mira's heart beat wildly when a hand touched her ankle. She kicked and rolled away.

The intruder, caught off guard, overbalanced and fell.

Was he conscious? *He?* Yes, she thought, it was a male's odour – humanesque, familiar almost. She tapped on the light and groped for the shortcast, but her hand froze in mid-motion. She stared down at the fallen figure.

'You!' Mira declared with enough accusation in her tone for a lawmon demanding a life sentence for a killer.

TRIN

Trin could not sleep. He see-sawed between shame and elation. Djeserit was a part-ginko and not quite an adult, yet he grew hard at the thought of her. Had her strangeness cured him of his need for bravura? He would know when he saw her again – and how he longed for that. Anticipation kept fatigue at bay: he should have been exhausted but still the energy flowed in him.

He dressed and went into the office where Nathaniel Montforte dozed over the desk.

Trin startled him awake. 'You had a visitor from Pell earlier. He grew tired of waiting and said that he must return to the mountains. He left you this.' Nathaniel yawned and pointed to a capsule on his desk.

Trin picked it up and turned it over in his hands. His data sponge was inside. He knew it. Joe Scali had been. 'Bene, Montforte. Have you had a meal?' he asked casually.

The young man shook his head.

'I shall watch the shortcast for you.'

'But the Capitano . . .'

'I will log it as my request. See.' Trin tapped an entry into the deskfilm's diary. 'It is hardly reasonable for both of us to be here when I am unable to sleep. Come back in a while when you have filled your belly.'

Nathaniel hesitated, then nodded his appreciation. 'Grazi, Don Pellegrini. The Capitano called me off my break cycle. I did not have time for food.'

Trin forced himself to smile: Nathaniel, at least, treated him with respect. 'Take your time, Montforte. My card is empty.'

When he had left, Trin attached the sponge to his deskfilm and searched for the file from Lotte Perrone's office. To his surprise the contents of the file were an audio-only record. He secured the coldlock to both doors before activating it.

Clearance level: **tau.**

Meeting between visiting dignitary (name available at clearance level: **psi**, *hereafter referred to in this recording as* **SUPPRESSED**) *and ambassadress for Araldis, Marchella Pellegrini.*

Recorded and sealed 20/14/4006.

'My apologies for any offence, Ambassadress Pellegrini: the sight of your beautiful planet excites my physiology. On my planet it is not a thing we hide. It prevents much deception when you can see what excites a person.'

'**SUPPRESSED**, please call me Marchella. I have arranged a tour of the main equatorial mines for you. Our transport will depart shortly after breakfast.'

'Will you be accompanying me . . . Marchella?'

'That would please mia fratella, **SUPPRESSED**.'

'But will it please *me*?'

(pause)

'The variety of minerals on Araldis is due in part to its unusual geography. As you may be aware, Araldis has no definitive polar land mass like most other inhabited planets. Large subduction plates collide at each pole, creating the maze of islands that sprinkle the breadth of each hemisphere, ending in the ranges that fringe the belted land mass on which we live and which we mine. Araldis's climate is extreme. While the polar waters are warm, due to the underwater volcanic activity, the islands are cool and wet. The Equatorial Belt, in the rain shadow of the ranges, is hot and arid.'

'I have familiarised myself with Araldisian geography, Marchella Pellegrini. It is part of what makes its minerals so . . . special. Please join me for a meal.'

'Thank you, **SUPPRESSED**, but I have eaten already.'

'Then I will be offended. I need a guide through your foods. Please sit, Marchella. I may wear less clothing than you are used to, but I am quite harmless.'

'This is kranse bread. It is our most successful crop and is very high in protein. The eggs are quark, and have an unusually dry texture – again, high in protein. The sea cucumbers are crisp. The roe is from the Tourmaline Islands and may be saltier than you are used to. I recommend that you drink it with wine. Araldisian Reds are our most

famous export, after our minerals, **SUPPRESSED**.
We have numerous varieties. Though the grapes
are grown in climate control, the Araldisian soil
that nourishes them makes for a piquant flavour.'

'Please join me, Marchella.'

<pause>

Recording resumed in AiV 197*

'And what of your family's operations, Marchella?'

'Below is Pellegrini A, and to the south
Pellegrini B. Each produces 60,000 tonnes of ore
per thirty-hour day. The ore is conveyored back
to Dockside and stockpiled. The Pellegrini
conveyors are some of the longest known. The
mining belt has the perfect geography and climate
for our conveyors, flat and hot – no frost to damage
the machinery. Subsidiary feeders from the smaller
mines join the main conveyor all the way along.'

'The process is very primitive.'

'Yes, but it works. Our society uses some gro-
technology to maintain its infrastructure but we
found it to be too expensive on the mining scale.
We are still a young planet.'

'And youth is so seductive, my dear. What of
the non-Pellegrini mines?'

'They use land barges to transport their ore, or
rent space on the conveyors.'

'So indeed your family has the monopoly?'

'The Cipriano Clan purchased Araldis after
seeing the assay reports from the first exploration
ships in this area. The Pellegrinis are the most
powerful of the Araldis Ciprianos, the royal family.
It is . . . our planet.'

'And what would it take for me to convince you that an exclusive minerals contract with me would be in the interest of the Pellegrinis' great name?'

'Orion lucre.'

'That is something I am in a position to offer.'

'What minerals do you want?'

'Only one little mine, Marchella. It is named Juanita, I believe.'

'Oh?'

'The one that produces a quantity of quixite.'

'Our financiers will negotiate with you on that issue, **SUPPRESSED**. But, if you'll pardon my frankness, there are others bidding for the same alloy.'

'May I enquire who that may be?'

'You know that I cannot disclose who bids against you.'

'Is there nothing that might convince you to short-cut this . . . this . . . bargaining?'

<pause>

'There is one small thing that would gain you favour in the bidding.'

'Which would be?'

'You are tyro to the Sole Entity?'

'Yes.'

'I . . . that is, we want one of our familia to be admitted to Belle-Monde to undergo testing by the Entity.'

'But only the very brilliant are chosen.'

'And you do not think there could be one so brilliant among us Latinos?'

'No need to take offence, ambassadress.'

'No offence taken, **SUPPRESSED**. But this point would be, in brutal parlance, a deal-breaker.'

<pause>

'Then perhaps it could be arranged, Marchella, once the terms of export are agreed. Do you have one person in mind?'

'I do.'

'Then I would say we are *close* to a deal.' His tone indicated that he was about to make a further condition.

'**SUPPRESSED?**' Marchella asked.

'There is one other thing I would also have, which would be, to use your words, a deal-breaker.'

'Si?'

<extended pause>

Trin sat transfixed as the final moments of the recording played out the unmuffled sounds of the dignitary's concluding negotiations. He then replayed the beginning, listening for the date – over a year ago.

Had the deal been struck, he wondered? And why did the dignitary wish to purchase minerals exclusively from the mine of Luna il Longa? What was this alloy that he, and others, so eagerly sought?

Trin stood and paced a little, noticing a sudden aching hunger in his belly. He searched the storage cupboards and found some dried fruits and a tube of sweetener.

As he ate he tried to open a farcast link to the OLOSS library on Scolar. The link bounced back with the message that the relay station at Dowl was indefinitely disrupted.

Indefinitely?

Frustrated, he replayed the trade negotiation. He had heard of the discovery of a strange Entity, out past Mintaka, but to believe that the creature was a god was so ... *unlikely!* Why had his tia loco wanted to send a familia to its tutelage?

When the answer did not come readily to him, Trin realised how little he knew of his familia's politics or what really lay at the heart of the trouble between Franco and Marchella.

His thoughts drifted to Djeserit. He checked the time. She would be waiting for him now but he could not leave until Nathaniel returned. The ragazzo was taking too long.

Trin allowed conscience and desire to war within him momentarily. But conscience had never been his ally.

Sole

manifestspace

watch'm secrets<luscious luscious>
cleave'm thoughts| bring'm danger danger
lose'm thoughts|round round
make'm| absurd absurd
try'm other
threat threat|on little creature.
watch'm secrets<luscious luscious>

TEKTON

'*What* privacy issues, Tekton? I am told that Sole Entity encourages competition between the tyros. And, to put it frankly, tell someone who cares. As long as you turn up for your assigned scans, you are free to bitch as much as you like among yourselves.'

Bitch? BITCH! Tekton toyed with the idea of opening his robe to share his annoyance with the Chief Astronomein but the Balol scientist's attention had already drifted back to the algorithm matrices rotating above his console.

Kick him, said his free-mind. *Slice tiny bits from his neck frill and stuff them up his olfactory orifice.* His logic-mind chipped in at this point with a cool observation that *free-mind is exhibiting signs of extreme liberation*, and warned Tekton that *following its suggestions could be construed as psychotic behaviour. Oh, and . . . the astronomein clearly has no legislative power over the tyros.*

In a rather disconsolate fashion Tekton made his daily pilgrimage to the ménage lounge.

To his surprise, Ra was there, playing 4D quoits with the uuli humanesquetarian specialist. Tekton hadn't seen him for weeks. The only other person in the bar was a particularly unkempt individual that Tekton's moud informed him was the famously famous Jo-Jo Rasterovich, mineral scout and Sole-discoverer.

Tekton experienced a surge of possibility that titillated both his minds.

'Cousin,' acknowledged Ra, amiably enough.

Tekton kept his tongue between his teeth lest he should hiss, and took a seat at the bar next to the scout.

'May I introduce myself and procure you a drink?'

The scout shrugged in a confused, thuggish kind of way. Tekton tried not to recoil from the sickly aroma of freeze-dried cabbage that clung to him.

'Jax and spritzer. And a teranu spliff,' he mumbled.

No cannabis if I'm paying, Tekton told his moud. *But put some adrenalin in the mixer – he seems half asleep.*

The moud relayed the message to the bar.

When the two drinks arrived sans boosted cigarette, the scout didn't seem to notice.

'I am Godhead Tekton of archi-Tects and I believe, sir, that you are somewhat of an expert in the field of mineral discovery?' said Tekton.

Jo-Jo took a sip and washed it around in his mouth. The movement displayed the elasticity of his skin and sent Tekton's free-mind skittering after thoughts of Miranda Seeward's jowls.

'Can't do, mate. Retired from all *that*, after all *this*.' Jo-Jo waved his hand around to indicate Belle-Monde.

'There would of course be some remuneration for any answers . . . any clues you might be able to give me.'

'Cheap as I might look, mate, I don't need your moolah.'

'What *do* you need?' Tekton was feeling unusually forthright – desperate, in fact.

Jo-Jo's answer, or lack thereof, was drowned out by Miranda and Jise entering the lounge, arguing loudly.

Lovers' spat, thought Tekton with a superior sniff and turned back to the scout.

Whether it was the effects of the adrenalin, Tekton could only guess, but suddenly Jo-Jo quivered with the alertness of a hunted animal. He stood and attempted to leave but stumbled backwards as if his body would not do as he told it – as if something held him firmly to the room.

His expletives were, thankfully, beyond the interpretation of Tekton's moud. He grasped Tekton's robe and dragged him close. 'You know that woman?' he whispered.

Tekton resisted pulling away, sensing that a bargaining point had presented itself. 'Indeed. We are colleagues.'

'She must not see me.'

Tekton pulled away a little and regarded the scout with a steely eye. 'How interesting that suddenly we both have something that the other wants.'

Jo-Jo Rasterovich gulped his drink and huddled down onto his stool, trying to make himself smaller. 'What would it take for you to get me out of here?' He glanced around wildly as if addressing someone unseen. 'What would it take?'

Tekton surmised that it was not the adrenalin and, in fact, perhaps Jo-Jo was a little deranged – but that was of no matter.

'That's very simple, Mr Rasterovich. It would take a rare mineral amalgam,' he said.

MIRA

The intruder, dressed in a once-white Carabinere fellalo, rolled onto his knees, clutching the back of his unhooded head.

'Trinder Pellegrini? What are you doing here? Dressed that way?' Mira heard the shrill fear in her voice.

'Mira Fedor?' he whispered, hoarsely. 'What in the cazzone are—'

A deafening explosion shook the room, knocking Mira to the floor, against Trin. After pushing him away, she scrambled for her boots and ran to the door.

'Stay inside,' he shouted at her. But she ignored him, flinging the door open.

Another explosion knocked her backwards as if she'd been kicked in the chest, robbing her of breath and hearing.

Stunned, Mira levered herself up onto her elbow to see Villa Fedor crumbling in the pink dawn light like a sand palazzo before a breaking wave. Fragments spewed outwards in a roar and a chunk of catoplasma struck her shoulder; gravel from the dry-garden stung her face. She rolled onto her stomach, moaning, fumbling to seal her velum.

A lull followed the shock, and in its aftermath came another noise. Worse. The cries of injured 'bini.

Mira's heart beat in painful spasms. Faja and Istelle. *Crux . . . oh, my Crux!* She climbed to her feet and ran outside. Fire consumed the ruins without conscience for those still alive who were trapped inside.

'Trinder,' she screamed over her shoulder. 'The Carabinere.'

But Trin did not answer, nor did he come outside.

'They'll burn to death,' she cried. What could she do? Nothing. She could do nothing. But what if Faja was alive? What if Istelle—

A segment of the villa wall cracked with a noise like a rifle shot and fell. The rest would follow. There would be no survivors when it did.

Mira ran towards the heat and rubble, the ground burning her as if she was walking barefoot on coals. Smoke and dust choked her breather, forcing her to take shallow breaths. She felt light-headed. *The cucina? No! Si! I think so. Crux. What is that? Ragazzo? Arm? Cannot tell.* Tears hampered her progress – no sadness, only panic – blurring her vision as they poured from her eyes.

Dining room, covered with beds fallen from the first floor. *Korm nest.* Smouldering. Other end of dining salon. Fallen cots from above. *'Bino in cot still.* Somehow. *Dead. Arms twisted. Istelle! Scrape debris away.* Istelle in her arms. 'Istelle?'

The woman coughed. 'Faja. Bambini,' she whispered.

Mira strained to lift the thin woman in her arms.

Istelle whimpered, clutching her robe around herself. Mira dragged her through the flames, legs shaking from the effort, staggering by the time she fell against the wall of the lodge. 'Trinder, please . . .' She thumped against the door.

Trin opened it and she fell inside. He took Istelle from her, carrying the injured woman to the bed.

Mira climbed to her feet. 'Where are the Carabinere?'

Trin's expression was strange, disconnected. 'I'm not there, so they cannot know.'

He made no sense but she did not wait. She returned to the villa, covering the same rooms: cucina and dining hall and back. More collapsed beds. Some bodies. 'Bini she didn't know or couldn't recognise. *Dead. All dead.*

One last glance at the cucina. A deep hole had appeared in the floor. *The cellar.* She lay flat on her stomach and crawled to the edge, her throat so choked with smoke that she couldn't swallow.

She heard a noise below. A chitter. A korm alive.

Mira plunged her arm down as far as she dared without toppling in. Smaller fingers grasped it. Elation suffused her with strength and she tugged the 'bino upwards.

Djeserit's frightened face appeared through the smoke. She bled from wounds on her cheeks and forehead. 'The korm is still down there.'

Mira dragged her away from the edge of the hole. 'She's much heavier than you. I will need something to pull her out.'

Djeserit called to the korm while Mira searched through the rubble for something to help them. She found it in what was left of the laundry amid the stench of smouldering chemicals – a roll of flex. She stumbled back to Djeserit but as she unwound it a prickling sensation crept along her spine. Nearby more explosions sounded. Were those other voices she could hear, calling out for help?

Mira tied the flex around her waist and told Djeserit

to grasp her. Together they pulled the korm jerkily up to the lip of the hole. Then the edge crumbled away with the weight and she dropped again.

Mira's weakness infuriated her. *I need a man's strength.*

Djeserit tugged her arm. 'Baronessa? Don't give up. Per favore.'

The ragazza's plea spurred her to try again. She planted her feet wide and began to pull backwards again. It was so hot now that it hurt to breathe. The flex bit through her gloves and pinched at her waist. Her muscles trembled uncontrollably with the weight of the load. Any moment now the fire would sweep through and take them.

Mira let obstinacy became her focus. The korm would not slip. This time as it reached the lip of the hole the korm gripped the edge with it strong beak and forearms and pulled itself out.

Mira did not wait to examine Djeserit's and the korm's wounds; she urged them from the ruins and back through the dry-garden to the lodge.

Trin was still inside, kneeling beside Istelle. In his arms he held a small bundle: a 'bino. His face crumpled with relief when he saw Mira. 'She had it in a sling under her arm,' he said.

Mira took the tiny shape from him. It was crying, a bleating noise so gentle against the chaos. 'Bino? I could have crushed you—'

The noise of another blast drowned her voice. The walls of the lodge trembled and Mira's ears popped. Instinct drove her to the floor.

Trin had fallen across Djeserit, shielding her with his own body.

Noble but tardy, Mira thought. If he had helped her before, maybe others would have lived – maybe Faja. She didn't need to look outside to know there would be no survivors now.

Closing her mind to it, Mira crawled to Istelle's side. The 'bino had fallen silent in her arms, its face wary like that of a tiny, scared animal.

'Where's the nearest medic, 'Stelle?'

The Pagoin woman didn't answer.

Mira ran her free hand over Istelle's head, feeling for wounds to her scalp and neck. The poor cara must have been feeding the 'bino when the blast had come. Where had Faja been? Did it matter? Faja was gone. Her sorella was *gone*.

But Istelle lived. *I must help her.* She stroked Istelle's hair in a soothing movement.

Djeserit stepped forward and tugged her arm away roughly.

'Istelle's dead, Baronessa. We must go from here and find help.'

Dead? What did she mean? Mira continued her stroking but Djeserit shook her again, insistently.

'*See* her, Mira!' The harsh voice belonged to Trin Pellegrini.

Mira had forgotten about him but his hostile demand forced her to examine Istelle's face; to watch her chest. Nothing. No airflow. No pulse. No life: only a trickle of drying blood at the corner of her mouth and a look of heartbreaking sadness.

Mira Fedor's world collapsed. She crouched, unspeaking, suffocated by the wretched beat of her own heart.

JO-JO RASTEROVICH

Jo-Jo reflected on his lucky escape over a squirt or ten of Noort-Cloud whisky. Not so lucky – for Jo-Jo, at least – had been the Lostolian fop's perspicacity in having Jo-Jo sign a contract before he agreed to help him from the ménage lounge and back into a taxi.

When that was done, the dreadful lethargy and fog that had taken command of his body and had brought him near to a close encounter with Dicter Thighs, seemed to abate. Jo-Jo booted *Salacious II* out of Belle-Monde's orbit like he had a supernova up his arse.

One complete resonance shift and a day or two of suffocation nightmares later, he began to settle back into his comfort zone. Or would have if the fop, Tekton, had not been on farcast to him.

'The need for this mineral is somewhat urgent,' said Tekton.

'Mate,' Jo-Jo said. 'You can stick your contract. I've got Lawmon all over Orion who could tie you up in court for years. Duress and all that.'

Tekton's expression remained unchanged apart from a small distortion of pixels that made his nose appear to jiggle. 'That is most unlikely, Mr Rasterovich.'

Jo-Jo eyeballed the farcast imager nonchalantly. 'I'm also halfway to Bellatrix. How exactly do you plan to catch me?'

'If you care to examine the contents of the contract shell in your possession, perhaps you will understand that I mean to hold you to it.'

'Not bloody likely,' said Jo-Jo with feeling. But as he terminated the farcast, a sense of foreboding grew in him. What had he signed? *A simple worthless contract*, he thought. In truth, he recalled little of those moments in the ménage lounge, aside from the difficulty he had had catching his breath, and the way his limbs had snubbed him when he had tried to flee the scene of his plight. Even now, the memories caused a great, anxious shudder to pass through him.

Annoyed and worried, he stamped along *Salacious II*'s velour-luxurious corridors to his laundry and rifled through several months' worth of dirty clothes. He found the shell in the pocket of the trousers he'd worn on Belle-Monde and took it back to his den.

After swallowing a sherbet of sniffing tobacco he cracked the contract shell open. An image transferred itself onto his deskfilm.

'Mr Rasterovich,' it informed him. 'You have agreed to the terms of a Hera.'

Fuck! Jo-Jo's heart stopped. 'Jesu and Crux.' *A Hera contract?* Only the expensive medites he'd purchased on Teranu prevented him from a full-scale coronary occlusion. Scrabbling madly to inflate his artery they brought him back to life in a few milliseconds. Which was a damn shame, he thought afterwards. If he'd agreed to a Hera contract he might as well be dead anyway.

The contract's image had thoughtfully paused itself while he recovered, and it cleared its throat before continuing. 'In brief, the terms are these: you shall deliver the agreed goods. Failure to meet the terms will result in the reclamation of all your wealth and the cancellation of any future rejuvenation. You will, in short, become poor and old. And you will die. Should you fulfil the contract all penalties will be withdrawn. It should be noted that Hera contracts have no process of appeal. The official version of this message can be viewed by forwarding to subsection B1.'

With the grudging manner of one who recognises inevitability and doesn't quite have the balls to spit right in its face, Jo-Jo called Tekton back.

The fop came on the farcast imager, calm and more than a trifle smug.

'Tell me what you want, prick,' said Jo-Jo.

'Aaaah . . .' Tekton's explanation of the mineral he sought was lengthy and colourful.

Jo-Jo condensed his waffling into three short categories: fluidly supple, resilient and beautiful in its natural form. *Impossible*.

For the first time in a long while, Jo-Jo set to work. He searched his databases for weeks, called every contact he had ever known, or thought he knew, but nothing came of it.

The galaxy was too small, he thought, to accommodate something of the kind. Its minerals were well catalogued.

Jo-Jo alternated between despair, feverish investigation, and fantasies of revenge to be taken on the fop. Between the times spent tracking down mineral assays from every lump of rock in the Orion system he gathered all the information he could on Tekton.

The smart, he vowed, would pay for his dirty trick.

So hectic did Jo-Jo's days and nights become that he had little time or inclination to spend with his sim-women.

One week, as he passed through various stages of despair, he decided to land on the invitation-only bordello pseudo-world of Vela.

Several days and many infection screenings later Jo-Jo found himself at Vela's most salubrious bar in no better mood.

That was until an OLOSS circuit judge started buying drinks and drugs for the entire place.

Jo-Jo rose to the occasion, deactivated his blood stabiliser, and imbibed enough to send any decent-sized sentient comatose.

At one stage during the thirty-hour binge, he Cossack-danced naked with the OLOSS judge (Samuel L.) on the back of a pair of stocky Balol twins. His toes bled from the frill pricks, but during the process he and Samuel L. bonded for life.

Hour twenty-nine of the binge saw them arm in arm on the lounge sofa, exchanging stories.

Samuel L., who was inclined to be verbose at best, and at this stage of the proceedings was melancholy with guilt, produced images of his family and children at home on their privately owned world in the OLOSS system of Betelgeuse.

As Jo-Jo surveyed the images through the smear of too many cocktails and not enough stimulants, something caught his eye. A rippling objet d'art the like of which he had never seen before. 'Tell me, mate,' he said. 'What the fuck is that?'

Samuel L got a rather sly look on his face.

Which made Jo-Jo wonder if he'd cheated on the binge and left his blood stabilisers functioning.

'That is an extraordinary little something I picked up from a planet way out west. Can't remember what it was called now.'

The 'little something' was a feature wall – in the entrance of his mansion – that shimmered and rippled and changed form. 'It's made of a shape-memory alloy: "quixite" is the common name. I've been on the circuit to some hick planets for a long time, never seen it in these quantities before. Rare combination of mineral. Did a little deal for it.' He winked. 'Course, it's not something I spread around. Wouldn't do for everyone to have one. The wife would never let me hear the end of it.'

At that point Jo-Jo produced a rather nifty recording dice of the entire binge, including Samuel L.'s attempt to give adequate cunnilingus to the bordello's mistress who had six state-of-the-art orifices. 'And I don't suppose she would let you hear the end of *this*, either.'

Samuel L.'s newly implanted hair stood stiffer in alarm than his erection ever had in passion.

'Now, mate,' said Jo-Jo. 'Where did you get that alloy?'

Mira

Trin led Mira to the front of the villa's ruins as if she were blind. Djeserit carried the crying 'bino and the korm limped behind her. Rumbles from more explosions across the city shook the ground underneath their feet. Shots echoed between villas, followed by shouts and screams and the whirring of AiV rotors lifting into the air. Familia from the nearby Villa Cabuto stood, peering through their fence.

Trin signalled for their help but they withdrew inside.

'Cazzone!' shouted Trin after them. 'Who are you that you would not help your Principe?'

'They don't know you,' said Djeserit. She rested a hand on his hip. 'It's us they avoid. They hated the Baronessa taking us in. They excluded her from their gatherings.'

Faja, thought Mira. *Faja.*

Trin made an angry noise and ran a few steps. He pointed to Villa Fedor's collapsed gate pillars. They lay across the back of his vehicle. 'We must walk further to get help,' he said.

'But the heat . . .' Djeserit shaded her head with her arms. She wore only an indoor robe and no velum. 'I can stand the heat but the sun . . .' She showed him her palms. Already welts had appeared on them and on her face.

The korm chittered as if agreeing, yet its reptile skin and patches of feather-fur looked as impervious as Balol skin armour.

Trin glanced up and down the viuzza. One direction led out of the city, the other, which ran past the Villa Cabuto, intersected other viuzzas at a vehicle shelter. 'There. The TerV-way.'

They moved quickly towards it, Trin pulling Mira along. With relief they found the coldlock still functioning as they crowded into the passenger set-down.

From an observer's distance that meant as little to Mira as the cuts on her feet and the scoured grazes on her face, she heard them discuss her condition.

'What is wrong with the Baronessa? Why won't she speak?' asked Djeserit.

'Shock,' said Trin.

'How long will this last?'

'I do not know.'

Another explosion rattled their shelter, raining debris on the roof. Trin ran to the coldlock and flung it open.

'Crux,' he cried, falling to one knee, pounding his chest. 'Villa Cabuto . . .'

'What is it?' said Djeserit.

'It is gone.' He stayed staring out into the hot daylight as if he could not believe it.

Djeserit began to cry in carking sobs. The korm crouched closer to her, making sympathetic noises. Djeserit fondled its crest with her trembling fingers.

Trin turned on them. 'Stop it,' he said harshly. 'Stop now.' He paced a little. 'We must go to the Carabinere.'

Djeserit's face twisted in fear. 'What will they do?'

'They have transport. They can evacuate us.'

Mira watched Trin pull Djeserit to her feet and draw her aside. 'We should leave them. They will slow us,' he whispered.

'Why would we?' Djeserit asked.

Trin hesitated. 'I can . . . I wish to help you.'

Mira felt only detached curiosity as she waited for Djeserit to reply. What would the ragazza say? And why would Trin make such an offer – a ginko above familia?

But Djeserit did not answer. 'The 'bino needs fluid,' she said. She disappeared into the TerV-way's washroom and came back with a wet cloth that she had torn from her robe. With it she dribbled water into the 'bino's mouth. It suckled at the material hungrily and choked a little. She repeated her action, returning to the washroom several times to rewet the cloth.

When the 'bino was sated the korm began chittering loudly, then left the TerV-way.

'Where is it going?' Trin demanded.

'There is a market nearby. She will try to get food for us.'

The idea of waiting agitated Trin but he seemed loath to leave Djeserit. 'As soon as the sun has set we must go. Things may get worse.'

The korm returned with a tube of lig honey and packets of latte. She told Djeserit the market had been ransacked by 'esques and that they had thrown rocks at her.

The 'bino sucked the latte in choking gulps and then vomited.

Djeserit squeezed honey into Mira's mouth, then

pressed her lips closed and massaged her neck. The honey stung the back of Mira's dry throat and she swallowed reflexively. It lessened her feeling of numbness and she began to tremble violently.

'We should leave here soon,' said Trin again.

Stiff words escaped Mira's lips. 'Si, *you* should.'

'Baronessa,' cried Djeserit with relief.

The korm trumpeted but Mira's attention stayed fixed on Trin Pellegrini. 'You may leave us now. I will watch out for them.'

Trin crossed his arms in a stubborn gesture characteristic of his papa. His manner, which Mira had always thought regal, now seemed intolerably arrogant. She wanted to strike him but she could not lift her arm. Her shoulder ached as though it was broken and her belly ached nearly as much, from hunger and shock and misery. The cuts and grazes on her legs and face seemed worse than either Djeserit's or the korm's. 'Please go.'

Djeserit tugged her shoulder. 'No, Mira,' she begged.

Mira winced in pain, her head spinning a little. 'He has no honour. All he knows is how to take.'

Trin gave a brittle laugh. 'And just who is the misfit? The Principe's son,' he thumped his breast, 'or the eccentric Baronessa Fedor?'

They glared at each other until Trin looked away. 'This is not the time for dispute,' he said.

Mira nodded, wondering at her own anger and the false courage it lent her. 'What is happening to the city?'

'There was a fire yesterday at the grain silos. Perhaps it was not the accident the Carabinere thought it was.'

'A *deliberate* fire?' said Mira.

Trin shrugged. 'Who would wish that? Everyone on Araldis – even the ginkos – understand how quickly our oxygen-rich atmosphere and dry winds can spread flames.'

Mira's stomach contracted into a hard, tight lump. 'Then obviously that was their intention. To create chaos; to destroy.'

'Baronessa, we must stay with Don Pellegrini. He can protect us,' interrupted Djeserit.

Mira's moment of complicity passed. 'Protect you? A moment ago he was ready to abandon a tiny 'bino and yet you would trust him.'

'All I wish is to travel quickly,' Trin objected. 'I would have sent Carabinere for you.'

'Liar!' exclaimed Mira.

'And again you forget yourself, Baronessa.' Trin slapped her face with deliberate force.

She staggered backwards, feeling blood on her face. The seam of his glove had cut a welt across her cheek.

'Stop!' pleaded Djeserit.

The 'bino began to cry.

Mira pressed her hand to her cheek, struggling to subdue her emotions. She had never felt this uncontrolled before. Her anger had become a molten, living thing inside her. She wanted to hurt this man, and the turmoil of the feeling would not leave her. Sealing her velum, she strode out into the sunlight.

Outside, the shadows of the TerV-way had grown longer. Mira crouched against the wall, letting tears flow until her velum was sodden with them.

Faja is dead. The words recurred like little explosions

in her head, scattering her thoughts to places where she could not follow. *Istelle*.

She got to her feet and picked her way through burning debris. The viuzza was empty. There were no AiVs in the sky, only great drifts of smoke. The fire from Villa Cabuto and Villa Fedor raged northward, driven by gusts of wind. They would need to move on before the nightwinds came and brought the fire back on itself.

Mira followed an intersecting viuzza towards the market. Villas that weren't damaged were shuttered or deserted. It was as though all the familia had left already.

One solitary man stood outside his gate façade in a full-weather fellalo, watching the purple sky. As Mira approached him he jerked a rifle up from behind his back and pointed it at her head. His skin was familia-crimson but his build was stringy. A syrupy scent clung to him, pervading even the smoke-tainted air. *A non-Latino servant*, she thought, *who has had a lifetime of melanin boosters*.

She lifted her hands in a supplicatory gesture. 'Signor, I am from Villa Fedor. They are all dead. May I use your shortcast?' she said.

He stared at her suspiciously. 'Sat's out. No 'cast,' he said.

'What about news? Can you tell me what is happening?'

He kept the rifle high and steady. 'Carabinere've deserted. Useless cazzone. Aristos have bailed out too.' He cocked his head to the side and gave Mira a sly look. 'Looks like they forgot one, though. You hungry? How about you come to my place?'

Mira shook her head, taking a step away. 'I have others with me. Waiting for me.'

His glanced around. 'Can't see no one.' He waved his rifle. 'Git inside.' He took a deliberate step towards her. 'NOW!'

Panic sent Mira stumbling sideways. If she ran he might kill her; if she went inside he might rape her. Her imprudent rage at Trin Pellegrini had brought her to this.

A noise sounded behind the man and two young 'esques ran towards them from between villas.

'There!' shouted one. He pointed behind the man. The man moved and Mira saw a partially excavated hole just inside the gate. The top of a large globular object was visible just below the lip of the hole. Something was buried in there.

The man swung his rifle around but the youths shot him before he could aim. He staggered backwards and fell. The shot did not kill him and he began to crawl towards the hole.

Mira wanted to run but her body remained frozen with fear and fascination as the young 'esques shot repeatedly at the man.

Still he struggled forward, clawing at the ground until he reached the lip of the hole. In a final action he plucked at the globe with his remaining strength, pinching its skin. The globe contorted and tore open.

One of the young 'esques shouted something unintelligible and fired at it, spattering its contents wide, some of which reached the hem of Mira's fellala. The action loosed her frozen muscles and she ran back down the viuzza.

In her panic she took the wrong turning at an intersection. Seized by confusion, she roamed among the deserted villas, dizziness coming and going. Her fellala's bio-check began a rapid blink to tell her that her body temperature had escalated. She sucked on the thin moisture tube inside her velum. The pouch wouldn't last long, maybe a few hours without replenishment. And then . . .

Mira stopped in the long shade of a wide gate-pillar and tried to create a mental map of the area but images of the globe crowded her concentration. What was it that the man had been digging out?

She coughed out the strengthening taste of smoke from her throat. Daylight was fading and the nightwinds would soon come, bringing the fire back. Now was the time for thinking, not for fearing. With tentative steps she retraced her path until she found the man's body lying in the gate of the villa, one hand outstretched. Nothing had changed, but the young 'esques had gone.

Mira glanced around. In the growing dark Loisa had become a frighteningly unfamiliar city. In her years of living here she had never been out at night on foot, never spent time in the nightwinds.

She walked to the closest intersection and turned in a different direction. Another turn and she saw the TerV-way lit and only a short distance away. Good fortune had left one of its solar panels undamaged.

As she entered the shelter a different kind of apprehension took hold of her. *Where are they?*

'Baronessa?' Djeserit's voice came out of the gloom. 'Where did you go?'

Mira unsealed her velum. The memory of Trin Pellegrini's belligerence flooded back. She was not ready to share what she had seen with *him*. 'I have spoken to someone on the viuzza. He said the Carabinere have deserted.'

'No. That is not possible. What else did he say?' Trin stepped forward from the shadows.

Mira kept her distance from him. 'He did not know.'

'Where is he now? Why did he not come with you?'

'He . . . went off on foot. He said it was the only way. The TerVs have stopped running.' She wetted her lips, forcing them to form the words that she needed to say. 'We should stay together, as Djeserit said.'

Trin's shoulders lifted slightly in satisfaction. 'A change of heart, Mira Fedor? What did you see outside that took the wind from your bravado?'

Mira shrank from his perceptivity. 'If you contact your familia they will help us.'

To her surprise Trin gave a mocking laugh. 'I am here because I was being punished. The Principe was teaching me a life lesson.'

'But you are the young Principe. Your safety is paramount,' she protested. 'Should anything happen to your papa . . .'

'Then where do you propose we go, clever Mira?'

'To Pell,' said Mira, suddenly longing for the safety of the enclave.

Trin gave a derisive snort. 'That is thousands of mesurs away. We have no transport, no food and little water. And what will we find there, anyway?'

'The Fleet is there,' she said.

'The mighty Cipriano fleet: five vie-ships and a dozen assailants. And what good is a fleet with no pilots or crew?'

The 'bino woke and gave a pitiable mewl as though it was too weak to really bawl.

Mira felt a stab of guilt. While she and Trin argued, the 'bino was starving. 'Pass him to me,' she said to Djeserit.

She took the 'bino closer to the fading solar light that hung above the TerV-way timetable. An orange-stained pannolino was stuck to the infant's skin. Mira recognised the acrid colour as a sign of dehydration. She laid the 'bino on its back and gently peeled the absorbent film away. Though its genitals were partially internal, she guessed it to be a ragazzo. He had long, thin limbs like all Pagoins and a solemn expression. *Too solemn*. He could barely cry now because of exhaustion. His thighs were raw from urine scalds; another day and they would be weeping with infection. His skin was already loose from hunger and the soft crown of his head was slightly shrunken.

Mira glimpsed her own fragility mirrored in his. How long would she survive without food and with little water? She had never been hungry or thirsty before.

'We should go to the Carabinere. Their emergency shortcast will be working,' said Trin.

'D'accordo,' Mira agreed cautiously. That made sense. 'It will it take us some time to walk there.' She thought of the youths with their guns, and the strange globe. 'We should leave soon.'

'Yes. Djeserit cannot travel in the daylight without a fellala.'

'Nor can the 'bino. And the wind has changed. The fires will come back.'

Trin nodded. 'Fill your pouch and drink your fill before we go.'

Mira diluted some latte for the 'bino in the TerV-way's washroom. The mixture seemed more palatable this time and the infant settled into sleep. She unfolded the outer layer of her fellala and wound him into it. That freed her hands so that she could move quickly if she had to. Just so long as she didn't trip and fall on him.

Djeserit watched. 'What if we lose each other in the dark? The nightwinds can make you loco.'

'If we are separated then wait where you are and I will find you. Do not wander.' Mira sounded more confident than she felt. How would she find anyone when she herself had been lost already?

Djeserit repeated the instructions to the korm.

'Has it no 'esque language?' asked Mira.

'It understands Latino but it can't form the words. It's beak is too . . .' Djeserit searched for the word. 'Wrong.'

'Teach it what you can. Without you, it won't be able to communicate.'

'But that won't happen. We won't get separated,' Djeserit said quickly.

Mira gave Djeserit's shoulder a gentle squeeze. 'Just in case. You understand?'

As every night, Tiesha rose before Semantic, casting its aloof light across Loisa. Tonight, though, the glow from the fires distorted the view of the city and several times they had to double back when the viuzzas were blocked with bomb debris. The blistering nightwind blasted into them until they were bent double against its drying force. Eddies of hot ash swirled past, choking them, and 'esques ran past them in the dark. A group of youths knocked Djeserit down but Trin pulled her from under their feet before she could get hurt.

No one would stop and speak with them. Mira called to the shadowy figures as they vanished among the churning ash-phantoms. The city had lost itself in the spin of a day.

Trin instructed them to stay close but in a single line: himself first, them Djeserit, then the korm, with Mira and the 'bino last. When AiVs with their night lights on flew overhead, he stopped. 'Cavaliere,' he rasped.

But Mira suspected his words to be more hope than anything else.

Without the protective filter of a fellala or suit Djeserit coughed constantly.

'We should rest a while,' said Mira.

Trin led them off the viuzza to a wall opposite a bomb-damaged bistro. They rested with their backs against it and watched the figures moving around inside.

The 'bino woke and cried with hunger. Mira unwrapped him and laid him on the ground, gently peeling back the absorbent film. She removed her gloves to gauge the level of saturation. His urine felt grainy and she smelled the blood in it. 'I need a clean pannolino.'

'Our people use cloth, not film.' Djeserit's voice in her ear was thick with the effort of breathing. 'I mean . . . my mother's people do.'

Of course, why hadn't she thought of that? Turning away from them, Mira unwound her fellala enough so that she could wriggle out of her undershirt. She wrapped it as best she could around the 'bino. He whimpered at her touch. The smell of his excretions clung to her fingers but she had nowhere to wash them. 'The bistro might have more latte. I will look.'

'No,' said Trin with determination. 'We should keep going.'

She could see his hooded profile in the moonlight, not his expression. 'The 'bino might be dead by then. He is dehydrated.'

Trin clicked his tongue with impatience. 'Hurry, then.'

A baying started up behind them. Trin climbed onto the wall. 'Cane,' he said. 'We are safe while it is yarded.'

Mira passed the 'bino to Djeserit, missing the comfort of his small body the moment she did. 'I will go.'

Trin climbed down and stooped to pick up an object. He pressed a chunk of catoplasma into Mira's hand. 'Don't be afraid to use it, Baronessa.'

Thoughtful advice or a taunt, she wondered, as she gripped the rough edges and walked slowly towards the bistro.

A circle of ragazzi with torches sat to one side, drinking wine from demijohns and talking loudly about killing ginkos.

Mira skirted them and found her way around the back of the bistro. The outer coldlock door had been torn away. She pulled back the inner partition and stepped inside, heart racing. Without her undershirt, rivulets of sweat drenched the inside of her fellala.

Dimming solar lights showed the walls to be standing but the roof had collapsed in places. The floor was littered with large chunks of catoplasma from the ceiling, just like the one she was holding. She unsealed her velum and climbed over a pile of rubbish towards the line of frijs. They had already been ransacked.

A ragazzo with a torch was picking through one. He drew back when he saw Mira.

'Nothin' left,' he said. His voice was soft. In the torchlight his skin looked sallow and tight like Djeserit's but he had no neck gills.

Mira moved slowly towards him and set down the chunk of catoplasma.

He retreated, clutching the light.

'I have a 'bino outside. I need food for it,' she said.

'Sure. Everyone's sayin' that. But there's no food coming in. No help. They're planning to starve us out.'

'Who?' Mira asked the question as she stepped over to the first frij. It was empty.

'Them ginks who want our planet.'

Mira took another step. He was right. All the frijs were bare. 'What . . . ginkos?'

'Haven't you seen 'em? Ugly maggoty things cracking out of eggs.'

The ragazzo was badly unwashed. Now that Mira was closer she could smell his body odour. 'What's your name?'

'Perche?'

She shrugged. 'I am Mira.' She gave up on the frijs and began foraging under the fallen catoplasma. Keeping her gloves on, she burrowed for a few moments while he watched.

'You're familia. I c'n see that. I thought you'd all gone. Left us to die.'

She paused, not knowing how to answer. He was

right – no familia had stayed to help. They stood in silence for a moment.

'I'm Vani,' he said finally.

Mira managed a smile. 'Come and give me a hand, Vani. I think I've found something.'

He stayed where he was, suspicious.

'I'll share it with you,' she coaxed.

Keeping the torch's beam on her, he moved closer.

'It's a small frij under the fallen roof, I think. You can just see the corner.'

Vani's hunger overcame his distrust and he put down the light and began to help her dig.

In a few minutes they'd cleared around the frij enough to open it. The smell of rotting food made her gag and her stomach hurt as it contracted. She doubled over in pain.

Vani took no notice, grabbing what he could.

Mira knelt down. In the door were little packets of latte. She scooped them inside her fellala. The corners scraped her skin where she'd removed her underclothes.

Vani was gorging on stale tramezzini.

'Don't eat any meat or eggs. You'll get sick,' she said automatically. 'Just peel the pane off them.'

He ignored her, eating it all.

Mira found another compartment in the frij with stale pane rolls left in it, and slipped them inside her fellala as well. Satisfied that the frij had no more to offer she straightened. Then the sound of voices sent her stepping back into the shadows. Three 'esques surprised Vani with his head still in the small frij.

'What ya got there, 'bino?'

They were older than Vani. And bigger. Each carried

a weapon of sorts, clubs and a pistol. The biggest was 'esque – a teranu, judging by his flat features. The others, like Vani, had sharp profiles.

'Nothin',' said Vani.

'Give us what you found. We need food,' said the biggest of them.

One of the smaller ones cuffed Vani.

He staggered.

'Next time it'll be this.' The teranu waved his pistol. It looked like a pulse device, not a solid-projectile gun. Mira guessed it probably had no charge, but Vani was terrified.

'Now gimme ya light and get outta my way.'

Vani handed it over. 'Can I have some food?'

The teranu grabbed Vani and bent him over, making obscene gestures. The others laughed.

Their crudity shocked Mira. She reached down for the chunk of catoplasma and then stepped into the arc of light. 'Vani?'

They turned on her, surprised. 'Familia,' said one of them and spat.

Mira lifted the catoplasma into view. Now she would find out if the pistol worked. 'We're hungry like you but there's nothing left here. We are leaving,' she said. 'Dai, Vani.'

She walked past them and climbed the pile of rubble. A few more steps and she would be out through the door into the night. She subdued her urge to hurry and leave Vani behind.

The 'esques did not move out of her way, nor did they stop her. Did she smell as bad as they did? Did she look as appalling?

Mira glanced back. Vani stood there, unsure. 'Dai. The 'bino will be hungry,' she called softly.

With another glance at the pistol, he scrambled after her.

She led him outside and down the side to the viuzza. The circle of 'esques had vanished and Semantic glistened distantly through the pall of smoke. Leading Vani by the hand, Mira searched for the wall where the others waited. She felt the stiff suspicion in him.

'Trin. Djeserit,' she called.

Across the wall the cane bayed at the sound of her voice.

The sound sent Vani into a panic. 'You lie. There is no one,' he said, pulling away.

Fear gushed into Mira's stomach. They had not left her – surely? 'They will be close by,' she whispered.

'Where? Where's the 'bino?' he demanded.

Mira climbed up onto the wall to get a better view of the shadowy yard. Semantic cast only dull light across the dust. As if sensing that she had crossed into its territory, the cane inside bayed louder. A small light flickered in a window and a moment later the cane raged out of the door across the enclosure.

Mira climbed down backwards from the wall, landing heavily. 'They can't be in there. Not with that—' She broke off her shaken whisper. She was talking to empty darkness. Vani had gone.

She took a few steps in different directions calling to him and the others. Across at the bistro, a commotion started up. Had Djeserit and Trin gone there looking for her? *No.* Perhaps she had taken too long and they had left.

Breathing unsteadily, Mira sank down against the wall. She could hear the cane pacing along the other side, snuffling and scraping its horns against the fence. She reached inside her jacket, broke off a piece of stale pane and threw it over.

Despite everything, her mouth began to water. Before she knew it she was cramming the last of the roll into her mouth. She forced herself to tuck the rest away in her fellala. The latte caplets scratched her bare skin, reminding her of the 'bino. She must stay here – that was what she had told them. *Don't move.* At least until daylight.

And then?

Fresh sweat broke out over her body. *Calm*, Mira told herself. *Calm.*

Maybe she dozed, or maybe her thoughts were tangled like dreams, nightmares of Djeserit and the korm being torn apart by a pack of animals. Gradually, though, the light of dawn came.

The cane had been whistled inside a while before. Whoever had been arguing outside the bistro had finished their business and gone.

Mira moved her limbs, rubbing circulation back into them. Should she wait? Should she move on? Where should she go? Thinking had become harder. Pangs of hunger and thirst sent her mind into a spiral of misery. She sipped her water bladder and drank one of the lattes but it curdled in her tense gut. By first light she was on her knees, vomiting.

Inside, the cane bayed as if it sensed her distress.

She rested back against the wall.

Then a hand touched her shoulder. 'Baronessa?'

She clutched Djeserit with overwhelming relief. 'Where were you?'

Djeserit pointed to the casa behind the wall. 'The 'esques who live there heard the 'bino cry. They came outside to see who it was – said we could come in. Then the shooting started. Don Pellegrini said I should stay inside. He said you would be all right until daytime.'

Mira gave her a weak nod. 'What about the 'bino?'

'He is sleeping. The woman gives him food.'

'I wish to see him.' Mira got to her feet, swaying.

She followed Djeserit along a narrow path that ran between two casas. The korm waited there. It chittered at her and dipped its crest for a scratch. Mira's hand trembled; she had never exchanged affection with an alien before.

They walked together along the narrow back viuzza until Djeserit stopped. An 'esque stepped from behind the rear gateposts. He was short and wiry, his crimson skin creased like folds in iron rock. The rifle he held was the projectile kind that miners favoured.

'This her?'

'Baronessa Fedor,' Mira said, tiredly. 'I went to look for food for the 'bino and we became separated.'

'Fedor?' He stared suspiciously at her. 'From the Pilot familia?'

'Si.' She waited. If the man refused to let her in, she might never see Istelle's 'bino again.

He chewed his lip for a minute, then waved the rifle towards the back door. 'Git inside. Sun's spoilin' to be fierce today.'

Relief again. Mira stumbled after Djeserit and the korm.

Djeserit stopped and waited for her, held her arm. 'Baronessa?'

Mira nodded reassurance. 'I-I am well. What about you?'

Djeserit looked away without answering.

The cane strained towards them from a tether on the portico. Its nostrils streamed with saliva that ran down its horns. The spit sprayed over her as it bayed its hostility.

Mira shrank away from it. Nothing could convince her that the animals made good pets. They were too clever and too savage.

The korm's crest bristled and it fluffed its fur in agitation.

Mira shuddered to think what might happen between them if the cane was freed.

Trin Pellegrini met them at the coldlock. Accusations rose to Mira's lips – he'd left her again – but this was not the time to speak them. As he stepped aside to let her in she saw no remorse in his face.

The casa was dark inside with the windows covered and barred. Mira loosed her clothing, soaking in the coolness as she followed the 'esque through the cucina to a sitting room where a woman rocked the 'bino. A little ragazza with cropped hair perched on the arm of her chair.

The woman glanced up and gave a tired smile. Her likeness to Istelle gave Mira a pang of sadness. She wanted to weep at the kindness of the woman's look. Instead she slipped her hand inside her fellala and removed the latte packets. 'For the 'bino,' she said.

'Sit down,' said the woman. She had her finger in the 'bino's mouth. He suckled it for comfort. 'Baronessa, you must be exhausted. I am called Loris. This is Jessa and you've met my husband Con.'

'Call me Mira.' 'Baronessa' suddenly seemed vague, unrelated to who she was.

'I've been nursing the 'bino best I can, but he's no great suckler. I have only a little left, from Jessa.' Loris removed her finger from the 'bino's mouth and patted her breast.

Mira glanced away. Such things were not spoken of so plainly among her class.

Trin entered the room. Con followed but stayed near the door, his rifle cradled in his arms.

Mira sank into the chair opposite, suppressing her impulse to take the 'bino from Loris's arms. Instead she turned her attention to the little ragazza. 'Ciao, Jessa.'

The ragazza scowled and moved closer to her father.

'Don't mind her,' said Loris. 'These last few days have taught her not to trust anyone much except her own.'

'Nothin' wrong with that,' said Con. He held on to his rifle with one hand and pulled the ragazza close to his side with the other. He did not trust anyone either.

Mira wanted him to tell him to put his weapon away, that it was dangerous, and that they would be no threat, but she knew it would be breath wasted. Her word meant nothing to this man – not now. She lifted her gaze to Trin. 'Have *you* learned anything?'

Trinder shrugged. He looked refreshed as if he'd had a comfortable sleep, Mira thought bitterly.

'The shortcast is still out. No one knows why. Water is still running but food is disappearing,' he answered. 'Most familia have left the city for Pell or the other towns.' He grasped the back of the chair that she was sitting on. 'If they had just stayed, help would have come.'

Mira thought his words through. No food was produced near Loisa – land barges brought it in weekly from the biospheres in the Pell Basin. Only pane was made locally. 'If the Carabinere have really deserted, then aid may not come. How long can we survive here with no food? It makes sense that they would leave,' she said.

Trin made an impatient noise, irritated that she had challenged him in front of the 'esques.

Mira no longer cared what he thought. In a few days the whole of the city would be on the road to some-where else. The thought of it made her tremble. She turned back to Loris. 'Thank you for taking us in.'

Con spoke for his wife. 'Heard you out there so I used my night 'scope. Recognised that you was familia.'

'How close are we to the Carabinere office?' Trin asked.

'Bout a few hours' walk,' said Con.

'I must rest before I can go further.' Mira ached to lie down; her tongue felt swollen in her mouth.

Outside the sound of weapon-fire started up again.

Trinder glanced at Con. 'May we stay with you today, signor?'

'Si, Don Pellegrini. Of course.' The miner's chest swelled with pride. He was seemingly pleased to be helping someone so important. 'Come and rest in my room.'

The men left the room together.

Trin was adept at getting what he wanted. Mira felt simultaneously irritated and gratified: anything to sleep for a few hours.

'Jessa has a bed you can lie on,' said Loris. 'I'll watch the 'bino. It's at the end of the hall, on the right.'

Mira nodded her thanks.

'What is his name?' Loris asked.

Mira had not even thought to name the child. Doing that would make him closer, more hers. She was not sure she wanted that but the other woman was waiting expectantly for an answer.

'Vito,' she said at last, choosing her father's name.

Loris seemed satisfied with that.

Mira dragged herself down the short corridor of the casa. In her exhaustion she opened the wrong door. Behind it was a storage cupboard – only it was filled with food: dried, canned and powdered, shelves of it, too much for a small familia's pantry.

Too fatigued to fathom the reason, she shut the door quietly and stumbled to the next room.

Mira awoke to a 'bino's cry. Outside it was getting dark, which meant that she had slept long. *Faja, mia sorella. Gone.* She sat up shivering, tears rolling down her face. In the quiet of little Jessa's room, she surrendered to them.

Loris appeared at the door unannounced, cradling Vito in her arms.

Embarrassed, Mira wiped her face with quick finger movements.

But Loris made no comment as she passed Vito over

to her. He was clothed in a tiny envirosuit of the type that 'esques favoured and which showed the tell-tale bulge of a fresh dryfilm. His solemn expression tugged at her heart. He gave a tiny cry of recognition and she slipped a finger in his mouth for comfort, the way Loris had done.

'They are waiting for you to wake.' The woman closed the door and sat stiffly near Mira on the bed. Her jaw was swollen with a fresh bruise. 'I have left some things for you in the thorngrass outside the gatepost. Your 'bino's underliner is clean and there is some food, and more dryfilm. The proper kind,' she whispered.

Mira was confused by the nervousness with which Loris had spoken of her kind gesture. She laid her hand on the woman's arm. 'What is wrong, Loris?'

The woman bit her bottom lip. 'My husband knows more than he's saying. He wants you to think that we've helped you but he hates the Pellegrinis. I'm not much for them myself. They've done nothing for us but this little one deserves no harm. There's a pistol as well. Can you use one?'

Mira shook her head, dumbfounded. 'At the Studium they instructed the men only.'

'Not much charge left in it. Enough for maybe a few shots: it's all I can do.' Loris stood up, trembling, and cracked open the window shutter.

'*What* does your husband know?' Mira whispered.

'A man came here, wanted to pay us to keep these . . . things for him. Never seen the like of them before. Big, rough and ugly, round like an agate, but sticky.'

A suspicion began to grow in Mira's mind. 'What colour?'

The woman stared at her.

Mira gripped her arm. 'What colour where they?'

'They was—'

The door opened. Con stood there, his rifle hitched under his arm, mistrust clear in his stance.

Loris's hands trembled but her face remained bland. Practised.

'You ready?' he asked Mira curtly.

Mira clasped Vito and stood up. 'Yes. And thank you, signor – few are prepared to take in strangers at this moment,' she said in formal tones.

Con's shoulders relaxed but not his tone. 'Don't you let Pellegrini forget it!' He spat the name out like poison and waved the barrel of the rifle at her. 'Let's go.'

Con ushered them out to the gate in the wall.

Mira passed Vito to Djeserit as they passed through the coldlock. When they reached the clump of thorn-grass, Mira dropped back behind the korm's bulk.

'Still, korm,' she breathed while Trin and Con made empty gestures of farewell.

It looked over its shoulder at her with curiosity.

She put her fingers to her lips and knelt down, feeling among the thorns. Spines pricked her through her gloves as she lifted a pack free and its weight tripped her forward. The korm caught her with one strong arm.

Con spun around. 'What is it?'

Mira hung the pack on the korm's armlet and stepped in front. She concealed her bloodstained glove. 'I tripped,' she said. Nothing more. Too much explan-ation would make it worse.

Con squinted in the fading light to see her. With little Jessa clinging to his legs, he pushed the gate open. He watched Mira with hard eyes as she went to pass by him. Suddenly he reached out to tug her arm. With quick movements he searched her, ignoring the others. Before she could utter any protest, he pushed her out of the gate.

Trin had already walked on but the korm was waiting for her with the pack hidden from Con's view. It whistled softly.

'Grazi,' Mira answered.

They moved on a way before Mira dared look back to the casa. Loris would be there, watching, she was sure.

She raised her hand in farewell.

TEKTON

Tekton had not experienced such a sense of jubilation since the Chancellor's daughter, Doris Mulek, had agreed to conjoin bodies – and that, of course, had not been because of love or some such blighted theory but because of the sheer pleasure of having set out to climb a rung on the ladder to exponential success and succeeding.

An abundance of shaped metal alloy on a virtually unknown rock on the edge of the Orion system – what a delectable coup!

Well, that was what his free-mind thought, anyway. And for some reason or other it seemed to get louder and more bombastic by the day. His logic-mind was also quite intrigued but busied itself planning ways to investigate this far-off planet without alerting the rest of the nosy snitches on Belle-Monde. It concocted an elaborate ruse of dejection and failure (Tekton's) and pondered ways to obtain a feed from the Scolar hub. It considered and discarded several options: seduce an astronomein to gain use of their coded farcast; bribe an astronomein; hold an astronomein hostage, etc, etc . . . none of which rated greater than a thirty-six per cent chance of success.

The seduction of course got his free-mind's attention and his logic-mind shuddering (all those flooding neurochemicals positively drowned out any sensible cognitive process).

It had been some time since Tekton had lain with Doris and the titillation of Dicter Miranda's thighs had been a teasing spray of water to his parched libido. *When oh when*, bleated his free-mind, *will I get some agreeable intercourse?*

When you've done the work you should, you tosser.

Tekton's free-mind subsided in a bit of a stink after that and his logic-mind gleefully took over planning. It began with a general, innocuous enough data rummage around Orion's inhabited planets.

While pretending to be comet hunting, Tekton scooped off a holo-atlas of the micro section of space that Jo-Jo Rasterovich had identified. It contained over fifty stars and three times as many planets. More detailed mapping could be, the overview said, accessed from the Scolar hub archives.

So who do I have to murder to earn a research trip to Scolar? Tekton asked his moud.

Murder? it replied, confused. *I'm not sure that would be apposite.*

For Sole's sake, order some wit to be instated at your next service, Tekton grumbled.

The moud flashed an extensive menu up onto his workfilm. *Certainly, Godhead. Please choose from the list.*

Tekton gave an irritable sigh. There was no Lostolian humour option so he checked some random squares. 'Now locate me an application for research leave.'

Approval for the trip took a toe-tapping, ménage-bar-quaffing month to come through. Not to mention the expense of several farcasts to Doris Mulek to ensure that his application received priority when it pinged across the chancellor's film. Unfortunately, Doris then decreed that she needed a holiday and would meet him there, at Scolar.

Tekton had only visited the famous centre for Orion's philosophers on one occasion and had found them audibly hostile to graduates from other Studiums – though, of course, based on the OLOSS advancement charter, archival information was free. The Vreal Studium had an equally extensive repository but Tekton found the transhumanists there so dreary that there seemed no option but to put up with the snubs and visit Scolar. He agreed to rendezvous with Doris on condition that she absorbed the expense of their suite. 'The Sternberg,' he told her. 'Nothing less.'

With arrangements well in hand, Tekton took a lotion bath and then made his daily pilgrimage to the ménage bar. Dicter Miranda was well in her cups, bosoms quivering in hyperbeat with her chins as she claimed him for conversation. 'What are you up to, Tekton?'

'Indeed, I might ask you the same, Miranda. You seem unusually jovial.'

'Cut the dishembling. I'm pished and misherable,' she slurred.

Tekton's logic-mind charged into making lists of possible information that it might be able to prise from her. His free-mind was still sulking, though Tekton got a whiff of its disdain at Miranda's mien. 'Problems with Jise?' he asked politely.

'That *heterotroph*!' she cried, with a majestic heave

of flesh. 'He's taken his wife to a Teranu beach reshort. Said he needed shome time away. *His wife*, no lesh.'

Two fat tears appeared at the edge of Miranda's tear ducts. Tekton followed their journey as they parted from the neurotic glint in her black eyes to travel across the cosmetically concealed dermatitis around her nostrils and into the rivulets of pucker lines above her top lip.

'Miranda,' he said, surprised enough to be honest. 'This is not like you to be so self-pitying. Let's talk about work. How is your project going?'

She opened her mouth and then closed it again and gave a gluggy laugh. 'Clever Tekton, knowsh how to take advantage of a girl. I've alwaysh admired that about you.'

Tekton experienced a fleeting moment of embarrassment. Was he so utterly transparent?

Miranda gave him a playful slap on the rump. 'Now tell me about you, you tight-shkinned devil.'

Tekton squashed his indignation at being treated like priced meat and wondered how best to distract her. *Coffee and stimulants, please, bar.* 'I . . . er . . . am also planning a break. A small research trip to Scolar.'

'Scolar,' she shrieked, losing all traces of inebriation. 'I insist that you take me with you!'

'I . . . er . . .' For the first time in Tekton's conscious memory, words deserted him.

'When are you going?'

'I am awaiting travel approval,' he hedged. 'Of course, I may not—'

'Bollocks,' Miranda roared. 'Of course you'll get

approval. Now, what's the weather like there at this time of year?' Her expression glazed as she accessed her moud.

Meanwhile Tekton floundered around for some way to divert her from her intent. But Miranda was not the type of woman to be put off.

'Summer. How fabulous. I shall pack my bikini,' she trilled.

'But Miranda,' said Tekton in desperation. 'I am meeting my . . . paramour. She is unlikely to approve of—'

'Nonsense, Tekton! Don't be such a prude. We could have a *scholarly* ménage. Ho, ho! That will get Jise snapping his jaws. He rather envies you, you know. Something about being unfettered by the constraints of evidence. Besides, I am sure I can find some research to attend to there.'

Snap! bawled Tekton's logic-mind. *The woman is playing you again. What does she want to access directly from the archives?*

But Tekton was having a hard time concentrating. His free-mind had surfaced and was painting lurid images of Miranda and Doris locked in a vigorous bout of bikini-clad *amour*.

MIRA

No one on the viuzzas stopped to speak, though some shouted words of warning about packs of cane. Mira strapped Vito into a sling around the korm's neck. The alien's night vision was keener than hers and she was exhausted already. She could have asked Trin but she didn't trust him.

They walked, aided by Tiesha's light, until Mira begged for a rest. Semantic would rise earlier tonight and for those few minutes when both moons were present in the sky it would seem like daylight.

'Here.' Trin herded them behind the wreckage of an overturned TerV. Its axle had broken and the canopy had ripped open.

Mira took Vito from the korm and sank to the ground. She searched Loris's pack for latte and slipped a proper cleated teat into his mouth.

'Where did you get that?' Trin demanded.

'From the 'esque, Loris. She believes that her husband is somehow involved in this.'

'Why did you not tell me before?'

'You might have acted . . . rashly,' Mira said.

'I would have found out more.'

'How so, Don? Beat it out of him. And his cane?'

Trin took some food from her without answering.

They ate in silence. Mira gave the korm some piol

nuts and offered the water bladder to Djeserit. The ragazza had not complained but her epidermis looked pinched and dry in the moonlight. Her tightly pored skin was less efficient at cooling than that of the others.

She nodded gratefully and took the water.

Mira stared into the night. She recognised the Duca's chamber from the bank of solar arrays along its flat top. The Carabinere office must be close. 'How far now?'

'Another hour. Perhaps less.'

She pinched oily cheese from a wedge and sucked it slowly. A pungent sweetness permeated her breather. It was not the cheese, she thought, for the scent had lingered on the edge of her consciousness since leaving Loris's casa. Now, suddenly, it had intensified and she sensed its danger. Perhaps she should share her fear with Trinder?

What fear? What would she say to him? That she had hidden in a biozoon carrying ginko artefacts? That she had bargained for her freedom with a smuggler?

'That smell? What is it?' Trin asked.

'Trinder, I—' Mira began with a rush. But the korm screeched, silencing her.

Something moved behind them under the TerV's damaged canopy. Trin shone his light onto it. A large, rough-surfaced globe lay nestled between two damaged crates, fluid dripping onto it from a ruptured water tank. The water formed no puddle around it – the moisture was evaporating in moments.

Figures came from the shadows to stare at the object, attracted by the korm's screech.

Mira wanted to speak to them, ask them what they knew. But the globe began to judder and distort. Its movement jolted Mira's memory into a shocked reali-sation. 'Crux,' she whispered. 'No!'

'Che, Mira? Che?' Trin said, urgently.

'I know. I remember,' she cried. 'Cryptobiosis. I only touched on it at the Studium. Even before when I saw the globe in—'

'Before? Cryptobiosis? What in Crux's name . . .'

'It's a dormant state in which living things hiber-nate.'

'*What* is hibernating, Baronessa?' Fear lent Trin's voice an imperious edge.

'Saqr.' As she spoke the name, the globe warped and split. A feeler of dark tubular flesh crowned by a bulbous maw uncurled. The maw trembled as if tasting the air and another rush of sickly-sweetness flowed from it. The globe split even wider, and a glistening, carapaced creature, as large as the korm, with six fore-claws and two hind claws unfolded from within it. Though it had no discernible head, mouth lobes protruded from the tube at one end of its body. Tiny eye-spots glittered in the light, in a semicircle behind the lobes.

'Saqr? But they are water creatures,' protested Trin.

'Then these have adapted. Or have been adapted.'

'Mira?' He sounded far less imperious now, far less sure. 'How can you be sure?'

Her only response was an intensification of the hollow fear in her stomach. Instinctively she began to back away but before she could urge the others to do the same the Saqr lunged at Trin.

Djeserit anticipated its action and threw herself in front of him. A foreclaw slashed through her robe and blood fountained from her leg. She screamed, arching her body.

Next to her the korm erupted into more screeches, enraged by her friend's injury. It went down onto its small forearms: haunches high, crest stiff, it launched itself at the Saqr.

With unexpectedly quick movements, the Saqr tried to slash the korm's flesh with its claws, while the korm countered with its slashing hind limbs. They traded attacks but the korm was weak from hunger and in a few short moments it tired of sparring. The Saqr caught the korm's forearm and pinned it to the viuzza with several claws. From its mouth lobes thin, needle-like stylets protruded. It pierced the korm's skin.

The korm screeched again, this time in agony.

Mira stood transfixed by the hideous scene. How could she not have realised? How could she not have understood what Jancz had hidden in the biozoon?

'There is a pistol,' she cried, suddenly.

'Give it to me,' Trin shouted.

But even in that moment she hesitated to trust him. He snatched the bag from her and fumbled for the weapon but when he pressed the discharge the pulse was weak and the beam glanced off the creature's thick carapace.

Thin rivulets of fluid streamed from the korm's arm wound and the Saqr's mouth lobes worked hard, sucking greedily through its stylets.

Trin crouched over Djeserit, tearing at the lining from his fellalo to bind her wound. 'Go,' he shouted at those around them.

Mira's legs still refused move.

The Saqr tightened its grip on the korm as a cacophonous baying resonated along the viuzza. In a blurr of shadows a pack of cane, drawn to the smell of blood, attacked the Saqr from all sides. It withdrew its stylets from the korm to counter them. Blood spurted from its mouth lobes and sprayed the cane. They became frantic, leaping, howling, and buffeting their horns against its hide.

The Saqr reared onto its hind claws and began to fight in earnest, clawing and screaming until it chased the cane away into the night.

No one moved.

Slowly the korm righted itself and sank, exhausted, into a roosting position. Its wounds leaked a clear fluid, the sight of which broke Mira's state of trance. Uncertain of what what else to do, she took water to it.

It gulped some down and chittered softly at her.

Mira then took the water bladder to Djeserit. Trin had bound up the tear in her leg with his royal ensign and hovered over her with concern. 'Is there probiotic in that pack?' he demanded.

'No. There is no medicine,' said Mira.

'I cannot walk on it,' said Djeserit. Her face was contorted, her eyes disappearing behind the folds of her lids.

Trin touched her face tenderly. 'Then I will carry you.'

The action stopped Mira's heart. His concern. His touch. Why had she not realised before? That night of the explosion at Villa Fedor, his presence in the lodge . . . *but Djeserit is only a 'bina. Surely even you, Trinder . . .*

Vito began to cry in her arms. Mira rocked him. The Pagoin infant had not uttered a sound throughout the fight, as if he had already learned when to be silent.

Trin lifted Djeserit in his arms. 'We are close to Carabinere headquarters. We must keep moving before the sun comes.'

He was right. It was all they could do – Mira knew. She slipped the water bladder over Djeserit's shoulder. 'Keep drinking. You have lost precious fluid.'

Djeserit nodded weakly. She clung to Trin's neck, her head sagging against his shoulder.

Mira's stomach clenched. Djeserit was a juvenile alien on a world that despised her kind and Trin Pellegrini was a privileged humanesque used to the finer things. What use, what attraction could he possibly have for her?

Trin walked on, leaving Mira standing with her thoughts. She hastened to the korm and urged it to its feet. If they lost sight of Trin, Mira knew that he would not stop for them.

'Behind those casas.' Trin staggered now under Djeserit's weight.

Mira looked up at the brilliant night sky. Tiesha and Semantic spilled their combined light across Loisa for a few precious minutes before Tiesha set. What Mira had thought were merely shadows of walls became tight huddles of 'esques, banded together for comfort and safety. Dawn was not far away now but its light would be harsh and unforgiving. They had to hurry.

By the time they turned along the viuzza to the Carabinere compound the sky was brightening to purple. A crowd awaited them: mamas with strained, desperate looks on their faces clutching their 'bini, and angry men with weapons.

Vito fretted at the noise and Mira jiggled him against her shoulder. His weight made her arm ache but she did not dare to sit.

A scuffle broke out as they tried to move closer to the compound's fence.

'There have guards at the gate entry,' said Trin.

'How will we get near them?' asked Mira. 'Everyone is here for help.'

Trin stared into the crowd. 'Use the 'bino,' he said.

Before she realised what he was doing, he snatched Vito from her arms and forced his way into the throng. Carrying both the 'bino and Djeserit, he bellowed to be let through. People made way for him, affected by his commanding tone and the young ragazza in his arms with a royal ensign as her bandage.

The korm whistled and chirped and lurched after Djeserit, leaving Mira alone. Again, people parted automatically for the large, bloodied ginko. If she didn't follow quickly . . .

She stopped. Trin had the 'bino and Djeserit, and the korm would follow. He would take them somewhere safe. Would it be so unforgivable if she lost them in the crowds?

If she were alone then she could find her way to Insignia and leave Araldis for ever. Without Faja here she need never come back.

The escape fantasy lifted the weight of Mira's misery.

She felt heady, a ludicrous sensation amid the heat and dust and panic – but an irresistible one. She began to edge her way out of the crowd but a woman grasped her arm, stopping her.

The woman had a 'bino in her arms and an older one clinging to her legs. 'I need food for my children. They're starving. Please. I'll do anything.' She wore only light robes and her crimson face was coloured almost black by the sun. Her expression was exhausted but stubborn. Something about her reminded Mira of Loris.

Without realising what she was doing, Mira reached into her bag and brought out the last of the pane. The woman took it with shaking hands, nodding her thanks, and broke off bits – some for the ragazzo, tiny bits for the 'bino.

'Eat it slow, mind,' she barked at the toddler.

The child ignored her, gobbling it, spilling precious crumbs on the ground. He fell on them, licking up dirt. His mother dragged him up by his arm, cuffing him lightly. The child wailed.

How unacquainted with hunger we are, thought Mira. A stab of pain that had nothing to do with starvation pierced her belly. There was no escape for her. She was trapped here with the rest, waiting. Faja had died here. Vito, the korm and Djeserit were her last connection with her sorella – she could not abandon them in the way that Trin Pellegrini had abandoned her. *No.*

She turned back and searched the crowd for the korm's unmistakable shape but she was too late. There was no sight of them at all.

TRIN

Trin forced his way through the crowd to press against the fence. The sun had only just risen but already the wire was too hot to touch. 'Seb Malocchi!'

The guard saw him and stepped closer, gripping his rifle with gloved hands. 'Pellegrini! You have a Principe's timing. The last of us are leaving soon.'

'Let me in the gate.'

He shook his head. 'Too risky. Go to the office and call the Capitano.' He nodded at the 'bino and Djeserit in Trin's arms. 'There will be room for you, Don Trinder, but . . .' He left the rest unsaid.

Trin's heart contracted. He couldn't leave Djeserit behind. He didn't have time to examine his reasons for thinking so – but from the moment he had seen her alive after the bomb blast at Villa Fedor he had wanted to protect her. He knew that if he lived, then so she must. But would Montforte allow her to be evacuated with them? And Djeserit would want the korm to come with them. And what would he do with the 'bino? He should have left it with Mira. Mira Fedor would find her own way. The eccentric Baronessa had the heart of a survivor.

'Where is the Baronessa Mira?' said Djeserit in panic. She struggled to look over Trin's shoulder, nearly overbalancing them both.

'Keep still,' Trin ordered. His arms had begun to grow numb with the strain of carrying her light body. Pain stabbed the muscles across his shoulders. He lowered his mouth to her ear. 'The Baronessa is close by. But I must get you away from the sunlight. In the Carabinere office there will be spare suits.'

She fell back against him, exhausted. The skin on her cheeks had erupted in ugly bubbles of fluid and the movement of her neck gills was sluggish. If she stopped land-breathing he doubted that he would be able to revive her.

Gripped by urgency, Trin pressed back through the crowd and along the viuzza. The redcrete outside the office was deserted. He placed his finger in the authenticator and carried Djeserit and the 'bino inside. The korm followed them, making odd noises. She leaked blood still from the puncture wounds on her arm, as though the blood refused to clot.

'Quiet!' Trin made a stern face, stifling a desire to shout at her. He'd seen what the korm could do, even injured and exhausted.

She chittered, unhappy about something.

He placed Djeserit onto a chair and laid the infant on his desk. Its arms flailed in fear of abandonment but it didn't cry.

Trin shortcasted to the Carabinere. 'It's Trin Pellegrini.'

Christian answered from the compound. 'Where have you been, Pellegrini? Your negligence has cost us . . . I will personally discipline you for desertion.'

'Not desertion, Capitano – Nathaniel was on duty,' Trin countered.

'Later I will find the truth of this but now we are evacuating. We have been recalled to Pell.'

'Si. I have been down at the compound gate. Seb Malocchi told me to go to the office.'

Christian made an impatient noise. 'Come to the inner gate of the service yard. I will let you through.'

Relief was like a first mouthful of wine: Trin had feared that Christian would refuse him. He raced into his tiny room and collected his few belongings into a valise, then ran back to Christian's office and removed the medkit. Thumbing through it he found the coagulants used for stemming blood flow in wounds. There had been more of them yesterday, he was sure.

Rummaging in the kitchenette he found a tray of leftover dried carpaccio – Nathaniel's meal, perhaps – which he pressed into Djeserit's hand. She took two slices and gave the rest to the korm.

While they devoured the food, Trin pasted analgesic from the medkit on her leg around the wound. 'We have a chance to leave here now. We must take it or perish. You need proper medical attention and the 'bino needs food,' he said.

Vito began to mewl at the smell of the meat. Djeserit reached for him and let him suck the taste from her finger. He screwed up his tiny face and coughed; a heartbreaking look of disappointment.

Tears leaked from Djeserit's eyes and she brushed them away with unsteady bloodstained fingers. 'Where is the Baronessa?' she asked. 'Why hasn't she come?'

'Mira Fedor has others who will help her,' Trin reassured her. 'Now you must put this on.' He held out a spare Carabinere fellalo.

As Djeserit repeated his words to the korm, Trin showed her how to wrap the cloth and thread the fluid tube. The korm listened to her intently, her crest inflating and flattening as if she was agitated or unsure. But when Trin lifted both Djeserit and the 'bino into his arms and headed out through the coldlock she followed.

Christian opened the connecting inner gate. 'Pellegrini – what in Crux's name—'

'Please?' Trin held out the 'bino.

Christian took the 'bino with bare, trembling hands. His face was sweating and his pupils had contracted to tiny pinpricks of darkness.

'Trade visitors. Th-they were staying at the Villa Cabuto,' Trin lied. 'Jus Malocchi 'casted to say they were in trouble. That's where I went. Their aide is dead and the female is injured.'

'What of the Cabutos?' Christian looked unconvinced by the story.

Trin shook his head. 'Gone, Capitano.'

'Cazzone.'

Around them the remaining Carabinere loaded rifles and supplies into the AiVs. A vehicle lifted off through the open roof as they entered, leaving only three.

'You. In that one,' Christian told Trin. 'We'll go now before they break through the fence.'

Trin experienced a pang of guilt about Mira. Would she survive? 'Can we take more of them?'

Christian's eyes glittered. 'And who might that be? Would you like to pick them? I am sure they will be delighted to wait in an orderly manner while you decide who will come with us. Idiota!' He slapped Trin across the face. 'A war has started, Pellegrini. Not just here but all over Araldis. Malocchi wants us back at Centrale as per the code. If you weren't the Principe's son I would leave you here for desertion. But you are our heir – *Crux help us.*' He spoke the last words softly.

Trin bore the blow and the insults without retaliating. He would remember, though. *Always.* 'What about the familia?'

'They have left already.'

Trin thought of the empty villas they had passed. Indeed the familia had left – without a care for who they left behind.

Christian began issuing final evacuation orders.

Trin carried Djeserit to an AiV on the launch pad and lowered her into the last empty passenger seat. She cried out with pain and gripped his fingers, not wanting to be parted from him. Trin saw the fear in her eyes. He wanted to snatch her up again and reassure her but Carabinere in the other seats watched them with grim, suspicious stares. Instead he passed the office medkit to the closest one. 'There are some coagulants left in there. Take what you need.'

'Get in the co-pilot's seat, Pellegrini.' The pilot began priming the AiV. 'The rest will fly with the Capitano and—' A roar from outside drowned his words. A volley of shots was loosed outside and two Carabinere ran into the workshop. One of them was Seb Malocchi. 'They're through,' he shouted.

Trin climbed aboard and the pilot sent their craft upward. Only Christian, the korm and the 'bino were left on the pad. Christian put the 'bino down on the platform near his feet. The korm was crouched low on its hind legs; its fur flattened with the blast from the AiV jets, showing patches of blue skin.

Christian calmly sealed his hood and climbed into the AiV.

'No!' Trin shouted at the pilot. 'He is leaving them.'

The korm jumped at the AiV and was knocked sideways as it lifted off. She fell heavily and lay still.

'Capitano!' Trin thumped his fists against the window. Behind him Djeserit cried out in another language. Trin lunged for the controls but hands grabbed him from behind, pinning him back against his seat. A cord whipped around his neck and another around his chest. He flailed against the restraints as the workshop flooded with 'esques. Then the AiV banked left and away.

Sole

little creature/ fixed fixed
time concealed/
break limits/how to?
burden burden/force change
play game <luscious luscious>

MIRA

Mira pushed her way back into the milling crowd, her heart thumping. *Where is he? What will he do with them?* She asked anyone who would listen about a 'bino and a ragazza with an injured alien and an aristo. One man spoke to her – maybe he'd seen a korm near where the guards were posted – and asked if she had any food?

'No,' she said. 'No food.'

Over and over.

Pressing blindly through the crush, Mira found herself pushed against the fence. She shuffled along, pleading to be let past. Most wouldn't shift from their position. She squeezed around people where she could. Someone spat at her velum. The wetness slid down to her sleeve. A few days ago such an incident would have appalled her but now she didn't care – she could see the gate.

But the crush got worse. So did the heat, and the resentment from people she didn't know. *Can't breathe.* Something pressed into her thigh. She glanced down, slightly dizzy, and saw the heavy lock. She tugged at it, calling to the guard on the other side. 'Trin Pellegrini. Have you seen him?'

The guard ignored her.

Mira shouted again – barely a whisper above the

noise of the crowd – rattling and kicking the gate now with the last of her energy.

The guard scanned the sea of faces, his face unrecognisable under his hood.

She yelled until her breath came in quick, hard gasps. *Hear me! Please hear me!*

The guard took a step towards her, staring through the mesh, recognising her fellala as familia.

'Trinder Pellegrini. The young Principe. He had a 'bino and an injured child. Did you let him through?'

The guard stiffened, gloves tight on his rifle. He began to walk away.

'I want the 'bino back!' Mira screamed after him. 'He's got my 'bino!' Tears ran down her face. She clung to the wire, spent, only dimly aware of the crush and the noise.

Around her a chant started up.

'PELLEGRINI! WE WANT FOOD!'

The chant rippled outward.

Word spread through the crowd. A Pellegrini had been let inside when the whole of Loisa was out here starving. They latched onto a purpose and the focus gave them energy.

A brawny, filthy man on her right shouted in her ear, 'We'll get yer little 'un back for yer.'

The crowd was still chanting. A roar. Mira watched parts of the fence-line ripple under the force of their pushing. Any moment it would buckle and then people would be trampled in the surge. Perhaps some had already. She slapped the big man on his shoulder. 'They'll be crushed,' she screamed into his ear.

He stared down into her face. 'Too late.' He gripped the fence, adding all his strength to that of the others.

The guards fired warning shots as the fence rippled again but people were already climbing up it. The guards retreated and Mira glanced at the sky. An AiV lifted from the top of the Carabinere workshop. She strained to see who was inside but the windows were shaded. Intuition told her that Trin was in there – but what of Djeserit and the korm? And what had he done with Vito?

In the next ripple, the chains on the gate broke. Propelled by the bodies behind her, Mira had to run across the yard to avoid being crushed. The doors to the building were barred but in moments people were being hoisted through broken windows.

The crowd divided. Some charged to the back of the compound while others inside unlocked the building's doors. Mira fell and the brawny man hauled her up on her feet before he vanished into the mob.

Mira stumbled towards the launch pad where one remaining vehicle sat. Others had the same idea as her and they swarmed for the airlifts. The guards sprayed fire down at them and the man next to Mira collapsed, his throat blown wide open. She fell to the floor alongside him, appalled, caught between her instinct to escape and the paralysing horror of his wound. How could the Carabinere fire on their own? How could they do this? The bones of his neck, his blood, and his breath . . .

She wanted to cry, and to hide from it all, but booted feet jabbed her thighs and stamped uncaring across her back. She forced herself to her feet and circled around a group who were trying to get a land barge started. The pad was empty now – the AiV had left and the airlifts had been abandoned. She climbed onto one and sent it upward to get out of the crush.

All that the Carabinere had left behind on the platform was a pile of worn track-liners and a smashed crate. Mira sank to the floor and stared down at the mêlée. It would not be long before they realised there was nothing here for them. And then what would happen? Would they leave the town or would they go back to their casas and wait for the Principe to send help? If his Carabinere had deserted it would be a false hope.

Then a faint chittering sound caught her attention. Somewhere close.

'Korm?' Her heart beat faster as she glanced around her. Behind the AiV track-liners? Crawling over to them she found the alien ragazza lying on its side, fluid seeping across the mat of its fur. The korm raised its head slowly and stared at Mira with solemn recognition.

'a,' the korm chittered softly, trying to form a Latino word.

Mira touched its forearm. 'Where's the 'bino? And Djeserit?'

In answer the korm rolled heavily away. In the space between its body and the floor lay Vito.

Mira cried out in relief. She patted the korm and snatched the 'bino against her shoulder. A shudder travelled the length of his tiny body as he settled against a familiar touch.

'Djeserit?' she asked the korm again.

The korm gestured to the sky.

Mira let out a weary, defeated breath. *Why her? Why did he take her?*

She patted Vito for a few moments while she tried to think. The crowd was beginning to thin out. Most 'esques, she guessed, would move along the viuzza to the next public utility building, or seek out the Duca's chambers. 'Come.' They helped each other to stand and moved over towards the airlift.

The korm made a series of sounds that Mira didn't understand. She hoped the alien's injuries weren't serious but she knew only a little about their anatomy.

When the airlift touched the ground, Mira saw that all but one of the TerVs had been taken. A small group of 'esques in inferior heat-protection gear clustered around the tracks. One of them stood guard with a rifle seized from a fallen Carabinere.

Mira walked towards their huddle. 'Please take us with you.'

Heads turned towards her and the rifle swung to target her head. 'I have some engineering knowledge. Flight engineering. It might be useful,' she said.

One of the 'esques stood. He wore his hood open and his crimson skin was as unlined as her own – not yet baked by dust and sun. His expression, though, was openly hostile as he wiped his nose with his hand. 'Don't see no AiVs around here.'

'Some things are the same.'

What d'ya want?' he said, with a distinct miner's drawl.

'To return with my . . . bambino to Pell.'

'How is it you didn't leave with the rest of the aristos?' His stare roamed her body in a way that made her stomach clench. 'And why should we take you? *Your* kind deserted us. *Your* Carabinere killed some of our people.'

She couldn't think how to reply. The fallen bodies were all around them and Mira could see the fallen man's open throat, glistening with darkening blood.

The man with the rifle slowly shook his head. 'I'm thinking you might be trouble, aristo. Besides, we ain't saving no ginkos.'

The door to the TerV cabin banged open and a woman climbed down, helping a toddler. 'We're all in trouble here, Innis. This woman gave me food earlier. Now for Cruxsakes fix this thing so we can get out of here,' she said.

Mira recognised her from the crowd – remembered the toddler grubbing on the ground for pane.

The woman stepped forward, pushing the rifle aside. 'Don't mind my . . . er . . . what's your word for it . . . *fratella*. I'm Cass.' She held out her hand. 'You gave me your last food. I wouldn't have taken it if I'd known you had children of your own.'

Cautiously Mira extended her hand and they touched palms. 'I am Mira Fedor.'

'Baronessa Fedor?' She slapped Innis's shoulder. 'She's from the Cip pilot familia – only damn ones that can fly the biozoons.'

'So?' he said sulkily.

Cass turned back to Mira. 'What happened to you? Your kind have all left.'

'My villa was destroyed by a bomb – mia sorella, everyone. I need to return to Pell.' *To find Insignia.*

'Pell, love? Well, Ipo's as far north as we'll go. But

you're welcome to come if you want.' Cass beckoned to her. 'Now bring the korm around here.'

Mira followed her to the back of the TerV. On her urging, the korm climbed in awkwardly and lay down. Its wounds seeped still.

'I am not sure how serious its injury is,' said Mira. 'I am not an expert on their physiology.'

Cass gave her a sideways glance. 'You talk formal. Heard the women were more so than the men.'

'You have never spoken to . . . one of us?'

Cass shrugged.

'But you know Latino?'

'Most of us do. But we know a few other words too.' She grinned. 'Now, if the korm lies still it can control its bleeding.'

'It is an orphan. It may not know that. It had no mama to teach it.'

'Instinct will guide it. Besides, we're all orphans now, Mira Fedor.'

The truth of the woman's simple statement gave Mira a sharp pain in her chest. As if sensing her distress, Vito stirred in her arms and gave a hungry cry. His lips quivered piteously. 'The 'bino's name is Vito.'

Cass slipped her tunic from one shoulder and bared a soft, limp breast. 'I'll give him what I can but I've heard they don't suck too well, these Pagoins. Funny mouth.'

Mira had to look away from the woman's immodesty but in spite of it gratitude welled inside her. Cass was the second woman to help Vito in a matter of days. Mira stood there, not knowing how to say thank you.

'Baronessa, love,' Cass said quietly, 'you said you had some learning. Go see if you've got any clues to help them fix the damn mover or we'll all die here.'

Mira stared over Innis's shoulder into the TerV's tracks. Her knowledge of electric motors was entirely theoretical but the problem seemed self-evident. 'The copper contactors have melted,' she said.

Innis scowled. 'So what?'

She gave him a puzzled look. 'There should be replacement components here.'

An 'esque crouched to one side of her tilted his head up. He had a broad face with flat, plain features. 'Can you recognise them?'

'I think so,' said Mira.

He stood up. 'I'm Kristo. I'll come and help you.'

They searched the workshop shelves for a replacement component with Innis hovering closely behind them.

'These,' Mira said after a time.

Kristo took them back to the TerV and began refitting them. Innis glowered over his shoulder while an 'esque they called Marrat worked to fix the rifle to a mounting on the roof of the TerV.

Shots outside made Mira jump.

'You scared, pilot?' said Innis.

She knew he wanted to say more, that he had disliked her from the first moment but Marrat burst into the conversation. 'Ginks outside know we are fixing it. Reckon they're gonna come and try to take it from us.'

Innis pushed Mira aside. 'Kris?'

'Load the spare solar panels and anything else you can find,' said Kristo. 'And get everyone in the barge.'

'But there's only four of us, and four bambini. We could take more,' said Mira. What sort of people were these? No worse perhaps than the familia who had abandoned them.

'*We* decide that, aristo . . .' Innis tapered off. 'Now get up the front there where I can see you.'

Innis drove out of the hangar with Mira alongside him. Cass, Kristo, the korm and the bambini were in the back. Marrat was on top with the rifle.

'Esques leaped at the sides of the TerV but Marrat fired at them. Seeing a woman in the cabin, a desperate mother lunged for the running board, hoisting her 'bino towards the window. 'Please take me and my child,' she screamed.

Mira leaned out to help her but the 'bino slipped from her grasp as Innis veered the TerV sideways. She watched, stunned, as the infant fell under the barge's tracks. The mother's scream pierced right through her.

Innis leaned across the cabin and hauled her back from the window. 'We take no one else!'

The crowd fell away behind the mover, screaming in shared anger.

Innis relaxed his grip on Mira as they tracked over the fallen fence and cleared the confines of the compound. 'This is no aristo world anymore, Baronessa. The rules are ours.'

Mira could think of no reply. In the rear-view mirror she could still see the mother bent over in grief.

Trin

Dodging between smoke pillars, the Carabinere AiVs flew a close formation towards Pell. Below them on the parched ground Trin glimpsed food barges overturned, their contents spilled and crates of spoiled food left to dehydrate.

Loisa wasn't the only place in trouble. The Carabinere transceiver band fired off numerous reports. Dockside was overrun and Station Central was lost. Trin listened as Christian repeatedly tried to contact Malocchi.

Trin glared across at the pilot. 'Tell Montforte that Malocchi has gone already. I know it.'

'It's possible he's right,' said a voice behind him.

Trin strained to see who had spoken but the bonds around his neck and chest held him tight. He couldn't see Djeserit though he thought he could hear her crying softly.

'Ragazza . . . are you well?' Trin demanded.

'Si, Don Pellegrini.' Djeserit's voice was barely a whisper.

Panic prickled the length of his body. 'She needs medic. Untie me so I can see her.'

The pilot shook his head. 'Can't trust you, Pellegrini.'

Trin sagged against his seat with frustration. 'Then tell Christian I said Malocchi's gone or dead already.'

'Do it.' The voice behind him spoke again.

The pilot shrugged and opened the Carabinere frequency. 'Capitano, Pellegrini thinks he knows something. Says Malocchi will have gone.'

'The beacon is on, calling us in. Jus Malocchi would never desert. You know the procedure for a crisis. That's where we will go. THE BEACON IS ON.'

Trin strained against the restraints again. 'Let me talk to him.'

The pilot glanced over his shoulder for endorsement. After a moment he held the toggle to Trin's mouth. 'Speak.'

Trin took a breath. He had been thinking about this since Villa Fedor and it was a relief to be able to say it. He must convince Christian, though – or they would all die. 'If you were going to invade a world, what would be the first thing you would counterbalance?' he said.

'Any opposition force.'

'Si – and Centrale is the heart of our force. Capitano, we are not equipped to fight a war – expel unwanted ginkos and maintain basic order, perhaps, but not halt a well-organised invasion.'

Silence.

'Why do you call this an invasion? What do you know?' said Christian.

'No more than you, but I know acts of terror. I see our food burned. If I wished to create panic and fear then I would do the same. Now there are reports that Dockside has been overrun by ginkos – these creatures that are hatching from the ground. If that is true then we are captive on our own world and we must retreat.'

Silence again.

The men waited, as he did, for Christian's answer. He sensed their attention, even approval.

'Capitano?' the pilot prompted.

'We go to Pell headquarters first,' said Christian. 'There will be no more discussion.'

Frustrated by Montforte's stubbornness, Trin strained harder. The cords around his neck and body abruptly loosened. 'If you are right, then what would you propose?' asked the voice behind him.

Trin took a moment to think as he slapped the circulation back into his arms. He must be right in what he said or they would follow Montforte. He twisted, trying not to stare anxiously at Djeserit. She huddled in her seat, eyes closed, shrinking as far away as she could from the men alongside her. Her neck gills barely moved at all. 'If Dockside and Pell are overrun with these creatures then our best option is to retreat to the underground mines,' Trin said.

The man who'd asked the question held out his hand. He bore the blunt features of the lower familia and had a wide, generous mouth. 'I am Juno Genarro. What are these creatures you speak of?'

Trin clasped Genarro's hand. 'They are hatching out of large globes buried in the ground. I saw them in the viuzzas. Mir— I believe, from my learning, that they are a creature called the Saqr.'

'What harm can they do us?'

'I have seen them suck the fluid from a live body. They are primitive – with no ability to reason.'

'So we shoot them all.' Genarro laughed. 'Easy enough, I say.'

'Their chitin is impervious to most forms of attack.'

'There are others ways.'

'You miss the point, Genarro – they are a tool. Unknown

to us, someone has brought them here and buried them in our soil. Someone has bombed our cities and set fire to our grain silos. This is planned. Carefully planned.'

Genarro's eyes lost their cavalier humour. 'What do you suggest, Don?'

'Survival. And information. We regroup in safety and find our stragglers – work out a way to gather food. Some of the underground mines run for mesurs. We can cover much ground and send out night-time searches.'

'The Capitano said you weren't worth the spit necessary to say your name. Maybe he just had a dry mouth at the time.'

Trin managed a tight smile. Some renewed energy suppressed the shivering fatigue in his muscles. He looked to the others who had stayed silent. 'Where are your familia?'

They all named areas of lower Pell. Only Juno Gennaro had left someone behind in Loisa.

'I'm not Carabinere – you have your tradition and your training. But I know where I would lead you.'

Gennaro nodded slowly. 'Let us see how things are first.'

TEKTON

Miranda turned out to be the most irritating of travelling companions. Not only was the cabin not lavish enough, according to her, but she bitched long and loud about the appalling state of the ship's cuisine while stuffing copious amounts of it into her mouth. It seemed almost as if her chins acted as repositories for the food, freeing her tongue to do what it did best – complain. Tekton spent the journey to Scolar in a state of deep regret, at the same time experiencing mounting trepidation about his impending tryst with Doris. What would she make of Miranda?

But in the tradition of the countless generations of males who had gone before him, Tekton had got it wrong. From the moment Miranda and Doris laid eyes on each other under the Kant chandelier in the lobby of The Sternberg, it was lust at first sight.

'I hope you don't mind me saying, but what fabulous chins!' gurgled Doris. 'You must sing *divine* opera?'

'Oh . . . well, not really . . . but, well, it has been said . . .' Miranda dissembled. 'And your bosoms are outstanding. Le Feuvre corsetry?'

'What an exceptional eye you have!' Doris cooed. 'Tekton would never have noticed it. You *must* see where I bought it. *Divine* little boutique on the corner of Chomsky and Heidegger.'

The pair departed The Sternberg without further ado, leaving Tekton to find his way to the suite alone. His ménage fantasies dissolved along with the epithelium he desquamated in his lotion bath and he consoled himself with the knowledge that he would have plenty of time to find the planet he sought.

After a fine meal of bison pâté and plum quosh he strolled the cherry-blossomed Boulevard Voltaire to the Orion Institute. Ensconcing himself in a vreal booth, he lost a good part of the day and night on a faux tour of the sector on Jo-Jo Rasterovich's recording – all to no avail. There was no sentient settlement of any note on record.

If that drug-fuddled lout has cheated me . . .

Weary and more than a little bad-tempered Tekton returned to The Sternberg to find Miranda quaffing champagne and eating oysters out of parts of Doris that not even he had visited.

'Tekton, good fellow,' trilled Miranda in operatic tones. 'Come and join us.'

Tekton's rush of akula was akin to a lava eruption on Mount Frenzy. He plunged after the oysters with a true connoisseur's enthusiasm and worked off his frustrations.

Later, in the serenity of post-coitus, enduring Doris's snores, a thought occurred to him. Where on Scolar had Miranda got to? The woman had been there for his performance – he was sure.

Throwing on a cloak, Tekton hastened back to the Institute. 'A woman with many chins,' he told the auto-librarian.

It droned back at him with an infuriating privacy

disclaimer, which made Tekton feel like sticking his well-moisturised finger up its authentication mortise. Instead, he caught the elevator to Floor 202 and lurked around the vreal cubicles listening for a clue as to tricky Miranda's whereabouts.

Vanity was her downfall – *Die Walküre*, to be precise. He heard her warbling her way through the third act.

'Aha,' accused Tekton, sweeping back the curtain. 'I thought so.'

Caught in the act of reviewing his search route, Miranda didn't bother to deny it. 'It's that cousin of yours,' she declared. 'He promised me *things* to spy on you. Did you know that he can *see* microwaves? Do you know what surgery I could perform with that ability? Bloodless, that's what. Magical.' A single tear collected in a corner of her eye and she lifted her skirt to display the full undulation of her thighs. 'Don't be cross, Tekton. I have not the faintest idea what you were searching for in such an uninspiring slice of the galaxy – nothing there but rock and gas. And I should know. My grandmama three times removed – the famous actress Shelba Lanzano – ran away to Latino Crux to marry a prince. Terribly romantic, and so on. Last I heard she and the prince had upped stakes and bought a dirty little mining planet out that way. Hot as Hades and not half as exciting.' She pointed to Tekton's holo-tour. 'Took the whole damn clan with him. Faux royalty you know – all inbred.'

Dirty little mining world. Tekton became very still. *Carefully, Tekton*, both minds warned him. 'Mining world? Out there? No. How fascinating? But I found no such thing on the records' he said casually.

'Hah!' Miranda's laugh was more of a snort. 'Of

course not. OLOSS are renowned for tampering with their records: a judge on the law circuit spots a little world he fancies as a holiday home, bribes the Registrar of Planets to delete it from the database and buys it for a song. You must know the sort of thing . . .'

Tekton felt his skin grow warm with embarrassment. Obviously he did not.

'If you want to know the truth on anything you have to use the Vreal Studium. Those extropists are nothing if not meticulous with detail,' she added.

The Vreal Studium.

'And I must congratulate you. Your prolonged erection this evening was quite remarkable. You must tell Jise how you do that.'

Suddenly Tekton felt a different type of heat. 'Indeed.'

'And now, my dear Tekton, you won't squeal to Ra that you caught me, will you?'

Tekton pulled the curtain closed behind him. 'No, dear Miranda – not if you lift that skirt of yours a little higher.'

MIRA

Mira watched Cass nursing Vito. Despite the heat and the lack of food there was no hint of hopelessness, no surrender in her face. Her resolve reminded Mira of Faja and the similarity was like a wound. She couldn't think of her sorella without her breath catching in her throat.

Cass's older ragazzo played nearby in the dirt with the korm. The korm's bleeding had stopped, leaving ugly grey lesions on its blue flesh.

In a few days they'd travelled most of the distance to Ipo: unbearable, hungry days and hot-wind nights. They'd taken the rougher mining tracks towards the place. Cass had pronounced the proper roads too dangerous and crowded.

In some ways Mira was relieved by her decision, for every person on foot they'd have passed would've been another person they should have stopped for, every ragazza another one at risk of being run over.

Mira found herself moving automatically through the days but at night, when the TerV's depleted solar cells forced them to stop, her mind swirled in an agony of confusion and denial. This could not be happening. Her world, as much as she had felt a misfit in it, was being torn from her and crushed. She grieved for her displacement and for the ugliness that desperation caused. What would be the end of it? What would be her fate?

Each of them had been allocated a watch period. Innis declared that he would share his with Mira but, to her relief, Cass overruled him. Instead she took her watch with Kristo.

On the second night they had stopped in a shallow gully at the side of the track to shelter from the worst of the winds. They'd seen no one all afternoon but, to the east and west of the track, lights dotted the night. Miners guarding their leases, Cass had said, and refugees.

Like us.

Kristo tapped his fingers along the barrel of the rifle in a release of tension and Mira worried that in the quickening dark he might shoot her accidentally. 'Stop that.' She couldn't keep the imperious edge from her tone.

'Innis is right,' Kristo said. 'You're a nervous type. Guess that's 'cause you're an aristo.'

'What do you mean?' She found she had little patience left for their ignorant bigotry.

'Youse aristo wimmen up on Mount Pell are protected from real life.'

Mira stared out into the dark. His criticism bothered her. Was she like the familia women? She didn't – had never – *felt* like them. 'I am not just aristo – I am a pilot.'

'All I know is you ain't like Cass,' Kristo said simply. 'Though I guess she's learnin' it hard since her man died.'

'What happened to him?'

'He was killed just a week back when the Juanita mine caved in. They set a blast at one of the open cuts close by. Shouldna done it. Area was too unstable. Brought the tunnel down,' Kristo said.

'How long have you been on Araldis?'

'I was born in Loisa. Ma and Pap came from Inkla's

World along with Cass's folk. We grew up here together. First-generation mining stock.' He thumped his chest proudly. 'I've been here as long as you.'

Mira stared out at the plains. Semantic and Tiesha would soon be up together, bathing the iron ridges with their scarlet light. 'I know the area. I have been there once.'

Kristo looked at her, surprised.

'It was a study trip from the Studium,' she said, embarrassed.

'Didn't think you aristos set foot off Pell.'

'I was made t— I lived in Loisa with mia sorella at the Villa Fedor,'

'I heard of that place. The aristo woman there's been taking in ginkos. You lose her – your sister?'

Mira nodded.

Kristo screwed up his face in sympathy. 'Lost my place too. Lost my ma. Pap's out on the mines somewhere. He doesn't even know.' He stifled a sound of sorrow and turned his head away.

'I will watch the other side.' Mira left him to struggle with his grief. She had enough of her own.

Mira and Cass shared water at daybreak while Marrat reattached the rifle to the roof. Mira felt a slight searching pressure on her back that was gone a heartbeat later, then Innis leaned in so close that his breath fanned her velum. She stepped away in alarm.

'I got news.' He seemed jumpy. 'Talked to some folk over at the next camp. They're holed up on their lease. They reckon those ginko things are everywhere. Swarmin' like ligs on a thorn bush. Rumour says a merc

brought 'em in. The merc set the bombs off in Loisa.
They're using ginkos to do the rest.'

'The aliens are called Saqr. I learned a little about
them at the Studium,' Mira said.

'The Studium, huh? Well, this ain't the learnin' room
now, Baronessa. They've gone and overrun Dockside
as well. Ipo's still holding, though. When we get there
we'll stand against the spit-sucking ginks.'

Mira turned away from his swaggering to face her
own realisation. *Jancz*. Jancz was the mercenary. Her
limbs became heavy and her mind thick with the guilt
of her knowledge. Could she have stopped this? Could
she . . . 'What would they want with us?' she whispered.

Marrat came to stand next to her. 'Where are all your
aristos now? Where are your Carabinere?' he jeered at
Mira. 'Dead, most like! Useless pricks.'

'The miners reckon the ginks have come to take us
because their own world is dead.' said Innis.

Kristo joined them as well. 'They're getting closer,'
he warned. 'You can hear the gunfire.'

Cass hauled herself up and passed Vito to Mira. He
squirmed in Mira's arms, uncertain now where his main
source of comfort lay.

'We'll find out more in Ipo,' said Cass. 'We need to
get there quick now. How much in the cells?'

Innis shrugged. 'A few hours. They're old. Not
holding too well.'

'What about the spares?'

'Smashed.'

'Why didn't you say something?' Cass said in exas-
peration.

Innis's face fell into its usual sullen arrangement.

Cass sighed heavily. 'Let's go.'

They climbed into the barge, Innis driving with Marrat alongside, Kristo atop with the rifle. This time Mira rode in the back with Cass and the bambini. Through the window she saw their pursuers strung out across the horizon like dark beads.

Cass watched from the other window. 'They're on the road. If they beat us to Ipo we'll be cut off.' She took a knife from inside her clothing and passed it to Mira. 'Keep this and use it.'

Mira tried to push it away. 'I could not. We do not arm ourselves.'

'What about your Vito? If these Saqr catch us he will die.'

Mira was spared the need to reply as the barge began to weave, tossing them across the floor. She heard a loud thump on the roof where Kristo clung to his rifle mount. *He will be thrown. Like the 'bino.* She couldn't bear that. Not ever.

Crawling over to where the korm lay, she wedged Vito under the alien's forearm and took a cable from a side-hook. Then she scrambled to the inside ladder and climbed to the roof hatch.

It snapped open with the force of the wind and bounced up, wrenching her arm with it. Mira moaned from the pain as it dragged loose from her fingers. Kristo slid across the roof, his boots scrabbling for purchase. *Not time for pain.*

She threw the rope out to him. It snaked, slapping against his side and away. She reeled it in and tried again and again until, finally, she felt the tug as Kristo caught it and reeled in the slack.

To one side of the barge the dark beads had grown into TerVs: a line of huge barges. They were coming. Mira half fell back inside, leaving the hatch open, and wedged herself next to the korm and Vito. Cass's knife pressed against her side. *Can I use it if I have to? No.*

JO-JO RASTEROVICH

To say that Jo-Jo Rasterovich was the kind to bear a grudge was an understatement and, as such, a marked contrast to his own appetite for exaggeration.

So when the Hera Guild of Lawmon and Bondsmen released him from the contract that he'd signed on Belle-Monde he vac'd the shell. He then spent several hours concocting and uttering a wealth of profanities that would best describe his feelings for Tekton.

As that wore thin, and his throat got dry, he got down to the serious business of planning his revenge.

He returned to the vicinity of Belle-Monde and hired a surveillance module (disguised as a catering multiworld) in which to lurk about while he stalked Tekton's movements and traced his research (something he was able to do with relative ease, knowing the infrastructure and inbuilt protocols of the ex-bordello pseudo-world in remarkable detail), building a picture of the smart's hopes, dreams, and his allies.

It was during that time when he became aware of another shadow in Tekton's life. A stalker of detail, rather like himself. He weighed the probability of it being friend or foe and fell heavily on the side of the latter.

It seemed that Tekton had not just one enemy – he had two.

But he's mine!

When Tekton boarded an OLOSS transport with Dicter Thighs, Jo-Jo hightailed it back to *Salacious II* (with some excellent new heat, shake and gobble recipes) and tracked him there.

The OLOSS transport puttered off to the re-shift point near Mintaka and Jo-Jo eased *Salacious II* out after it with the skill of a plain-clothes detective on his preferred beat. He could have got closer but knowing that Dicter Thighs was Tekton's travelling companion Jo-Jo decided that surveillance was the smarter part of valour.

As they approached the J. Rast shift point (yes, named after him!) Jo-Jo snuggled up close to it in the busy queue and deployed a rather snazzy poaching programme, which informed him that Tekton was off to the philosophers' planet Scolar.

Jo-Jo res-shifted through a different route and still beat Tekton there. He then hung out in Scolar space until he was forced to enrol in an external philosophy course to keep the Scolar marshals off his back.

So while Tekton and Dicter Thighs went about their business, Jo-Jo inhaled Aesthetics and learned whole new meanings for the words 'sublime' and 'disgust'.

The agony and ecstasy of it all went on for several weeks until at short notice, Tekton hired a re-shift cruiser. Jo-Jo dumped Vatsyayan, Confucius and Mi as the cruiser's stolen coordinates tumbled into *Salacious II*'s nav system and brought up a distant system on his holowad.

Jo-Jo's high-heeled-legs pointer danced about before settling on one of the system's three inhabited planets.

A set of pouting scarlet lips formed to rattle off a short briefing.

> Araldis World has been settled for two hundred and three years. Its major export is mineral. Haulers operating on the mag-beam network cart ore to the Dowl res-shift station for sale and distribution through the wings of Orion.
>
> Owned and settled by Cipriano Clan (aristocratic families from Latino Minor with ideologically Machiavellian roots) originally from Latino Crux.
>
> Racial breakdown: Latino humanesque 72%, other humanesque 26%, alien 2%.

The pointer legs and lips vanished while the system diagram continued its elegant rotation in front of him.

Jo-Jo propped his elbows on his knees, sank his chin into his hands and gave a gargantuan sigh. 'The only things I hate more than tax collectors and Hera contracts,' he said aloud, 'are frigging aristos.'

MIRA

'You're the last in,' a voice shouted.

Mira and Cass peered out through the dirt-smeared windows. Ipo was only a few mesurs ahead of them. A small TerV pulled up alongside where they had stopped between huge hydroponic tents and an 'esque with crimson skin and gold miner's tattoos across the bridge of his nose leaned out of the open door. He wore no protective suit, only a thin insulating robe with an open hood.

'We're sealing off the town – bunkering in. Then we saw youse coming. We only got a few minutes.' He gestured back over his shoulder. 'Anyone outside the fence's on their own. What you got in the back?'

'Nothin' 'cept a couple of women,' said Innis.

Marrat opened the doorbridge for him to inspect the vehicle's interior and Cass and Mira climbed out of the barge to stand next to Marrat.

'What fence are you talking about?' asked Innis.

The 'esque pointed to the array of tripods posted at intervals to their left and right. 'We've rigged a laser around the town, using the mining levels.'

'But half of Loisa is behind us on foot. What about them?' Mira protested.

He gave her a hard look and then shrugged. 'Count yourselves too lucky.'

Too lucky? Too lucky – to see a child crushed under the tracks of a TerV? Too lucky – to lose mia sorella? 'The Saqr will kill them.' Mira looked for Cass to add force to her protest but the woman avoided her gaze, fussing with the seals of her 'bino's oversuit.

'You cannot deny them entry,' persisted Mira.

'Shut 'em out or die, Rast says. Pretty straightforward. Now youse best go further in to town now. Gonna be some bazoom out here,' said the 'esque.

Behind them a dull glow sprang to life across the road – a tinted distortion of the dawn like a not-quite fire. It spread in a wide circle around the town and high into the air.

'All the way around.' He laughed. 'They won't even know it's there until they're on it.'

As they watched the fence flicker, the wind gusted, blasting them with dust and grit. Another TerV pulled alongside and its driver leaned out. This one wore a full but hard-worn protective suit.

'These are the last ones, Catchut,' said their escort. 'Get 'em into town.'

Mira glimpsed Catchut's face behind the film. It was pale and space-soft. *An un-native who hasn't bothered with melanin therapy. Not a miner. Not a farmer. A soldier, perhaps?* But there were no soldiers on Araldis, only cowardly Carabinere.

'Yessir.' The miner slapped his fingers to his leathery forehead in mock salute.

'*Now*, Rast says. Everyone away from the fence,' said Catchut. He drove off.

Mira and Cass climbed back into the barge and Mira checked on the korm. Vito was asleep, tucked against

the large alien's forearm. The scar bubbles left by the
Saqr wound seemed smaller today, and the korm
seemed content to lie and let its body self-heal. It
needed food, though, like they all did.

As the barge drove past the rows of hydroponic tents
the guide wires sang in the wind. Mira pressed against
the window. *How much food is in them? Enough to feed
the town? For how long?*

They wound along Ipo's well-compacted dirt roads,
so different from the redcrete viuzzas of Loisa, and
skirted a small rectangular bore-field before entering
the town's centre. Mira knew of Ipo's reputation as
the harshest of the plains towns, a place where the
hydro-farmers and the miners lived in uneasy proximity. The miners were mostly 'esque but not familia,
not Cip. Like Cass and Innis they came from planets
all through the Orion system. They'd built their
shanties – gumes, they called them – from materials
discarded from the larger mines like Pellegrini A and
B. In Ipo, the shanties outnumbered the catoplasma
buildings and the mud-and-cellulose casas tenfold.

It was easy to spot where the few familia lived. Their
villas, though crude in comparison to those in Loisa,
were solid, comforting outlines in the flat red-brown
townscape.

As they passed the quark battery, Mira caught a
strong sulphuric stench and glimpsed people standing
in line outside the pens. 'They're queuing for eggs,'
she said to Cass. The notion shocked her.

Cass rocked her 'bino in time with the sway of the
barge. 'Never had to queue for anything before, eh,
Baronessa?'

When the barge slowed and stopped Cass climbed out ahead of Mira.

Catchut was waiting for them in a space half-filled with barges and trucks. 'We need your TerV.'

Cass gave him a steady look, one hand on her hip, the other still nursing her 'bino. 'Who wants it?' Innis and Marrat joined them – Kristo stayed with the rifle.

'Rast,' said Catchut, as if that should explain everything.

Cass smiled suddenly. 'Perhaps I'd better talk to *Rast*, then.' She turned to the others. 'Innis, you and Marrat stay with the barge. Don't let anyone take it anywhere. Get the rifle down. Kristo, see if you can find some food for us. Mira, bring Vito and come with me.'

'Cass—' Innis began. But she had already walked away.

Mira followed her and Catchut down a wide dirt road lined with gumes on either side and across a dusty piazza to a large flat-topped catoplasma structure that looked like a public-utility building – the town salon, perhaps. As they stepped inside the coldlock, the recycled air made her shiver. At least some places were still cooled. She had never spent such a prolonged period outside and her body had felt constantly overheated and coated in a layer of dirt and sweat. Her fellala could not be working well. Or was it simply exhaustion that made her legs tremble with the effort of the walk?

Vito mewled with hunger. She jiggled him tiredly.

'Here,' said Cass. She held out her own infant. 'Take Chanee while I feed Vito.'

Mira suddenly realised she had not even known Cass's 'bino's name.

With Vito still suckling at her breast, Cass walked calmly into the large middle room. One corner of it was furnished with stools and a hand-tooled metal table, the rest was empty. The walls were covered with shimmer maps of mine geography. At one end of the table sat an 'esque with a battered combat hood half-pulled over stark white hair. Her pale face was so lean and hollow that it seemed as if the flesh barely covered the bone. Across her cheekbones she bore the red markings of a tattoo.

'Rast,' Catchut said, with obvious deference.

Rast glanced up in irritation from a thin sheet of film. 'Don't—' She broke off her sentence in mild surprise. 'Well, if it isn't Cass Mulravey – I might have known you'd survive.'

Cass sat down, detaching Vito from her breast and settling him against her shoulder. 'Loisa is lost to the ginkos.'

Rast gave Catchut a dismissive nod before she replied. As he left the room her gaze settled on Mira. Her stare was an assault of evaluation and immediate censure. 'I know. Who's this?'

Mira forced herself to speak up. 'Mira Fedor. I am trying to get back to Pell. The signorina helped me out of Loisa.'

'Actually, *she* helped *us*. Picked up on the problem with the barge's motor. Otherwise we'd be ginko shit by now,' said Cass.

'Fedor, eh? Not the Pilot family?' Rast tapped her fingers on the table. Half of one – a little one – was missing.

Mira nodded.

'Heard about them. What does that make you? A princess or somethin'?'

'My title is Baronessa.'

'Well, things are bad at Pell, pilot-Baronessa. The bears have either overrun the place or destroyed it.'

Mira's stomach lurched at the blunt news. 'They are called Saqr.'

Rast gave her a curious look. 'You know about them?'

'A little. I am Studium-educated.'

'You and I better have a chat, then. Maybe you know something I don't. *Or* it may be that you don't.' Her lips curved in a cold, sneering smile that caused Mira to stiffen.

'What do they want?' asked Cass.

'Pretty damn obvious what they want.' Rast's eyes narrowed in a way that made her look less womanly. 'Your world is what they want. Why they want it? Aaah, well, you'd have to ask Franco Pellegrini that.' She took a slightly ragged breath. 'But he's dead.'

'Dead.' Cass repeated the word tonelessly.

Dead. The word had Mira trembling all over. *The Principe is dead.*

'Mad damn scramble to find his son now – apparently he was out in one of the border towns doing penance for something. Talk about timing. Anyway, no one'll be leaving here for a while anyway. We're bunkered down until help comes—'

'What about all the others out on the plains? There were so many behind us. On foot,' Mira interrupted. She did not mention her knowledge of Trin. She did not want any reason to prolong a discussion with this woman.

Rast's expression became even more unpleasant. 'Let's get one thing straight, pilot. I'm not much for planets. I came here to do a job that's gone arse-over and I plan to get my crew out. At the moment that means holding this shit-hole until we get some AiVs to get out of here.'

'You're going to fly the whole town out in AiVs?'

'Let's just say I plan to get us some help.'

Rast's hood began to ping loudly enough for Mira, on the other side of the room, to hear. 'Want to watch the show?' Rast slid the film along the table.

Mira drew closer to Cass. The screen showed what looked like flares being set off indiscriminately on the outskirts of Ipo. Except they weren't flares – they were Saqr, incinerating as they stumbled upon the laser fence.

'Your idea, I suppose.' Cass seemed older and suddenly weary.

Rast gave a mock half-bow where she sat. 'Just working with what I've got, Mulravey. My speciality, you could call it. We collected all the laser levels and sights in the town, any damn thing that could excite a proton, and set them up around the perimeter.'

'But how can you keep it running?' asked Mira.

Rast tapped her temple. 'Did you learn anything practical at your Studium, Baronessa? Or was it all manners and good taste? This town's electricity runs off francium and fluorine gas, not hydrogen.'

Mira raised her eyebrows. She had no real knowledge of chemistry. What surprised her was that this uncouth, uneducated woman did.

'Apparently they keep things stabilised with zirconium and something like it . . . hafnium, I think. We can run the barrier all night by a reversal process but it means diverting all the town's power there. Ever had a candlelit dinner, Baronessa? Not bad if you can stand the smell of ligs.'

'How long can you maintain it?' asked Cass.

'Indefinitely. Food is the main problem, along with folk's mental states. In my experience, people hate to be trapped.' Rast worked her jaw a few times, changing options on the combat hood. The deskfilm flickered through viewpoints along the fence in synch with her movements. 'This is a primordial species we're dealing with. They eat and shit and fight. Maybe they'll get bored and go elsewhere.'

'Why do you want to use my barge?' asked Cass.

'*Your* barge? Oh, you mean the one with the Cip crest on the side.' Rast showed a glimpse of pale teeth.

Cass held a steady, guiltless gaze. 'Cips don't rule here any more, Rast. You said yourself that Franco is dead. I'd say the vehicle belongs to me now.'

Cips don't rule here any more. Mira felt sick. *The Principe is dead.* How could they sit there discussing it so . . . casually?

'We're rotating guards inside the fence perimeter. Your barge can fit a lot of bodies in it. It would help me to get them out there and back,' said Rast.

'First I want to know more about what's going on.'

Rast visibly controlled her aggravation. She glanced to the window where dawn had turned to blazing light. More sound leaked from the hood. She rolled up the film and stood, sealing her protecsuit. She was a head

and a half taller than Mira, and muscular. A quick pred-
ator type that you didn't usually see on Araldis. Araldis
was two distinct things: court and custom, dust and
mining. Not pseudo-military efficiency.

'You'd better come with me, then. We'll talk again,
Mulravey, later: after the first wave. When you've had
a chance to squeeze out your milk brain.' Rast's insult
hung in the air after she left.

'Who is she? Who has agreed that she should make
the decisions?' demanded Mira hotly.

Cass dragged herself out of the chair wearily and
handed Vito back to Mira. 'She is a mercenary,
Baronessa. And I say better her than the rest.'

They followed Rast the short distance to a glinting
bore-tower with a narrow platform at the summit.

Mira had to squint to see the tower properly. Her
velum's light-filter was malfunctioning and she
wondered how many harmful rays it was allowing past.
'But what is a mercenary doing on Araldis?' she asked
Cass.

'All I know is I'm damn grateful for it.' Cass said no
more as she slung Chanee across her back and prepared
to climb the ladder.

Others were already up there. Mira recognised
Catchut among them. He handed a 'scope to her as
she took her place among the spectators. She pressed
the magnification button until the blur defined into
something she recognised. The hydro-tents. She lifted
the 'scope higher, past them, until she settled on a
growing line of TerVs, all with the same cargo. Saqr.
Hundreds of them.

War. It was being said over and over around her but some part of her had refused to believe it, because she had not wanted to, until now.

The sick feeling returned. Could she have stopped them? How had these Saqr adapted to survive outside their water home? 'Why?' the whisper escaped her lips.

'Si, Baronessa-pilot, your planet is mineral-abundant but why is it worth an invasion?' Rast had moved to her other side. Sweat stood out on the strips of exposed flesh at her neck as she mouthed quiet instructions into the combat hood. 'Deactivate the fence.'

'What are you doing?' exclaimed Cass from behind Mira.

'Watch.'

Mira put her eye back to the 'scope. As the fence glow dissolved, Saqr climbed from the TerVs and examined the burned remains of their first scouts. After a few moments one of them crawled back and forth across the line of the fence without harm.

'Come, pretty, pretty . . .' murmured Rast.

The individual returned to the group and after some moments a group of them shuffled across the line.

'Now,' breathed Rast. The fence flamed in a bonfire of incinerating chitin.

Jubilant shouts rose from the watchers on the tower but Mira didn't join in, didn't feel their sense of triumph. How could she celebrate the deaths of primitive sentients with little capacity for strategy or planning when those responsible for the bombs were alive? And what of herself? If others knew what she had seen and not shared, would they hold her accountable?

'Hope you got some tricks in your suit for when they

come from the air, Rast,' said Cass when the shouting quieted. She had moved to the other side of Catchut now. She shifted the weight of her infant on her back.

Mira suddenly felt the pangs of a different kind of fear. Chanee's oversuit hung so baggily on him. She reached behind to touch Vito. Had dehydration and hunger permanently damaged him?

'Their motor dexterity is limited. They are aggressive but they cannot operate machinery. What I want to know is, who is managing the auto-drives on the TerVs?' said Rast.

Mira watched her disappear down the ladder. *I know.*

One by one the other observers followed Rast.

When Mira reached the bottom she was surprised to find the mercenary waiting for her in the narrow strands of shade.

'Tell me what you know about the Saqr, pilot.'

'They are classified as a giant tardigrade and they come from a planet called Saqry, the largest moon of the gas giant Saqrshoanl. I read a case study . . . an OLOSS envoy went to determine their level of sentience. They removed all his body fluid and returned him perfectly intact to his planet of origin.'

'They sound intelligent enough to me,' said Rast.

Mira couldn't decide if she was joking. 'They have a basic social structure but, as you said, it is designed around survival.'

'Yeah, well, most things are.' Rast began to walk on.

With difficulty Mira and Cass kept step with her. 'Is that why you are here?'

This time Rast did laugh. 'You have an interesting sense of humour, Baronessa. Let's just say that the

Principe had some concerns that he didn't have faith in his own to deal with.'

Cass made a contemptuous sound. 'He was right. The cowardly cazzone left the city to burn, and us to die.'

Rast shrugged. 'Some might call it smart. Now tell me, Mira Fedor: if the Principe and his son are dead, who does the title fall to?'

Mira shook her head. 'I-I am not sure. That is . . . I am not sure that he is dead.'

Rast took her arm and pulled her into the shade of the town hall roof overhang. 'You've seen him?'

'His son? I think so – at the Carabinere compound. He left when they evacuated.'

'Deserted!' snorted Cass.

Mira felt the blood draining from her head. She could no longer think well enough to keep ahead of the inquisitive mercenary. 'We need food for our bambini.'

'We've got a temporary mess set up in the bistro off that dust bowl of a town centre you're all calling a piazza, past where the TerVs are parked. We eat in shifts.'

'I'll tell Innis and Marrat,' said Cass. She walked off leaving Mira.

Rast watched her go. 'She's tough, that one. We pulled her man out of the Juanita mine collapse only a week ago. She came and identified him. Never showed a thing, no tears, no screaming.' Rast's voice was tinged with admiration. 'You were lucky to hook up with her.' She slipped a casual arm around Mira's shoulder. 'I've known a few pilots but never an aristo. I like refined women.'

Mira clutched Vito tighter. She would not let Rast intimidate her. 'I haven't eaten properly for days.'

Rast let her arm drop. 'You might still score breakfast if you hurry.'

The mess was a jumble of chairs and tables collected from the casas and spread through the market place's all-weather tents and adjoining bistro. Innis, Marrat, Kristo and Cass sat at a table in the bistro section room, enjoying plates of kranse bread and farfalli.

Mira went to the food-server. The room sweltered as the environmentals struggled against the heat from the overworked ovens and the constantly opening coldlock. She saw the korm squatting in a corner of the cucina, chewing at a mound of raw kranse.

The korm raised its head and chittered. Though still crusted with blood, it seemed more lively; its crest looked less shrivelled.

Mira went to help herself to a plate of stewed quark eggs but was stopped by a solid Latino-looking woman with a determined face. Her protecsuit was stripped back to her waist and her crimson skin glowed with the heat. Sweat dripped freely from her forehead, down her cheeks and onto the neck of her undershirt. 'Just so you know. It's one plateful only. Some have been taking more than their share. Sign for your meal here.' She pointed to a touchpad.

Mira placed her finger on the pad and it moulded around her finger for an instant.

'Do this each time,' said the woman. 'If you don't . . .' She glanced behind her to an 'esque rocking back on a chair, a rifle resting across his thighs.

Mira nodded, took her one slice and one plateful and went to Cass's table, not sure that she could eat the food. She bit into the bread and moistened it in her mouth.

'I can't feel my feet,' complained Kristo.

Mira looked under the table. Cass's older child was asleep on the floor, head resting on Kristo's feet. Mira felt a sudden softening towards the man, guessing that he had also seen to the korm.

'Your ragazzo,' she said to Cass.

Cass got down on her knees and moved the 'bino's head, freeing Kristo's feet.

Kristo nodded his thanks and smiled at Mira, stamping the blood back into his feet. The warmth of his expression should have meant something but her tiredness and grief had suddenly gone beyond something she could explain, beyond civility, beyond manners and breeding. She could not care at that moment. All she knew was that the food hurt her stomach and the thought of the woman's sweat dripping from her face made her feel sick. She wanted to eat and yet she wanted to vomit. She lowered Vito to the floor and slumped in her seat.

'Baronessa?' Cass stared at her.

Mira forced herself to take another mouthful of bread. She chewed it mechanically. When it reached the pit of her stomach the nausea abated some. She found herself longing to lie next to Vito on the floor. Her thoughts began to wander a little. Where had Trin taken Djeserit? *Why* had Trin taken Djeserit? Desire didn't seem enough of a reason. Not for Trin Pellegrini.

It had not been enough for him before when he had

taken Mira to the Tourmalines. Their date drifted to
the surface of her mind – the gently warm sea water,
and the cerise sand that had been vivid against her
white bathing skin. She had felt unsure of herself,
unsure of whether she liked the young Principe or not.
Certainly she had been flattered, and excited. But then
he had left her abruptly, after they had shared a kiss.
It seemed so trivial now – the event that had caused
her such embarrassment – but the water . . . how she
longed to feel its honeyed touch.

Lost in the memories, she failed to notice Innis shift
his seat closer, until he draped his arm over the back
of her chair and breathed wine into her face.

Her focus sharpened onto the empty jug and the
two men who'd been drinking from it – Innis and
Marrat. Kristo and Cass and her children, she realised,
had left.

'My sh-ister's taken to you,' slurred Innis.

Mira leaned away from him instinctively.

He tried to pull her closer. 'You ain't got much to
be stuck-up about now, Baronessa. Your type don't run
the place no more.'

Mira didn't like his tone or the way heads were
turning to listen and her skin crawled at his touch.

'Anyway, how come you know so much about
ginkos?' He poked a foot at the sleeping Vito, startling
the infant awake.

Mira shrugged off Innis's arm and bent to Vito.

'Do not touch my ragazzo. Do not touch me.' She
spoke the words loudly and clearly so that the message
was unmistakable to Innis and to everyone else within
earshot.

His mouth pinched tight. '*Aristo-bitch*,' he hissed softly.

'What are you gabbing about, Innis?' Cass was back, standing beside them, taking in the empty jug and Mira kneeling protectively over Vito. 'Have you been drinking?'

He pouted like a sulky ragazzo. 'All I said is . . . how come she knows so much about ginkos?'

In front of everyone there, Cass slapped his face; a sharp, belittling sound that brought tears of embarrassment to his eyes. 'I told you not to drink again. Ever. Not after . . .'

Mira stood up, clutching Vito tightly against her body. *Not after what?*

Cass held out a latte bladder. 'I got this from the market next door. Basic amenities are being pooled and shared out. The kitchen will fill it for you.'

Mira took it from her, not trusting herself to speak, and went to the cucina.

The woman who had served her the eggs filled the bladder from the spout of a drink dispenser. 'It's not vitamin-enriched – we're all out of additives. But it will do. That 'bino of yours looks half-starved. And you look half-dead. I've finished my shift now. I can show you where the closest dormitory is.'

The korm gorged down the last of the kranse stalks and brought the empty bowl over to them, looking for more.

The woman shook her head. 'No second helpings for anyone. Two meals a day and that's all. May get down to less than that if this drags on.'

Mira took the bowl from the korm and passed it to her. 'Grazi, signorina,' she said.

The woman frowned, as if the polite form of address displeased her. 'I am not a signorina. I am Mesquite.'

Mira followed Mesquite down the dirt road, past the flapping market tents to a flat-topped structure that had been a leisure club. Coldtanks and deskfilms had been pushed aside against the walls and every space was crammed with thin roll-up bedfilms. Only about half of them had covers.

'The men have got the same thing. They don't like it. Most of them want to sleep near the TerVs,' Mesquite rolled her eyes, 'or with a woman. But we separated them up to cut down the trouble. Don't know that it worked but when your population goes from one to five thousand in a couple of nights you got to try something.'

Mira gave a small smile and held out her hand. 'Mira Fedor.'

'I know,' said the woman. She shook Mira's hand, then began folding covers. 'Word travels quicker here than most places. You're from the pilot familia?'

Mira took a bedfilm and cover from her. 'Si.'

'Well, that's your corner over there.' Mesquite disappeared outside, then returned with an armful of kranse stalks and some rags. 'Korms need to roost, don't they? Keep it tidy. Some of these women are real prejudiced against aliens. More so now.' For all her abrupt manner, Mesquite hadn't used the word 'ginko'. It stood her apart from just about everyone else.

Mira pulled her bedfilm away from the corner and with fatigue-numbed fingers built a nest for the korm wedged between her and the wall. Then she coaxed the korm onto the jumble of rags and the alien roosted instantly, exhausted.

Laying Vito on the bedfilm Mira curled herself around him and went straight to sleep.

TRIN

Juno Genarro handed Trin a rifle and a combat web to fit under his hood. The landing pad on the top of Malocchi's enclave was deserted apart from the four Loisa craft. Smoke drifted across from the fires burning below at Dockside.

'You might be the last Pellegrini alive. I'd hate to have the death of the newest Principe on my conscience.'

Trin listened for the humour in Juno's voice. When he couldn't hear it, resurgent dread shivered through him. Malocchi's enclave was eerily quiet and he didn't know what to do about Djeserit. She slept now, curled into her seat, gills moving only faintly.

'Someone should guard the AiVs,' he said, fumbling with the safety on the rifle. He'd had basic instruction at the Studium but it was not something he'd ever taken seriously. The Cavaliere were his protection. Had been.

'You would volunteer, I expect.' Christian loomed at his side, his expression obscured by the distortion of the combat webbing.

Trin tried dissuading him again. 'We've had no communication from Malocchi. There are fires all over Dockside and the pad is deserted.' He looked along the edge of the building to the blunt edge of the stairs. 'Where are ther TerVs? Where are the Cavaliere?' His voice sounded thin and high with fear.

The Carabinere gathered around, waiting for Christian to respond. Trin could see Juno Genarro moving among them, whispering.

Christian also noticed. 'Juno, you stay with the AiVs,' he said, frowning.

Genarro shook his head and slapped the butt of his rifle. 'I'm more use to you in there, Capitano.'

Trin thought Christian wavered, knowing he was right. 'Vespa Malocchi will stay then. Seb will lead one team, Genarro another. I will take the third. Test your shortcasts.'

Trin struggled not to panic as he activated the webbing. It moulded tightly over his nose and he felt something thrust into his ear and tug at his lip as the audio settled into place. He forced himself to breathe deeply a couple of times, and the membrane over his nostrils and mouth thinned enough to allow the passage of air. It still didn't feel comfortable, like trying to breathe in a dust storm.

Remembering his basic instruction he worked his jaw to find the shortcast frequency. Static crackled on most of the channels but one was filled with unintelligible shouting. He clicked on until he found Christian's voice.

The Capitano divided the groups. Trin listened to his simple plan and watched a display flicker alive and steady in his right eye. The webbing was a more advanced version than the ones they had practised with at the Studium and he couldn't interpret many of the icons.

'Pellegrini, you are the only one without body armour. You should stay behind here as well,' said Christian.

Trin felt a prickling suspicion. Why the sudden change of heart?

'I'm more use to you in there.' He deliberately used the same words as Genarro. 'I know the building well. I worked here, remember.'

Christian only hesitated for a few seconds. 'Bueno. I want it on record that you chose to come in.'

So that was it. 'I choose to enter Carabinere head-quarters of my own volition.' Trin made sure his words were crisp for the web's recorder.

'I'll watch him, Capitano,' Juno volunteered.

'One sweep and out on my order.'

'Where will we go then?' asked one of the others.

Christian didn't answer.

Inside the coldlock they split up, one team heading for Malocchi's office, another to the main office floors, the last to the beacon.

Trin's thoughts turned to Joe Scali as his team of six, headed by Juno Genarro, crept towards Technology.

'Don Pellegrini, come up here behind me and call out the floor plan. Anyone starts shooting, you find the floor.'

Trin could barely hear Juno's order over his own ragged breathing. Spots faded in and out before his eyes. Hunger and exhaustion had begun to steal his sense of reality. He gripped Juno's shoulder.

Genarro tensed under his fellalo but didn't look back at him. 'Your biostats are weak. Bite down on the pickup. You've got a small reserve of water in the web that has glucose in it.'

Trin did as instructed and moisture squirted into his

cheeks. He tongued the sweet flavour and his vision cleared almost instantly.

'You can probably do that twice more before you run out.' Genarro paused. 'Will that be enough?'

Trin let go of his shoulder. 'Si.'

They crept into the labyrinth of offices, finding no one. Some desks looked as though they had been cleared for the day, others were abandoned as if the person had left suddenly.

The pattern was repeated through every office on every floor. Each window gave them another panorama over Dockside with the same view: smoking fires and the absence of orbital traffic in the purple sky. For the first time since its settlement nothing was coming in or going out of Araldis.

Seb Malocchi's third group reported in that they'd found the beacon unattended, but intact and functioning normally. No signs of damage.

Christian ordered them to rendezvous with Juno's group. He was at the door to Malocchi's office but couldn't get in.

'Nothing here either, Capitano,' said Juno.

Trin felt clammy and claustrophobic under the webbing. The glucose was wearing off fast and he desperately wanted to get out of the building and back to Djeserit but something stronger than this urge compelled him to push the search further. 'What about the refectory? We haven't looked there.'

'You think maybe they're all taking a siesta?' said Juno.

Laughs congested the shortcast.

Trin waited until it quieted. 'It is the largest space

in the building. If someone wanted them all in one place . . .'

'Capitano?' asked Juno.

'Rendezvous with Seb, then check it out. We're nearly through breaking this seal. Should be in Malocchi's office in a few moments. I'll know more then.'

The clamminess that had beset Trin turned to unrestrained sweating. He gripped the rifle hard to keep it from sliding in his grasp. Spots danced before his eyes again and he bit again on the glucose release.

Juno gestured an order to his team, pointing for Trin to take the position at his shoulder. 'On the bottom floor?' he asked.

Trin nodded.

Seb's team met up with them on the stairs above the bottom level. Juno and Seb exchanged the barest of tactical instructions. Juno would count them in from opposite doors. They would enter low and cautious.

'I can smell food.' Someone broke the agreed silence.

Trin could smell it too. His mouth watered so violently that he dribbled. He felt slight pressure from the web as it absorbed the moisture.

Genarro slid open the double doors and crawled in, rifle first.

'We're in.' Christian's voice broke shortcast silence again.

Weapon fire started up almost simultaneously.

Trin froze with the confusion of noise. *Who's shooting?* He was pushed down onto the floor as the shortcast channel clamoured with competing voices:

'What in the Crux's holy—'

'Juno. I need back-up!'

'Principe be our father. Care for us in our unspoiled world and deliver us from—'

Someone was praying. Trin tried to sort through the cacophony for a voice he recognised. The weapon fire, he realised, was up on Malocchi's floor.

But the prayer came from Juno inside the refectory. Trin forced himself to crawl through the doors after him. Juno was on his knees, fingers steepled together, rifle discarded.

At one end of the large room tables and chairs were piled high against the windows. To the far side, over-cooked, dehydrated food crackled on the warmers. In the space between the two lay a mound of casually heaped bodies.

Trin's gaze was drawn to the matted clots of dark-ness in their faces. They seemed untouched apart from the bleeding holes that had been their eyes.

Automatically, without wanting to, he sifted the muddle of flesh, seeking out familiar faces. *Not Joe Scali. Not Rantha. Please . . .*

Rising acid burned away the glucose taste in his mouth. He wanted to run back to the launching pad, to Djeserit and escape this. *Swallow or suffocate.* He grappled with his bodily reactions for a few moments, trying to subdue his gag reflex. When he could, he called out hoarsely. 'Genarro.'

His team leader had stopped praying and was watching Seb Malocchi's team who had entered through the other door. One of Seb's men ran to the pile of bodies and fell onto it.

'Nathaniel!' shouted Seb.

But young Nathaniel ignored him and began plucking at the mound of flesh, mumbling names. 'Kosta, Lorrena Scali—'

Trin knew exactly what the young Carabinere was doing and the sight transfixed him.

Genarro climbed to his feet, purposefully, the shock waning. 'Nathaniel, the Capitano needs our help. These people do not,' he said.

'What if there's someone alive?' Like a drunken dancer changing partners Nathaniel struggled to move the bodies. A woman in his grip slipped to the floor, her head rolling slightly askew.

Trin saw the face. It was Rantha's.

His horror threatened to swallow him. He tore off his hood, peeling back the web to be sick. *Rantha. No.* She would never again hate the man who made her pregnant, never date Joe Scali, never hold her 'bino. *Rantha.*

A hand grasped Trin's shoulder and pulled him roughly to his feet. He stared into Juno Genarro's mesh-distorted face. 'Both teams upstairs to assist the Capitano. *NOW.* Except you.' He shook Trin. 'Can you fly?'

Trin barely made sense of the words. 'Si.'

'Go to the landing pad and tell the Pescares to have the AiVs ready to leave. You prepare the third one. You saw that woman's head. These people haven't been dead very long . . .'

You saw that woman's head. Rantha's head. Instinctively Trin knew that Juno was right. The Saqr were still near. Maybe this had happened just as they landed, or as he'd put his webbing on, or as they crept through the quiet, empty corridors.

'Nathaniel,' said Seb again. 'We must leave now.'
He approached the young Carabinere.

'No,' said Nathaniel. He lifted his rifle and waved
it at Seb. 'My familia are here . . . my friends. I wish to
see them.'

Seb Malocchi nodded his understanding and edged
slowly back to the door. The background noise on their
shortcast was beginning to lessen.

'*Rapido!*' shouted Juno Genarro.

The Carabinere disappeared, pleased to move, for
the same terror was upon all of them.

Trin was left alone with Nathaniel and the dead.

'The Saqr did this.' Nathaniel released his grip on
Rantha's body.

Trin wanted to run from what he could see. *But what
about Joe Scali?* an inner voice nagged. *Where is your
friend? Is he in that obscene pile of flesh?* 'How do you
know Saqr?'

'I worked in Alien Ethnicity. Signor Malocchi thought
the department was a waste of time but Principe Franco
insisted that we keep it. Those holes in their eyes are
caused by stylets. They bore for their food.'

'I know,' said Trin shortly. 'I've seen them. Nathaniel,
we must go to the AiVs now.'

Nathaniel smiled absently at him and nodded. But
he didn't move.

Shock. Trin recognised it. Mira Fedor had been the
same. He retreated to the door and glanced out. There
was a noise on the stairs. On the shortcast Juno
murmured instructions to his team as he tried to raise
the Capitano. But this noise was not made by the
Carabinere. *Something else.*

'Nathaniel,' Trin urged. 'Now. Prego.'

But Nathaniel was back on his knees among the bodies, laying them out in neat rows.

The sound got louder and Trin panicked. He ran through the cucina to the directors' refectory. The security director was at a table nearby, his torso resting on a tabletop, dried trails of black blood in stripes across his clean scalp where tiny holes had been bored.

Trin ran past him without stopping. *Malocchi is dead. Malocchi is dead.* The realisation pursued him down a forgotten, malformed corridor. He bit down to extract the last squirt of glucose as he ran. When he reached the door of his office he hammered at the lock. As the door slid open, a deep-rooted survival instinct sent him dropping to his knees.

A pistol discharged into the empty air where he'd been standing.

He scrambled against the wall, feeling warm wetness flood his groin. Trin Pellegrini had never in his adult life pissed himself before. He fumbled with his rifle, jamming the charge in his haste. Visions of himself on the pile with the others, his discarded flesh being laid out by Nathaniel, took control of his mind. *No.*

His rifle flickered in readiness. He lifted it and fired at the doorway. The pulse hammered into the ceiling, blasting out chunks of catoplasma. Fear racked him and he couldn't bring himself to move any closer to the door.

'Familia?' a hoarse voice called into the silence.

Trin's heart lurched and he began to breathe again. He knew that voice. He knew it. 'Scali,' he rasped. Then again. 'Scali, is that you?'

'Don Pellegrini?'

'Si. Si, Nobile.' Tears of relief spurted from his eyes.

Scali stepped into the doorway, sobbing too. His fellalo was torn and soaked with blood.

He saw Trin on the floor and fell down beside him. They stared at each other in silence.

'You stink, young Principe,' Scali finally said, hugging him. 'But you came for me, Don. I will never forget that. You knew where I'd be hiding. I hoped Rantha would think of it. Have you seen her?'

Trin swallowed slowly and painfully. 'No, Nobile, I have not. She must have got away. Now you and I must do the same.'

MIRA

The Saqr encircled Ipo like maggots working the edges of a carcass. Rast tried to keep order, organising work parties, but many wanted to fight away their fear.

Mira volunteered to pick grain from the crops in the hydro-tents. At the end of her first shift, Rast was waiting for her outside, sitting in a TerV. 'Get in.'

Mira ignored the mercenary, walking back towards the town centre behind the truck that had brought them to the tents. Now it was loaded down with kranse.

Rast rolled the TerV alongside her. 'That's an order, Fedor.'

'I do not take your orders,' Mira said softly.

Rast raised her rifle and pointed it casually out the window. 'Do as I say, Baronessa.'

Mira stopped still, biting her lip. The others on the work detail walked on, heads averted, not wanting any part of her problem. She stood, undecided. She found the mercenary abrasive and rude but she sensed it was not wise to test Rast's anger so she climbed into the TerV.

'Your manners are appalling,' she said in her stiffest aristo tone.

'Manners?' Rast laughed so hard that she sent the TerV jerking from side to side of the track as she drove it past the tents toward the east end of the town.

They pulled up near a section of the fence through which they could see a handful of Saqr tending a row of yellow globes half-buried in the ground. Mira could smell the cloying sweetness.

'Tell me what these things are – everything you know about them, and how you know it,' Rast demanded.

Mira paused to collect her thoughts. It seemed hard to remember things and harder to concentrate, as if a heavy impermeable shroud had been cast across her mind. 'I studied other sentient cultures at the Studium and the Saqr were one of over five hundred life forms I referenced. I did not receive a neural fact-augmentation because it was not deemed necessary. Not for a woman who would never truly hold a position of importance. So I can only use ordinary recall and it is possible that I may be confusing them with other species. My knowledge hardly qualifies as expertise.'

'Try,' said Rast.

'I believe the globes are cysts.'

'You mean eggs?' Rast asked.

'No. Each one is a fully formed Saqr in a state of cryptobiosis. Hibernation,' Mira said, softly.

'Impossible. The globe is too small.'

Mira shook her head. 'I saw one hatch in Loisa. They are capable of compacting their bodies.'

'Why do they do that?'

'Cryptobiosis is used to survive extremes of temperature and other conditions.'

'Then what is the sweet stink?'

'I've been trying to remember. I think it has something to do with the alteration of their body fluids. In cryptobiosis the water in their bodies is replaced by glycerol and sugars. It protects their membranes. Usually, though, they would enter hibernation if conditions were very dry. Somehow that has been reversed . . .'

'By someone.'

'Si.'

'What of their social habits?'

'Their culture, as we discussed, is based on reproduction and survival.'

Rast snorted. 'Do they take orders?'

'Perhaps. I'm not sure about their organisational hierarchy, though I believe it is possible to communicate with them. OLOSS has attempted to do so. I do recall one other thing. After hibernation they are voraciously hungry and hostile – depending on how long their hibernation has been.'

'So someone has bought them here and released them in their most aggressive form. I wonder,' said Rast, staring through the fence, 'who that might be.'

Mira clasped her arms around herself, holding tight to the guilty weight of her conscience.

That evening Rast called a town meeting in the piazza to set up a maintenance turnaround to keep the TerVs ready to move. She also insisted that all available weapons should be stockpiled and distributed according to the duty-watch roster. Though, on the face of it, the miners and farmers agreed, Cass told Mira that many of them had other weapons hidden.

They stood together at the edge of the crowd, among the women and 'bini. The segregation had occurred naturally as if the women sought comfort in each other as they listened to some of the men lobby to attack the Saqr.

Rast's mercenaries prowled through the crowd, fully armed, while she talked the aggressive faction down. Mira wondered how long she could restrain them.

Rast sought Mira out again after the meeting 'I want you on a maintenance shift. You've got engineering knowledge.'

'Theoretical,' Mira countered.

The mercenary gave her a withering stare. 'Your *theoretical* aristo manner will likely get you strangled in this climate, Baronessa.'

Mira's heart quickened and she instinctively stepped backwards.

Her reaction set Rast guffawing. 'That stiff little act of yours is getting brittle, Fedor.' She made a snapping noise with her tongue as she strode off.

'Rast is attracted to you,' said Cass. 'Maybe we can use that.'

We? Mira pondered what that meant as she walked back alone to the dormitory. Cass had met a man and moved in with him. Her Thomaas was a scrawny, unsmiling person who owned a gume close to the dorm. Was that the 'we' she spoke of?

'Someone digging your grave?' Mesquite was outside in the dark with her hood off, smoking. The nightwinds whipped the smoke straight up into the sky where Tiesha was already waning. Semantic would rise later.

'What do you mean?' Mira found the woman's forth-right manner disconcerting.

Mesquite moved casually closer to her. 'Cass Mulravey's fratella has been outside, watching for you. I saw him, though he has been hiding across the way,' she whispered.

Mira couldn't stop herself peering into the dark.

'You need to learn how to protect yourself, Baronessa.'

'Aristo women do not use violence,' Mira said auto-matically. 'We made that choice when we left Latino Crux.'

Mesquite ground the butt of her smoke underfoot. 'So the women made that choice? Or the men made it for them? You have the Inborn Talent? What can you fly?'

'Anything. Though I am most skilled with the Intuits.'

'What about assailants?'

'Si,' said Mira, puzzled.

'What are they built for, then? Leisure trips?'

'Of course not.'

'Oh, so you're trained to fly a warship but you do not take up arms?'

'That is different. I would never *see* my enemies . . .' Mira trailed off limply.

Without warning Mesquite hooked Mira's ankle and knocked her flat on her back. She shoved the point of her boot into Mira's throat.

Mira struggled, trying to wrench Mesquite's foot away, but the woman pressed harder, cutting off her airflow. In a bid to breathe, Mira twisted sideways, over-balancing Mesquite.

The woman fell heavily onto the ground.

Mira sat up, holding her throat. 'Are you l-loco?' she gasped.

Mesquite rolled over slowly to face her. 'Aristo women do not fight, eh? Well, aristo thinking will not keep you alive through this, Mira Fedor,' said Mesquite. Her expression became suddenly apprehensive. 'It did not save the Principe, or his familia.'

But Mira cared not for her philosophies. 'How dare you touch me?' She climbed to her feet, furious enough to strike the woman.

Mesquite brushed the dust from her protecsuit, unfazed by Mira's reaction. 'Adapt if you want to survive.'

Mira left her and went inside. She took Vito from one of the cluster of makeshift cradles that was serving as a nursery and thanked the young familia woman who'd been minding him. He snuggled into her arms.

'He doesn't eat much. Dribbled out most of his latte,' said the minder.

Mira sighed. 'He is Pagoin. They cannot metabolise it so well.'

The woman nodded doubtfully, as if she didn't understand. Then she frowned. 'Did you have a fall, Baronessa? Your fellala . . .' She gestured at the fresh red smears on the back and side of Mira's robe.

'Si. An accident. Please, my name is Mira.'

The young woman smiled this time. 'And I am Josefia.'

Mira took Vito to her corner where the korm was roosting, one eye closed. She retrieved the knife that Cass had given her from the small bundle of clothes that she had been allotted and secured it inside her underliner. Then she lay down on the bedfilm, cradling Vito close to her. He squirmed a little. He was stronger now that he'd had some food, but his expression stayed solemn.

Mira lay there, trying to picture him in a few years. *Wiry and serious*, she thought, *no easy laughter for Vito*. Her heart ached for that young man. Would she be there to see him like that, to tell him about this terrible time and where he had come from?

She knew she wanted to be, and in that instant Mira felt Faja close to her.

The following night Mira took the korm to the early sitting at the mess. Mesquite surprised her by producing a meat-extract soup that the korm could digest. Mira watched the alien gulp the food, avoiding Innis's sulky glares. He seemed sober though Kristo told her he'd been drinking behind Cass's back. Kristo had taken to calling for Mira at the dorm to walk her to meals. She welcomed his company and his unobtrusive manner.

'G'd,' said the korm. It had collected some rudimentary 'esque words but its palate wasn't designed for speech. It replaced some letters with whistle sounds, making its pronunciation difficult to understand.

'Dj^s^r^t?'

Mira shrugged. 'I don't know where she is.'

The korm's crest filled and coloured. Mira had come to recognise this as a sign of emotion in the child.

'F^nd?' it insisted.

'Where would I find her?'

'F^nd h^r!' The korm lurched to its feet, upset, body quivering. It fell into a fighting crouch – the same one that Mira had seen it adopt in Loisa, against the Saqr. Its action knocked over the table, which tipped onto the next. Marrat's dinner crashed to the floor, Innis's spilt across him.

The korm rushed out, leaving Mira.

Marrat began to clear up the mess but Innis was at Mira's side immediately, his face only a breath away from hers. 'That ginko of yours is no more'n an animal. Should be kept outside with the quarks and the cane,' he said.

Mira's fingers curled into the skin of her felalla. Why did he come so close? 'The korm is upset. It has lost its friend. We have *all* lost someone.'

Innis's expression became petulant. 'You been turnin' my sister against me.'

Mira stared at him in honest surprise. 'How could I do that? Why would I care to?'

Innis's glower lightened into something slightly more amenable at her answer. His hands fell to his sides and he took a step back.

'I guess I've been riding you, Baronessa. Maybe we could work things out better. Don't need it to be like this. Not with the ginkos out there jus' waiting to get in at us.' He gave her a would-be appealing smile that only made her nervous.

'All right,' Mira agreed cautiously.

'Let's talk outside.'

She glanced around. The korm had gone – back to the dormitory, she hoped, but she couldn't be sure. She should follow, she thought: collect Vito from the nursery and see what she could do to calm the korm. Or should she let Innis have his say?

Mira took a deep breath and nodded to him.

Innis led the way outside, away from the refectory and down a dirt road to the north that was lined with gumes. One fading street solar and the occasional flicker of activity inside the huts lit their way. Marrat tagged along close behind.

Halfway along, Mira suddenly stopped walking, uncomfortable with the distance they were from the refectory and the dorm. 'Speak your mind now.'

'You sleeping with my sister?'

Mira opened her mouth, astonished. 'That is ridiculous.'

Innis came closer to her, his face puckered like that of a ragazzo about to cry. 'She thinks I'm useless. Why else would she think that, 'cept if you're poisoning her?'

Mira found herself wordless in the face of Innis's accusation. She held out a gloved hand in protest. 'Your sorella and I have no such relationship – she is with a man. You have seen him.'

But Innis was sunk low in self-pity. He slapped her hand away with force and grabbed her shoulders. 'I'll teach you 'bout men,' he said, ripping at her robe.

Fear made her react without thinking. She reached for the knife inside her fellala, the one that Cass had given her, and slashed at him.

Innis staggered back a few paces, surprised. Blood flowed from the wound.

But Marrat seized her, pinning her arms to her sides, forcing the knife from her hand.

'Aristo b-b-itch. Ginko-fucker.' Innis coughed. He kicked her in the stomach.

Mira crumpled over in Marrat's arms. The pain made her vomit up the food in her stomach.

'The bitch is sick, Innis,' Marrat complained. 'Let's dump her.'

Innis laughed, sounding a little loco. 'Better. Let's give the ginko-fucker to the ginkos.'

'How?'

'I know how to shut the fence down,' Innis whispered. He sounded excited.

Mira's heart pounded so loudly in her ears that his voice sounded distant. Then she felt his hands on her fellala, ripping at it.

'That's jus' stupid, Innis. Next thing the ginks'll be on us,' said Marrat.

'Only needs to be off for a snap. I'll switch it off; you shove her through. Ginks won't even know what's happened.'

'What if you turn it on too quick? What if you fry her?'

'What if . . .' Innis was smiling.

A wave of loathing swept through Mira. He didn't care if she lived or died. He had no thought for Vito's survival. He'd see her dead because of his stupid jealousy.

'Cass will know what you've done,' she whispered hoarsely. 'What will she think of her little fratella then?'

'Shut it, ginko-lover.' Innis slapped her mouth.

'Innis. Quash it.' Marrat was getting nervous.

'Juanita, Marrat. Remember Juanita.' Innis's reminder was an explicit threat.

'Yeah, Innis. I wasn't the only one. Remember that, too.'

Mira knew that her fate was being decided in the silence that fell between them. *Stand up to him, Marrat.*

'Amico?' said Innis in a more cajoling tone.

Marrat let out a long, troubled breath. 'Give her to the ginkos.'

No! Sagging back against Marrat, Mira kicked out at Innis.

Enraged, he threw himself at her, toppling the three of them to the ground.

Mira flung herself from side to side. *Help! Help!* Fear robbed her of breath. She couldn't shout, couldn't breathe at all. Stabbing pain where fingers dug into her throat. Choking dread. *Don't strangle me. No.*

Then the grip loosened. Weight peeled off her. Different hands touched her and a light shone into her eyes. Rast peered down at her. 'You alive, Baronessa?'

'Si,' Mira whispered. She heard Rast's sharp, relieved breath and felt a vague surprise.

'Lock the prick up. Get her to the temporary infirmary in my building. Find Cass Mulravey and bring her to me,' ordered Rast.

Cass was sitting beside her, Mira knew. She could see her through half-closed eyes, as the woman read the infirmary log and bladder-fed Vito. Mira tried to swallow and coughed instead. She wished Cass would leave but she didn't have the energy to say so.

This time the korm was there as well. Mira wanted to say that she was well enough but that meant speaking aloud. Speaking to Cass. She'd rather sleep. *Why is Catchut guarding the door?*

Next time the world was sharper. So were the aches in Mira's throat and head. She lay still, orientating herself. *Innis. Rast. Cass.* She placed them in order of events.

'Mira?'

Slowly, painfully, she turned her head. Cass was in the same spot as before. This time Vito slept in her arms. The korm was there too, on a makeshift roost in the corner of the small room.

'Medic's pretty basic. Rast said a few more hours with pain relief – no more. That's all she can spare.'

'What's wrong with me?' Mira rasped.

'She thinks you're on the right side of a broken skull. And there's heavy bruising on your neck where he tried . . . he tried . . .'

Silence.

'Speak it.'

'. . . Strangle you,' Cass whispered.

'Where is . . . he?' Mira couldn't say Innis's name.

'Rast has locked him and Marrat up. I'm so sorry, I feel responsible but—'

Yes, you are.

'—There are things about him you don't know . . .'

'And there are – things you don't know – as well. He would have killed me – he wanted to – push me through the fence to the Saqr. What would have happened to – Vito if he had?'

Shock registered on Cass's face. Mira had never seen her in such distress and she felt a moment's pity for the woman. Innis was a burden that she didn't deserve.

The korm stirred on its roost, its crest filling at the sight of Mira awake. It stood up and loomed over the bed. 'K^rm b^d. M^r^ h^rt.'

Mira held out a hand. 'Korm misses – Djeserit. I – understand.'

'M^ss M^r^ t^ ^f d^^d.'

Mira managed the smallest smile. 'Not – dead,' she whispered.

Vito woke and blinked, looking around in alarm. When he saw Mira he gave a little cry and reached out. Her heart contracted with pleasure and sorrow. *Am I all he has in the world?*

Cass laid him on the bed next to her. 'My brother's scared. We all are. And that Marrat is not the sort of friend . . .'

'It was not – Marrat's idea. Innis forced – him too. Blackmailed him. And I know what it is. So tell your fratella, if he comes near me or my – bambini again I'll make sure the whole of Araldis knows. Rast in particular.'

Cass faltered, confused. 'Wha-a-t do—'

Mira watched her distress intensify. 'I know it was – him. He caused the Juanita tunnel – collapse.'

Cass trembled violently and began to cry into her hands. 'I've protected him always. I always will. Promise me you won't speak a word of it outside this room.' Her voice was fierce, despite the tears.

'He caused people to die. He is a – criminal.' And Cass protected him. What did that make her? It made her nothing. Nobody cared about criminals in this world now. There were no Carabinere. No familia judges. No law. Suddenly Mira felt exhausted and depressed. She took Vito in her ams and turned the other way.

When Rast came to see her, Mira was dressed in her fellala, sipping sweetened water to soothe her throat.

'Enjoy the rest? Get up. I need the bed,' Rast said.

Mira eased herself to the side of the cot and stood. Someone had repaired the skin of her fellala where Innis had torn at it. She ran her hand over the patch. It seemed sound. 'How did you find me? I was almost . . .' She couldn't bring herself to say it.

Rast sat in the chair previously occupied by Cass and put her feet up on the bed. 'I've had you watched.'

'Perche?' Mira asked, startled.

'Not just you. Mulravey's lot. I had a feeling about them and it paid off, it seems. For you, leastways.' Rast tugged her white hair thoughtfully. 'You know I lost two of my crew in the Juanita tunnel collapse. I kinda took the whole thing personal. Really stuck in my gut that we couldn't find the killer.'

'Killer?' Mira's heart fluttered. Should she tell Rast what she suspected?

'Yeah. To my mind it wasn't an accident. We were all supposed to be down that tunnel . . . for various reasons. I pulled most of the team out at the last minute to quash a fight that had started up top in the wet mess. Left two down there on the job. When we investigated it turned out that there'd been no permission to blast in that area, and no blast clearance. It was damn obvious that the charges were set too close to the boundary of the underground. Apparently that sort of things's never

marianne de pierres   297

happened before. Never happened since. What's the odds of that, I wonder?'

'What does that have to do with the Mulraveys?'

'Maybe nothing. Maybe something. Sometimes you have to trust your gut instinct about people and other times you gotta ignore it. I haven't decided which camp they fall into.'

Mira opened her mouth but the words stuck in her throat. She had no evidence. No facts. Rast might have saved her life, but Rast was a mercenary. That made her as much an adversary as Innis. Mira fumbled with the bed cover to hide her indecision.

Rast watched her closely. 'Why don't you move up here with me? Be less crowded than the dorms.'

Mira dropped the cover in surprise. 'W-why would you suggest – that?'

'I like your voice. And your body.' Rast got up off the chair and sat close to Mira on the bed.

Mira closed her eyes. How desperately she wanted some privacy. Some space. Here with Rast she would not have to share ablutions or listen to the moans of women who were scared even as they slept.

But then she would be indebted to Rast and that was something she could tolerate less than the over-crowding or the intimate touch of another woman. Araldisian women did not exchange physical love with each other.

Mira stood up, drawing a deep breath. 'No.'

'You came for me.' Tears filled Scali's eyes again.

'Lower your voice, idios. I knew that if you were alive you would think of here.' Trin ignored the twist of his conscience. He would never tell Scali he'd thought only of saving himself and that he'd left Nathaniel Montforte behind for the same reason. *Never tell anyone.* Familia prized sacrifice and courage. Joe would be for ever indebted to him and that could be useful enough.

Trin pushed his friend back inside the office, locking the door. 'Malocchi is dead. I've just seen him at his table in the refectory.'

'I always wanted to sit there,' Scali said.

But Trin was distracted by the conversation on his shortcast.

'They're still in the building,' Genarro was shouting.

'Capitano. Capitano.'

'He's dead. Leave him and get out.' Genarro again.

Trin grabbed Joe Scali's arm. 'We must leave.'

Scali moved towards the door but Trin stopped him. He stepped across the office to the shelves and wrenched them away from the wall. The hole was still there.

'What's this?'

Trin kicked away his makeshift patch and peered into the gap between wall and mountainside. Rock had fallen, blocking the path to the light. He thrust his gloved hands in, tearing at the pile until he had created a space. He climbed into it and repeated his actions, scooping rocks back into the office. When there was enough space for them both he called Scali. 'Nobile. Follow me,' he said. 'I will pass the rock to you, and you drop it here like so.'

The bigger man hesitated. 'I cannot fit.'

Trin stifled his impatience and edged back to the hole. 'You have to.'

Joe shook his head. 'I will go the other way, through the building. I will look for Rantha.'

Trin reached for his hand and squeezed it. 'You saw the ginkos, Nobile?'

'Yes, for a moment before I ran. Great thick-crusted creatures with claws and many mouths. But they were slow. I could run past them.'

Trin tugged his hand fiercely. 'You are scared and not thinking. Theses ginkos are called Saqr. Their many mouths are lobes and inside them are needles. They herded everyone into the refectory and pierced their skulls and their eyes. Then they sucked the life from them.'

'Everyone?'

Trin nodded, panting. The narrow gap he had created squeezed his chest, making it hard to breathe.

'But you said Rantha-'

'I lied.' Trin knew how harsh his words were but cared only that they shook Joe from his paralysis.

A great sob broke from Scali.

Trin tugged his hand again. 'Now come, Nobile. Please.'

This time Scali climbed after him into the small space.

Trin shuffled sideways, scraping ahead with his gloves to clear the fallen rock, ignoring the pain of his compressed flesh and the panic of claustrophobia. His only thought now was to get back to Djeserit.

Sole

little creatures| juices juices
call'm hormone|flowing flowing
cause'm|deeds deeds
secrets <luscious luscious>
mak'm progress| little creatures
use'm|hormone hormone

TEKTON

Tekton stepped energetically from his immersion bath, his free-mind filled with a sense of prescience. Beneath it his logic-mind flowed with its usual lava of inexorable reason. The tension between the two left him aroused. He turned to the Araldisian diplomat without bothering to cover his body.

Her skin heated. He sensed the rise in her body temperature, bringing it closer to something he might want to touch. Un-Lostolian humanesques were so cold and slippery. Like fish. This one, though, was approaching her monthly fertile peak. She wore the signs like a banner.

This will help my negotiations.

Tekton stood patiently silent as his aides applied lotions to keep his skin from drying in the harsh Araldisian climate. The window of his guest chamber gave him an inspiring view of a harsh, red-barren territory, blemished by the clumsy workings of mining.

At the sight, his free-mind swamped his body with a rush of *akula*. It left him rigid-tight with pleasure.

The ambassador's embarrassment deepened.

'My apologies for any offence, Ambassadress Pellegrini. The sight of your beautiful planet excites my physiology. On Lostol it is not a thing we hide. It prevents much deception when you can see what excites a person.'

Marchella Pellegrini made a small choking sound.

Tekton felt a small irritation at being attended by a diplomat with such obviously limited experience.

But she is a Pellegrini, his logic-mind reverberated up through the current of *akula*.

She cleared her throat. 'God-Tekton, please call me Marchella. I have arranged a tour of the main equatorial mines for you. Our transport will depart shortly after breakfast.'

Tekton acknowledged her inaccurate use of his title with a gracious smile. How would a savage know that he wasn't – yet – a God? 'Will you be accompanying me . . . Marchella?'

'That would please mia fratella, God-Tekton.'

'But will it please *me*?' he teased, half serious.

Marchella stared through the window, putting distance between them. 'The variety of minerals on Araldis is due in part to its unusual geography. As you may be aware, Araldis has no polar land mass like most other inhabited planets. Large subduction plates collide at each pole, creating the maze of islands that sprinkle the breadth of each hemisphere, ending in the ranges that fringe the belted land mass on which we live and which we mine. Araldis's climate is extreme. While the polar waters are warm, due to the underwater volcanic activity, the islands are cool and wet. The Equatorial Belt, in the rain shadow of the ranges, is perennially hot and arid.'

'I have familiarised myself with Araldisian geography, Marchella Pellegrini,' said Tekton, feeling his *akula* quicken as she spoke.

The knowledge of the raw materials on this planet

stretched his arousal painfully. His free-mind rampaged through new designs and diagnostics for edifices that would use Araldis's resources, carefully storing them for sharing with his builder sycophant.

But he must be careful not to show his lusts. Archi-Tects were regarded with suspicion throughout the galaxy: their known avarice for raw materials was a delicate matter. And Tekton had only one purchase in mind. Something he must have. *Quixite*. Large amounts of it!

How amusing to think that this unassuming orb on the outer galactic arm would have what he so desired: this place of ridiculously crude architecture and primitive conditions. Even the mines, according to his moud, were a catastrophe of dangerous non-planning. Yet from the moment when Tekton had seen Araldis from the viewer on his space transport, his blood had thrummed in passionate chorus.

Now he must negotiate.

Delegating the job of ambassador to the Principe's sorella, Marchella, puzzled the second-Godhead. But he allowed the question to subside under the tide of his *akula*.

While his logic-mind puzzled, his free-mind cart-wheeled through rough sketches of buildings with nuance and flair. 'Please join me for a meal, Marchella Pellegrini.' Tekton modulated his voice seductively as he sat himself at a table near the window.

'Thank you, God-Tekton, but I have eaten already.'

'Then I will be offended.'

Marchella hesitated, unsure at the brevity of his response.

Tekton noticed the play of tension along her

musculo-skeletal frame, and admired the dense, compact look of her. Like a basement with load-bearing joists, Marchella looked like she could bear weight. Tekton found that alluring – imagining what he could build atop her.

'I need a guide through your foods.'

She stepped forward immediately, peering under serving covers.

'Please sit, Marchella. I may wear less clothing than you are used to, but I am quite harmless.'

Marchella seemed doubtful, but seated herself opposite. 'This is kranse bread. It is our most successful crop and is very high in protein. The eggs are quark, and have an unusually dry texture – again, high in protein. The sea cucumbers are crisp. The roe is from the Tourmaline Islands and may be saltier than you are used to. I recommend that you drink it with wine.'

At her gesture Tekton took a minute mouthful of roe, followed by a swallow of the frothy red liquid served in a crude glass decanter. He must remember to bring his own dining accoutrements on outworld visits, he told himself.

The wine, surprisingly, was sweetly palatable.

Marchella warmed at his expression of pleasure.

'Araldisian Reds are our most famous export, after our minerals, God-Tekton. We have numerous varieties. Though the grapes are grown in climate control, the Araldisian soil that nourishes them makes for a piquant flavour.'

'Please join me, Marchella.'

Marchella nodded and sipped heartily from the glass

that his moud proffered her. The red fluid spilled from one corner of her mouth.

Tekton was amused by her indelicacy. If Marchella Pellegrini was indeed typical of her world, then Araldisian women were some of the most primitive he had encountered, despite their pretensions to nobility. Again his *akula* throbbed. It somehow seemed in keeping with the rawness of the planet.

He allowed the wine to relax him, enjoying the heightened glow it brought to Marchella's crimson skin. He sent a direct logic-mind instruction to his moud. *Make sure we have wine for the tour.*

After dining, they left the embassy in a small liveried AiV, peeling away from the landing docks cut into the imposingly violet ranges. By the time they had skimmed low to a more intimate viewing height, Marchella had shared the full decanter of wine with him. She began to lose her reserve, enthusiastically pointing out the more significant landmarks.

They drank steadily through several carafes, until Tekton judged her to have completely relaxed her guard.

'And what of your family's operations, Marchella?'

She gestured at the AiV pilot to sweep lower over a large scar in the ground. 'Below is Pellegrini A, and to the south, Pellegrini B. Each produces 60,000 tonnes of ore per thirty-hour day. The ore is conveyored back to Dockside and stockpiled. The Pellegrini conveyors are some of the longest known. The mining belt has the perfect geography and climate for our conveyors, flat and hot – no frost to damage the machinery. Subsidiary feeders from the smaller mines join the main conveyor all the way along.'

'The process is very primitive.'

Marchella sighed. 'Yes, but it works. Our society uses some gro-technology to maintain its infrastructure but we found it to be too expensive on the mining scale. We are still a young planet.'

'And youth is so seductive, my dear. What of the non-Pellegrini mines?'

'They use land barges to transport their ore, or rent space on the conveyors.'

'So indeed your family has the monopoly?'

Tekton's provocation caused Marchella no embarrassment. 'The Cipriano Clan purchased Araldis after seeing the assay reports from the first exploration ships in this area. The Pellegrinis are the most powerful of the Araldis Ciprianos, the royal family. It is . . . *our* planet.'

'And what would it take for me to convince you that an exclusive minerals contract with me would be in the interest of the Pellegrinis' great name?'

'Orion lucre,' Marchella said quickly and bluntly.

We have her! Tekton's free-mind sang joyously, drunk on the proximity of the minerals and the unbridling effect of the wine. 'That is something I am in a position to offer.'

'What minerals do you want?'

'Only one little mine, Marchella. It is named Juanita, I believe.'

'Oh?'

'The one that produces a quantity of quixite.'

Marchella nodded thoughtfully. 'Our financiers will negotiate with you on that issue, God-Tekton. But, if you'll pardon my frankness, there are others bidding for the same alloy.'

'May I enquire who that may be?'

'You know that I cannot disclose who bids against you.'

Tekton inclined his head, his logic-mind running lists of possible competitors. Or perhaps there were none. Perhaps she had more negotiating finesse than he thought. 'Is there nothing that might convince you to short-cut this . . . this . . . bargaining?'

'Unlikely.' Marchella shook her head, showering him with the musky perfume of her velum. 'Though there is one small thing that would gain you favour in the bidding.'

Tekton's arousal became painful again. Marchella was indeed much less naive than he thought. Desire began to agitate the waters of his *akula*. He reclined into the envelope of his seat, giving her the full benefit of his arousal.

'Which would be?'

'You are tyro to the Sole Entity?'

'Yes.'

'I . . . that is, *we* want one of our familia to be admitted to Belle-Monde to undergo testing by the Entity.'

Tekton hid his surprise: such ambition for a backwater family with no scholarship. 'But only the very brilliant are chosen.'

'And you do not think there could be one so brilliant among us Latinos?'

'No need to take offence, ambassadress.'

'No offence taken, God-Tekton. But this point would be, in brutal parlance, a deal-breaker.'

Tekton's minds streamed alongside each other, considering her request. Perhaps his influence stretched far enough to give Marchella what she was asking for. If it meant he could get what he wanted, Tekton would do almost anything.

Unconsciously he stroked himself, exhilarated. Araldis called to him. He wanted to land the AiV and rub the dirt on his skin, taste it in his mouth. He wanted to ingest this planet and build from its lifeblood the greatest-ever structures. 'Then perhaps it could be arranged, Marchella, once the terms of export are agreed. Do you have one person in mind?'

Her expression softened – a peculiar juxtaposition in her square, pragmatic face. 'I do.'

Marchella's words resonated deep inside him as though significant in the scheme of things. Tekton pondered them and his future. 'Then I would say we are *close* to a deal.'

He reached out a hand to touch her. The texture of Marchella's skin on his felt rough in comparison to that of a Lostolian female – and yet not unpleasant. He smelled the light perspiration on her brow, could feel the minerals she sweated from her skin.

She withdrew from his grasp and he felt an instant loss.

'God-Tekton?' she said.

'There is one other thing I would also have, which would be, to use your words, a deal-breaker.'

'Si?' Marchella gave him a look of earnest enquiry.

With the confidence of one used to getting his own way, Tekton reached for her, running his tongue along the side of her face, tasting the bitterness of iron and the tang of copper. He then shuddered into a seated position and pulled her down to him. With her face pushed to his thighs, he sent his logic-mind diving under the sea of his *akula* and began building magnificent cathedrals in his free-mind.

MIRA

Mesquite was folding a pile of underliners when Mira returned to the dorm. She spared no moment for courtesy. 'What did I tell you, Mira Fedor?'

Mira avoided the older woman's gaze. 'I had a weapon – a knife – but no knowledge of how to use it. I do not wish that to happen again. I want the other familia women to understand how to defend themselves. Can you call them together?'

'Si. But how do you think you will persuade them?'

Mira unwound the neck-folds of her fellala. The dark bruising was a stark contrast against her vivid cerise skin. 'I will show them this.'

Mesquite swallowed hard, blinking tears from her eyes. 'I will set up the meeting for tonight, here. But remember this: you are not the first person to be bruised by a man, Mira Fedor. Some will not care about your plight.'

After the mid-evening meal sittings, most of Ipo's women packed into Mesquite's dorm, sitting on the floor where they could, or standing and leaning against the walls. Mira stayed on the opposite side of the room to Cass. She couldn't find it in her to relinquish her anger. Innis had tried to kill her and she held Cass in part responsible for her fratella's actions.

Mesquite stood in the centre of the room and called for quiet. But the women had their own ideas.

'When's this gonna end, Mesquite? We're low on detergents. Soon we'll be washing by hand. It'll be more damn primitive than the early days,' called out a tall, thin woman.

'What about the food?' another said. 'It can't last. We should fight the ginkos, or we'll starve.'

Nods from many.

Mira watched them, trying to sense their mood. They were mostly humanesque, with a small proportion of lower-caste familia: Galiottos, Cabones and Genarros. The familia women clustered together, distinguished by their traditional dress and their diffidence. They did not look comfortable crushed alongside the miners' wives and they held their bodies stiffly.

'It's not safe to be out walking on your own. These men are getting damn restless,' piped up another. 'This week I had two of my women attacked near the north-end dorm.'

Mira reached automatically to her throat. Now was the time. She threaded her way between the women to join Mesquite at the centre of the room. As she unwrapped the neck of her fellala and turned a slow circle, she could barely control her fluttering hands.

Those closest gasped. Others strained forward, unsure what it was she had revealed.

Mira glanced across to Cass and read the pain on her face. It seemed the smallest, meanest of retributions.

'Baronessa Fedor was attacked by a man a night ago. If the mercenary and her people had not come, she would have joined the many who have already gone to their graves,' said Mesquite.

Upturned faces regarded them both, waiting.

'I think we should take up weapons,' Mira said quietly.

The room stilled. Above all, she sensed Cass's surprise.

'You mean . . . fight?'

Mira couldn't see who had spoken but she answered anyway. 'We do not know what the Saqr want. We do not know how long this will last or what it will do to our world. I have to protect my – my 'bino and I have to protect myself. I have my wits but that is all. Knowing how to use a weapon may not save me – but then, it may.' She sat down again on the nearest bed. The short explanation had exhausted her.

Around her the conversation of the others buzzed. Some of the women were unimpressed – the miners' wives to whom weapons were no taboo. And yet, as Mira dropped her hands from her face to look around, she saw the flicker of something in the faces of the rest. As palpable as Mesquite's heavy breath, Mira felt their minds open to possibility.

'Who will teach us?' called the young woman who had minded Vito.

Her question prompted a range of expressions on the other women's faces: some puzzled, others disapproving. A handful looked keen – the younger ones, mainly. How easily youth married with change. *Thank Crux.*

Cass Mulravey's reaction fell somewhere in the middle. She was hesitant, Mira could tell. She stood to speak, commanding attention. 'You think it might save you. I think it might get you killed.'

'You're entitled to that thought, Cass Mulravey.' Mira heard the defensiveness in her answer. 'But you are the one who put a knife in my hand.'

Whispers followed this. Mira Fedor might be a native of Araldis, but she was also a crown aristo. Privately, many respected the gap between her and them.

Mesquite saw the way things were going and clapped her hands. 'Well, I believe her to be right. What happens if all the men are killed? What happens if we are the only ones left? Who will save the bambini?'

'The men will never agree to teach you,' said Cass.

Mira forced herself to her feet again. 'I will do the asking.'

'What difference will that make? Why would they listen to you?'

Mira waited a moment before she answered, allowing the tension to build. 'Because I may be your next Principessa.'

Her bold statement was met by calls of derision from many, until one of the familia women came and stood next to her. A ragazza younger than Mira but old enough to have children pushed the velum back from her face. Josefia. The one who had minded Vito. 'I am Josefia Genarro and I wish to learn.'

Mira looked at the other familia women. One by one they voiced their agreement. Her skin prickled with emotion.

Soon non-familia females joined them until over half the room had spoken up in support of Mira.

She took a deep, shaky breath. 'Come with me.'

Cass caught up with her as they walked through the daytime heat, past the town salon and the vehicle bay and on to the Men's Depot. The bay was filled with

TerVs, from the smallest all-terrain vehicles to the enormous land barges.

'I think you are mixing things up. You are choosing this because of what Innis has done to you. But that is different to the matter of the the Saqr,' said Cass.

Mira did not look at her as they kept pace with each other. 'You have great endurance, Cass Mulravey. I do not have that kind of strength. I must take other steps to protect myself.'

Cass seemed surprised. She sighed. 'Perhaps you are right. Perhaps fortitude is not the only way.'

Mira felt a fragile bond re-emerge between them. Despite Innis's attack, Cass Mulravey was a reasonable person.

They paused to watch the men taking turns to practise with e-m rifles under the tattered shade cloth at the back of the Depot. Faded targets stood at the far end of the range, while Catchut and several of Rast's people gave instruction from the benches at the other.

'Rast has the projectile rifles under lock and key so that they can't waste the ammunition,' whispered Cass in Mira's ear.

Mira nodded. It could not be said that Rast was a fool.

The men stopped when they saw the women and shouted coarse suggestions.

Mira quickly led their delegation inside before her nerve failed. The depot itself was a shabby gume filled with rough furniture and a makeshift bar. She walked directly to the largest, most crowded table.

A bank of curious stares followed them, some openly

hostile. Everyone knew that Mira was a crown aristo. Perhaps the only one left alive. That possibility was a knot inside her.

'We want to learn how to use your weapons,' Mira said.

Their laughter was vociferous and their dismissiveness offended her but she kept her expression calm. 'I nearly died because a man attacked me. What will happen when the Saqr come? I want a chance.'

'And who are you?' said a big man with a beard and a barrel chest.

'I am Mira Fedor.'

'Aaah, the pilot aristo.'

'It does not matter who I am. What matters is that when you are all dead, your children will be next.'

The big man slapped his chest. 'Well, I am Brusce, Mira Fedor, and no ginko's getting past me to my woman. Besides, giving a rifle to you means one less for a man. I know whose hands I would prefer it in.'

Mira glanced around the other faces. She saw curiosity in some. The fact that not all of them mirrored Brusce's arrogance gave her the courage to go on. 'You should be teaching your women everything you can,' she said.

'Who are you to be speaking for all these women? You aristos don't dirty your hands. Your don't lift a damn finger to do anything.'

'Hear her out,' said a wiry man to Brusce's left. 'I've seen her on the work detail.'

'Nothin' to hear.' Brusce thrust his finger at the women standing behind her. 'Now go back to your work and leave us to make the decisions.'

Some of the young women edged nervously towards the door but Mira did not move. 'Is that what you have told the mercenary?' she said. 'Isn't *she* a woman?'

A few of the men hooted and Brusce waved them quiet. He spat at Mira's foot. 'Mercenaries ain't real women and maybe you're not one either. Maybe we should find what's under that fine robe. You're sure damn skinny for an aristo.'

Mira trembled. Would he rape her? Would he kill her in front of this crowd? She watched the sweat on his forehead trickle to his eyebrows.

The silence became a thick, dangerous thing.

It was broken by the click of boots on the floor. A rifle butt thumped onto the table. Some of the men eased back but the big man stayed where he was.

'What's your name, cazzone?'

Rast. Mira felt faint with relief.

The big man leaned across the table, his fists clenched and threatening. 'Brusce is my name.'

'What's the problem, Brusce?'

'This loco aristo bitch wants to teach women to fight.'

'To protect themselves.' Mira choked the words out.

'That is our job,' he spat back at her.

'Quiet!' Rast thumped the rifle on the table again. She eyed Brusce. 'Have you ever been in a war before, son?'

The big man rocked the table with his clenched fingers as if he might pick it up and throw it.

Rast ignored him and sat down at it, one leg hooked over the other, the rifle laid casually across her knee.

From the corner of her eye Mira saw Catchut climb onto the bar.

'Well, I've been in four of them and there's one thing I've learned: there are no rules. When your life is threatened – whether you're 'esque or ginko – you're capable of anything. Fedor here might save your carcass one day and you'd be lucky, because *I'd* leave you to die,' said Rast.

Suddenly she dropped her feet to the floor, lifted her gun and shoved the muzzle into the soft part of Brusce's neck. 'Teach the women who want to learn.'

But Brusce clung to his belligerence. 'Piss on you, mercenary. This is our world and we would have defeated these ginko bastards if you had not interfered. You tell us we must wait. Waiting is for cowards and *women*.'

Rast's expression became so hard and so intent that Mira wanted to run from it.

Without warning she shot Brusce through the neck. His body flopped off his chair to the floor, spouting blood.

Mira sagged against the woman behind her, appalled. This was worse than seeing the 'bino who had fallen under the tracks of the barge. Too close. Brusce's blood was all over her.

Rast swivelled in a quick, tight arc. 'Anyone else like to suggest I am a coward?'

Catchut slipped the cover from his rifle and pointed meaningfully at the crowd. Their gasps told Mira that the gun was no ordinary weapon: around her she heard whispers and grunts of disbelief.

'I've said over and over that we need help to fight the Saqr. We wait until it comes. I'm not going to be responsible for a mass slaughter, though Crux knows why I care.' Rast pointed her rifle at the man closest to her. 'Now, you prehistoric pricks, teach these women to defend themselves.'

She grabbed Mira by the arm and strode out, pushing her ahead.

In the shade of the Depot the mercenary rounded on Mira, her fists clenched in frustration. 'What in Orion's arsehole did you think you were doing, going in there?'

'Why did you kill him?' whispered Mira, dazed.

'I mean, what do you think you're *doing*? This town is wound tight as a screw and you want to start a cultural revolution.'

'Why did you—?'

Rast took an impatient breath. 'I killed him because they need to know that I mean what I say. And because . . . he would have raped you to make his point. Men like that can't let things go.' She spat on the ground and thrust her blood-spattered rifle at Mira. 'You still want to learn to use this?'

For a moment Mira thought Rast meant to shoot her. 'W-we need a . . . a chance,' she stammered. 'That is all I want.'

'Then make sure you understand what that might mean.' Rast withdrew the rifle as Cass and Mesquite joined them, one on either side of Mira.

'She is right,' said Cass.

'Si, mercenary,' said Mesquite.

Rast eyed the three of them angrily. 'Well, Mira Fedor, I got you your chance. Use it.' Then, inexplicably, she laughed. She slapped her rifle into its magnetised sheath and strode off.

'Sure of herself, that one,' Mesquite said heavily. 'And brutal with it. I wouldn't like to sleep nights with her conscience.'

'When you've seen . . . lived . . . most things, then conscience fades,' said Cass wearily, as if she knew from experience.

'How will the men react to the killing?' Mira turned to them, sick in her stomach from the blood and the tension.

Mesquite shrugged. 'They'll either accept what she said, or they'll mutiny. Either way we still need to know how to protect ourselves.'

They began rifle training the next night, Mira and ten young women, with Cass and Mesquite. One of the teachers was the wiry man who had spoken up for her. She knew she should thank him but the words would not come. Gratefulness had deserted her.

In a few days their class grew to thirty.

They also began a nightly women's meeting, which Mesquite let them hold in her dorm.

'We should plan for ourselves,' Mesquite declared at the first meeting. 'Prepare for the worst and not rely on the men to save us. Cass Mulravey, you have a barge than can carry many?'

'The mercenary takes it to post her guards,' replied Cass.

'And between times?'

'It sits in the parking bay. My brother and his friend live in it.'

'Can they be persuaded to serve us when we need it?'

Cass nodded, keeping her gaze averted from Mira. Most knew that it was Cass Mulravey's brother who had assaulted Mira Fedor.

'Can he be trusted?' asked Josefia Genarro.

'He will do as I tell him,' Cass said stiffly.

'Will he truly, Cass Mulravey?' Josefia turned to Mesquite. 'And what of our own men? They are likely to harm us before they fight the Saqr. It is unsafe to walk at night – there are too many of them without women and the fear of waiting makes them erratic.'

'My man is not like that,' argued Cass.

'Then he is a rare one,' muttered an older woman.

Mesquite let their argument run back and forth until the heat left it. Then she took control again. 'Use your common sense and you will be safe. Stay away from the drunken ones, walk in groups. Mira Fedor knows the mercenary. She can seek help from her.' Mesquite looked to Mira.

'Why would Rast listen to me?' But even as she said the words, Mira knew the answer. Rast had already demonstrated the attraction she felt.

Mesquite did not bother to contradict her. 'If the Saqr come we must be ready. Collect your things from the dorms if there is time, then go to Mulravey's barge in groups – in numbers we are stronger, more threatening. Group leaders?'

'Mira Fedor,' called Josefia Genarro. 'She should be one.'

Mira gave Josefia a startled glance. She had not expected such a thing.

'You, Mesquite,' said another, older woman.

'Cass Mulravey.' Another.

Voices called more names until a vote was cast.

After the meeting dissolved, Mesquite moved among the women, answering their worries, calming them. When they had gone about their business, Mira followed her into the makeshift laundry that was lit only by a small solar torch.

Mesquite began to beat the dust from the clothes. The women's underliners were heavily stained with red dirt now that there were no soaps or sterilisers left.

'You share little about your past, Mesquite, but you think for everyone. Where are you from?' Mira asked.

'What might that mean, Baronessa?'

'The way you speak, your appearance . . . is it possible that you have ties to the familia?'

In the torchlight Mesquite's face was sombre. She stopped beating the clothes. 'I have a feeling it is not long now, Mira. The Saqr will find a way to get to us soon, and the women will need you to get them through this. Cass Mulravey is strong, but she has ties and customs that blind her. You can make her see things. She will *let* you make her see things.'

'What about you?'

Mesquite fumbled inside her clothes for her tobacco. She deftly rolled a smoke and lit it. The acrid smell filled Mira's lungs. 'I cannot see my future but I know about yours.'

'Who are you, Mesquite, that you can read my future?' Mira laughed.

Mesquite sighed heavily. 'A person who pays daily for the sins of her ancestors.' She inhaled deeply, then let the roll-up hang from her lip. The smoke curled up into her dark hair. 'When it happens, you run. I will hoard a little food in Cass's barge but there is not much to spare. You take as many of the women from this dorm as you can – and get out. Go to the Pablo mines south of Pellegrini B.'

'Why there?'

'Provisions have been made for this kind of... occurrence.' Mesquite hesitated as if she might share something more but the moment passed. She turned and began hanging more liners out. 'You must accept this and trust me.'

More questions sprang to Mira's lips but in the end Mesquite's steadfast self-possession silenced them all.

That night Mira went to the town salon to see Rast.

Catchut patted her down against the wall in the large room they had first been taken to.

Mira stood stiff against the contact, wishing it to be over.

'Nothing on you, but what about *in* you?' Catchut's smile was cruel.

Acid rose in Mira's throat – what did the mercenary mean? She took quick nervous sideways steps until she knocked into something – the weapon that had so intimidated the miners.

Catchut pounced on her, rescuing it from falling.

'What is it?' asked Mira. 'Why were they so scared of one rifle?'

Catchut moved the rifle to the table, placing it carefully in the middle. He raised an eyebrow in surprise. 'You aristos don't get out much, do you?'

Mira thought he might even laugh but the hint of humour died as his stare rested on the covered rifle.

'GRG. Gamma-ray. Best you go and see the Capo. Save your questions for her.'

Rast was in a smaller room that she was using for sleeping. She wore a soft grey underliner that showed the lines of her hardened muscles. Her combat hood and protecsuit were next to her feet.

Like Mira, her possessions were few – a spare underliner, some personal effects and a tube of cleaning gel. Parts of her rifle were spread across a low bureau in precise order. She selected a part and squeezed a small trail of gel onto it. 'How fare the warrior gentry?'

Mira ignored the sarcasm. She leaned wearily against the door – she'd worked in the hydro tents through the day and had taken her rostered turn in the laundry. Clothes were becoming a problem. Some of the liners in the protecsuits needed replacing and the familia who wore fellalas needed the skins repaired.

Rast saw her fatigue. 'I hear you've been getting your hands dirty, Baronessa' she said. 'You want to watch out, you'll be getting a reputation.'

'I suppose you would know about that,' Mira countered.

Silence fell between them, which Rast showed no interest in breaking. She carried on methodically cleaning her weapon.

Mira straightened her back and took a deep breath. 'I have come to ask you for guards on the dorms. The women are no longer safe.'

'Safe?' Rast's eyes narrowed and she shook her head. 'Can't do, Baronessa. I only have twenty people here that I can trust and I can't spare them to babysit.'

'Bodies are turning up around the town every

morning. There won't be anything left for the Saqr – we're killing ourselves.'

Rast's expression became unreadable. 'It happens like that. But we need to wait.'

'For who? What help will come here?'

Rast seemed about to answer but instead she put down a rifle part and came over to Mira. She ran a hand down Mira's arm. 'You've lost weight.'

'We all have,' Mira retorted, edging back.

'You look more real every day.'

'Real?' asked Mira, puzzled.

'I like the look of you here . . . and here . . .' Rast leaned over and caressed Mira's neck.

Mira stood absolutely still, like a hunted animal. 'The men think you are weak. They will do something whether you like it or not.'

Rast dropped her hand to her side. 'The Saqr don't fall down dead in front of ancient .44 Winchesters and electromagnetic pistols, Baronessa. Their skin is too tough.'

'What about your fancy rifle that everyone is frightened of?'

'Even with that we will be butchered if we fight them now.'

'The miners don't think so.'

'What do *you* think, Mira Fedor?' Rast asked softly. Her eyes gleamed with an intensity that made Mira want to curl up.

'I think we may starve to death. But before that we will kill each other. We are living on a diet of kranse and quark eggs. The high protein will send us all loco in the end anyway.'

'As I've said at the town meetings, I have scouts out. One of them, Latourn, has just located some surviving Carabinere. They will be here within days to assist us. If they can launch a counter-attack we shall stand a better chance.'

'And if not, one night you and yours will just disappear and leave us to our fate.'

Rast suddenly looked tired. She rubbed her eyes. 'I can't save all these people, Fedor. Not without help. But if I can save my crew, I will.'

'We have assailant craft on Mount Pell. If I could somehow get these I could come back here and assist you to break the impasse with an air attack.'

Rast gave a humourless grin. 'And what would your experience of this sort of thing be, Baronessa? A handful of virtual hours on a simulation programme? How do you think you might survive a journey to Pell? Do you think the Fleet is still intact? And if, by some miracle, you succeeded and got to them, would you come back? Wouldn't it be easier to just disappear?'

'I would never do that. Even a woman has honour.'

'Even a woman?' Rast narrowed her eyes. 'You might have made a soldier – but you would be a terrible mercenary.'

Mira straightened her shoulders. 'And you would disappoint as a Baronessa.'

Rast belly-laughed until her hood began to beep. She picked it up and slipped it on. 'Yeah.'

'Capo. An AiV's just flown in on the north-side perimeter. I think you should see who is in it.' Mira heard the voice as clearly as if she was wearing the hood herself.

Rast jumped to her feet, pulling her protecsuit on. 'No, you can't have a guard. Now get yourself back to the dorms.'

Mira reacted to being dismissed. 'If it is to do with the Saqr maybe I can help?'

Surprisingly, Rast didn't argue. 'Sure. If you keep up,' she said as she closed up her hood.

By the time Mira had sealed her velum and followed her from the building, Rast was reversing her TerV. Mira scrambled into the passenger seat as the mercenary leader started to weave between pedestrians before heading quickly to the northern perimeter.

Within moments Mira could feel the heat burning her skin even through the TerV's canopy. Her eye-display told her that her fellala needed re-skinning.

She would not be the only one with such a problem. And she had heard that the melanin boosters were running out as well. How long before people started dying from heatstroke?

'Are you sick, Baronessa?' Rast had pulled the TerV alongside the northern guard post and was staring at her.

'I'm due for a melanin booster.'

Rast took out her 'scope and trained it on the AiV that had landed some mesurs back on the other side of the laser fence. 'Well, I got some bad news for you there.'

Mira nodded. 'They are finished?'

'Yep.' Rast tapped the focus toggle. After a moment of intense scrutiny she swore in cold, hard words that brought more heat to Mira's body.

'What is it?'

Rast brushed her arm as she handed her the 'scope. 'See the 'esques? There's only one reason for them to be here.'

Mira placed the 'scope to her eyes, altering the focus. Her hands shook so much that the mechanism struggled to compensate. She braced herself against the door of the TerV and reset the eyepiece. 'What reason is that?'

'Killing.'

Mira swept the scope along the figures standing on the other side of the fence near a recently landed AiV – a dozen Saqr and two humanesques.

Jancz and Ilke.

TRIN

'Where would you have us go, Don Pellegrini? If Christian Montforte and Jus Malocchi are dead then what of Franco? Is it likely that you are now the Principe?'

The question came through the shortcast from Juno Genarro who was piloting the AiV that hovered on Trin's right wing. Trin sensed he was asking it for the benefit of the other Carabinere listening in.

Trin did not hesitate – he could not, if he were to take the lead. 'It is very likely,' he said gravely.

Are you dead, papa? He did not stop to probe his own feelings – they were too tangled. But he knew where they should go. 'My tia Marchella has stockpiled her mine with food. Pablo also has many subsidiary tunnels. We can withdraw underground to the south if necessary.' His voice sounded confident even though his mind was skittering through a thousand possible tragedies.

'What about the Fleet?' someone asked. 'You are Pilot First. We could use the Fleet's weapons to rid ourselves of these creatures.'

A strangling sensation rose in Trin. He would never admit to these men that he could not command the Fleet, that he was unable to fly the Insignia because its systems were too intuitive for him. 'If this invasion has been well planned then the Fleet will be gone: destroyed or sequestered. We could scout the Fleet base but it would be time wasted when we have injured who need medic. The Pablo mine will contain much of what we will need.'

Voices crowded the shortcast, trading opinions.

Trin let them debate for a few minutes before he cut across their talk. 'It will be this way. Juno Genarro will take one craft to Dockside to see if the Fleet survives. I will lead the others to the Pablo mine.'

There were no objections to his decision. Trin felt energised: these men were listening to him.

Genarro immediately altered his direction to Dockside while the three remaining AiVs set their course south, for Pablo.

They flew for several hours across the great red plains, spotting only occasional burned-out ground vehicles among the dust swirls and quivering mirages.

Trin switched to autopilot and made a show for his Carabinere passengers of closing his eyes, though his thoughts rebounded between Djeserit, the fate of his papa, and the extent of his resources. Four AiVs and forty-five men – three injured – did not make an army. *Are you dead, papa?*

'Principe?' Seb Malocchi roused him from his reverie. He gestured below.

Trin glanced out of his window. They had reached the beginning of the iron dunes outside Loisa where rocks jutted like rows of broken red teeth. 'Si?'

'Our visual scans are showing a TerV on one of the dunes. They are signalling for our help.'

'Search the lower frequencies.'

Seb sent his scanner flicking until he located an 'esque voice.

'—ed assistance. Repeat. Need assistance.'

Trin toggled the shortcast. 'This is the Araldis Carabinere. Identify yourself.'

'Thank fuck,' the voice said in a muffled aside. 'It's the Carabinere.' Then louder. 'My name is Latourn. I've been sent from Ipo to scout for help. The Saqr have surrounded the town. We got over three thousand 'esques trapped there. We've rigged a laser fence around from the town's power cells and a team of eighteen IH are holding everything together. How many men do you have? Do you have weapons?'

Interstellar Hire. 'What are IH doing on Araldis?' Trin demanded.

'The Principe hired us. We arrived a bare week ago.'

Trin sensed the men behind him glancing at each other. 'I know nothing of this,' he said.

'Can't help that, mate,' said Latourn dryly. 'Can you help us?'

'What do you propose?'

'Our Capo wants a distraction coming from behind them. She reckons we can get most out that way. Needs to be coordinated through her, though. We've got combat-com and one GRG. Things are getting desperate, though: food is short. The miners are fixing for a bloodbath, which wouldn't be so bad – if the town wasn't full of women and bambini.'

'She?'

'Our Capo is Rast Randall. Best IH in the business,' he added.

Trin took a moment to think. Why had papa hired mercenaries? Had he suspected that danger was imminent? 'We must collect some resources at one of our mines and then we will hasten to Ipo. Stay on this frequency. Give us two days.'

'The quicker the better – I'll tell the Capo that the cavalry are coming.'

'Carabinere.' Trin corrected Latourn humourlessly, and signed off.

They continued south but this time Trin returned to manual flight to distract himself from his hunger pains and his fears. Djeserit had not uttered a sound since Pell and he fought his compulsion to glance anxiously at her. Hovering over a ginko was not the way to keep the respect of these men he was leading.

As they descended towards the Pablo site, they flew over the giant excavation machinery at Pellegrini B, which stood inert and abandoned: vari-loaders, scrapers, and haulers, their paint blistering under the sun. Many, dust blowing from their half-full buckets, looked as if their operation had been suspended mid-action.

'Looks like everyone's deserted, Principe,' said Seb Malocchi.

A sensation of unease grew inside Trin. Was he the only one who knew of Pablo's food and medic stores?

They set down on the landing pad by the Pablo site office and spilled from the AiVs, gathering in the shade of two haulers. Joe Scali stood next to Trin like an anxious fratella. 'Bring the ginko, Nobile. You will have to carry her,' Trin whispered to him.

His friend nodded and returned to the AiV.

Better that he himself kept his distance from her,

Trin thought. 'Where is the entrance to the main shaft?' he asked.

'Behind the water tanks,' called an Ascanio. 'But there are only these two TerVs left. We will have to walk or do repeat trips.'

Trin glanced around. Apart from the gusting swirls of dust and the men's voices, the mine was unnaturally quiet and without movement. 'Together,' he said firmly. 'Use the TerVs to follow with the injured.'

Again there was no argument from the men.

They walked into the main tunnel minutes later. As the light faded behind them, Trin found himself breathing too frequently. Even though the tunnel was wide and the descent gentle, it was as if a weight of rock pressed down on him and the oxygen in the air had diminished.

They zigzagged downward along the road for an hour or so before they reached the bottom of the main shaft. The road opened out into a large cavern into which entry was blocked by a line of electric crawlers, diggers and spiders. The line was too perfect, too tight, as if the vehicles had been set there as a deliberate boundary.

'Wait,' Trin told the Carabinere.

He motioned Seb Malocchi to follow him as he climbed onto a giant track of one of the machines. Behind it, the cavern was pitch black.

Malocchi pressed a torch into his hand.

Trin shone it up to the rocky ceiling and then along and down one side.

'In front of us,' whispered Malocchi. 'Some movement, I think.'

Trin swung the light directly in front of him. Anxious faces peered back at him from the gloom. Hundreds of them.

'Don Pellegrini,' shouted a voice in relief. 'Thank Crux – it is the young Principe.'

MIRA

The Saqr broke through the fence before dawn.

There were just shouts at first: unintelligible noise that could have meant nothing more than another fight at one of the clubs.

Then, as Mira started awake, the shouts became hoarse but distinct words that filled her with a sick kind of fear.

'Fence's down!'

'Wake up. Wake up. They're through!'

'The Saqr are coming!'

Mira rolled from her bed and began pulling on her fellala. The korm woke a moment later and gave a loud screech. Across on the other side of the room Mesquite was shaking women awake, directing them to stay calm and collect their things. They were assembled in a handful of minutes, clutching their bambini and their meagre possessions.

Mira slipped Vito into a harness that Cass had fashioned from kranse stalks. She put her hand on the korm's forearm to quieten it down.

It blinked its large eyes.

'Stay near me,' Mira said, 'whatever happens.'

The alien stopped screeching and chittered.

Suddenly Mesquite was next to her. 'Cass will be waiting with her land barge. You take these women there. Go to the Pablo mine, south of Pellegrini B.'

'Perche?'

'Because it has many subsidiary tunnels that lead far south underground. With enough water you should make it nearly to the islands. If any of the Carabinere are alive they will go there as well – the smart ones. If Franco is dead, as they say he is, someone will have assumed leadership. Perhaps Jus Malocchi. Perhaps Trinder, my young nipote.'

'Nipote?' Mira wanted to shake her head to clear it for with every word she spoke Mesquite's voice had lost its standard 'esque accent and acquired something more cultured – more familia. 'Who are you?'

'I am Marchella Pellegrini,' she said simply.

Mira stared at Mesquite – Marchella – in astonishment. Of course – how could she not have seen it? 'B-but . . . aren't you coming?'

'There are five other dormitories in Ipo like this one, plus the women who have taken others into their homes and those who chose to stay with their men. I will get as many out as I can. These are your responsibility, Mira. Keep them together. The Saqr are less likely to attack a large group.' The woman gave her a rough push. 'Don't let me down, Faja Fedor's little sorella.' With a quick squeeze of her shoulder, Marchella disappeared.

Faja! There was no time to reflect on what she had learned as fifty or more expectant frightened faces turned to her.

She forced herself to speak. 'W-we will meet up with Cass Mulravey at the parking bay. She will have her barge waiting. But we must stay together. No matter whom you see that you know, *we must stay together*. Do you understand?'

The women nodded fearfully.

'We will walk four abreast. Stay close to the ones in front and behind: 'bini in the centre. I will lead. I want all those who have trained with me to take a position on the outside of the group.' Mira picked out one of the young familia women. 'Josefia, you come in the last line.'

Josefia Genarro nodded.

Mira addressed them all again. 'If you break away from the group you will become lost. Now . . . *Crux help us*.' The familia women crossed themselves.

Chaos met them outside. Men running in all directions, some armed with shovels and picks, others with rifles. The Saqr were heading towards the town centre, they said, and they shouted for the women to 'git back inside'.

But Mira ignored them, leading the group by the most direct route to the parking bay. She'd instructed the korm to take Vito and find Cass or Mesquite – Marchella – if she, Mira, was injured or killed.

'Stay close!' She shouted the words over and over as they moved forward but still some of the women panicked and broke away to join with others. A woman to her right fell as another group of women charged into them at an intersection.

The two groups dissolved into a milling crowd. 'Bini wailed as they became separated from their mamas.

'Stay close!' Mira screamed again. She ran along one side of the group, pushing them together.

Josefia Genarro added her voice to Mira's from the other side. 'We will make it,' Josefia cried. 'We will. Stay together.'

The women began to grab each other, interlinking arms, thrusting the 'bini back into the middle.

Mira ran to the front and urged them to follow her. The group lumbered forward again.

Rast drove past her, heading out of town, with Catchut at her back nursing the GRG. '*Fortuna!*' Rast shouted.

Or was it Mira's own cry? She no longer knew if she was speaking aloud. Her throat was dry with ragged breathing and her body was prickling hot and cold. On all sides now they were jostled – everyone seemed to be moving in the same direction towards the bay. Everybody wanted an escape vehicle. Some grabbed at the women, begging for help. Others attached themselves to the group, pulling Mira's people back as they attempted to keep up.

Mira stumbled over broken packing crates of food that had fallen from the back of a TerV. She snatched up a jagged shard of crate and waved it aloft so that the women could see. Some of them stooped to arm themselves, causing the group to spread dangerously.

'No. No. Stay together,' Mira cried.

But they did not listen.

Panic began to overtake Mira's purpose. *Will Cass wait for us? What if Innis has taken the barge? What if the Saqr are already at the parking bay?* Her fear mounted. Marchella Pellegrini had asked her to do the impossible – save these women from the Saqr. *I cannot save anyone.*

A TerV passed them, blaring its horn, and she felt an impulse to throw herself under it. She stepped towards it.

Josefia called after her. The korm screeched. Sheets of dust sprayed from the TerV as it braked to avoid her. None of it meant anything until Mesquite's voice pierced the confusion. '*Vito!*' she roared as she led another group of women in from a side road, carrying a rifle.

Vito! Vito! The 'bino was on her back. Panic had made her forget him. Instantly Mira threw herself sideways to avoid the grinding metal tracks. Vito bawled as she landed heavily on her side, trapping one of his legs.

Marchella ran to her and dragged her to her feet, gripping her arm with strong, unforgiving fingers. 'Think of the women,' she whispered fiercely. 'Think of Vito.'

Mira reached behind, cupping Vito's leg, feeling for breaks. He gave little grunts of discomfort but no hurt-animal cry. 'I-I . . .'

But Marchella pushed her back towards the women.

They huddled around her and Marchella, drawn back together.

They would think she had not seen the TerV. They would not know what she had intended. Only Marchella knew . . .

Marchella raised her voice and her fist. 'The barge is close. We will survive! We will survive!'

In a moment they joined with her, chanting the words as she led all of them around the final corner.

Ahead, between them and the parking bay, ten or more Saqr clustered around a TerV. Some crawled, others wavered awkwardly in an upright stance as if they had just hatched from their globes.

Ilke, Jancz's pilot, stood among them, puncturing their chitin with hypodarts from a large pistol. She wore no protecsuit and her stocky Balol shape and long spines were unmistakable.

'What is it? What is the Balol injecting them with?' asked a woman behind her.

Marchella shook her head, then turned to Mira. Pulling her velum aside, she stared into Mira's velum. Her eyes were bloodshot and ferocious. 'There is a name you must remember. It is Tekton.'

Mira nodded, confused.

'Say it. Say the name.'

'Tekton,' said Mira.

'He owes me a debt. He owes this world a debt. Go to him and free our women. Now lead them around the Saqr and DO NOT STOP.'

'Marchella—'

But she had already lifted her rifle and turned towards the Saqr.

Mira felt another intense surge of desperation. A mesur away she saw Cass standing on the back of the barge's doorbridge. 'There!' She pointed to the women.

Several of the Saqr changed direction away from Marchella towards Mira and the women. Kristo fired on them from the top of the barge as the women raced over the last stretch.

Cass and Thomaas helped them inside. The barge was already crowded with women and 'bini from another dorm.

Mira was the last to get there. She grasped Cass with blood-slick hands. 'We have to wait for Marchella.'

'Who?'

Mira struggled to recall her other name. 'M-Mesquite.'

Cass pointed across the dust of the parking bay. Several 'esque bodies lay sprawled in the awkward angles of death. The Saqr were bent over them, mouth-needles prodding their flesh. 'She fired on them. I didn't see what happened but we have to go now. Medic is strapped to the inside of the hatch.' She slapped the doorbridge mechanism and it began to close.

Mira scrambled to get down. 'No—'

But Cass shoved her hard off balance into the mass of bodies. Before Mira could recover the door had clicked into place.

Mira's flight to Ipo paled beside the flight out. The suffocating dark, the smell of bodies crushed together so tightly that breathing was difficult. And the noise: the agonised cries of the injured women and 'bini, the faint whine of the barge's motor, the squealing Saqr rage as their prey escaped.

Bodies thumped against the barge's canopy, climbing the outside. The barge began to slew back and forth. Then the external noises stopped abruptly. Mira's thoughts flashed to the ragazzo in Loisa who had fallen under the tracks. Who had just died?

The barge rumbled for an interminable time before she could shake the numbing horror from her mind. She tried to think of what Faja would do. Or Marchella. What would be practical? Useful?

She folded back her velum and touched the woman next to her. 'There is a medi-pack on the door. Can you help me?'

The woman took Vito from her and leaned hard

against the next female, giving Mira space to uncramp her legs. She grasped for finger holds on the wall as she stood up and pulled the pack free. Hands reached out to steady her as she sank back. The barge whined on and weapon fire started up again. She raised her voice above it.

'Pass the word to shuffle the worst-injured to me,' she said.

The instruction echoed into the depths of the barge. While some protested that it was too cramped, others began the process of shuffling bodies around.

'Is anyone trained in medico?' Mira asked.

No one spoke up but a woman close to her passed an injured body across. 'It's my daughter. Please see to her first.'

'What is her name?' Mira asked.

'Davina. The things . . . they clawed her head. Save her, Baronessa Fedor.'

Mira started. 'You know me?'

'Si. Most do.'

Davina moaned and twitched.

Mira stripped off her gloves and felt carefully over the child's head. Blood trickled from wounds. *Nothing serious*, she thought. Then, as she moved her unsteady fingers down one side of the ragazza's skull, her finger dipped into a warm, sticky hollow. Mira's heart faltered. 'I need light!' Hysteria made her voice sound sharp. She did not want to see the injury. She did not want to stare at death.

The child moaned and her arms spasmed.

Mira fumbled blindly in the pack for a skin adhesive and antibiotics. As she sprayed the synthetic membrane over the fracture the child convulsed and went still. *Too late*. And now she had wasted precious medic. Mira found herself clutching the small body, wishing that she could peel the adhesive off. She made herself let go, shocked by the callousness of her own thoughts.

'Davina is dead,' she said flatly. 'Who is alive?'

As the barge lumbered on, she blocked out the moans from Davina's mother as she clutched her ragazza's body.

Other injured people were passed to her and she laboured on, doing what little she could to help them.

When the barge finally stopped, Mira was drifting, no longer sure if the darkness before her eyes was the crowded barge or a state of waking sleep.

Cass opened the doorbridge and peered in. 'The Saqr stayed in Ipo. We're on our own now and Kristo has found us a water station.'

Water. Fresh water.

A small cheer went up and Mira's spirits lifted. The women surged down the doorbridge. When the last of them was out, Cass peered in again.

'Fedor?'

Mira crawled out and blinked at the light.

Cass recoiled. 'Crux. Look at you.'

Mira's fellala was dirty and blood-soaked and flecks of human tissue had dried between her fingers and under her nails. 'I couldn't do anything for her.'

'Who?' Cass herself was covered with the white sap of Saqr blood. It had dried on her arms like peeling scabs.

Mira looked for the distraught mother carrying her dead ragazza among the crowd of women. 'They put a hole in her head. My fingers . . . my fingers touched . . . do you know what I thought?'

Cass waited in silence, letting her speak.

'I thought . . . I *wished* I had not wasted the antibiotic on her.'

Cass gripped Mira's shoulders and shook her a little. 'What you thought was practical, Mira. Practical is what we need.'

'Is it?' Mira said hoarsely. 'And afterwards . . . who will I be?'

Cass let go of her and looked at her squarely. 'Just who's guaranteeing an afterwards?'

The bore had been sunk at the base of a rocky dune, surrounded by a light scattering of rust-brown thorn bushes that survived on the hint of spilled underground water. From the top of the dune it could be seen that the plains stretched all around, bare and red. Heat shimmers distorted the horizon and Ipo might have been on another world – there was no sign of it, nor of anything else.

Cass asked Josefia to find women to keep watch from the roof of the barge while she and Marrat unloaded the little stockpile of food that Marchella had insisted they should hoard. They began dividing the kranse into bite-size sections and laying it out on the flat housing of the bore. The able-bodied women queued to wash and drink at the small trough, scaring away the spiny lizard-brown checclias lurking around the pump.

Mira took her place in the line.

'Shame we can't eat 'em,' muttered the woman ahead

of her. 'Only meat in these Crux-forsaken plains and it's poisonous.'

'I have never seen so many,' Mira said. 'They were eradicated on Pell.'

'Yeah, I hear you had purrcocks and laba-deer. Only civilised animals for you aristos,' she jeered.

Mira wished she had not spoken. She waited in silence for her turn but sluicing the blood from her hands and fellala made her feel no less filthy. Afterwards, though, a peculiar and inexplicable vigour took hold of her. She sought out Marrat, who was checking the ammunition.

'Which implement will allow me to dig?' she asked abruptly.

Marrat gave her a curious look. 'Tool compartment sits above the tracks. Help yourself but make sure you put it back when you've finished.'

Mira located the box and wrenched it open. She selected a long-handled tool with a sharp metal end and walked a short distance from the barge into the thorn scrub.

Kristo followed her. 'What are you doing, Baronessa?'

'We can't take the dead with us when we move on.'

He glanced back towards the barge and the small row of lifeless bodies laid out underneath it. One was so much smaller than the rest. With a sigh he disappeared back to the barge and returned with another tool. 'You loosen the ground with the pick, then I'll shovel it away,' he instructed.

They worked together in silence. After a while Mira insisted that Kristo should take the pick and she shovelled inexpertly until the shallow hole was wide enough to hold the dead, and her underliner was sweat-soaked beyond absorption. Her arms trembled fiercely with the exertion and she had to stop.

'It's right to respect the dead,' said Kristo. 'You thought well.' His breathing rate had not altered with the digging. He was a strong man, Mira realised, and his few words lifted her spirit.

While he finished, Mira went to find Cass.

She was delving into the medico pack. 'Precious little here,' she grumbled.

'We should bury the dead now, before the midday heat. Kristo and I have prepared a grave.'

'You?'

Mira ignored her surprise. 'Waiting . . . will make it worse.'

Cass nodded, put down the pack and climbed the open doorbridge to address the women. 'We should bury our dead. Come.'

They assembled in an exhausted fashion along the sides of the single large grave. Kristo and Marrat laid the bodies next to each other. Davina's was last.

Davina's mama howled in sorrow and threw herself down among the bodies, pulling them apart from each other.

Cass, Kristo and Marrat – everyone – stared helplessly.

Only Mira reacted. She knelt down at the side of the grave and took the woman into her arms. 'What is it?'

The woman slumped against her, sobbing. 'You canna leave her on the edge. She'll be scared. She's just a 'bino.' She gripped Mira's velum, pleading for understanding.

Mira looked to Kristo.

He nodded and lifted Davina into the middle of the grave.

'Thank you,' the mother whispered, weeping quietly into her fingers.

Mira helped her up and away from the grave. They leaned against each other in the shadow of the barge, listening to Cass.

'Rest here in Araldis's soil, mia sorellas. We will all be together again, soon enough . . .'

They rested inside the barge and under the bore housing through the afternoon heat. At dusk, before the nightwinds sprang up, they ate small servings of kranse bread soaked in glutinous gravy.

Kristo and Marrat removed the barge's outer canopy and settled it on the ground, pegging it down. When all were fed they spread across it and slept.

Tiesha rose, casting a pale light. When Semantic joined her later for the brief minutes before Tiesha set, the sky would be almost as bright as daylight.

Cass stirred the men from where they sat near the trough to keep watch over them. Marrat and Kristo walked to opposite ends of the camp but Innis refused to get up.

'Why do they get to sleep?' he complained.

'Everyone will take their turn,' Cass said with tired patience. 'Tonight, though, these women need to rest.'

Mira listened to their conversation from where she lay on the edge of the canopy. She had not been able to settle, even though her body ached with fatigue. Vito slept next to the korm's roost, a frail bundle of bones that appeared barely to breathe. She could not bear to watch him. 'I will go.'

She climbed to her feet and went to a third point near the barge. As her eyes adjusted to the deeper dark, she could just make out the scrapings of the grave. She rubbed her fingers together, trying to rid herself of the lingering viscous feel of Davina's brain tissue.

Without warning, Cass appeared next to her. She handed the rifle to Mira. 'It is best that you have it. You or Kristo.' She did not have to say any more.

Cass turned and climbed up onto the barge's huge metal tracks, peering not at the graves but up at the night sky.

Mira shifted her own gaze upward to Tiesha, wishing she were there. Araldis's moon looked so serene.

'Where do you think we should go?' asked Cass quietly.

'Mar— Mesquite said we should head south of Pellegrini B, to the Pablo underground.'

'Back in Ipo you called her something else.'

Mira shrugged. 'Marchella Pellegrini, her real name. She had only just told me.'

They sat in silence while Cass digested the information. 'Franco's sister?'

'Si.'

Cass gave a low whistle. 'Why underground?'

Mira considered how to answer. Cass was no friend of the Pellegrinis, nor was she loyal to the familia, and Mira knew that Marchella would have had good reason for giving the directions she had. 'We will find out when we get there.'

'You would go there on faith?'

'Si.'

'And what if Franco's sister is wrong? Pellegrini B is over three hundred mesurs from here. If the winds stay down we might make it. Food is the main problem.'

'How many are we?'

'You brought forty-two. I had forty-six. Then there are the men.'

Forty-two. Marchella had given her charge of fifty. When their groups had mingled near the parking bay, it must have been closer to a hundred. *Forty-two out of a hundred.* 'Are there any other survivors?'

'Marrat is listening on shortcast for any news but we can't afford to use the cells for long at night.'

Silence fell between them again.

Mira's thoughts fell to food. The plains were devoid of most anything edible. The terrain ahead of them would be fine powdered dust, thorn scrub and, along the mapped roads, the occasional water bore. There would be no hunting for fresh meat, or collecting edible plants. Vito could have Mira's ration of bread but the korm would need meat.

'Go and sleep,' said Mira, suddenly tired. 'Or I will.'

Cass nodded and climbed stiffly down from the tracks. 'I'll make sure someone comes to relieve you. And I'll check Vito and the korm.'

'Vito needs more fluid,' said Mira.

Cass nodded again and disappeared.

Mira settled with her back against the barge and hunted through her mind for thoughts that might keep her awake. She settled eventually on the enigma of Marchella. If she truly was a Pellegrini then what had brought her to Ipo? Mira tried to recall all she knew of

the woman. Faja had called her the Villa Fedor's bene-
factress. Franco's sorella was known for her eccentric
ways. She had not been seen in Pell for some time. A
rift had occurred between her and the Principe – a rift
that would now never be mended.

Mira felt the familiar ache rise in her chest, the one
that told her how much she missed Faja. She pressed
her hand to the soreness.

'Baronessa?' Josefia woke Mira from a doze with a gentle
shake of her shoulder.

Mira blinked and peered around in the dark.
Semantic was high now but dawn was still hours away.
The winds blew hard and hot, sending drifts of dust
over the barge.

'Pardon, I—' Mira began.

But Josefia touched her arm. 'No matter, Baronessa
– it is quiet enough and I could not sleep. Davina's
mama cries and cries. What is happening to our world?
Why have these Saqr creatures come here? I want to
kill them all,' she said fiercely.

Mira wiped her sleeve across her facefilm and stood.
On awakening, the leaden feeling had returned to her
chest. She did not share Josefia's desire; death was not
on her mind. Only escape. She knew that she wanted
to leave Araldis for ever.

Josefia took the rifle from her. 'Thanks to you, I
know how to use this. First sight of them . . .' She
jerked the gun viciously.

Mira left Josefia to take a drink from the trough but
the young familia woman's words haunted her. Had she
been wrong to insist that they learned about weapons?

No, she told herself, *weapons by themselves do not make hate.*

She laid down the scoop and bent against the nightwinds to reach the canopy. Her fellala was barely cooling now and she wanted to strip its sodden weight from her, yet she knew hotwinds would rip all the moisture from her body in a matter of hours. Better that the garment stayed on her skin.

She searched for Vito among the sleeping bodies and found him in the crook of Cass's arm where she slept near Thomaas, her own bambini between them.

Mira did not have the heart to move him. Instead, she found a space next to the korm and settled herself on it. The alien roosted on the ground uneasily, jerking and chittering softly in its sleep. Of all of them, the korm was in the greatest danger of starvation. As she drifted off to sleep, Mira reproached herself for not paying closer attention to its needs. What could she find for it eat? Little enough lived on the plains . . . little lived.

They gathered to talk at dawn. Cass drew a map of their position in the dirt but the wind spun little spirals in it, distorting her lines. It had not dropped at daybreak like a normal nightwind.

'We've heard that the Pablo undergrounds near Pellegrini B will be safe but we have little food and water is scarce,' said Cass.

'How far?' a woman asked.

'Maybe three hundred mesurs. We have one compass only. The navigation aids must have been destroyed.'

'What about going to Dockside?' suggested someone else.

'The mercenary told us that it is the worst of all. Overrun by Saqr,' said Cass.

'What happens if the Pablo mine is not safe?'

Others voiced similar fears.

Mira climbed up onto the doorbridge. The hundred or less women and 'bini and the few men crowded in a semicircle around Cass. Despite having washed and eaten a little the night before, their faces looked as ragged as their protecsuits.

The korm roosted at the very back, near the trough, weak with hunger despite Mira's morning attempt to make an edible paste from thorn-scrub roots.

'What do you think, Baronessa?' called Josefia.

Mira shifted Vito's weight to her other arm. 'I swear we shall find help there. If we ration ourselves – one portion of food a day for the adults, two small portions for the children, we shall have enough to last four days at our present travelling speed.'

The group murmured among themselves.

'What about dust storms? We're in the season,' called a tall woman.

Mira looked into the distance. The wind was gusting abnormally, lifting the tattered trim of her fellala. If it turned to a storm, it was likely that most of them would perish long before they reached Pellegrini B. Long before they reached anywhere. Was that why the Saqr had not pursued them, she wondered? 'That is why we must decide and move on.'

'I want to go to Dockside. My family is there,' demanded the tall woman.

'What about Chalaine?' Marrat suggested.

Chalaine-Gema lay at the foot of the southern ranges.

Neither their food nor the barge would likely see them that distance. 'Perhaps. Yes. But not without more food. We would starve,' Mira said flatly. 'The Pablo mines have subsidiary tunnels that run for mesurs in that direction. We could travel underground. We must vote now. Pablo or Dockside?'

Only Marrat, the tall woman and three others voted against Pablo. Innis didn't vote at all. He sat apart from the meeting toying with a rifle.

Mira worried at his lack of interest. She also worried that the sudden fierce dryness in the back of her throat wasn't triggered by thirst. *Dust.*

Cass must have sensed it too for she added her voice to Mira's. 'Fill everything you can with water,' she told them all. 'We should move on.'

The women and 'bini packed tight into the barge again, leaving the side vents open for airflow. But within a few hours they were winding them shut.

They journeyed for two days in a pall of mounting red haze. At night they huddled on the canopy in the lee of the barge, stomachs sore from hunger, stale bread and dirty water. Few slept for the noise of coughing and the wind-howl. Some already struggled for each breath. With no storm filters to attach to their protec-suits Mira feared for them.

Unable to rest, she stood guard over the shadowy mass of bodies. Cass had told her it was pointless to set a watch but she could not sit there among the suffering.

'If the dust thickens much more the cells won't work.' Cass said quietly. She stood close enough for Mira to sense that she was crying.

Those worst affected should travel in the cabin, Mira thought, listening to the gasps. The filter in her velum was more efficient than those in many of the protec-suits and yet she still felt the tightness at her chest, could taste the dust with every breath.

Cass moved closer. 'Mira?'

'We must keep going.'

Cass lifted her arm in a gesture of helplessness. 'In this?'

A fierceness rose in Mira. 'Maybe the mine is closer than we think. Or maybe the dust storm will blow out tomorrow. Are you wishing us dead?'

The other woman stiffened and anger replaced her tears. She turned and walked away without replying.

Mira returned to watching and listening, straining to discern anything over the burning howl of the wind. She wondered if she'd said enough to provoke the other woman. If Cass lost belief, so would they all.

They travelled slowly the next day with the dust whip-ping screeds of gravel against the sides of the barge. Mira sat crammed against the doorbridge with Vito and the korm.

Innis was only a few bodies away from her; she could hear his voice. They'd argued when Mira had insisted to Cass that those with breathing difficulties should replace the men in the cabin. Marrat and Cass's man, Thomaas, had supported Innis. Only Kristo had backed Mira.

'The Baronessa is right. The environmentals in the cabin are better. They will help filter the dust,' he'd said. While they'd argued he'd disappeared inside the barge and returned, carrying a 'bino. Her breath had rattled and her neck had been corded with the effort of breathing.

Suddenly the others' argument had lost ground.

The child whimpered as she crawled inside the cabin.

'But I'm the driver,' Innis whined.

Mira felt gut-sick from having even to speak to him. 'And you take up enough space for two.'

'Who do you think you are to tell me what to do, Baronessa? Your brains would've been sucked dry by the Saqr if it weren't for us.'

Cass stood between them, unsure of what to say. Mira knew that she was still angry from the night before.

The tall outspoken woman, who Mira had learned was named Liesl, strode into the centre of their huddle. 'What's the hold-up? I might not want to go to the undergrounds but I surely don't want to stay here.'

Innis suddenly changed tack. 'I'll ride in the back,' he announced.

Mira watched, perplexed, as he disappeared around the back of the barge.

Cass shrugged. 'It's decided, then.'

They quickly transferred the worst cases into the cabin and Cass climbed behind the controls.

Now Mira sat pressed against the ramp with Kristo and Josefia next to her, wondering what had caused Innis's change of heart. She listened to the tone of his voice – his words were muffled – and realised it was punctuated by low, warm responses from Liesl.

* * *

Sometime during mid-afternoon the barge came to a sudden halt, rocking violently in the wind. Long moments passed and no one came to open the doorbridge.

'What is it?' Frightened voices clamoured for an explanation.

Kristo wound the latch on the small inset open and peered out. Thick dust blasted in, sending most of them into coughing fits.

'Can't – breathe out there,' he spluttered when he could speak.

Mira hugged Vito for a moment, then handed him to Josefia. 'I will go,' she shouted to Kristo over the roar. 'My – filter – better. Close – hatch. Knock – when – I return.'

Kristo nodded. 'Stay close – barge,' he shouted back as he boosted Mira through the hatch.

Outside, the sky had turned solid. Mira could see nothing through the hail of sand and grit that blasted past her. With her body halfway through the hatch she knew that she'd made a mistake. The wind tore her out and away from the side of the barge. Gasping for breath, she clawed at the ground to find a hold, digging her boots deep into the sand. Despite her velum, her eyes streamed. She closed them and took shallow breaths while she convinced herself that she wasn't suffocating. Her lungs felt as if they'd been coated with hot ash.

When Mira opened her eyes again she couldn't see the barge. She began to crawl in the direction where she thought it was. Pebbles bounced off her shoulders and back as she crawled forward, counting the number of her movements. After half a dozen in one direction, she reversed back to her starting point. A sound whipped past her – her name, she thought – but from where? She didn't have the breath to call back. Rotating through a quarter-turn she crawled in that direction.

No luck.

Panic took her easily now, tossing her heart around. She wanted to curl into a ball but logic told her that if she stayed still she was likely to be buried. Already she could feel a dirt mound building against her legs. The thought of being buried alive kept her trying her clockwise forays. Just short of the full circle her hand touched something hard – the barge's tracks. Relief was a sharp pain in her stomach.

Staying on her hands and knees, Mira crawled the length of the barge, clinging to the top of the tracks, until she reached the cabin. She reached upward, feeling for the door but before she could open it a thought stopped her – if she opened the door it might well be torn off altogether, and that would endanger those inside who were already suffering.

Recognising her folly, she dropped back to her knees and retraced her movements to the doorbridge.

The climb up the doorbridge taxed her muscles to the point of total exhaustion and Mira clung to the ladder without the strength left to bang on the inset. In a few moments she knew she would fall and there would be no fight left in her body to crawl back to the protection of the vehicle.

Then strong fingers grabbed her from above. Kristo was leaning out of the hatch, struggling against the storm to drag her in.

Mira reached for him as if he were . . . Insignia.

Sole

manifestspace

learn'm|learn'm|little creature
push'm push'm|more more
each'n versus each'n
watch'm alter <luscious luscious>
<LUSCIOUS>

MIRA

The storm blew out more quickly than it had started. The women stayed still, as if afraid of what might follow. Some sobbed, but most stayed silent, worn out from the exertion of breathing.

The doorbridge began to open but became jammed on the build-up of sand. 'It's over,' Cass called to them from the small opening. 'It's over but we shall have to dig the sand away.'

Innis was the first to move, pushing roughly over Mira and Vito to help Liesl out.

Kristo raised a hand to ward him off but Mira stopped him – she had no heart for such confrontations. She felt more concern for the korm who roosted next to her, barely moving.

The barge emptied slowly, two at a time, until only Mira and Josefia were left. Cass waited for them on the mound of sand.

Outside, the dust-filled air filtered the sting of the sunlight. Visibility had increased to several mesurs and Mira could see the squat outline of thorn bushes scattered along the base of the dune. 'Are we near water?' she asked, hopeful.

'Perhaps – I haven't looked yet. I couldn't open the door until the wind had dropped. Had to dig sand away from it, too.'

'Why did you stop?'

'Cells ran down when the storm got bad. One of the young ones . . . she . . . died in my arms.' Cass gave a raw, shuddering sound – something much deeper than a sob – and walked around the side of the barge.

Mira turned to Josefia. 'Everyone needs a ration of food and another drink.' She handed Vito to the young woman. 'Give him my bread but soak it in water first. Little pieces so he won't choke. We won't be able to move until the cells charge. Make sure that the rest understand to stay near the barge – the dust will take days to settle.'

Josefia nodded, calling others to help her.

'Kristo?' said Mira.

'Si, Baronessa.' He was hovering close behind her still.

'There's a . . . body in the cabin. Can you . . . bury her? Quietly.'

Kristo nodded and disappeared around the side.

Mira felt immeasurably grateful to him, not simply because he had pulled her inside the barge but because she did not have to explain herself to him. At some level, despite their differences, he saw things as she did. She had not experienced that before.

She found Cass crouching alongside the tracks, her hands on her knees, facefilm open. Even in the thick air, Mira could see that she had been sick, could smell it.

She stood behind Cass on trembling legs, unable to think of anything to say.

Eventually Cass straightened. Tears had left dirty tracks down her cheeks and chin. 'It was one of the older ones. Katia. Her face went—'

Mira held her hand up to forestall the explanation. She could not stand to hear it, no matter how much Cass needed to give it.

'How long until the cells are charged?' she said gently.

'A day, perhaps – it depends on the dust. If we take the canopy off, everyone can rest. We'll start again tomorrow.'

'The korm needs something to eat. I will search a little among the thorn bushes.'

Cass nodded, understanding. 'Take the pathfinder from the cabin. We won't be able to come looking for you if you get lost.'

Mira collected her rationed drink and checked on Vito. He grizzled as Josefia sat on the ground trying to feed him. Clear fluid ran from his nose and mixed with the dirt and spittle on his chin. He reached for Mira but she resisted picking him up. 'I must look for food for the korm, can you watch him?'

Josefia made an unhappy noise. 'I am so tired, Baronessa, and he is not my 'bino.'

'I'm sorry. I know. Please.'

Josefia nodded wearily. 'Do not be long.'

Mira threaded her way through bodies, looking for the korm. When she could not find it, she returned to the barge where she found Kristo replacing the shovel. 'Have you seen the korm?'

'She watched me bury the ragazza. I tried to get her to leave but . . .' He shrugged. 'She's probably still there.'

Mira had a sinking feeling. 'Where is the grave?'

Kristo pointed to the ridge in front of the barge.

Mira fetched the pathfinder from the cabin and walked in that direction. She found the korm scratching feebly at the grave, turning over the sand with which Kristo had covered the body.

'Korm?'

It whistled weakly but would not look at her. Even in the dull, dust-laden light Mira could see that its crest was flat and dry. Patches of fur had rubbed off and the blue skin was covered in small grey sores.

'S'ck,' it said after a time.

Mira took a step closer. She brushed caked dirt from its back with her glove. It flinched in pain. 'You cannot eat our dead. They will hate you for it. They might harm you. What can I find for you?'

The korm made a weak, swerving movement with its forearm. 'Ch'cl'.'

'Checclia? But they are poisonous.'

The korm shook its head.

'Then I will catch some.'

The korm stopped scraping at the grave and sank into the dust. It made a sound that frightened Mira – a dying sound. She ran back to the barge. The canopy was down and Cass sat near an edge with Thomaas, chewing slowly through the last of her pane. Near the doorbridge, some of the women had already begun digging the sand away with their hands.

'I need the rifle to hunt with; the korm must have food.'

Cass didn't argue, just nodded in Marrat's direction. He was on the opposite edge, close to where Innis lay with his hand on Liesel's thigh. Mira walked around to him, aware that people's gazes were on her. Most had their facefilms open and she could see their dully curious expressions. Would they care that the korm was dying?

'There might be checclia out after the storm. I need the rifle,' Mira said.

''Esques can't eat checclia,' Marrat objected. 'Stinkin', spittin' poisonous things.'

Mira lowered her voice. 'But korms can.'

He shook his head, scowling at her. 'Unlikely to hit a checclia with a rifle – waste of ammunition.'

'Please,' Mira begged.

'Innis—' Marrat called.

She grabbed his arm urgently. 'The korm will die if it does not eat. It has had nothing while we've all had *something*.'

Marrat became still, surprised at the contact.

'Have my pane ration,' Mira whispered. 'But let me use the rifle. We cannot travel today. Not until the dust has settled.'

Innis had sat up and was looking over at Marrat. 'Yeah?'

Please, no. Mira implored him with the pressure of her hand.

Marrat hesitated and waved Innis off. 'Nothin'.'

Innis gave them a wary look and lay down again next to Liesl.

Mira's relief was like a shot of kiante. 'Grazi.'

Marrat stood and walked Mira around the corner of the barge, out of sight. He handed her the rifle. 'You bring it back to me quietly. Don't want everyone knowin'. They won't understand about our deal.'

* * *

Over the next ridge Mira lost sight of the barge, though voices drifted out to her. She confirmed her pathfinder obsessively as she searched among the scant, stubborn thorn bushes.

On the Studium interactives she had seen the different shades of flora of other worlds, which the programs had told her were due to different pigments in the photosynthesis process. She tried to imagine living on a green world as she stared into Araldis's iron-stained reds and browns.

After climbing only a few ridges Mira's energy was spent. She sank wearily onto the sand, wondering how she would find the energy to return to the barge. They would not look for her, Cass had said. Her eyes hurt so much that she closed them for a while. The thoughts that came to her were filled with hopelessness. They had no more food. Pablo was days away and what would they find there? More of them would die before then, she knew. Had she been right to trust Marchella? If Trin's tia was with them now so much might be explained. And she would know how to bolster Cass. She would know how to bolster them all.

A tiny noise bought Mira out of her reverie. A lig had landed on the thorn bush closest to her. It rubbed the base of a thorn with its spiny abdomen, seeking moisture.

Her spirits lifted a little. Ligs might mean checclia. If she waited quietly . . . *aah* . . . a slight depression in the sand began to sink further a short distance from her outstretched legs. Slowly, with delicate, tasting care, a red-skinned checclia the size of her forearm burrowed up into the air.

Mira barely breathed as the lone creature eased its long body all the way out. It rested for a second, then collapsed its body into a tight coil. It sprang right up into a thorn bush, catching the lig in its feet. With precise, quick movements it curled, pressed the lig under its stomach flap and swallowed it whole. Then it dropped and rolled back into the well of sand.

Mira crawled forward on her stomach, propping the rifle against her shoulder. She sighted on the sand well the way she had been shown and waited – reflecting on how inhospitable Araldis was compared with other worlds. The fragile ecosytem of the plains would never sustain even the hardiest humanesques. The Latinos had produced all their protein from cuisine-culturers that had come on the original familia vieships. That was the one thing that the Cipriano habitat-developers had not cut corners on.

Mira's mouth watered involuntarily. Her stomach contracted with intense hunger pains. How must the korm feel, if her own body was so weak? She must not give up. Not yet.

She waited.

After a time more ligs buzzed in. Their wax scent was almost as strong as that of the Saqr.

The checclia ventured out again but as Mira moved the rifle to target it a cramp seized her leg and the animal disappeared as she writhed in pain.

The game of silence and patience continued between them until Mira's shoulder blades stung and her fingers became numb from holding her position. Her body refused to stay alert and she dozed, waking

with a start to find the checclia three-quarters of the
way out of its tunnel.

She jabbed her finger on the discharge button but
nothing happened.

The checclia sensed the movement and went
springing away.

Mira crawled onto her knees, weeping with frustration. The korm would die because she was so inept. She
took the rifle and swung it at the thorn bush in a storm
of fury. The spikes quivered but clung to the bush with
the same will that had defeated the dust storm.

'Leave your rifle. Move away from it.'

The sound of another voice was so unexpected that
Mira did just as it asked. 'It is malfunctioning,' she
said. The anger drained from her in an instant and she
turned around, unable to stifle a dry sob. 'I need food
for my korm. Please . . . help me.'

A ragazzo stood there, pointing an ancient rifle at
her. He stared at her, looking for something that would
identify where she'd come from.

Mira didn't care that he seemed nervous enough to
kill her because tiredness rose up in her like the wall
of dust that had just blasted the plains.

'Where's your korm? I don't see no one else.'

She couldn't answer. Her tongue felt swollen and
unnatural in her mouth, like a lump of unchewed food.

The ragazzo became agitated by her silence. 'Tell
me where the others are or I'll kill you.' He glanced
over his shoulder repeatedly. 'Where are you from? How
did you get here? You one of them?'

His questions ran together faster than Mira could
think, and standing had become much too difficult. She

felt her limbs begin to give way. Would he shoot her if she fell down?

'Stand still.' He lifted the rifle to his shoulder.

But Mira could not.

The rifle followed her movement.

'*Alt.*' Another voice.

A figure moved into Mira's dimming vision. 'Alt. I know her,' it said.

Mira tried to control the lolling of her head. It was hard to make sense of the blurring outlines. 'Djeserit?'

TRIN

Trin waited at the top of the Pablo mine, 'scoping the plains. He saw them when they were still mesurs away, a smudge on the dust-tinged horizon.

Djeserit had sent word ahead that she'd found Mira Fedor and a hundred or more Ipo refugees – women, mainly – alive but suffering from dehydration and hunger. After speaking with the Scalis and Cabones Trin had sent what water and food they could spare on the back of a TerV, enough to last them until the cells on their transporter regenned.

Now he watched the barge's progression with mixed emotions. Ipo had fallen to the Saqr before he could bring help. His world continued to disintegrate around him.

My world. Franco was dead, he was sure. Whether he approved of his son or not, the succession had passed to him. *Or the ruins of it*, thought Trin bitterly. For what had been left him? A ragged community of 'esques – more than half of them not even familia – and some uneducated ginkos.

When he had learned the proportion of ginkos hiding in the mine he had wanted to cast them out but knew he could not, not when his own woman was one.

Trin was pleased enough that Mira Fedor had survived. But what trouble would she bring with her? She was a Crown aristo and had certain rights in the eyes of others.

He had never expected to see her again, but this was not the first time he'd thought that about Mira Fedor.

Joe Scali stood next to him, straining to see into the distance with his naked eye.

Trin slipped the 'scope rig off and passed it to him.

'How will we feed them?' Scali asked.

'We cannot – for long – while we stay here.' Trin turned to his friend. 'You think we should fight the Saqr?'

'What choice is there, Principe? We will either starve or they will come for us. Perhaps our only advantage is to take the initiative.'

'We are not fighters.'

'We have to be. Or they will wipe us out.'

Trin stared into the distance. Joe Scali was right. They would be wiped out. He would never govern his world. Never have a true heir. Unless . . . 'I will wait below. Tell Djeserit to come to me.'

Trin sat in the one of the many niches along the main tunnel. In the last few days this one had become his and Djeserit's own.

'Mira is here. Don't you want to see her?' Djeserit stood at the opening.

He stood up and pulled her close to him.

She stroked his hair. 'You were worried about me?'

A shudder passed through his body. 'Your leg is still not healed. You must not go out again – I fear the Saqr are too close.'

'If I hadn't gone out, those women would be dead.'

Better them . . . he wanted to tell her. *Better anyone than you.*

Djeserit knelt on the thin film that they used for a bed, beckoning him. He sank down next to her, opening the front of her suit, roaming his hands across her body, examining her for further hurts. She smelled unwashed. Mixed with the naturally acrid scent of her skin, it both repulsed and attracted him, as everything about her did. Her skin felt hot. 'Your suit is not working properly.'

'None of them are. There are too many of us and not enough means to replenish them.'

She was right. They would not be able to stay here in Pablo much longer. Already the environmental converter was struggling to pump cooler air through and provide enough water for them all.

Djeserit sat up. 'Don't you want to see Mira?'

Now she was here, he did not. Trin did not want to hear her censure, her judgement of his decisions. He rolled away from Djeserit and pressed his fist into the rock wall until the physical pain brought unsheddable tears to his eyes. 'Si.'

The condition of Mira's group, even in the dim light of the main cavern, appalled Trin. Their suits were ragged and without exception they were weak and dehydrated. Joe Scali and Seb and Malocchi moved among them, organising food and lig water. Kranse bread and dates for those who could digest them; lig water for the others who had gone beyond that. They were low on medic already and there would be no help for the second group if they did not heal of their own accord.

Djeserit went to the korm and stroked its crest, encouraging it to swallow the meat proxy. Trin felt a stab of jealousy at the soft noises of pleasure she made.

A woman in the centre of the group climbed wearily to her feet.

Mira.

She helped someone next to her to stand up, a smaller, gaunter woman who was un-familia. They picked their way through the sprawling bodies towards him.

Trin didn't hold out his hand in welcome. She wouldn't take it, he knew.

'Baronessa. Do you have the strength to tell me what happened in Ipo?'

Mira glanced down to those sitting closest and he realised that she did not want others to hear what she had to say. 'Si.'

'Come.' He beckoned her to the side of the cavern where several TerVs sat.

Mira and the other woman followed him with painful slowness. He did not offer them his arm to lean on.

Djeserit joined them.

Panting, Mira sank into a seat and nibbled at her dates.

Trin waited for her to speak. With her hood down, her face looked thinner than it had ever looked before and the skin under her eyes was dark with strain.

She finished her mouthful and swallowed with difficulty. 'This is Cass Mulravey. She is the reason why we are alive. She and Marchella Pellegrini.'

Trin stared in astonishment. 'Tia Marchella?'

'Si. She is the one who told us to come here.'

'Eccentric, that one.' He remembered their dinner at the palazzo.

'Not eccentric. Clever and brave,' Mira corrected him. She put another date to her lips and sucked at it.

Trin sensed an indifference in her towards him that not even her exhaustion could explain. Something had changed in her.

He felt a sudden compulsion to apologise. To say that he was sorry about Loisa, to explain that he had panicked, and then that the decision had been taken out of his hands. But he had no wish to bare himself before the woman with the sharp eyes. He settled into the seat next to Mira. 'Tell me what happened.'

Mira closed her eyes for a long moment, summoning the energy, the clarity. 'In Loisa they broke down the gates at the Carabinere compound. I-I was lucky.' She stared straight at him. 'If you can call it that. I was able to help Cass and her familia repair one of the TerVs. We used it to get to Ipo.'

She paused, panting again – so fragile.

'How many familia survived with you?'

'A few Galiottos and Scali. More Cabone and Genarri.'

'Tia Marchella?'

'No,' said Mira quietly.

The woman called Cass Mulravey spoke up. 'The rest of us are teranu and inklan. Honest miners for the most. And there's a korm.'

Trin felt a rush of urgency. Mira Fedor was the only unrelated Crown aristo female left.

Djeserit's gaze rested on him, as if she could read his thoughts. 'It does not matter, Principe, *who* they are. Only that they are alive,' she said.

He smiled at her and nodded. 'Of course.'

This time it was Mira's eyes on him. Wary eyes that he could never deceive again.

'And Ipo?' he asked quickly.

'We were there for some days.' Mira looked at Cass Mulravey. 'Weeks, was it? There was a mercenary there who had devised a way to keep the Saqr out of the town. A laser enclosure, I think. Something happened at the end, though. They got through.' She closed her eyes, as if remembering it.

'Are you all that survived?'

Mira shrugged. 'What news do you have?'

'Dockside and Pell have been overrun. Malocchi is dead – I saw him. Franco is dead.' Trin did not mention Jilda. In truth, he did not know if his mother still lived – nor if he cared. 'We came here when we realised. Others had already thought to do the same. The tunnels run a long way south.'

'The dust storm stopped the Saqr. But they will come. We cannot stay here.'

'The Principe will lead us to safety, Baronessa,' said Djeserit.

Trin nodded. 'Rest now. I have more men returning tonight. We will make decisions tomorrow.'

Mira agreed.

Seb Malocchi approached them. 'We have beds for those who need it.'

Cass nodded her appreciation and followed him back to the group while Djeserit returned to the korm.

Mira climbed down stiffly from her seat. She stopped and looked up at him. 'And if I sleep, Trinder Pellegrini, will you and your Carabinere still be here in the morning?' she said softly. 'Or will you leave me to die – like before?'

Trin lay awake next to Djeserit, listening to her troubled dreams. The weight of her faith in him was as heavy as the Araldis rock between him and the sky. He longed to be outside and free of these tunnels. Every creak of the catoplasma struts, every minor rockfall, had become in his mind the footsteps of the Saqr or the prelude to a shaft collapse. He did not want to die underground. He did not want to die.

He sat up and eased away from Djeserit, leaning his back into the wall. Not eating tonight had been easy. There was little enough food to go around with the new influx of women and no one had noticed the Principe skip his ration.

Lig honey had been set aside for those too distrait to eat, and had been harder to acquire. Trin had been forced to take it from one of Mira's injured 'esque women.

Now, with difficulty, he put all thoughts from his mind and slipped into meditation. The trance took some time to get right. He had not practised it since he had come into his potency. It had seemed unnecessary.

As Trin struggled to find the exact inner route, he wondered if he had been foolish in neglecting the ritual. Familia males practised daily before their potency commenced, so that they had command of themselves when it burgeoned. Once the rush was on them, the lessons were never as well learned: the mastery never as complete.

In silent mime he began the fertility mantra. When he was satisfied that his body was prepared he took the borsa from inside his fellalo and removed from it a pliable strip. He carefully broke pieces from one end and chewed the dried plant in delicate bites.

Djeserit murmured in her sleep, calling his name. But Trin's mind had roamed to another place, and he could not answer.

In the main cavern Mira Fedor sat rocking the 'bino she had rescued from Villa Fedor, talking quietly with the woman Cass Mulravey. Trinder beckoned to her across the sleeping bodies.

She passed the 'bino to Cass and stood hesitantly, not trusting Trin: never trusting. After a moment she made her way over to him.

'I must speak with you alone. I have had word from my scouts,' he said.

'Why alone?'

'There are reasons that you will understand. Please, Baronessa. Mira?' He took a few steps toward a TerV.

Mira glanced back at Cass Mulravey, then followed him.

Trin drove them to the top, past the sentries and out into the nightwinds. Tiesha lit the unending pattern of the plains in either direction. When Semantic rose, the moments of brilliant twin moonlight would reveal the line where the silky shifting sand dunes changed to the hard rock ridges. Trin stared out to the horizon, to the row of flickering lights. He climbed down from the TerV and walked a distance from it, waiting for Mira to join him.

She did so reluctantly, her arms wrapped tight

around her. He wondered if she sensed something in him, or if her natural reticence had grown into a habitual suspicion.

'What are those lights?' she asked.

'My scouts tell me that Saqr are hunting the Ipo refugees. But I believe they are pursuing more than that. They are coming for these mines.'

'Then we must move on now,' Mira said, alarmed. 'How many can you transport?'

'Some – mainly your women as they are too weak to walk. We will follow the tunnels as far south as possible and then we must travel overland. I have only enough vehicles to transport fifty. Then your barge: another hundred. We have five hundred or more people spread through the shafts. I will pass the word along soon. When we reach the end we will bring the tunnels down behind us.'

'What makes you think that these people will do as you say?'

Trin turned to her, shocked. She had her velum sealed against the nightwinds and seemed impervious. 'Because I am the Principe and I command the Carabinere.'

'The Carabinere? A few tired men against an invasion? What if these people wish to go elsewhere?'

'There is no *elsewhere*. I have been to Pell and Dockside. I saw Malocchi with his brains sucked dry. I saw Rantha . . . Pell is dead.' Trin paused while he controlled an upwelling of emotion. 'Loisa and Ipo are lost.'

'What of the Fleet?'

'I sent a trusted man – a Genarro – to seek out its fate. He has reported it destroyed.'

'Insignia?' Mira cried.

'That is our secret – yours and mine. Insignia is hidden at the palazzo on the Tourmaline Islands, near the beach where . . . where . . .' It seemed so ridiculous now – that night on the beach and his fear of her. He would have liked to see her face now, to know if she felt the same.

'Thank Crux!' Mira breathed.

'Papa had some foresight after all.' Trin spoke as much to himself as to her.

'It is difficult to know everything about a person,' she proffered.

He wondered of whom she spoke. His tia Marchella, perhaps? 'There is one difficulty though. The royal lozenge is in my palazzo on Pell.'

Mira dropped her hands to her sides, her gloved fists curling. 'Why are you telling me this?'

'Because someone must go to the OLOSS worlds and tell them what has happened here. They will send forces to free us.'

'Will they listen? Will they care?'

Trin reached inside his fellalo and took a small data sponge from his borsa. 'Take this to them. It is the record of an interview, a trade negotiation with Marchella Pellegrini. I believe that this is the reason for the invasion. Have you heard of quixite?'

Mira shook her head.

'A Lostolian was here some time ago. He purchased all the exported material from a mine that produces a rare naturally occurring alloy of that name. The mine is owned by Franco's . . . concubine, Luna il Longa. Tia Marchella negotiated the deal. I believe this invasion is somehow connected to the deal that was struck.'

'What was the Lostolian's name?' Mira demanded.

'The name was blanked from the recording.'

She turned the data sponge over in her fingers. 'Marchella Pellegrini saved us in Ipo. She could not have caused this invasion.'

Trin felt none of the distress that showed in Mira's voice. He wanted to survive; he did not want to feel sorry for those lost. 'Yet this mine – her mine – was stockpiled with food and medic. A mere coincidence?'

'She is a clever woman: a woman with foresight.'

'Or maybe she is a scared woman? A woman of guilt?'

Mira made an impatient, unhappy noise.

Trin changed tactics. 'You are the only one who can fly Insignia, Mira Fedor. The only one who can take word of this atrocity to OLOSS.'

He saw her tremble. 'You would have stolen my Inborn Talent, Trin Pellegrini. Torn it from me and left me to drift into insanity. And yet now you ask me to rescue your world with it.'

'Your world as well, Mira. Your sorella's world. Your papa's world.'

Mira's trembling increased. 'Do not speak of Faja. Do not use my familia. I am no longer a ragazza like Djeserit who will worship your royalty.'

'Djeserit is not a ragazza, she is a woman.'

'If that is so then you have forced her to be so – you have stolen her youth from her. It is indecent, what you have done.'

Trin took an angry, impatient breath. Mira's forthright manner offended him even though he knew her for an eccentric. 'I have an AiV ready for you but you must leave now.'

'What of Vito?'

'He will stay here. Djeserit will care for him.'

'No,' Mira said. 'I will do nothing without the 'bino.' Her voice took on a cold, stiff quality that familia women used against their men.

'If you refuse to do this then we have no chance of survival,' Trin said.

'You would blackmail me?'

He stepped close to her. 'I would do far worse than that, Baronessa.' *And will. And will.*

Mira shrank from him, but her voice stayed firm. 'You cannot coerce me, Trinder Pellegrini!'

'And you *will not* fail me. Your Vito is my guarantee that you will go to OLOSS and make them listen – make them come.' Trin's voice rose to a near-shout. 'I swear that Pellegrinis will not lose this world to ginkos.'

Mira turned to run from him.

Trin saw her intention and raised his hand in a beckoning gesture. Vespa and Seb Malocchi appeared behind her, each seizing one of her arms.

She tried to pull away from them, but they held her fast. 'What is this, Trinder?'

'Listen,' he hissed. 'We will retreat to Chalaine-Gema. If the Saqr are there we will cross the southern range to the Islands and wait for help.'

'What else do you want?' Mira whispered. 'What does that dogged face you present to me mean?'

Trin hesitated one last moment. 'There is no manner in which I can make this less brutal, Mira. I have thought it through. You can resist or you can accept.'

'Accept what? To go to OLOSS?'

'No. That is decided already . . . I wish to make a bambino. Now. An heir.'

'Loco,' she whispered in horror.

'I am truly,' Trin agreed. 'But there *will* be another Pellegrini and he *will* be Cipriano. You are the only patrician blood left.' He reached into his borsa again and selected his last remaining bravura. As he slipped it under his tongue he began the silent release mantra that would trigger his fertility.

Seb and Vespa Malocchi wrestled Mira easily to the ground and held her there. One of them pushed the filthy hem of his fellalo into her mouth.

As Trin forced Mira's robe open, and himself inside her, it was, at last, his turn to cry.

MIRA

The AiV flew on autopilot out of Pablo. The dust had begun to settle and Mira watched dawn became a blazing mid-morning sun from a position of numb awareness. *What has he done? What has Trinder Pellegrini done?* She couldn't bear to think of it and yet her senses were ablaze with her violation.

Beneath her the Araldisian plains unfolded, their endless flowing rock and sand punctuated with dark flecks that might be bodies or wreckage. An invasion seemed impossible with so much earth and so few living things. So much that had happened seemed impossible.

Mira knew that she should be thinking ahead but the rhythm of the AiV's engines was like the comforting lull of her sorella's voice and a profound lethargy crept upon her. Without wishing for it or knowing what, she succumbed to a deeply exhausted sleep.

Mira woke again as the autopilot sensors detected smoke and arced sharply. It brought the present back to her with a jolt. *Trin. Vito. OLOSS. Insignia.* She forced herself awake this time. *Insignia.* Trin's confirmation that the biozoon had survived was the one coherent thought she could catch and hold. She would survive to be with her ship. She would survive to come back to Vito. She would survive to see Trin Pellegrini descend into his own hell.

She magnified the AiV's ground view and peered into the viuzzas of Loisa. The extent of the devastation assaulted her mind. Fires had eaten wide, dark furrows through the city and Saqr crawled in and out of villas, searching for bodies. She hoped that no one had stayed behind. She prayed those that were left were already dead.

As the AiV passed over the edge of the city and crossed the first of the iron ridges, Mira noticed a flurry of movement on the ground. With a sigh that was almost satisfaction, she released the autopilot and took the controls. The AiV felt light and responsive beneath her touch and sent a tiny surge of life through her. She had not flown an AiV since the Studium, and then only in clandestine circumstances. Yet the thrust and tilt felt so familiar.

She swung it around to make another pass of the area and studied the scanner. Some 'esques fended off Saqr from behind the cover of a wrecked AiV that had broken fins and fire damage. More Saqr approached from the ruins of Loisa, crawling across the hot ground like slugs.

The 'esques signalled frantically to Mira.

She circled once more, dropping her speed to hover above them. What she saw brought her mind fully to the moment. Her heart thumped so hard that it felt cramped in her chest.

Rast.

Mira engaged the fin rotors, curtailed the safety protocol and dropped the craft down behind the damaged AiV. It sent a whirlwind of grit pelting out but she kept the rotors spinning. Already she could see

Saqr cresting the dune. Rast would have to come quickly or—

A shout startled her and a bloodied face pressed against the cabinplex. Fists thumped it. Mira opened the door and Rast and two of her mercenaries scrambled in.

'Allez! Vai! Whatever the Crux it is, *go*!' Rast bellowed.

Mira assigned full power to the fin rotors so that the craft wouldn't drift as it lifted. Pummelled by grit and blasted by sand they rose into the air. She heard a crack and felt a sudden searing pain in her elbow but she didn't look. Not until they had gained enough altitude to be out of the Saqr's range. By then she had begun to feel sick.

'Your arm,' said Rast as she tumbled into the front passenger seat, still clutching her rifle.

Mira glanced down at her elbow. The hole was gaping and bloody. She reset the autopilot, pushed back from the controls and vomited down the side of her seat. It ran into a puddle around her feet.

'Pressure the wound,' Rast barked at her. 'You're losing one fuck of a lot of blood.'

Mira fumbled behind the seat for the medic kit. All the painkillers had been removed but the pseudo-skins were still there. She rolled back the sleeve of her fellala. The pain made her moan but as she placed the skin over the wound and watched it grow the agony receded a little. She lay back in her seat and waited for the dizziness to pass.

'If you've finished fussing over that scratch, Baronessa, pass the medikit to Catchut before Latourn bleeds to death.'

Mira felt her skin burn with embarrassment.

Catchut reached to take the kit from her and rifled through it. 'Nothing in it, Capo. A few skins, that's all.'

'Do what you can.' Rast turned to Mira. 'Can't think of anyone I've ever been gladder to see, Fedor.'

Mira did not think she could return the sentiment, and yet in some odd way it was good not be alone. 'What happened to you in Ipo, when the fence broke down?'

Rast dragged off her hood. Her short white hair was plastered to her skull and her pale skin was stained crimson with heat and dirt. 'It didn't break down. Someone interfered with it.'

Mira stared at her in shock. 'Who would do that?'

'Who would beat up one of their planet's last remaining royals and try to feed her to some gizzard-hungry ginko?' Rast shrugged. 'A loco.'

'But why?'

'Lucre, mebbe.'

'What did you do? I saw you drive past . . .'

'Same as everyone else – we got out. Only made it this far, though. Damn AiV dropped a middle rotor. If I was of a paranoid nature, I'd say someone fixed it to happen, seeing as it was my AiV.'

Innis. She was talking about Innis.

'I know what you're thinking but don't waste your time. It could have been him but it could have been anyone. I don't make many friends – I make memoirs.'

Mira thought of the man, Brusce, that Rast had killed outright. Rast was right. Mira reached out to disengage the autopilot and heard a tiny whirr. A muzzle pressed against the soft part of her neck.

'Before you touch that, tell me where you are going.'

Mira saw no reason to lie but she also saw no reason to tell Rast everything. 'I'm going to Pell. The Fleet's been destroyed but one ship is hidden. I will take it to OLOSS to plead for sentientarian help.'

'You're telling me there's a way off this dry rock?'

Mira nodded carefully.

Rast gave a short, joyous laugh and eased the rifle back onto her lap. 'Baronessa, it was a fine day, the day we met.'

Mira couldn't suppress a shudder as she took back manual control of the AiV. She did not, in any way at all, share Rast's sentiment.

They passed no air traffic the rest of the way to Pell, only TerVs carrying Saqr.

'Beats me how Jancz got so many of them in here without anyone noticing,' said Rast.

Mira swallowed nervously. 'Jancz?'

'The 'esque who joined the Saqr at Ipo. He's IH, like us. He was my capo in the Stain Wars. Afterwards he went chasing pots of gold in Latino Crux. I didn't like the fight. I choose my battles but Jancz's only god is his pocket,' she said.

'What did he do there?'

Rast shrugged. 'Latino Crux was about clan wars, wasn't it? One of your kind wanting to be dominant. I guess Janez just fought for whoever paid him the most.'

'But why would he bring Saqr here?'

Rast shrugged again. 'The only thing you can be sure of is that someone's paying him to wipe you Cips out.'

Mira's guilt throbbed harder than the pain in her arm. How could she have been so naive, so indifferent?

If she had alerted the Carabinere would the invasion have been thwarted?

Rast fell into a doze, her head lolling.

In the back of the AiV Catchut attempted to patch up Latourn's wounds. Mira caught snatches of his monologue over the thrum of the rotors. Despite having lost most of their team, Catchut was animated by the conflict. How could anyone relish such terror?

Suddenly Mira yearned for the Studium palazzo and the cool comfort of her room. She yearned to see Faja and drink wine with her. Things that she could never have again.

Those longings intermingled with something else that had begun to burn deep inside her. With the cold, logical part of her brain she understood why Trin had done what he had. But her being – her *self* – was outraged and sickened. Mira knew that she was carrying Trin Pellegrini's 'bino. And that, one day, she would dance on his regret.

JO-JO RASTEROVICH

Jo-Jo was having trouble putting the whole Hera death-contract thing behind him.

Even though the fop Tekton had stamped the agreement and Jo-Jo had duly disposed of the contract shell, he couldn't let go of the edginess. He vac'ed the remains just to be sure and then got so drunk that his HealthWatch took evasive maneouvres and brought him back from near-coma.

The edginess was his reward for still being alive. And the thing eating at him was the hunger for revenge. Payback. Vengeance. Retribution. Call it what you like. Jo-Jo was itching to kick fop arse.

He recognised, despite having a giant hangover, that he had to be clever about it. The contract had been perfectly legal and Tekton lived the life of a protected species on account of his being a god-in-waiting to the Entity. Jo-Jo could not go after Tekton with guns nor would he pay someone else to do the job.

No, this was personal.

So Jo-Jo tagged Tekton from Belle-Monde to Scolar and then on to the hick planet called Araldis.

Jo-Jo parked in one of Dowl's executive bays and got properly, bad-tempered sober. Then he collated everything he'd learned about Tekton.

When he got bored reviewing the information he

stretched his legs and hung out at the kafebars, listening to gossip. It confirmed most things he already knew and coloured in a few extra pictures. Araldis was run by inbred aristos who couldn't organise a jar of piss in a tavern.

Jo-Jo found the best bar tucked in a corner of the station that had a view of the res-shift zone and a pervasive smell of av-oil. He reset his HealthWatch to low sensitivity and idled away more hours brooding about Tekton. The fop had played the wrong guy for a sucker. Jo-Jo's rejuve was in good shape and he was rich enough not to have to do anything but plan.

Everything he'd dug up on Tekton reeked of privilege. There was the upper-class Lostolian family with over a thousand spare epidermises each in secure store (the average Lostolian tight-skin had three, maybe four). That meant the fop would probably be as long-lived as Jo-Jo himself, barring accidental death.

Then there was the brilliant academic career as an architect, distinguished by his contributions to the design of the Latour Moons Bridge and various other God-awful constructs. Jo-Jo thought of them as God-awful because he was an old-fashioned guy when it came to messing with the universe. That was the reason he'd become a minerals scout. All that artificial crap on the civilised worlds wasn't for him. Giant gas formations and meteorite-cratered worlds were his type of architecture – and were what God had intended.

The frontiers of space were Jo-Jo's idea of romance and beauty – or they had been. Since actually discovering God, though, he seemed to get a lump in his chest and a pain in his frontal lobe every time he tried to think through the wonders of space. It wasn't a good pain. Not a 'Shit-this-is-too-big-to-contemplate' pain: more like a 'Something's-not-right-and-I-can't-for-the-life-of-me-put-a-finger-on-it' pain.

It was as if something was trying to stop him thinking in a certain direction. Jo-Jo wasn't in the least given to superstition or speculation of the metaphysical kind but his trip to Belle-Monde had become a kind of blur. He remembered the details of being there but not why he'd actually gone there. If he didn't know better he'd think that substance abuse had finally wreaked its havoc.

No, he consoled himself, *not with* my *HealthWatch model*.

As Jo-Jo watched shifters resonate in and out of the station space he pondered the best way to crush a humanesque. Tekton had risked his reputation by using a Hera contract to get what he'd wanted. Then he'd forced Jo-Jo to search out a metal alloy that had the properties of liquid and the strength of steel.

What for?

Somehow the fop needed that to better his position on Belle-Mode. If Tekton lost his position, what did he have left? A failed career and shame to take home to Lostol.

Jo-Jo had already learned that returning to Lostol wasn't optimal for Tekton. It seemed that the fop had left back there a disgruntled Dean's daughter who was relying on him to come up big in the godhead stakes to save her pride. Tekton had wedded and bedded her to get to Belle-Monde and everyone knew it. The only way to make that less tawdry was for the fop to be a hit with the Entity – and then all would be well. The Dean's daughter could justify her choice of husband and Tekton could stay away as long as he damn well liked.

Tekton had narrowed his options before Jo-Jo had even got started on narrowing them for him. That notion gave Jo-Jo a shiver of excitement. Which got him looking around for a drinking buddy.

The only other humanesque in the bar was sitting next to a singularly ugly Balol female. It reminded Jo-Jo that his feet still hurt when he went barefoot. Last time he'd walked on a Balol female's back he'd ripped his tender soles on her spines. This one didn't look like the back-walking type. In fact, she looked as though she'd as soon rip his feet off than let him walk on her. That kind of turned him on too.

The humanesque, though, had a different kind of effect on him. He had antagonist stamped all over him – in not-so-obvious ways. Jo-Jo found himself caught somewhere between wary and randy. Ugly could make an 'esque as damn horny as beauty.

After a pathetically one-sided struggle Jo-Jo allowed his sexual urge to win and moved along the bar.

'Buy you and your mate a drink?'

The humanesque gave him a hooded look. 'My *mate* might eat you.'

'That's what I was hoping,' replied Jo-Jo.

The humanesque laughed spontaneously. 'You berthed on that luxury yacht. Fancy gear for someone who drinks in bars alone.'

'*Salacious II* is company enough for most. It's station-side when a bloke gets lonely.'

'I'll have blood juice. My shipmate likes OP rum. What business would you be in, then?'

Jo-Jo spoke to the Table Order before he answered. 'An easier one than you, my friend.'

The humanesque gave him a sharp look. 'How do you reckon that?'

'Your clothes tell me you don't like to dress up, and the ship you're in on is known for shuttling mercs. I'd say you're on your way to a job. Probably Dash or Latino Crux.'

'You're a smart man . . .'

'Ivan.'

The merc laughed at the false name and held his hand out. 'Jud.' He took his blood juice to a small table by the window and sat back to watch Jo-Jo woo his companion.

Later, when Jo-Jo's HealthWatch began to whisper in his ear that his sexual function would be impaired if he imbibed further and the Balol merc had begrudgingly told him her name ('Ilke, but you may not use it'), Jud rose and bade the pair goodnight.

Jo-Jo took But-you-may-not-use-it-Ilke back to his room-in and let her walk on him.

She did it with a vehemence that forced him to raise his endorphin levels to cope with the pain. 'Outstanding,' he gasped as she pressed her spines into his buttocks. 'Truly illuminating.'

Jo-Jo, an armed intruder has entered shipzone. The quiet mindmessage from *Salacious II* snapped him out of his ecstasy.

He shoved But-you-may-not-use-it-Ilke onto the floor and pulled on his clothes.

She stood up, showing fully flushed arousal and growling menacingly. 'You do not run out on Ilke.'

Jo-Jo pulled a revolver from the pocket of his suit. 'Put your clitoris away, Balol. If you have anything to do with this, I'll come back for you and rip those charming spines out, one by one.'

She remained motionless as he backed out of the room, a tiny smile hovering around her false lip.

Salacious II was parked on theta arm in a secure bay for luxury craft. The ship's port entry was wide open as if someone had left in a hurry.

Why is the damn door open?

The intruder damaged a portion of my senses with a virus. I cannot tell what hatches are closed or open, I cannot . . . I cannot fly. The last sounded like a sob. *I am trying to grow new sensors but as you know—*

Yeah, yeah – it takes time. Well, hurry up, you're buck naked and ready to pluck.

I fear I may already be plucked.

Jo-Jo dragged the hatch across manually but could not make it seal. *Fuck it. I'm going in to have a look. Where was the main action?*

My subsidiary sensors detected that the den was entered.

The den! Jo-Jo ran the decks to the heart of his ship.

A quick scan told him that the room had been searched – not so that it would appear so, but with a singular purpose in mind. He checked his log vault and his credit crystals.

What else? What could the merc have been after?

Then he noticed the Carabinere.

'Mr Rasterovich?' A station-security man stood in the doorway, fidgeting in an officious manner.

'You're too late. He's gone. But I know which ship he was on.'

The Carabinere didn't move. 'We have a warrant to search your vessel.'

Jo-Jo's jaw dropped. 'For what?'

'Our information is that you have an undeclared life form aboard.'

'What life form?' Jo-Jo felt his heart change rhythm.

The Carabinere glanced out into *Salacious II*'s corridor.

Another officer appeared and handed him a sample bag.

He opened it and waved the contents under Jo-Jo's nose.

It smelled and looked like a decayed jellyfish. 'Uuli.'

'Yes, sir. Place your hands on your head and keep them there until I say otherwise.'

'But you don't understand,' said Jo-Jo as the Carabinere pressed a pistol into the small of his back and marched him off *Salacious II*. 'I wouldn't . . . I couldn't . . . I'M ALLERGIC TO THE DAMN THINGS.'

The courtroom on Dowl was a grimy basement in the station's underbelly. The closed-circuit screens provided most of the light and the only humanesques present were the Latino defence lawmon and the court custodian: a paid witness slept in a corner. The defence lawmon zapped Jo-Jo awake with a laser-pointer.

'All stand for the judge,' rumbled the custodian.

At one time, courts had been conducted via uplink but too many proven cases of fakery had occurred and OLOSS had chosen to go back to the old-fashioned face-to-face ways. It saved a fortune in disputed convictions.

Jo-Jo had prepared his defence using Dowl's executive-lawmon suite, knowing that its legal-aid wrap would be more than sufficient for anything a circuit judge's automated prosecutor could deal him.

He stood, confident and impatient, his mind on the two scores he had to settle. Tekton, and now the unknown mercenary: Jo-Jo Rasterovich planned to live for a long time.

The ceiling opened and the judge descended into the room in a darkened protective-sealed transparent capsule. He was already seated and shuffling deskfilm.

'Presiding today will be Samuel L. Frattini-Longbok-Speaking-Goh,' said a disembodied voice.

Jo-Jo experienced a frisson of shock like a cold hand on his balls. *S-samuel L.?*

The capsule lit up and the judge fixed Jo-Jo with a neutral stare. 'Proceed!'

The court's auto-pros read the charges.

'Mr Josif-Josif Rasterovich. How plead you?' said Judge Goh.

Jo-Jo ran angles as fast as his brain could manage. The lawmon dangling before him in the large capsule just happened to be the same man he had blackmailed to obtain the location of the shape-changing alloy. The blackmail had involved compromising snaps of Samuel L. and his attempt to give cunnilingus to a Balol madam with six orifices.

Perhaps he won't recognise me. Perhaps he has recognised me. Perhaps he—

'Speak or be held in contempt.'

'Um . . . not guilty . . . Judge Goh.'

'On what grounds?'

Jo-Jo launched into his version of events, letting his wrap dictate the necessary phrases. As he recounted his story, Samuel L's face remained in a frozen 'judgely' expression.

'Have you finished?'

Jo-Jo nodded. To his consternation, a hint of a smirk twitched the corners of Samuel L's mouth.

'The OLOSS court finds Josif-Josif Rasterovich guilty of neglecting to declare a Class Three life form, and cruelty to a Class Three sentient species. The penalty for such an offence is two years in confinement. The defendant will serve that sentence on Dowl resonance-shift station without cause for appeal or transfer. Good day.'

'No!' bellowed Jo-Jo.

The court witness woke with a start, the newsfilm slipping off his knees.

Samuel L darkened his capsule as effectively as if he were drawing the curtain on a stage.

'Goh, you fat, dirty prick! You can't do this to me. I'll find your wife and tell her about your—'

The capsule shot upwards into the gap in the ceiling and the hatch snapped shut with a smooth click at the precise time that auto-restraints snaked around Jo-Jo's neck and ankles and secured him to his chair.

The court witness got to his feet and stumbled over. 'Haven't always worked here,' he said, conversationally picking his nose. 'Caretaker for most of my life.'

Jo-Jo stared at him. *What was the dumb fuck on about?*

The court witness patted his head. 'And for a small

fee I can bring you excellent food and women, ersatz or genuine.'

Jo-Jo strained at his bonds in mounting fury. 'My ship,' he demanded. 'What will happen to my ship?'

'Oh, that,' said the witness with bored assurance. 'It's been missing for two days.'

MIRA

'Cheap,' said Rast suddenly.

Mira had thought she was still asleep. Indeed, her eyes remained closed.

Below them smoke snaked from Malocchi's building along and up the range to the Studium and the Principe's palazzo.

'This is a cheap invasion. No AiV capacity other than what they commandeered. Basic weapons. Lots of groundwork done, though. All those little accidents beforehand. Distractions. Get the local Carabinere running around stamping out groundfires and they don't see that the forest's about to be burned down.'

Mira didn't understand the mercenary's odd analogy. 'Other than the climate, Araldis would not be a difficult planet to plunder,' she allowed.

'Yes. One minimalist fleet and a toothless enforcement agency.'

'That is why you were here?'

Rast gave a mocking salute. 'Touché, Baronessa. Yes, we hire out as security. Obviously the Principe had cause to worry.'

Mira returned her attention to the scan. Sprawling out along the bottom of Pell, Dockside looked normal enough. 'It's overrun with Saqr, according to what I've been told.' She stopped short of using Trin Pellegrini's name.

She felt Rast's gaze on her. The mercenary sensed that she had been about to say more.

'You look different, Baronessa. Where did you get this AiV? Catchut saw you and Mulravey take some women out of Ipo on a barge. What happened then?'

'We were caught in the dust storm. There are some survivors hiding out among the smaller mines. One of them found us after the storm. We were fortunate, I suppose.'

'Fortunate? Hmm.' Rast lapsed into a moment's silence. 'So who did you kill to be the only one getting off this planet?'

'I-it was agreed. I am the only one who can fly Insignia.' Again, she avoided mentioning Trin's name. 'If she is still intact. If I can get to her.'

'Her?'

'The biozoon is not inanimate. Only a fool would treat them as such.'

'If *she* is intact, I'll get you to her,' Rast said grimly. 'But I want out of here. If you try and blow me off, Baronessa, I'll kill you. Is that clear? I lost most of my crew and only got part of my payment. I'm not feeling generous.'

Mira nodded. What absurd impulse had made her stop to help the mercenary? *Because she can kill and I might need her to do that.*

As they descended towards the royal palazzo Mira saw that the main landing pad was strewn with debris, as though an AiV had exploded on take-off. Chunks of metal and melted plex spread in a wide, relatively even circle. Saqr crawled over the remains.

'I cannot land there.' Mira climbed again until she could execute a more horizontal sweep of the palazzo. The alternative pad on the mountainside had collapsed and torn a chunk out of the foundations.

'Crux. It looks like the entire palace is cracking away from the side,' said Rast. She and Catchut had their faces pressed to the cabinplex, peering below. 'Where is this res-ship?'

'The Tourmaline Islands. It's the Principe's Insignia craft. It's kept separate from the rest of the Fleet.'

Rast fell back from the window and turned to Mira. 'Then what in the Crux are we doing *here*? The place is crawling with Saqr.'

'It can't be flown without the Insignia lozenge. And that is in the Principe's vault.' Mira banked the AiV in an unnecessarily steep turn just to see the mercs clutch their seats. 'I think.'

'*You think*.' Rast closed her eyes.

'It is possible that the Principe had it with him when he died. He may have removed it from the vault,' said Mira. 'Anything could have happened to it, really.'

'*Really.*'

Rast's mimicry irritated Mira.

The mercenary expelled a deep breath. 'I think I know why the little aristo stopped to pick us up, Catchut,' she said in a raised voice.

Catchut grunted. 'Capo, Latourn's bleeding won't stop.'

'The Insignia craft has comprehensive automedic,' said Mira quickly.

'Where are the Principe's rooms?'

Mira could see what Rast was thinking. 'I will have to come with you. I'm not sure exactly but it will take me less time to find them than it would you.'

'If we land this thing and leave it, it won't be there when we come back. Catchut? Keep it in the air and then come back for us?'

'Yes, Capo.'

'Can you use a rifle, Baronessa?' Rast asked.

'Si.' *Not to kill, though. Not to kill.*

'Then hurry up and put us down.' Rast began checking over her rifle while Mira searched for a spot to land.

The AiV's hydrogen cells were half depleted and the back-up cells had been removed. Much longer in the air now and they wouldn't make the distance to the Tourmalines without another cell. Mira took one more pass to make a decision.

Switching to descent rotors, she sent the craft plummeting between two water tanks perched above the Palazzo. The gap was scarcely big enough: any drift and they would crash against the tanks sides. But she would not let Catchut fly this AiV.

The proximity alarms tripped off in an obnoxious blare. Tingling adrenalin made it difficult for Mira to keep her hands steady, yet some part of her brain relished the precision of it. She dived into the gap and stayed there, seeing every lump in the seams of the tanks, every crack in the white lettering on the blackened sides.

'What are you doing?' shouted Rast, clutching her armrest.

Behind them, Catchut muttered what might have been prayers.

Mira counted off altitude in her head, comparing it with the display. With total concentration she slid the AiV flawlessly but too swiftly between the water silos. It thumped down onto the sloping platform and slid forward. She stalled the rotors and braked hard.

They skidded to rest on the 'creted lip of the tank platform. The sheer drop to the palazzo below got her heart fluttering. She'd thought that the base was wider.

'Crux, Capo, I can't fly out of here,' said Catchut.

Rast gave Mira a hostile look. 'It seems the Baronessa is used to getting her own way. Pass me the E-M.' She thrust Latourn's rifle into Mira's hand and opened her door.

Mira scrambled out her side the AiV. Now that she was standing her legs felt muscle-weak and her stomach ached for more food. Could she find the Principe's chamber now that they were here? The royal Palazzo was a maze of corridors and porticos.

She peered down over the lip. Like the landing pad, the stairway access between the silos and the Palazzo had been destroyed. Rast had not waited for her, taking the direct route, belly-crawling, rifle first.

Mira followed hesitantly. As she stepped down, scree tumbled free. Her feet slid out from underneath her and she fell heavily. The ground burned through her gloves and fellala and the sun burned into her skin as if she were naked. More than anything else, she wanted a cool drink but she could not stop her momentum and she slipped and slid to the bottom.

Below her, Rast had already scaled the portico. She crouched there, waiting impatiently. The mercenary uncoiled a short thick cord from her suit and threw it down. 'Tie it under your arms. When I take the tension, brace your feet against the wall. I'll pull – you walk up.'

They tried several times. The cord bit into Mira's skin and her legs trembled and collapsed when she tried to walk. She felt the tears of frustration and exhaustion mounting. *This is useless. I am useless.*

Rast muttered unrecognisable oaths. 'Face away from the wall and tie it around your waist.'

The cord slipped from Mira's fingers as she tried to knot it and her body ached in every imaginable place. She picked the rope up and tried again.

Rast began to haul her up slowly, grunting and swearing with the effort. Partway between the portico and the ground she dropped Mira.

Every part of Mira's body felt bruised until the welcome numbness of endorphins washed over her. She wasn't even sure if she was conscious until Rast hung over the ornate balustrade and called, 'Crux, Baronessa. Are you dead or napping?'

The stupid insult stung her enough to make her move. Fedor tenacity got her to her feet and she reset the cord under her arms. 'I will climb.'

A sudden waft of sweet Saqr scent lent another surge of adrenalin to her exhausted body. Her arms and legs found strength from fear and anger.

When Mira reached the underside of the portico Rast reached down a hand and hauled her bodily over. Mira tumbled over the balustrade, landing on her injured elbow. Without consideration or care Rast pulled her to her feet.

The mercenary's face swam before her eyes and Mira experienced a gush of nausea followed by a rushing sound inside her skull.

'Don't you faint on me, Baronessa!' The mercenary shook her so hard that her neck snapped back.

Mira gritted her teeth. 'I – am – quite – fine, thank – you,' she panted. 'Each floor has a central corridor. I – imagine the Principe's room – is on the front side of the Palazzo . . . the crown floor . . . no, probably the second floor from the crown.'

Rast let go of her and moved to the row of windows. She fumbled inside her suit and brought out a tube with a long nozzle. She squeezed the contents onto the transparent catoplasma in a wide circle. The substance spread, eating away a large section with little fuss or noise. Rast thrust her boot into the panel and popped it inwards.

Mira watched in astonishment.

Rast gave a short laugh. 'Yeah. Shitting expensive, too. Don't brush against the edges – it will eat your skin away.'

Bending low, Mira followed Rast through the hole. They entered a lesser reception hall: an elegant room with a gold-filigree reproduction of Latino Crux inlaid into the black marble walls. Each star glittered, casting a halo across the dark background.

Chairs had been overturned and toppled. Not wilful damage so much as incidental harm caused to anything standing between the Saqr and the satisfaction of their hunger. Their sweet smell lingered in the air as if they had secreted it on every surface they had touched.

The lesser hall led into another, and another, each

one with varying degrees of damage. Mira and Rast threaded their way through the debris until they found the central corridor.

'Uplifts are spaced along the wider corridor,' Mira panted.

Rast ran ahead, fuelled by something that Mira would never experience: the ecstasy of danger. The mercenary again waited impatiently for her at the first uplift.

Mira tried to catch her breath as they rode it up to the fifth level and was still trying as they stepped into the splendour of Franco's private wing. The floor-to-ceiling doors had been lovingly packed and brought out from Latino Crux. A hand-painted Pellegrini familia crest adorned each one. Their value was inestimable: genuine polished wood in a world of catoplasma and mud. Unlike the lesser halls, the walls of Franco's rooms were cloaked in soft materials – velvets, silks and rich corduroys. On one wall of the ante-room hung a vast parcel-gilded mirror that reflected a delicately crafted fauteuil set and gilt-bronze bureau that sat opposite.

Rast raced in and out of each room, searching for the vault. 'Where would it be? Bedroom? Office? How many damn rooms can one person have?'

Mira followed slowly, feeling guilty about their invasion and strangely saddened by what the emptiness meant. The Principe was truly gone.

She veered into the service chamber, not wishing to see the Principe's innermost room. A Galiotto servant lay motionless on the travertine floor, spidery trickles of blood across his face. His fellalo was torn open at the chest and a sliver of precious wood protruded from his temple.

While Rast ignored the body and went about over-turning drawers and upturning statues, Mira knelt by the servant. The expression on his face was pained, one hand clenched tight as if he had died in terror. The evidence of his suffering set free tears that she had been holding back. They poured down her face as she straightened his fellalo to give him some dignity.

'The vault's been opened, Fedor. There's fuck-all in here.'

'Si,' said Mira, as she gently prised open the Galiotto's fist. 'That is because it is *here*.'

The Tourmaline Islands were as serene and picturesque as the last time Mira had seen them but now there was no Studium crowd to litter the beaches. Would Trin bring the survivors here, she wondered? Or would he go further south to the cooler, uninhabited Galgos? She hoped that he would have the sense to go the Galgos. If Jancz wanted to destroy every last Cipriano on Araldis, he would know to come and search the vacation Mecca of the aristos.

Trin had told Mira that the Insignia craft was hidden on the Principe's island so she flew once over the area to visually confirm her bearings before landing the AiV high on the broad, flat beach on which she and Trin had kissed. The memory of it had become dim now, overshadowed by the horror of the present.

As the AiV sank into the sand Mira half-expected the Principe's Cavaliere to emerge, but the island seemed deserted. Preceded by Mira, Rast and Catchut carried Latourn up the beach to a line of brown salt-scrub. As they approached the Principe's chalet two frightened Galiotto servants appeared.

Mira called out a traditional greeting. She recognised the stout woman wearing a royal household fellala as one of Jilda Pellegrini's own. Was there a chance that the Principessa was here?

'Galiotto, we have news,' said Mira. 'I am Baronessa Fedor. I come from the young Principe.'

The Galiotto woman wailed. 'Don Trinder? Is he alive? Thank Crux. You must come to the chalet.' She glanced around wildly as if danger might fall on her from the sky.

The Galiotto male was less trusting. 'Who accompanies you, Baronessa?'

'Interstellar Hire. They help our cause.'

'What cause is that?' he asked suspiciously.

'Araldis has been invaded by creatures called the Saqr. The towns have been captured or destroyed. I have come from the royal palazzo. The Principe has been killed.'

The woman sobbed loudly. 'We have prayed for better news. Our shortcast is no longer functioning. The Cavaliere left us and went to—'

'Hush,' the man told her. He pulled out a rifle from behind his back.

Mira's throat tightened. 'The young Principe has asked me to take the Insignia ship to OLOSS. Our world needs sentientarian aid. Without it we will all perish.'

'The Insignia will not fly without a sanction.'

Mira reached inside her fellala and pulled out the lozenge. 'The mercenaries made it possible for me to retrieve this and reach here alive.'

Beside her, Rast shifted impatiently. Latóurn mo ed
in their arms.

'Baronessa, you may enter the chalet but the mercenaries must stay here.'

'My crewman needs help and somewhere to lie
down,' said Rast.

'We shall return with some medic,' said the Galiotto
man.

'No!' Rast took a step towards him.

The man raised the rifle. 'You may not enter.'

'Please,' said Mira to the Galiotto. 'Let them come.
They will do no harm—'

But the male servant fell forward before she could
finish, his rifle discharging into the sand near her feet.
Blood flowered across his hair and spattered the sand.
The woman at his side made a small inarticulate noise
and fainted.

Mira turned on Rast, appalled. 'What have you done,
animale?'

'Latourn will not die on this beach because of a
scared servant. Your oath might be to your people but
mine is to my crew. Now pick up that rifle and move.'

In that moment Mira did not care if Rast killed her
as well. She went to kneel by the woman.

Rast stared at her. Then she shrugged, picked up
the rifle herself and marched up the dune to the chalet.

Mira stayed by the Galiotto woman until she regained
consciousness but she could not persuade her away
from the body.

'Mia fratella,' the woman moaned, over and over.

Mira held her until her sobbing subsided.

'What is your name?' said Mira.

But the Galiotto pressed her hands across her face and curled into a ball.

Mira grasped her arms and shook her hard. 'Listen! Saqr have invaded our world. I want you to stay here until the young Principe comes. Tell him that I have done as he asked and that he should go on to the Galgos. The Saqr will not like the water.'

The Galiotto quietened, listening to her.

'Do you know somewhere to hide?'

'Si. I know because the Principess—' She broke off, cupping her hands over her mouth.

'The Principessa is here, isn't she?' Mira shook the woman again, her tolerance as low as her energies. '*Isn't she?*'

The Galiotto nodded tearfully.

Mira put her face close to the servant's ear. 'The mercenaries must not know that she is alive. Go to her now and tell her what I have said to you. Stay hidden until we have gone. Whatever happens, her son must not stay here. He must go further south. Capisci?'

'Si. Capisco.'

Mira helped the woman to her feet.

'Are you a traditrice, Baronessa?' the Galiotto asked hoarsely.

'Not traditrice, Galiotto. Incinta.' She touched her belly with a trembling hand. 'Tell the Principessa that if I survive she will have a nipote. The Pellegrini line will continue.' *Tell her that her son is a rapist.* 'Now go to her without being seen.'

Mira left the woman and struggled up the red beach, across the patches of sand-thorns to the paths around the chalet. Heat exhaustion was upon her, the nausea greater with each step, the headache more intense. But now she had something to keep her going. Insignia's voice was back in her mind. Its return was like a feast to someone who was starving.

She threaded her way through several archways until she found Rast and Catchut in the chalet's infirmary. They were removing Latourn from a blood-sluice.

'Why is everything here so primitive?' Rast stormed.

Mira took a long, steadying drink of water from a faux spring by the window. It tasted faintly briny, as though the desalinator needed servicing. 'This is not the Palazzo; it is a holiday retreat. The Ciprianos spent their fortune to purchase Araldis. They could not afford unlimited technology.' Mira was not sure why she bothered to speak at all. This mercenary had just killed familia for little reason.

'Where's the servant woman?' asked Rast.

'On the beach still. She wished to stay with her fratella . . . with the body,' said Mira.

'She might know something useful. I'll get her,' said Rast.

Mira's heart fluttered in panic.

'Capo? He's slipping away.' Catchut's tone came close to pleading.

Rast hesitated. 'You said the ship had decent medic?'

Mira nodded. 'Si.' She led them back through the arches, across the polished iron courtyard to the spiral outside paths.

Rast and Catchut carried Latourn between them. As before, he was too weak to stand.

The hangar doors opened at the touch of the lozenge. Inside, the kite-shaped black Insignia craft with its golden Cipriano emblem seemed to suck the light from the air.

'Open her up and then prepare for lift-off,' ordered Rast. 'You do know how?'

Mira glanced around the hangar. It was like a miniature version of the Fleet's base on Mount Pell. 'Of course.'

Rast nodded. 'I'll be back to help you when we've got Latourn hooked up. And hurry. I got a feeling that I don't like gnawing at me.'

What gnawed at Rast, Mira thought, was the guilt about those she had murdered because they had got in her way.

While Rast and Catchut carried the dying Latourn on board, Mira limped across the hangar to elevate the launch pad. The pseudo-skin's anaesthetic had worn off and her elbow throbbed painfully in an ugly, pulsing rhythm.

She placed the lozenge in the seal on Insignia's hull. *Bonjourno, bella*, she whispered to the ship.

You are here?

With Insignia's words Mira's mind came alive. Things she needed to account for streamed into place: weather conditions, stabiliser integrity, g-thrust analysis, environmentals. The Insignia was rated for deep space but it had been many years since it had seen such a journey. Had the res-shift been hummed recently? Was the ship's grown still healthy? Degradation from neglect was a possibility. Had the shipskin retained suitable integrity?

The hangar flattened, settling into its lift-off position while Mira stood in the flooding sunlight. Quotes from her instruction-manual download whispered to her. *The result of an inexact res-shift is catastrophic and will have an irrevocable impact on humanesque tissue. Vibration calibration must be precise or molecules in the tissues will implode the flesh.*

A shiver of anticipation finished in a flush of heat that left Mira feeling faint. She had stopped perspiring. Serious dehydration was imminent. In careful order she slipped the last tethers. *Where is Rast?*

Insignia replied. *There is a humanesque in Secondo vein. I am obliged to listen.*

Mira started towards the loading door in a panic as Insignia's elevons began to flex. 'Rast.'

An AiV buzzed in low over the hangar and past the chalet, coming from the north. The wind from its rotors stirred a dust whirl. It arced out over the water and circled back towards her. When it reached the point of descent it come down like a flake of meteorite in the atmosphere.

Mira scrambled onto the platform-lift. *Insignia. I am coming.*

Saqr screams sent her stomach into a clenching spasm. As the lift reached Insignia's wing they were already in the hangar. She felt along the biozoon's scales for the one that would give her admission.

'Turn around,' a voice ordered. 'Slowly.'

Jancz was on the ground below the Insignia's elevons. Ilke stood next to him.

'So dirty and dishevelled, Principessa?'

'It's Baronessa,' she said coldly. 'You should know the difference by now. You have murdered enough of us.'

'Touchy, these aristos.' He spoke to Ilke but his stare never left Mira. 'Now come down from there.'

Mira felt frantically along the scales. *Which one? Tell me which one.*

'Now, Baronessa!' Jancz raised his weapon.

A scale twitched under her fingers and she sank into it, letting it draw her in. It sealed behind her and she picked herself up and stumbled though the twisted, sloping aisles to the flight stratum.

Rast was in the Secondo vein, only her face uncovered, eyes darting, unfocused. Cathcut and Latourn were absent – in the medic stratum, Mira supposed. Rast didn't move her head.

'You were going to leave me,' Mira said accusingly.

'Yeah. Well, I didn't. Vein up. There's more Saqr coming and the 'esques have some type of incendiary. We'll have to cold start. The planet's nav-sat is out. Dowl isn't responding either.' Rast's voice sounded thick, like she was eating something sticky.

Cold start. Mira found that she had trouble breathing at the thought. She collapsed into the Primo vein and felt the couch pucker around her. She fought off the claustrophobia and tried to relax as grow-receptors skittered over her skin and burrowed in for the beginning of the inflating procedure that would protect her against g-forces.

For a moment she felt as if her throat was closing over. She swallowed repeatedly until the feeling faded. It was replaced by a sensation of body-bloating, as though she had consumed too much liquid. She flexed and contracted her muscles, knowing that the movement would release the pressure. Again the sensation faded. Nausea mounted in her throat and she found herself swallowing repeatedly.

All normal adjustments to vein-sink, Mira told herself. She concentrated on the tingling at the base of her skull where the vein insinuated itself into neural lanes. *Hurry.* The tingling became colour bursts before her eyes. They steadied and resolved into nothing.

Absence.

Then whispers became a flow of information, absorbed into her hindbrain with terrifying speed. Mira knew at once and intimately that the ship systems were burgeoning; that Catchut was leaning over Latourn in medic, crying; that the Saqr had positioned themselves around Insignia; that Jancz and Ilke were fixing a patch onto her underbelly.

Insignia? Prime and Exfoliate, she told the ship.

Exfoliation while Primed is counterintuitive, Insignia replied.

Wassat mean? Rast/Secondo interjected.

Mira ignored her. *It is preferable to obliteration.*

Agreed, Insignia thought back.

Then proceed.

Yes, Primo. It should be noted that if skin isn't regrown by mesopause, irrevocable tears may occur, thought Insignia.

It will be all right, Mira soothed. *Proceed.*

The tremor that ran through the ship mirrored itself in her body – so did the contortion, as the ship began to shed skinscales. The sensation was a hundredfold worse than vein-sink, as if her own skin had been inverted and the raw tissue exposed. Bare nerve endings prickled and shrieked.

Rast/Secondo moaned and whimpered like an animal.

At some level Mira was aware that the mercenary

had urinated, just as she knew that Rast was also drooling helplessly. She instructed her pelvis to tighten against the same impulse. She would *not* disgrace herself.

Exfoliation crest imminent, Insignia informed her unnecessarily.

For a time Mira/Primo's organs seemed to be in a tug-o'-war with each other. But even at the height of her pain, she maintained focus on the individual scale that held the incendiary. When it peeled off and dropped to the ground, she rejoiced.

Prime, she ordered.

Very well, Insignia sighed.

The ship lifted in a burst of beach sand, shedding iridescent scales like large moulting fish leaping from a stream. Mira/Primo felt the rush of cooling altitude on her fins, followed by heat on her belly as the incendiary detonated below them.

The plume of fire peaked and receded like a flung wave, leaving them untouched and free.

Rast/Secondo's thought came to her, weak but marvelling. 'Well, fuck me, Fedor! I didn't think you had it in you.'

Mira/Primo didn't bother to send a thought back. For a singular and infinite moment she had found herself at home.

THE VATTA'S WAR SERIES

An explosive military SF adventure

Elizabeth Moon

Kylara Vatta was a military cadet destined for great things, until an act of kindness incurred the Academy's wrath and ended her career. Instead of the expected disgrace, her trader family gave her captaincy of a small ship, to sell for scrap. But in typical flagrant disregard of orders, she saw the opportunity to make a profit and save the ship.

Several upgrades later, she is determined to retain her independence in the cut-throat world of interplanetary trading. But a complex political situation becomes increasingly dangerous, and she becomes far more involved with the military than she had planned in her new career.

She must keep her wits, and trade on every bit of her hard-won experience, or she – and her family – could lose everything.

For high-octane action read:

TRADING IN DANGER
MOVING TARGET
ENGAGING THE ENEMY
COMMAND DECISION

SATURN RETURNS

Book One of Astropolis

Sean Williams

It's time to die – for the second time.

When former mercenary commander, Imre Bergamasc, awakes in the 879th Millennium on the edge of the galactic rim, with large portions of his memory missing, he understandably has a few questions – not the least of which is: why is he now a woman?

It seems that Imre's body has been resurrected from the fragments of a bizarre time capsule. Unfortunately, the drum was all but destroyed in an obvious attempt to erase all that remained of him, leaving his record – and his memories – incomplete. After it becomes clear that his rescuers' motives are not entirely altruistic, Imre steals a ship and flees back towards civilisation – or, at least, where civilisation used to be when he was last alive.

Now Imre must piece together both the fragments of his memory and the story of civilisation's fall. Was the Imre Bergamasc he no longer remembers an unwitting pawn in the fall of civilisation? Or was he, in fact, the architect? And if unknown parties have gone to such extreme lengths to resurrect him, why are they now trying to kill him? Again.